THE BABY SOLDIERS

THE BABY SOLDIERS

GERRY R. LEWIS

PALMETTO
PUBLISHING
Charleston, SC
www.PalmettoPublishing.com

Copyright © 2024 by Gerry R. Lewis

All rights reserved

No portion of this book may be reproduced, stored in a retrieval system, or transmitted in any form by any means—electronic, mechanical, photocopy, recording, or other—except for brief quotations in printed reviews, without prior permission of the author.

Hardcover ISBN: 979-8-8229-4800-6
Paperback ISBN: 979-8-8229-4728-3

DEDICATION

TO THE MEMORY OF

CATHERINE McCLOSKEY

MY BELOVED GRANDMOTHER

CHAPTER ONE

Julie Newman stood shivering outside the Nelson Clinic. The windbreaker covering her white nylon uniform offered little protection from September's unexpected cold snap. Other members of the staff joined her, muttering about the cold wind and the whereabouts of the lazy guard, who held the keys to another day in paradise.

A convoy of automobiles and pickup trucks rolled along the circular driveway, braking just long enough to discharge their passengers, then moving on to the parking lot behind the building. Julie studied each vehicle warily, wondering if any of them held terrorists, like those responsible for blowing up other family planning clinics in the Tidewater area.

The Nelson Clinic had opened barely three weeks ago, and the staff had received more than a dozen threatening calls. Julie shuddered, thinking about the call she'd received her first week on the job. The caller had spoken so softly she could barely hear him, but his message had been crystal clear. Anyone entering an abortion clinic was sinning against God and man. If the clinic did not close immediately, it would be blown to bits.

The caller had frightened her so badly, she wanted to pack it in right there and leave. But Julie needed her job. She wasn't as fortunate as those, who could run home to mama whenever things got tough. Her parents had been killed in an auto accident when she was ten. Afterwards, she'd been shuffled off to Baltimore to live with an old maid aunt. For a long time, Julie wished she had died in the accident, too. When her older brother graduated from medical school and invited her to live with him in his condo in Virginia Beach, everything changed.

Julie's happiness was short-lived. It ended abruptly when her beloved brother was shot and killed, leaving a clinic where he'd spent countless evenings counseling pregnant girls. Now, she had no one.

Julie listened to bits and pieces of the conversations from people gathering near a barren maple tree several yards away. Her calculating blue eyes shifted from one male face to the next. How stoic they appeared. She bet they didn't look quite so grim when they were sweet-talking their girlfriends into having sex with them.

Her attention shifted to a wiry man in greasy coveralls, who danced from one foot to the other while glancing at his watch. Suddenly, he turned to the shivering woman at his side and grumbled. "How long will it be before someone shows up to open the damned door? Christ, it's freezing out here."

Julie watched the woman flinch. She was obviously afraid of him.

"The lady I spoke with yesterday said the clinic opened at eight o'clock. They must be running late this morning."

The trembling girl winced when he grabbed her arm. "That was half-an-hour ago! I can't spend the whole day waiting around here for you to get fixed. I do have a job, you know."

The woman lowered her head and whimpered. The man yanked her so hard their noses were touching.

"Don't start that whining shit again," he growled. "I'm sick of it!"

Julie turned away in disgust. "What a bastard," she muttered, thankful she lived alone and didn't have to put up with a prick like him.

A chartered bus squealed to a stop near the end of the long driveway. The doors clattered open and a boisterous troupe of men and women emerged. They carried large signs made of poster board and stacks of colorful pamphlets. A few wore dark jackets with faces of smiling babies painted on the back.

"Just what we need," Julie whispered to a nurse standing nearby. "A pro-life demonstration."

THE BABY SOLDIERS

A stocky woman, wearing a long wool coat and lace up boots, emerged from the rear of the bus. She acknowledged the nurses with the same disdain she would dog feces. Then she bellowed a string of orders to the others.

One of the nurses nudged Julie. You got an extra smoke?"

Julie reached in her handbag while watching another busload of demonstrators enter the grounds near the opposite end of the driveway. They stopped about seventy feet short of the building and proceeded to set up folding tables and chairs.

The nurse lit her cigarette and said, "You don't suppose they're going to have a bake sale, do you?"

"I wish they would," Julie retorted. "If I had something to chew, maybe it would keep my teeth from chattering."

Two of the demonstrators raised a bright colored banner proclaiming, *Sinners Will Go to Hell!*

Julie couldn't help but notice the fearful way the demonstrators eyed the building. The bomb threats at the clinic were no secret. The protesters were probably as worried about being blown up as she was.

A ruddy-faced man with slouched shoulders and a beer belly sauntered toward the front door. His windbreaker billowed open, exposing a revolver strapped tightly to his chest and a heavy ring of keys fastened to his belt.

"Hallelujah!" Julie dropped her cigarette into a concrete cuspidor.

"Ben, where in the hell have you been?" she snapped. "I've been standing out here freezing my ass off for nearly an hour."

The guard winked at her as he raised the keys and slipped one into the lock on the wrought iron gate and another into the front door.

"I'd be happy to warm that up for you," he teased.

Julie rolled her eyes. "Just hurry up, will you."

Ben glanced over his shoulder at the swarm of people making their way across the grounds.

"What's going on?" He mumbled wryly. "You guys running a two for one special?"

— 3 —

Julie tapped her foot impatiently as the door finally opened. Ben bowed theatrically and said, "After you, sweet thing."

The technicians within earshot hooted loudly.

Julie stepped inside the confines of the building, greedily sucking warm air into her lungs. While a throng of people stood in line to check in, she glanced outside and saw four couples lagging behind, obviously frightened by the taunting protesters. She pushed Ben aside and stood in the open doorway. "Come on, people. It's still a free country."

The couples glanced timidly at the protesters and then hurried inside.

As the last couple approached the building, Julie noticed a late model Chrysler pull to a stop near one of the busses. Immediately, the protesters stopped waving banners and chanting.

Two men sat in the front seat of the car. Julie prayed they didn't have a bomb with them.

One group of demonstrators quickly gathered up paraphernalia and hurried toward a waiting bus, while the other group began taking down signs they had just put up.

She felt colder now, than when she was standing outside. The men in the Chrysler didn't make a move. Julie couldn't imagine why they were just sitting there.

The last young couple approached the clinic, holding hands. Julie thought they must be in love. The boy was tall and slender with curly dark hair. The girl at his side was nearly his height and blond. Her long tresses floated on the wind behind her. Julie imagined them walking down a church aisle, ready to embark on a wonderful life, rather than coming here to destroy one.

The men in the Chrysler were watching the young couple…a little too closely. Julie wondered if one of them were related to the girl. Her father perhaps.

Kerry Trivane clutched Robbie's hand tightly. She couldn't believe she was actually going through with the abortion. She had never killed anything in her life. The thought of killing something growing inside her own body was so horrible she couldn't comprehend it.

She pulled the woolen scarf tighter around her neck, wishing she had waited until she was older to have sex. But she loved Robbie so much, and she never dreamed she would get pregnant at fifteen.

She knew other girls, who got pregnant at fifteen, but she always thought they were dumb. She never thought it would happen to her. It wasn't like she and Robbie had sex all the time, or that Robbie had forced her to have sex with him. She wanted it as much as he did. And they'd only done it a few times.

Robbie stopped walking and placed his hands on Kerry's shoulders, turning her to face him. He pressed his forehead to hers. "I love you so much," he whispered. "Whatever happens in there, I promise I'll be with you every step of the way."

Kerry grimaced. "I wish we didn't have to do this," she replied. Then they continued walking toward the clinic in silence.

The young couple passed the maple tree, which only minutes earlier had been surrounded by disgruntled men eager to get the day's sorry business over with.

Suddenly, Robbie gripped Kerry's hand.

She spun around as heavy footsteps pounded the ground behind them. Two men ran toward them. One was holding a gun. Robbie's eyes widened fearfully. "Run, Kerry!" he yelled, pushing her toward the clinic. "Hurry!"

Kerry stood frozen, like a glass-eyed mannequin, as the two men closed the gap between them. The taller man holding the gun fired twice. The sound was deafening. Kerry covered her ears and screamed. Then she saw Robbie falling. She tried to grab him and hold him in her arms to keep him from falling, but he was so heavy.

"Robbie!" she cried, tugging his shirt. "Robbie, please get up!"

She dropped to her knees as blood gushed from his chest and trickled from the corner of his mouth. The shorter of the two men grabbed her arm and pulled her to her feet. "Shut up, damn you," he muttered.

Kerry squirmed and lashed out at him, raking his face with her long nails. The tall man put his gun away and grabbed Kerry's arms, pinning them behind her back. She kicked and screamed and grunted ferociously, but she wasn't strong enough to break free. The men dragged her to the curb and shoved her into the back seat of the Chrysler. The shorter of the two slid in beside her and put his arm around her neck to immobilize her. She got in one last kick before something pricked her arm.

The protesters stood trance-like near the buses. She gazed helplessly through the closed window, wondering why no one would help her. Her mouth was so dry she couldn't swallow. She tried to cry out one more time, but no sound escaped her lips.

Julie raced across the yard. The security guard at her heels. He wrapped his arms around her as the car sped away.

"Julie, don't be crazy," Ben growled. "They have guns and you don't. Let's go back inside and call the cops."

Deflated by what she'd seen, Julie lowered her head and followed him.

CHAPTER TWO

Detective David Williams hurried toward the ringing phone in the bedroom, a damp towel wrapped around his torso. He snatched up the receiver while gazing helplessly at the trail of water along the hardwood floor he'd just refinished. It never failed. Somebody always called when he was in the shower.

It was Friday. His first day off in over a month. The moment he heard Lieutenant Woolard's voice, he knew his plans to go fishing with Buddy Mason had just gone down the toilet. He grabbed a pen off the night stand and jotted down the information the lieutenant gave him.

"Jesus... Jesus," he mumbled, shaking his head as he hung up.

David finished drying and slipped into a pair of khakis and a white shirt, tossing the jeans and sweatshirt he planned to wear on Buddy's boat back in the drawer. As he read the words over again, he tried to convince himself it was true. At nine-o-five this morning, Kerry Trivane had been kidnapped and her boyfriend, Robbie Kelsey, murdered outside the Nelson Clinic. "Sweet Jesus," he mumbled. "What next?"

David slipped a notebook and a couple pens into his shirt pocket and headed downstairs. It was times like this he wished gang violence was still the city's biggest problem. Fighting over a piece of turf was something he had grown apathetic to, not this.

Lieutenant Horace Woolard had instructed him to talk to the parents of the victims and visit the crime scene. Just once, David wished Woolard would visit a crime scene and get a taste of what the real world was all about. The lieutenant had become a master of skirting the worst problems facing the community. Woolard had absolutely no sympathy for anyone connected to an abortion issue. On more than one occasion, David had overheard him saying any 911 calls from abortion clinics were a waste of time and should be treated as such.

Considering the kidnapping and murder involving the children of two prominent families, Woolard couldn't avoid an investigation. Even though he probably believed they got what they deserved.

David backed down his narrow driveway and turned west on Prescott Street. As he glanced in the rearview mirror, he noticed a few new lines etched into the corners of his hazel eyes. A mournful sigh escaped his lips. Next week, he'd be forty-two. A forty-two year old sergeant with nothing to show for the years he'd invested in the police force but a house older than himself, and a Honda Civic well past the hundred-thousand mile mark. He thought about his wife, Ann, and his daughter, Ginny. Once he'd had a loving family. But they'd vanished without a trace more than four years ago.

He could have understood Ann leaving him had he been a heavy drinker, or if he'd cheated on her. But she had no reason to leave. He was a good husband and provider, well...better than most. One day, she just up and disappeared, taking their teenage daughter with her. He tried tracking her through DMV records, credit cards, and countless contacts with relatives and friends, but nothing turned up. No one could imagine what happened to them...Even Ann's mother, who had an opinion on everything, could shed no light on the mystery.

Not long before disappearing, he remembered Ann saying she was afraid their daughter was in terrible danger, but she wouldn't explain why she felt that way. Ann would never go anywhere without telling her mother where she was going. But every lead turned into a dead end. And after four years, David had given up the chase and decided to pull together the shambles of his life and move on.

This morning, the disappearance of his family weighed around his neck like a rusted anvil. Kerry Trivane's kidnapping touched him deeply. His daughter and Kerry had attended the same school. Now they were both gone.

Priscilla Trivane sat on the edge of the sofa, sobbing fitfully, an open box of tissues on her lap. Even though her deep blue eyes were red and puffy, and mostly hidden behind a yellow cluster of tissues, the sergeant always thought they were her most outstanding feature. Her husband, Bernie, paced the length of the room, his long legs making the trip in six easy strides. He looked helplessly at his wife. "David, she hasn't stopped crying since I picked her up at the hospital."

David and Bernie had served in the Navy together in another lifetime. Most people had mistaken Bernie's bulky frame as a sign of clumsiness, but David knew better. Bernie had the stealth of a cat, a stealth that had been responsible for saving his life. They'd been fast friends ever since.

"I don't know what to do, or what to think anymore," Bernie said, running his hands through wavy dark hair. His brow furrowed as he stared at his tormented wife. "I feel like this is all my fault."

David looked at his old friend, a puzzled expression on his face. "Bernie, how could you even think something like that?"

The husky man dropped listlessly onto the sofa beside his wife. After a moment of quiet contemplation, he leaned forward, resting his forearms on his knees. "When Kerry came to us and told us she was pregnant, I went nuts."

David's eyes narrowed.

"Yeah. You heard me right...typical father. After Cilla calmed me down, I told Kerry the best thing she could do was have an abortion. I was embarrassed," Bernie said, lowering his head. "Not for her sake, but for ours."

David remembered a time when nothing in the world could embarrass Bernie Trivane. His attitude seemed to have changed after being promoted to supervisor at the shipyard. The new job brought a lot of extra baggage into Bernie's life. He started taking everything anyone said to him as some kind of personal affront. David felt his old friend's limited education had a lot to do with the way he felt. Bernie had never taken more than a few courses in business management at a local community college. Most of the fellows who worked with him, as well as under him, had degrees up the ass. David hadn't seen much of Bernie and Priscilla in recent years. In the old days, he and Ann would get together with the Trivanes at least twice a month to play cards, or go out to dinner and a movie. Ann's disappearance had put an end to the good times. He'd become the odd man out, and no one knew exactly what to do with him. The sergeant shifted uncomfortably, unable to bear the pain in their eyes. He knew what it was like to lose someone you loved. He sat in the reclining chair facing the sofa and sighed heavily.

"Priscilla," he said, wishing there were some way he could get around the questions he had to ask. "I heard you were on duty in the emergency room when the rescue squad brought Robbie in this morning?"

Priscilla closed her eyes tightly and moaned. "Oh, David, it was so horrible. I recognized his shirt…we bought it for him last Christmas. It was drenched in blood." She shook uncontrollably. "I couldn't believe it was Robbie lying there."

Bernie took her hands in his. "It's okay, babe. It'll be okay."

She pulled away and brushed away the tears streaming down her face.

David studied the couple closely. How devoted they were to each other. Priscilla had witnessed an awful sight, one he was certain she wouldn't forget as long as she lived. He looked at his weary friend, knowing exactly what Bernie was thinking. Bernie was afraid the police would find Kerry in the same condition as Robbie Kelsey.

David hated this part of his job. But he knew it would be far worse for his friends if they had to go over all the intimate details with a complete stranger.

"When was the last time you saw Kerry?" he asked.

Priscilla's small feet peeked from beneath the hem of her skirt, then slid limply to the beige carpet. "This morning," she replied, sniffing. "I was going to fix her and Robbie breakfast before they left...before they went to the clinic."

She grabbed another tissue and wiped her nose. "Kerry told me she wasn't supposed to eat anything until...until the procedure was over."

David thought it interesting that Priscilla couldn't even bring herself to say the word abortion.

Bernie rubbed her hands. "Christ, if I had known anything like this was going to happen, I'd have told her to go ahead and have the little bastard!"

David's head jerked up, startled. Bernie was the last person in the world he expected to say something like that.

"How well did you know the Kelsey boy?" David asked, already aware of the answer.

Bernie's jaw tightened. "Apparently not as well as our daughter did."

Priscilla scowled at Bernie, then turned to face David. "We've known the Kelseys for years, David. You know that. We were all good friends...once."

David pursed his lips, remembering. "Sorry I had to ask. I don't remember seeing Robbie around much back then."

Bernie snorted. "He was probably away at boarding school so he wouldn't interfere with Sybil's social life."

"Do you think Kerry's pregnancy had anything to do with your friendship with the Kelseys cooling off?"

Bernie shook his head, his face grim. "It died way before that. When James took over as editor of the newspaper, he became too busy for his old friends. We weren't exactly the class of people he and Sybil chose to socialize with after that."

Bernie reached over and took a mint from the candy dish and popped it in his mouth. "It was no secret how I felt about Sybil,' he said, chewing. "Not seeing her on a regular basis was a blessing. She always had her nose stuck in somebody else's business. It got worse after she joined that radical church group. You couldn't even talk to her without starting an argument."

"Sybil wasn't the same person anymore," Priscilla said, lowering her head.

David frowned. "What do you mean, she wasn't the same?"

Bernie's eyes flashed angrily. "All that crazy shit Sybil heard at that church changed everything. After awhile, she started acting like she was better than the rest of us sinful mortals. She prattled on like a complete idiot about anything and everything that preacher Jacobson said.

"Bernie took a deep breath and continued, "I got the impression that James didn't want any part of him or his preaching; he just went along with whatever Sybil said to keep peace in the family." He scoffed. "That is, if there is such a thing as peace, living with a bitch like Sybil Kelsey."

"You said Sybil would go off over anything?" David asked curiously. "Can you give me an example?"

Bernie huffed. "She used to come over here, uninvited I might add, and jump up and down like a lunatic, criticizing whatever television program we were watching. She said they were all the work of Satan. She claimed her wonderful preacher was going to have them all banned."

Bernie shook his head. "David, you were here one night when she barged in and started spouting that shit?"

David grimaced. "Ah, yes. The X-files. How could I forget?"

Priscilla groaned softly. "Sybil really hated that show. The thought that people could possibly believe in something that was beyond human intelligence."

She turned from David to Bernie and added, "I wonder if she ever thought about God? He isn't human, either, and she believed in Him."

Bernie shook his head. "I don't believe Sybil ever thought anything out completely. Once she got over her crusade to ban television programs, she started in on homosexuals. She wanted them all ostracized." He paused remembering. "But the abortion issue was always front and center."

David watched Bernie curiously as the big man got up and began to pace once more. "Who in the hell did they think they were, telling people what they could and couldn't do with their lives? To tell you the truth, Sybil made me feel like we were living back in the forties and Adolph Hitler was running the show."

"1 can't say I'm sorry I missed out on all that," David said, loosening his tie.

"You know something interesting?" Bernie said. He sat back down, cupping his large hands over his knees. "No matter how much that crowd yapped against abortion, I never heard tell of a single one of them offering to adopt one of them precious bastards."

"Bernie, please watch your language! "Priscilla cried.

His shoulders slumped. "My language used to be just fine until people like Sybil Kelsey got me all riled up."

David cleared his throat. "Mind if I get a drink of water?"

"Help yourself," Bernie said. "I've got something stronger, if you want."

"No thanks," David said, walking toward the kitchen. "If anybody at the station got a whiff of liquor on my breath, I'd be facing retirement without pay. But I would like to ask you both a couple more questions."

"It's all right, David. We know you don't want to be doing this either," Bernie mumbled.

David returned from the kitchen holding a glass in his right hand. He looked at them thoughtfully. "Did Kerry mention receiving any threatening phone calls the last few weeks?"

Priscilla squinted thoughtfully. "Not that I'm aware of. I'm sure she would have told me if she had. Not many people knew about her pregnancy. Just us…and Robbie of course…and his folks."

"Are you sure there was no one else?" David asked pensively.

Bernie leapt to his feet, knocking the coffee table at an odd angle. "Sybil called here the other night, taunting Kerry about her preg-

— 13 —

nancy. Telling her what a sin it was to be thinking about abortion." He turned, facing Priscilla. "Don't you remember, babe?"

Priscilla licked her lips. "After all the years we've known Sybil, I've learned not to take anything she says seriously."

"Sybil is definitely one of a kind," David muttered. "I guess we should all be grateful for that anyway."

"Sybil probably told Kerry she should have the baby and raise it herself. It was the right thing to do." Bernie chortled.

Priscilla turned away, embarrassed.

David walked out to the kitchen and placed the empty glass in the sink. "I haven't talked to the Kelseys yet," he said, returning. "They weren't home when I stopped by earlier. Their housekeeper said they had gone to make funeral arrangements."

Priscilla's face paled as she broke into tears once again. "That poor baby."

"I'd better be going," David said, his eyes shifting from Priscilla to Bernie. "I got a list of people a mile long I have to talk to. If there's anything I can do to help, please let me know."

Bernie walked him to the door where the two men shook hands. "Find our little girl, David. Find her and bring her home to us."

David nodded grimly and walked out. He wondered if he'd have any better luck finding their daughter than he'd had finding his own.

CHAPTER THREE

The Kelseys had returned from the mortuary. The two-car garage stood open and David could clearly see a fresh coat of wax on both luxury cars inside. Running the Ledger Star must pay better than he thought. He wondered if it was too late to change careers. Then, he wondered what possible difference could it make now? In a couple more years, he'd be retired. Then, he could buy that fishing trawler he had his heart set on and spend the rest of his days fishing and drinking beer.

David remembered the first time he'd seen the boat of his dreams. It was skimming along the Inter-Coastal waterway in Chesapeake. The captain had a gaudy mustard yellow For Sale sign taped on the side. David had jotted down the number and called him that same day.

He'd taken Buddy Mason along to have a look at her. Buddy ruffled the captain's pride when he said the boat looked more like a dinghy than a fishing trawler. David had to get him away from there quick, before the old man raised his price. Hell, he didn't care what she looked like, as long as she'd float.

Tucking in his shirt, David walked up to Kelsey's front door and rang the bell. The housekeeper opened the door and, once more, gazed at him as though he were Jack the Ripper. She turned up her nose and said curtly, "You may come in now. The Kelseys are back."

David figured a smile would probably break her jaw. Silently, he followed her into the study.

James Kelsey sat with his back to the open door, staring out the window. David glanced out the window in the same direction. It was a nice yard. Shrubs stood like soldiers at inspection on either side of a wide cobblestone walkway. A heart-shaped pool lay beyond a rose garden on the far side of the grounds. Yeah. A real nice yard, he thought.

"Hello, James," David said, clearing his throat. "I can't tell you how sorry I was to hear about Robbie. This is the worst thing that can happen to a man."

Silence filled the air like an invisible poison.

"James, I hate to intrude at a time like this, but I've got some questions I need to ask—if you feel up to talking?"

Kelsey turned around slowly. His face was chalk white and his brown eyes were as red and swollen as Priscilla's had been.

"I've been expecting you," he said hoarsely. Mildred said you called while we were...while we were out."

David seated himself in a straight-backed chair, too rigid for comfort. He knew Sybil had selected the rattan furnishings on purpose. She didn't want company to get comfortable and stick around past her endurance.

"I know this is an awful time." David said sympathetically.

Kelsey nodded.

"James, were you aware that Robbie and Kerry Trivane were going to an abortion clinic this morning?"

Kelsey's face turned crimson. "If that little tramp hadn't forced him to have sex with her, he'd still be alive."

David cocked a brow and removed the small note pad from his shirt pocket.

"James, I've already talked to Bernie and Priscilla. They're as upset about what happened to Robbie as you are."

The newspaper editor snorted loudly. A wisp of thinning brown hair swayed limply over his brow. "They have no idea how it feels to lose a child! There isn't a scrap of decency between them. After they found out their daughter was pregnant, they insisted she go to

THE BABY SOLDIERS

the clinic and have an abortion. It didn't matter what anyone else wanted. If they had taught her anything at all, she wouldn't have gotten herself in that kind of fix to begin with."

The sergeant grimaced. It was obvious that James Kelsey didn't hold Robbie the least bit responsible for Kerry's condition. "Tell me something, James. If Kerry had decided to have the baby, was Robbie prepared to marry her and help her raise it?"

"That's irrelevant," Kelsey grumbled, his eyes blinking rapidly. "The child was a living thing. It had a right to be born."

"But if Robbie and Kerry were planning to marry, an abortion wouldn't have been an issue. Would it?"

Kelsey's mouth gaped open. "David, you can't be serious. I had Robbie enrolled in Yale, for God's sake! He had his entire future to consider. Being saddled with a no- account child wasn't part of it."

David clenched his fists. "Let me see if I understand this correctly. If a child goes hungry, or cold, or is unwanted by its parents, it doesn't matter as long as it gets born. Is that what you think, James?"

"Every child has a right to live," Kelsey murmured.

David closed his eyes. He had lost count of the number of times he'd heard the same answer.

"James, do you have any idea who may have done this? Do you think there's a remote possibility that the zealots who demonstrate against everything that comes down the pike could be behind Robbie's murder...and Kerry's kidnapping?"

James rubbed the stubble on his chin. "Well, it certainly is obvious it was someone who didn't want her to go through with the abortion." He lowered his head. "Why didn't they just take her? Why did they have to kill my boy?"

David looked directly into the editor's bespectacled eyes, unable to believe they had once enjoyed each other's company.

"Before Robbie started seeing Kerry, he was a good Christian boy. He didn't use drugs, or drink liquor, or do any of the evil things the rest of them did. She changed all that. She should have been the one to die, not my Robbie!"

— 17 —

Kelsey lowered his head and wept so hard his entire body trembled.

David rose to his feet and slipped the notebook in his pocket.

"James," he said hesitantly. "I'd appreciate it if you would call me if you think of anything that will help us find the people who did this."

"That won't be necessary," James snapped. "I've hired a private detective to find out who killed Robbie." He turned his back on the sergeant and resumed staring out the window. The query was over.

David Williams walked down the solar-lighted hall toward the front door. He didn't see Sybil lurking around anywhere, although he felt her presence. In a way, he was relieved she hadn't made an entrance. After talking to James, there seemed little point in having her parrot his words.

David drummed his fingers on the steering wheel as he drove the fifteen miles to the Nelson Clinic. He knew he'd probably hear a thousand different versions of the same incident, but that was his job, a job he was beginning to hate more with each passing hour.

The highways were fairly clear of traffic. It was the best possible time for driving along the beach—after the snow-birds had gone home, and before Christmas shoppers swamped the highways.

Ben nodded curtly when David flipped his badge before entering the clinic. David walked directly to the information desk. A middle-aged woman with orange hair pinned on top of her head looked up as he approached. "May I help you?" she asked snippily.

Sergeant Williams whipped out his ID once again. "I'd like to speak to the members of the staff who were present this morning when the shooting occurred. Can you help me with that?" Then he forced a patronizing smile.

The carrot-topped woman's smile mirrored his. "Here's the list," she replied, handing him a legal sized sheet of paper. The administrator figured you'd be asking for it." Then she gave him directions to the various offices in the clinic, as well as the window washer, who happened to be clinging to a scaffold on the second floor outside the main entrance when the murder took place.

After speaking with several technicians and doctors, who knew little or nothing about the incident, David questioned the maintenance man, who couldn't remember seeing anything but the frightened demonstrators scurrying into their buses when the shots were fired.

David was growing more frustrated as he walked down the hall past the elevators to the employees' lounge. Some nurses were sitting near the windows on the far side of the room. He gave them a quick once-over, noticing they were giving him the same. Their uniforms were spotless and wrinkle-free. He wondered how it was possible to work such long hours and still manage to look like you just stepped out your front door. The nurses were mostly slender and blond. One of them looked vaguely familiar, but he couldn't remember where he'd seen her before. Two were sitting at another table and looked enough alike to be sisters.

He dropped four quarters into a vending machine and retrieved a Styrofoam cup steaming with coffee. He walked over and placed the cup on the table where the look-alike nurses were sitting.

"My name is Detective Sergeant David Williams. I'm here to investigate the incident that took place in front of the clinic this morning. I was told you may have some information."

The young woman seated on his left, whose blond hair was a tad shorter than the other said, "I can't help you, Sergeant. I just missed it. When I came inside, I went directly upstairs to my duty station."

"Then you didn't see the car drive up, or anything unusual?"

The same nurse crushed an empty Sprite can in her fist. "I saw the car pull up to the curb. It was one of those fancy luxury cars, a Chrysler, I think. At the time, I thought it was odd, a car like that showing up here. Most of our patients come by cab, or some rickety old vehicle that won't draw any attention. That Chrysler was a cream-colored honey."

She turned to the other nurse. "Julie, I asked you about the car, remember? You mentioned it might belong to one of those groups that go around bombing clinics." She glanced at David and shrugged. "Julie was suspicious of the car right from the start."

David glanced at the paper Carrot-top had given him. Julie Newman ripped open a bag of potato chips. "I called 911 right after I came inside. It took them forever to get here."

"Can you identify the men?" David asked patiently.

"There were two of them," Julie answered thoughtfully. They both had dark hair and wore dark jackets and sunglasses. When they got out of the car, I saw one was taller, regular frame. He was the driver. He shot the young man with the girl. The other man was shorter and stocky. He grabbed the girl and dragged her to the car."

David scribbled the descriptions onto his pad.

"One other thing," she said, remembering.

David looked up.

"They were both smokers. I saw them tossing butts out the windows of that fancy car." She bit her lower lip. "I smoke too, but it makes me mad as hell when people dump cigarette butts and other trash all over the grounds."

The sergeant slid to the edge of his chair. For the first time since Woolard called this morning, he felt he might actually have a lead.

"Can you show me approximately where the car was parked?" he asked.

"Let me borrow a sweater from somebody," Julie replied. "I'll show you the exact spot."

David followed Julie Newman across the patchy grass, stopping to pick up a leaflet the demonstrators had dropped during their hasty retreat. His eyes darted over the inflamed words before giving it to Julie. "Looks like you had more to worry about than a couple fellows smoking cigarettes this morning?"

Julie folded her arms across her chest, shivering. "We had two camps of protesters show up at the same time. You'd have thought those guys would have blasted a few of them while they were at it."

THE BABY SOLDIERS

Julie pointed to the ground near the curb. "This is where the Chrysler was parked. Look at all those butts. You'd think this was a trash site."

David turned from the cluster of spent cigarettes to the old stone building, thinking a trash site was exactly what a lot of folks did think it was. He counted eight filtered cigarette butts as he scooped them into a plastic evidence bag. Then, he looked at the paved street to see if he could make out any discernible tire tracks. There were too many; it was impossible to tell if any of them were from the Chrysler.

He thanked Julie for her help and gave her one of his cards before walking back to his car.

CHAPTER FOUR

After turning the cigarette butts over to the lab, David transcribed the information from his notebook onto his computer. He was about to call the lieutenant and brief him on the day's events, when he remembered Woolard would be playing golf with the mayor and the city's youngest congressman today. He grinned maliciously, knowing how much the lieutenant hated playing golf with "that little twerp." David didn't think it was so much because the congressman was so much younger, but because he had to let him win. And everybody knew Lieutenant Woolard didn't like anybody getting the best of him.

He checked his watch and exhaled heavily. It was almost four o'clock. Too early to catch up with Buddy Mason at home. He grabbed his jacket and stopped by the dispatcher's desk to let him know he'd be home if anyone needed him. Then he walked out of the station house, just as the sun disappear behind a dark cloud.

A storm was brewing in the east. He hoped that Buddy would make it safely back to shore before it struck. David didn't make friends easily, and couldn't afford to lose any more of the ones he already had.

CHAPTER FIVE

No matter how desperately Kerry tried, she couldn't wake from the most horrible nightmare she'd ever had. The dream started when she first became pregnant. She didn't want to tell her parents, but she was so frightened, she didn't know what else to do. Wondering what their reaction would be made her so nervous she couldn't eat or sleep. When she fainted at school one morning and the nurse instructed her to see her family doctor, Kerry knew she couldn't hide it any longer.

The Trivanes were the greatest parents any kid could ever have. She knew how much they loved her...and trusted her. Kerry never wanted to do anything that would disappoint them.

Her boyfriend, Robbie Kelsey, offered to go with her when she delivered the bad news to her parents. She loved Robbie so much. If only they could get married the way they'd planned. But that wasn't going to happen, not after Robbie told his folks about her pregnancy. His mother had reacted far differently than they'd expected. She had never given any indication that she didn't like Kerry. Sybil Kelsey even treated her like the daughter she'd never had. But Sybil told Robbie that marriage was simply out of the question. He was nothing but a child himself and had no business considering marriage to anyone, least of all a Trivane. Then Robbie told Kerry his father had jumped on the bandwagon as well. A lot of strings had been pulled to get him into Yale and nothing was going to screw it up! His father told him that once he got his sheepskin, he could marry anyone he wanted. Kerry was devastated.

— 23 —

Kerry had felt the unbearable weight of contempt and disapproval bearing heavily upon her narrow shoulders. No matter how much Robbie professed his love for her, she knew he would never go against his parents' wishes. He told her they could run off and elope, but Kerry worried that they'd end up in some homeless shelter, begging for scraps of food, like the winos she saw outside the mall. She had no choice. She had to tell her parents.

Bernie Trivane was building a fire in the fireplace. Priscilla was busily going through brochures on places to go this summer, when Robbie and Kerry walked in.

"We thought you were going to a movie?" Bernie said, glancing over his broad shoulder. "What happened, Robbie, that new hummer of yours break down already?"

Robbie shoved his hands in his pockets. "No, sir. The jeep is running fine. Ah, we came back because we need to talk to you."

Slowly, Priscilla placed the brochures on the cocktail table and stood up. "Let me get you both some hot chocolate. You look half frozen. I didn't realize it was that cold outside."

Kerry reached out, touching her mother's arm. "Mom, Dad, please sit down. We don't need anything to drink…really."

Bernie cast her a sidelong glance, wiping his hands on the rag dangling from his back pocket. Then he joined his wife on the sofa. "Well," he said, "You have our undivided attention. What's this all about?"

Kerry faced her father, then her mother, unable to say the words. Robbie took her hand in his, and stammered, "We came…because… we wanted to tell you we're going to have a baby…and I…"

Bernie leapt to his feet. His hazel eyes wild and glaring. "What? Is this some kind of joke?"

Robbie shook his head. "No, sir. Kerry really is pregnant. She's already seen a doctor."

THE BABY SOLDIERS

Bernie paced the length of the room, while the others silently listened to the floorboards creaking beneath his heavy footsteps. He spun around glaring accusingly at his daughter. "Kerry, I can't believe this. I can't believe you'd do this to us. Haven't we always given you everything you wanted?"

Tears filled Kerry's eyes. "Yes, Daddy," she muttered softly.

Bernie frowned. "Then how could you do such a thing?"

"I love Robbie, Daddy. We were going to get married."

Bernie's eyes narrowed critically. "Well, now that you're pregnant, there isn't much choice. You'll have to do it right away."

"Please, Mr. Trivane, don't be angry with Kerry," Robbie pleaded. "It's all my fault. I really want to marry Kerry." He lowered his head and mumbled, "But my folks won't let me."

Bernie stopped pacing. His arms folded over his massive chest, like a Greek soldier prepared for battle. "What do you mean, they won't let you? You're not exactly a child, Robbie. You're old enough to get my daughter pregnant. You should be old enough to own up to your responsibilities."

Robbie bit his lip. "I really do want to marry her, Mr. Trivane. Please believe me. If it were up to me, I'd marry her right now."

Bernie chortled. "Yeah, I can just see tomorrow's headlines. *Editor's Son Forced into Marriage. Bright Future Flushed Down the Toilet.*

Bernie's breath came in short ragged gasps. "Kerry, what are you planning to do about this?"

Kerry shuffled her feet, looking at her mother. "I don't know. I wish that I had never..."

Bernie snickered. "It's a little late for that now."

Priscilla rose from the sofa and put her hands on Kerry's shoulders. "There must be something we can do. How far along are you?"

"Dr. Jennings says about six weeks."

Bernie gasped loudly. "You mean you actually went to our family doctor about this? Now everyone in town will know what you've done!"

— 25 —

"Bernie, calm down, Priscilla said. "What did you expect her to do, go to a fortuneteller?"

Bernie ran his fingers through his hair and mumbled.

"Dad...Mom..." Kerry said. Robbie and I came here because we thought you would help us. We want to do the right thing. We really do. We just don't know what that is. We can't count on Robbie's folks. They're too upset."

"I can't imagine why," Bernie muttered, refusing to look at them. Then he turned to Priscilla and said, "I know you're not going to like what I'm about to say, but it's the only solution that makes any sense."

Priscilla looked at him questioningly."What is it, Bernie? Tell us."

He sighed heavily, glancing from his wife to his daughter. "I think you should get an abortion - - - and get it done right away. You're only six weeks gone. It won't be that big of a deal."

"An abortion!" Kerry cried, the color draining from her face. "I can't do that."

"You certainly can," her father answered sternly. "I'm not going to have a bastard living under my roof, because its father doesn't have the balls to marry you!"

Robbie stepped forward, placing himself between Kerry and her father. "That's not true," he said defiantly. "I told you I'd marry Kerry today if I could."

Bernie waved him off dismissively. "You just can't afford to walk away from all that money and security, can you? My daughter isn't good enough for you to make that kind of sacrifice."

"That's not fair!" Kerry cried.

Bernie studied her tear-stained face. "They say you're growing up when you realize that life isn't always fair." He flopped back onto the sofa, staring down at the floor. "You do everything you can for your family. You work twelve hour a day at a job you despise, with people who look down their noses at you, because it's the right thing to do. You do everything just the way you were taught. Then you get your guts torn out by your own family." Then he looked at Kerry, blinking back tears that flooded his eyes. "Somebody you loved and trusted with all your heart."

Priscilla wrapped her arms around her daughter, stroking her long hair. "Bernie. I think we've all heard enough. Kerry made a terrible mistake. We should have talked to her long ago about using protection. We're just as much to blame as she is. What we have to do now is decide the best way to solve this problem."

Bernie looked at the stricken faces in front of him. "I've already told you the best solution. She gets an abortion, and she gets it damn quick."

Priscilla sighed heavily and nodded. "I think your father may be right, Kerry. If you had a baby right now, you'd have to drop out of school and give up so much. We'd hate to see you destroy your life that way."

Robbie took Kerry's hand and squeezed it gently. "Maybe...maybe they're right," he stammered. "Maybe we should think about it."

"Think about it hell!" Bernie roared. "You're going to do it... tomorrow if possible. I don't want you dragging this out until it's too late."

Priscilla guided Kerry and Robbie toward the kitchen. "I think I know some people who may be able to help us. Let me call around and see what I can find out."

Kerry and Robbie sat motionless at opposite ends of the kitchen table while Priscilla talked to someone on the wall phone beside the refrigerator. Kerry was more terrified than ever when her mother hung up and announced, "Kerry, you can have the abortion tomorrow morning at the Nelson Clinic. You'll be home, safe and sound, by tomorrow afternoon." She walked out, leaving the teenagers alone.

Kerry had heard so much about what happens during an abortion from other girls at school. They told her how much it hurt, and how empty you felt afterwards. But what choice did she have? She didn't have any money of her own and neither did Robbie. Kerry walked into the study, where her mother and father were waiting. Reluctantly, she agreed.

The next morning, Robbie drove Kerry to the clinic. He didn't want her to go through with the abortion any more than she did. His hands were trembling and his face was whiter than she'd ever seen it before. On the drive across town, they talked about other things, things that would distract them from concentrating on the pressing issue at hand. They talked about a future they still planned to have one day. Robbie promised Kerry that, no matter what happened, they'd get married as soon as he graduated from medical school. She wanted so badly to believe him. He was everything she'd ever wanted, now and forever. She assured him that someday, they'd be the happiest people alive and have lots and lots of children.

CHAPTER SIX

Kerry thrashed in her sleep, the dream more real and frightening than ever before. Two men racing toward them across the grounds outside the abortion clinic. One man holding a gun. Robbie telling her to run. She couldn't move. One of the men fired at Robbie. He was falling in slow motion, trying to tell her something. He was going away. She cried out, begging him to come back. The men pushing her into a car with cold leather seats. Strangers gawking at her. Protest signs dropping from numb fingers. No one tried to rescue her. "Help me," she cried as the car sped away.

Startled, she opened her eyes and gasped for breath. It was so dark. She didn't know where she was. "Oh, God," she moaned. It wasn't a dream."

Her clothes were soaked with perspiration. She turned her head, squinting to see. The room smelled awful. Where was this dingy place those men had brought her?

The shuffle of feet followed, and two men appeared in the lighted doorway. She gasped, recognizing them instantly.

"Well, what do you know? Sleeping beauty woke up," the squatty one named Fritz said. "Let's get her over to the camp so the guardian can inspect the new merchandise."

Kerry tried fighting them off, but she was so weak. They pulled her to her feet. She could barely place one foot in front of the other. She was still groggy from whatever they'd given her earlier. She didn't understand what was happening. What was she doing here?

A sour lump formed in her throat, making it difficult to swallow. These men killed Robbie and kidnapped her. But why?

She thought about Robbie the last time she'd seen him. Tears filled her eyes. She shook her head, fighting them back. She didn't want to give the men the satisfaction of knowing how badly they'd hurt her.

A thrust of cold wind whipped her face. Fritz yanked her from the storage shed. His fingers dug into her skin so deeply, she yelped. Pauly, the taller one, yanked her hair and told her to shut up and keep moving. Then he pushed her so hard she nearly fell.

The glare of sunlight burned her eyes. Kerry lowered them as Pauly roughly nudged her forward. She lost her footing on a clump of dirt and stumbled. Fritz caught her before she fell. About a hundred feet ahead, stood a long metal building with a rounded roof. It looked like an airplane hangar, the kind she'd seen in old movies her dad used to watch on television. The dull paint was chipped and worn, leaving huge patches of rust all over. High, narrow windows ran the length of the structure. Kerry noticed most of the windows had bars on them. This was no airplane hangar, she thought horrified. It was prison.

When Pauly shoved her inside, she tripped on the leg of a metal chair near the door and spun around. He grabbed her by the shoulders and laughed wickedly. "We can't have you falling down. Damaged goods aren't worth much around here."

In spite of her fear, Kerry was surprised by how warm and bright it was inside the building. The men lead her to a small room on the right side, not far from the front door. The room was sparsely furnished, containing a long metal desk and two folding chairs. A row of filing cabinets stood against the far wall beneath the windows. Kerry studied the windows. Too high to reach and too narrow to climb through.

Pauly pushed her down in one of the chairs. "Stay put," he snapped. "The guardian will be here soon."

The men walked out, locking the door behind them. Kerry's hands were trembling. Soon, her entire body joined in the frenzy. "Help me, Robbie. I'm so afraid."

Kerry's head snapped up when the metal door burst open. She hugged herself tightly, trying to control the spastic gasping brought on by her grief. A somber faced stranger stood in the doorframe, broad chest straining the uniform's seams. The stranger had penetrating dark brown eyes and short-cropped hair. Kerry assumed this was the guardian the men spoke of. At first glance, Kerry thought the guardian was a man, but on closer inspection, she realized it was a woman wearing a man's uniform.

Her somber gaze burned straight to Kerry's soul, making her feel as helpless as a three-year-old child.

The woman's voice was gruff. "I'm Margaret Hatchey," she said cutting the ropes binding Kerry's wrists. "Who might you be?"

Kerry flinched, touching her raw wrists. "I'm...I'm...Then she broke down and cried.

"We don't have time for blubbering here," the guardian snapped. "Now, get out of those nasty clothes so I can examine you."

Kerry's blue eyes widened fearfully. "Right here?" she stammered.

Hatchey placed her hands on her wide hips. "Listen, missy; I don't have time to coddle you. Just do as you're told and we'll get along fine."

Kerry stood up, her legs trembling worse than before. "But...I...I never"

Margaret Hatchey threw her head back and laughed. "Don't give me that I never bullshit. If you were so pure, you wouldn't have gotten yourself knocked up to begin with now, would you?"

Seeing her protests were getting her nowhere, Kerry began to disrobe.

The examination the guardian gave her wasn't much different from the one Dr. Jennings had given her the week before. Although the woman probing her private parts was far more gentle than her family doctor had been. The main difference she could see was that the doctor's office had a regular examination table. Here, she discovered the versatility of an office desk.

"You're not that far along," Hatchey said, snapping off the rubber gloves. "You're going to be with us for quite some time."

Kerry raised up on her elbows, so she could see the guardian's face more clearly. "What...what do you mean by that?"

"I mean that you'll be staying with us until you have that baby you're carrying. Offhand, I'd say that would be about seven months from now."

"Seven months!" Kerry cried out. "You can't keep me in this place for seven months!"

The guardian smirked. "We do a lot of things here. You're not so special, you know. Girls like you come through that door every day. And they do exactly what they're told." She shrugged nonchalantly. "Once their babies are born, they're free to go their merry way."

Kerry gasped loudly. "You mean...after I have my baby, I can leave here?"

"You can go to Egypt for all I care," Hatchey replied.

"I don't believe you," Kerry said brazenly. "If other girls were forced to stay here until their babies were born, they would have had sent the cops back. They'd be crawling all over this place the minute they got out."

Hatchey sighed tiredly. "Let me tell you a little secret, missy. We don't fear the police here."

Kerry clutched her blouse to her bare breasts. "You mean the police know what you're doing?"

The grim lines in Hatchey's olive face softened. "You might even say we have their blessing. The powers that be figured this is the perfect way to solve the problem of all you little twats who want to get rid of your babies."

Kerry slid off the desk and pulled on her panties and jeans. "I want to go home! I want to go home right now!"

The guardian wrote something down on a clipboard and then eyed Kerry as though she was a fly sitting on the rim of a glass. "Get this into that empty skull of yours, once and for all. For the next seven months, this is going to be the only home you know."

Kerry gawked at her, a thousand questions glimmering in her frightened eyes.

"Now, finish dressing so I can take you to your room."

Kerry zipped the jeans slowly, noticing it took more effort than before. "I'm not staying in this place. You can't make me," she said defiantly.

Margaret Hatchey grabbed her arms and shook her till her teeth hurt. "Listen to me, you spoiled brat. You will do exactly as I say. We have rules here and everyone is expected to follow them. You wouldn't be here at all if that boyfriend of yours had done the proper thing and married you."

The color completely drained from Kerry's face. "We wanted to get married, but his parents wouldn't let us. They wanted him to go to college and study to be a doctor."

"Sounds to me like he's nothing but a pantywaist coward," Hatchey quipped.

"Robbie's not a coward!" Kerry cried. "I loved him more than anything in the world. And he loved me, too."

"Is that so?" the guardian replied snootily. "If that fellow of yours loved you so darned much, why wasn't he around when you needed him most?"

Kerry lowered her head, unable to stop the tears that trickled down her pale cheeks. "Because those men who brought me here killed him."

Hatchey froze; her dark eyes riveted on Kerry's tortured face. "What? What did you say?"

Kerry glared at the guardian and repeated the agonizing words. The woman folded her arms, clutching her fingers into her thick waist, her laser eyes darting from side to side. It was only then, Kerry realized Margaret Hatchey didn't know about Robbie's murder. The guardian continued to stare at her, but asked no more questions.

After Kerry laced her shoes, she meekly followed the guardian down the open corridor that stretched the length of the building. Thin sheets of paneling partitioned the square rooms on either side of the corridor. One of the doors was left ajar. Kerry peeked inside and saw four empty bunks, much like the one in the storage shed where she'd been held the night before. They were stacked like bunk beds, two on either side of the room.

She thought about an old fort in North Carolina her parents had taken her to see the previous summer. The rooms here were about the same size as those at the fort, and decorated similarly. The smell of disinfectant was so pungent, Kerry thought she would puke if she stayed in this place another minute.

When they reached the end of the long corridor, the guardian pointed toward a small cubicle on the right side. "This one is yours."

Kerry stared idly at a girl sitting on one of the lower bunks. Her long legs stretched halfway across the room. Her stomach billowed from her breasts to her knees. Her stringy red hair fell forward, covering her face as she filed her nails, oblivious to the rest of the world.

Margaret Hatchey turned to Kerry. "Since you arrived so late, you missed having breakfast with the others. I'll have something sent in for you. We want to make sure that baby of yours is perfectly healthy when it gets here."

The guardian crossed the room and kicked the soles of the girl's feet with the tip of her heavy boot. The girl moved her legs closer to the bunk without comment.

"Look what we have here, Amy. Another roommate for you to teach all your sneaky tricks."

Kerry jumped, clutching her chest, when the door slammed shut behind her.

Amy glanced up at her. "No worries. You get used to the sound of that after awhile."

Warily, Kerry studied her new roommate. She guessed Amy was about eighteen or nineteen. She was huge. She looked big enough to deliver twins any day at all.

Amy stood up awkwardly, using her muscular arms for leverage. "Welcome to the greenhouse," she said sarcastically. "I'm Amy Patterson."

Kerry looked past Amy to the narrow cots and the single metal chair between them. "I want to go home."

"Yeah, yeah," Amy said, sauntering toward her. "We all want to go home, kid."

Kerry glared at her. "If they won't let me leave. I'll run away."

Amy snickered. "Aren't you a little young to be in a place like this? What are you, fourteen?"

"I'm almost sixteen," Kerry retorted defensively. "And I don't like being called a kid!"

"Feisty, too." Amy arched a brow. "You know something, kid. I like your spunk."

Kerry crossed the room and plopped down on the bunk across from the one Amy was using. "My name isn't kid. It's Kerry...Kerry Trivane. I've got to get out of here. My folks are going to be mad as hell when they find out somebody kidnapped me and brought me to this...this dungeon."

Amy leaned against the door, filing her nails as she studied Kerry. Then she yawned.

Kerry narrowed her eyes. "I guess you never tried to escape."

Amy grinned. "I tried to break out of this joint lots of times. They always caught me though." She lowered the file and rubbed her swollen stomach. "That's one of the perks of being pregnant. If you do something they don't like, at least they don't beat the shit out of you."

Kerry stared at Amy in disbelief. "But if you weren't pregnant, you wouldn't be here to start with?"

Amy cocked her head to one side. Her long red hair draped over her breast. "You got a point there, kiddo."

Kerry stood up slowly. "That woman, Margaret Hatchey, told me that once my baby is born, I can leave here. Is that true?"

Amy pursed her lips. "Sure. You can leave, but you can't take the baby with you."

Kerry folded her arms protectively over her stomach. "No...that can't be true."

Amy sat on the solitary chair and tried unsuccessfully to cross her legs. "Since you're a novice, let me explain how things work around here." She grunted, letting her foot settle back to the floor. "You have the baby and then you're free to go. The guards take the baby off to some secret place where it will grow up, never knowing about you or where it came from."

"No, they won't," Kerry replied. "When I have this baby, I'm going to raise it myself. My baby is going home with me."

Amy snapped the wooden file in two. "I'm afraid that's not the way it works. Here, we're nothing more than breeding machines. They feed us and see we get plenty of exercise and make us clean up after ourselves. Oh, we balk all right. Some of us don't like being pushed around. But we're not strong enough to push back, not yet, that is. This camp is run by a huge organization...like the government. The major decisions are made by a group of perverted assholes nobody really knows, and we are expected to keep our mouths shut and follow orders."

Kerry was speechless.

"After they take your baby," Amy shrugged her shoulders. "You're no longer of any use to them, so you're free to go about your business. A lot of girls ended up committing suicide once they got out, or living in some shit hole."

Kerry shook her head more vehemently than ever. "Not me! I'm not living in any shit hole."

Amy scoffed. "Suit yourself. You can live on the streets or in a cardboard box, if that suits you better."

"I live in a nice home," Kerry said indignantly. "I have a mother and a father and a little brother, too."

"Well congratulations," Amy quipped. "By the time you get out of this dump, they'll be long gone, moved so far away you'll never find them."

THE BABY SOLDIERS

"My family would never move away without me," Kerry said. "Not ever! Once I get out of here and tell them what happened to me...and Robbie...they'll have the cops here so fast it'll make your head swim."

Amy laughed so hard she had to hold her stomach to keep it steady. "Don't," she groaned. "Stop it. I can't go on laughing like this. It's killing me."

"I wasn't trying to be funny," Kerry said, leaning over her. "Look at you. You're due anytime at all. Doesn't it bother you that those creeps are going to rip your baby away, and you'll never see it again?"

The laughter stopped.

"I have another question, Amy. How is it you know so much about this organization?"

Amy rubbed the back of her neck. "I've been here a long time, too long." She scowled. "I wasn't much farther along than you when they first brought me here. You'd be surprised how much you can learn by just listening and keeping your mouth shut."

"What kind of things?" Kerry asked.

"Things like what happens to the babies once they're taken away from us."

"Nothing is going to happen to my baby," Kerry said boldly.

Amy looked at her with the pity she normally reserved for the grossly ignorant and the terminally ill. "Interesting, you're being so concerned about that baby, when only yesterday, you were planning to abort it?"

"That was before," Kerry said, her voice trembling. "Before they killed Robbie."

Amy frowned. "Robbie?"

"Robbie was my boyfriend. He was my whole life," Kerry murmured softly.

"They...they killed him?" Amy stammered.

Kerry could tell that Amy was just as shocked by what had happened to Robbie as the guardian had been.

Kerry grimaced. "Those bastards took Robbie away from me. But no one is going to take my baby." She glanced down, caressing her stomach. "I'll come up with a plan. You just wait and see."

Amy studied her for a long time, and nodded. "I got a plan or two of my own."

"What kind of plan?" Kerry whispered.

Amy eyed her suspiciously. "What makes you think I should trust you? You might walk out of here and blab everything you know to the guards. I don't trust anybody that much. Even the walls in this place have ears."

Kerry shrugged and turned away. "Suit yourself," she replied smugly. "I don't need your ideas, or your help. I don't need anybody. Whoever is responsible for killing Robbie and bringing me here is going to pay big time. I promise you that."

Amy smiled thinly. "You got balls all right. If I had more time, maybe I'd be around long enough to trust you. If you're half as serious as you claim, we could make those bastards sorry they ever tangled with the likes of Patterson and Trivane."

Kerry shook her head. "I'm not saying another word. Anything I tell you could put me in danger, too."

"Yeah," Amy muttered. "Even getting up in the morning can be dangerous. Look what's happened to you since the last time you woke up in your own bed."

Kerry lay on the lumpy cot and thought about the last morning she'd slept at home. Was it only yesterday? It felt more like a hundred years ago.

She remembered saying goodbye to her mom and dad. She remembered holding Robbie's hand while he drove to the clinic. She remembered feeling the heat from his body as they walked along the yard in front of the clinic. She remembered him saying he'd always love her, no matter what. She remembered those men and the awful sound of gun shots. She remembered screaming as the men, who killed Robbie, but they dragged her away and she couldn't touch him anymore. She opened her eyes as tears streaming down her face.

— 38 —

THE BABY SOLDIERS

"Whether you believe it or not, I can be trusted," she told Amy. "All I want to do now is get even."

Amy believed her. "For now, just eat what you're supposed to eat and get plenty of sleep and exercise. If you're going to be any good to yourself, that baby you're carrying, or anybody else, you have to keep up your strength." Amy looked longingly at her stomach. My little one is anxious to bust into this lousy world. As soon as that happens, I'm out of here. And once I get out," she said, her eyes filled with fire. "Those bastards better look out!"

"How will I get in touch with you?"Kerry asked.

"Don't worry," Amy replied. "If you're serious about making good on those threats of yours, I'll find you."

Two pregnant teens sauntered into the room, unasked questions in their eyes. Kerry figured they were the tenants of the remaining two bunks. They nodded stiffly at her and then turned to Amy, waiting for answers. Amy walked toward the window, her eyes even with the bottom of the glass. She gazed blankly through the bars. Kerry took Amy's indifference to them as a sign that they couldn't be trusted. She introduced herself, not wanting to burn any bridges she may need later, then climbed onto one of the top bunks. The drugs the men had given her still hadn't completely worn off. The moment she closed her eyes, the nightmare started all over again.

CHAPTER SEVEN

David Williams fought to stay awake long enough to watch the eleven o'clock news. When the doorbell rang, he turned the volume down on the remote and went to answer it. Danny Woolard stood on the porch shivering. David appraised his nocturnal visitor, glancing left and right.

"I'm alone," Danny assured him.

David motioned for him to come inside. "Why are you out so late? It's freezing and you're not even wearing a jacket."

Danny followed the detective inside. "I...I'm sorry. I didn't have anywhere else to go."

David grumbled. "It must be thirty degrees, and you're running around wearing nothing but a T-shirt and jeans."

"My car has a heater," Danny stammered, inching closer to the fireplace.

"Sit down," David said, nodding toward the worn sofa. "You want something to drink? I got water, sodas and instant coffee."

Danny rubbed his arms. "I could use a slug of brandy."

David eyed the young man furtively. "Nice try. Your old man would have me strung up for delinquency."

"Yeah, knowing him, he probably would," Danny mumbled, mesmerized by the flames. "I don't need anything. I'll be okay."

"You sure don't look okay," David said. "You look like somebody stole your best girl."

"I don't have a girl," Danny replied softly.

David glanced at the TV screen and sighed heavily. He'd missed the weather report. He turned the television off and looked at Danny. "Well? Are you going to tell me what's going on, or do you plan on keeping me in suspense the rest of the night?"

While continuing to stare at the flickering orange flames, Danny replied hollowly, "It's dad."

David sat back in his recliner and grunted. He had a bad feeling the lieutenant was behind this. "What has he done now?"

Danny replied tersely. "He and Mom were arguing about something. He hit her, David. I was in the garage when it happened. He hit her so hard I heard her bouncing off the wall." He turned his back to the fire, shaking his head. "I told him I'd kill him if he ever touched her again."

David jumped from the chair, his fingers coiled into fists. "Is Adele all right?"

Danny lowered his head. "I guess so." Then he quickly added. "She said I shouldn't worry about her." He rolled his eyes. "You know how she is? The perpetual martyr."

"Is Horace still at the house?" David asked.

"I guess so. I got out of there as soon as I said my piece." Danny stood and rubbed his legs. "I shouldn't have come. I never should have left her alone with him. He's getting worse, David. I don't know what's wrong with him anymore."

David couldn't count the number of times he'd heard that over the years. "Was he drinking?" David asked, already knowing the answer.

Danny's green eyes grew misty. "When isn't he?"

David combed his fingers through his dark hair. "Maybe you'd better give your mom a call - - - just to be sure she's okay?"

Danny glanced nervously at his watch. "Would you mind calling, David? If...if my dad answers, he'll hang up on me."

David lifted the receiver and grunted. "That's six-four-nineteen, isn't it?"

Danny smiled. "As many times as you've called our house, I figured you'd know that number by heart."

David chuffed. "If I was any good at remembering numbers, I wouldn't be a lowly public servant."

Danny turned back toward the fire as David made the call.

The moment David heard Adele's voice, he breathed a sigh of relief.

"Adele. It's David. Is Horace there?"

"No he isn't, David," she answered hesitantly. "Is something wrong?"

"You can answer that question better than I can," he quipped. "Where did he go?"

"He just left for Baltimore. He said something about urgent business."

"Urgent business, huh," David said, wondering what was so urgent it couldn't wait until daylight. "Adele, Danny's here. He told me what happened over there earlier."

"Oh, David," she replied, embarrassed. "He shouldn't have done that. I don't want him to worry you with our problems."

"You're my friend, Adele," David said comfortingly. "We go back a long way. I'm not happy about what's going on between you and Horace."

"I'm not happy about it either, David, but I really don't see what anyone can do. Horace is…Horace is going through a rough time right now…some kind of crises at work," she explained. "I'm sure as soon as he straightens everything out, he'll be just fine again."

David couldn't think of any crises at work that would upset Horace badly enough for him to go off the deep end, particularly with anyone as sweet as Adele. He shook his head from side to side. "Come on, Adele, you don't believe that any more than I do."

"I have to believe it, David. I keep hoping that someday things will be the way they used to be. It's the only thing I have to hold onto. It's not just me. I have the boys to consider."

— 42 —

THE BABY SOLDIERS

David wished she were standing in front of him right now, so he could try to shake some sense into her. Danny had already told him Horace was getting worse. What did she want him to do, beat her to death before she realized that he was never going to change? "Adele, I'll call and check on you tomorrow. I'll send Danny home just as soon as he gets warmed up."

"Please do," she replied. "I have some things I need to talk to him about."

David hung up, his fingers drumming lightly on the end table.

Danny turned around and caught David frowning. "David, is she all right?"

David couldn't understand why a woman like Adele would put up with someone as insensitive as Horace Woolard. She hoped Horace would change into the person he used to be. As far back as David could remember, Horace had always been a mean son-of-a-bitch. "Danny, your mother said Horace left town, unexpectedly. She also said she needs to talk to you when you get home. She sounded anxious. Any idea why?"

Danny shrugged. "Not really. I guess I'd better be going."

David put his arm over the boy's shoulder and walked him to the door. Suddenly, he stopped and clicked his fingers. He opened the closet beside the front door and removed a black jacket. "Here," he said, giving it to Danny. "I used to wear this…before my washboard stomach turned into a full-sized Maytag. I don't want you to catch pneumonia."

Danny rubbed the soft leather. "Thanks, David. I'll take good care of it."

David watched the boy shove his powerful arms into the jacket's long sleeves, surprised by how well the jacket fit him. Danny wasn't a little boy anymore. Suddenly, he felt older than he had that morning. "Danny, if you need me, call."

Danny zipped the jacket and nodded. "I will."

David stood at the open door and watched Danny fold his long legs into the VW, wondering where the years had gone. He closed the door and thought about all the children growing up. His thoughts centered on Kerry Trivane, the missing teen.

Kerry was younger than Danny - - - and already pregnant. He hated to see them grow up too soon. Then he thought of Robbie Kelsey, lying in the hospital morgue, and was cruelly reminded that some of them didn't grow up at all.

CHAPTER EIGHT

Kerry Trivane moped around the camp for weeks after Amy Patterson was released. The only hope she had to cling onto was the day when she would be free to leave this awful prison and destroy the people responsible for kidnapping her and killing Robbie Kelsey. She tried to remember everything Amy had told her to do in order to keep from losing her mind. She kept busy scrubbing floors, changing linens, and the other duties that Margaret Hatchey had assigned to her. As the weeks rolled by, Kerry found even the simplest tasks increasingly difficult to perform. The bouts of morning sickness she'd experienced since the very beginning of her pregnancy hadn't let up, but continued to drain her strength and willpower well into the afternoon.

Kerry couldn't help but notice the way the other girls avoided her in recent weeks. Even the few who had been cordial before, now turned the other way when they saw her coming toward them. She wondered if the guards had warned them to stay away from her. The guards didn't like her because she was Amy's friend. They knew Amy was a troublemaker.

Kerry forced a smile remembering how Amy didn't help the situation very much, carrying on the way she did. Amy would think nothing of tripping a guard, or dumping sugar on him, then defy him to touch her. By the time Amy left the camp, Kerry couldn't have cared for her more if she'd been her own sister.

Amy was strong and brave, and had refused to cry, even on her last day at the camp, after they'd taken her baby away and told her she'd never see him again. Kerry shuddered when she thought about the ferocious look on Amy's face. For one single moment, her face transformed into something sinister. There was no doubt in Kerry's mind that Amy could have killed the whole lot of them. Kerry lay awake many nights, worried that Amy hadn't been set free at all. She was afraid the guards had taken Amy off somewhere and shot her, the way they'd shot Robbie.

Although Kerry was forbidden to contact anyone on the outside, she missed her family so much. She wondered if they thought about her and missed her, too. She thought about Robbie constantly and wondered if his parents blamed her for his death. If only she hadn't become weak and bowed to her parents' wishes. If she had refused to have the abortion, Robbie would still be alive. Not an hour of the day went by when she didn't blame herself for what happened to the man she loved. If she hadn't gone to the abortion clinic that day, not only would Robbie still be alive, but she wouldn't be wasting away in this awful place.

Her stomach churned when she felt the baby kick. Gently, she caressed it, knowing it wouldn't be long before the child that no one wanted would be born…and taken away, like Amy's baby. She never believed she could become so attached to something she had never seen, something she would not be permitted to hold or love. She'd never forget the hatred in Amy's eyes the day she left the camp.

Amy had confided that she'd never agreed to have an abortion. Her parents had forced her to go to the clinic. All Amy wanted was to have her baby and raise it herself. As badly as Kerry felt for herself, she knew Amy was going through so much worse.

Amy had sworn she'd get her baby back one day. Kerry wanted to believe that with all her heart. Each day, she prayed Amy would find the support she needed to carry out her plan. Before Amy left, she made Kerry promise she would keep her ears open and try to find out the names of the people responsible for putting them through hell. Amy had already warned her that the organization was extremely powerful, and she should be very careful. Amy had hinted that one of those crazy right wing religious groups was most likely behind everything. Kerry hoped she was wrong. No one who believed in God could possibly do the horrible things that had been done to her and the others.

CHAPTER NINE

Margaret Hatchey didn't normally feel compassion for the girls at the camp, considering most of them were responsible for their own predicament. But she made an exception in Kerry Trivane's case. Having a child in a place as desolate as this, and being locked away from your family and everything familiar was bad enough, but witnessing the murder of the child's father was monstrous. She scowled, thinking of Pauly and Fritz, his faithful corporals. That's what Reverend Jacobson frequently called them. She wondered if the Kelsey boy was the first person they'd ever killed. Somehow, she doubted it.

Margaret couldn't stop thinking about the troubling number of missing persons over the past ten years. Statistics had shown that teenage girls accounted for the largest percentage of the missing cases in Virginia alone. She realized that some of the girls had been picked up on their way to abortion clinics. But what had happened to the others? Margaret wondered if they could have been on their way to the camp, when something went wrong…and the guards had murdered them. She hated men and their pagan needs. How many times had she walked into one of the rooms to check on a pregnant girl and found a guard in the process of raping her? She thought about Clifford Jacobson's perfect society and snorted. It would never work - - - not as long as men were in charge.

Margaret vowed to keep a close watch over the Trivane girl. None of those filthy animals were going to touch her, not if she had anything to say about it. Margaret opened a stick of chewing gum and popped it into her mouth. Ever since Amy Patterson left the camp, she noticed the Trivane girl had withdrawn. She kept up with her chores, but the spark was gone from her eyes. After witnessing Fritz and Pauly shoot her lover, it was a miracle the girl hadn't snapped completely. She could still remember Kerry's face the day she said the guards had killed her boyfriend. Margaret wanted to call Clifford Jacobson right there and then to let him know what his men had done. But she knew it would be a waste of effort. He wouldn't have any objections to a few people being trampled underfoot, as long as his orders were carried out. But it mattered to Margaret Hatchey. And sooner rather than later, she was going to have to do something about it.

She looked at the headline on the front page of the afternoon paper. *Spontaneous Bombings Reverberate Through Community!*

In the beginning, the bombing incidents were scantily reported, making them appear insignificant and unrelated. It wasn't until the bombing in the Kempsville area of Virginia Beach had made the front page of the Virginian Pilot that people began to realize the destruction was well-planned, and the bombings always took place when the clinics had the largest number of people present.

Underneath the headline, Margaret read, *Twelve Maimed, Nine Dead.*

Margaret wondered how it had come to this. In the beginning, the group she served had fought for the rights of the unborn. Now, it seemed that no life was safe, born or unborn.

Even her own family wasn't free from the insanity taking over the country. The leaders of the organization had moved her aging parents to a secluded woodland in the middle of the state. They'd been accused of harboring those who refused to accept the New Order. When Margaret protested, Jacobson assured her it was a necessary move and no harm would come to them. She had good reason to worry. Clifford Jacobson wasn't a man known for keeping his promises. Her sister, Peggy, had learned that the hard way. And now, Peggy, Margaret's impetuous sister, had vanished as well.

CHAPTER TEN

Due to its support of the abortion movement, radio station WKJL had received numerous threats in recent months. This particular day, a group of parents, whose children were reported missing, had come to the station in an attempt to go public with their stories.

Tim Barnes, moderator of the public concerns forum, introduced the first set of parents. The Simms couple stated their daughter was twelve years old when she was raped by a violent criminal who'd been paroled by the system. They said he should have been executed for his crimes, but the right-to-lifers had fought to keep him alive, all the way to the state supreme court. Eventually, the fiend was set free to rape again.

When the parents learned the monster had impregnated their daughter, they contacted an abortion clinic and made arrangements to spare their child the curse of carrying a rapist's offspring. Jack Simms told the listeners that on the way to the clinic, a truck had forced their car off the road. He said he and his wife were beaten, and left bloody and dazed. The men who had beaten them had kidnapped their daughter. They hadn't seen her since. He added that they had been contacted by someone who warned them not to breathe a word of what they'd seen to anyone, or they would not walk away from the next accident. After remaining both terrified and silent for three long years, Mr. and Mrs. Simms said they couldn't keep quiet any longer. They had to come forward and share their story as a warning to others, even if it meant they would be killed.

Each parent who followed the first couple to the microphone had a tale more ghastly to tell than the one before. They all claimed they had gone to the police, even their congressmen for support, and had received no satisfaction. Feeling they had nowhere else to turn, they decided to go public. WKJL was their last resort.

Callers swamped the lines. The reactions varied from disbelief to heartfelt condolences. But in the end, nothing had been resolved, although the group felt some satisfaction in knowing their message was out. They were no longer alone, or afraid of the maniacs who had stolen their children. They were ready to fight back.

CHAPTER ELEVEN

Amy Patterson was in top physical form, ramrod straight and lean. Since leaving the camp where she'd been held prisoner, she'd worked toward gathering the forces needed to destroy the heartless animals responsible for kidnapping her and stealing her baby. Four months ago, she learned her folks had high-tailed it to Nevada shortly after her abduction. She wasn't surprised to find they didn't stick around to find out what had happened to her. Amy figured they'd chalked up her disappearance to divine intervention. Her absence probably didn't upset them nearly as much as her condition had.

Amy had never forgotten the way they carried on when she told them she wasn't planning to marry the fellow responsible for her pregnancy. For a brief moment, they looked relieved. They assumed she would have an abortion. She knocked their socks off when she explained she wanted to have the baby and raise it herself. Her mother actually fainted. Then they began pressuring her to have an abortion.

Amy thought about them suffocating somewhere in the Nevada desert. The little girl's voice in her head giggled. Nevada was perfect. She couldn't think of a single place that could possibly be any more uncomfortable to live. While she was at the camp, she'd heard rumors that the families of the other girls, who'd been kidnapped, were forced to move away. They didn't have to force her folks, she thought grimly. The Pattersons would have been all too happy to escape the scandal.

She was surprised to learn her parents had done one decent thing before leaving Virginia. They had opened a savings account in her name...in the event she did come back from wherever she had gone. It wasn't a huge amount, but at least she didn't have to beg for food, or check into a homeless shelter like some of her less fortunate peers. After paying a modest deposit and the first month's rent on an efficiency apartment, and splurging on a gym membership to keep in shape, Amy set out to find other victims, like herself, who were seeking retribution.

Listening to WKJL was the bright spot of Amy's day. She enjoyed listening to oldies music, and the DJ's cheerful banter with his call-in audience. She particularly enjoyed his edgy opinions of politicians and certain members of the clergy. She was driving across town, trying to find one of the women she'd met at the breeding camp when Tim Barnes announced his show today would be different. Amy leaned forward and turned up the volume.

"Today," he said, drawling his words to pump up the suspense, "we're interviewing some mighty angry folks. They've come here to tell you their harrowing stories., demanding to know the whereabouts of their missing daughters."

Amy was so shocked her foot slipped off the brake pedal. She nearly drove the Plymouth's long hood into the back of the Cadillac in front of her. Her heart pounded as she listened to the agonizing stories the men and women told about the tragic ways their children had been taken from them—and the threats to their own safety. Amy longed to hear a name she would recognize. If any of the girls had been kidnapped and taken to the camp, she would call the radio station and tell them. Finally, she could tell someone the truth, someone who would believe her. Perhaps, she'd even find someone brave enough to help her get her baby back. But none of the parents' names set off any bells. How odd, she thought, especially since the girls had supposedly disappeared from the same vicinity she had. She remembered the names of all the girls who were at the camp the same time she was, even the ones she didn't like. She had heard, by way of the grapevine, that the greenhouse where she'd been held was the only one of its kind operating in the state. She didn't think the

— 54 —

goons who had kidnapped her would have taken those other girls all the way to Maryland or Carolina. Amy was more curious than ever. Exactly what had happened to the other missing girls? The puzzle was growing larger and more distorted, and the pieces were getting smaller and less defined.

Amy spent a lot of time traveling to homeless shelters, where the overwhelming scent of disinfectant made her want to puke, and abuse centers, where the sight of battered and broken women made her want to pull her red hair out by its roots. Occasionally, she found someone who would talk about the camp, but more often than not, the women she met were too frightened by what had happened to them to even discuss it. All they wanted to do was forget the past, no matter how painful, and get on with what was left of their lives. Amy's plan to bulldoze the organization that had caused irreparable harm to so many wasn't going to be easy. Since leaving the camp, she had enlisted a mere twelve people. She needed thousands.

She thought of Kerry Trivane often, and wondered how she was coping with the guards in the greenhouse. Kerry had mentioned one of them coming onto her right before Amy left. Amy had taken it upon herself to mention the problem to Margaret Hatchey.

Hatchey was a miserable bitch in a lot of ways, but she didn't tolerate guards who thought the pregnant girls were there to provide their personal amusement. Hatchey had rescued her on more than one occasion.

When Amy wasn't busy gathering recruits, or working part-time at the library, she scouted for a place to use as an operating base. A place where she could hold meetings and house the girls who were having a difficult time coping with life after the greenhouse experience. She would have preferred finding a location close to the beach, but decided it would be more prudent to settle for something in an older suburb, where the group wouldn't be as likely to attract attention.

Early one evening, after narrowing the selection of homes she could lease down to three, she stopped at a restaurant to grab a quick sandwich and a beer. A couple of men were seated in the booth directly behind her, their voices grew louder with each round they ordered. When she heard the name Jacobson, she stiffened. When she was little, a man named Clifford Jacobson had been the pastor of the church her folks attended. She remembered the way he would pat her on the head every Sunday morning after the service ended. He'd plaster on his phony smile and tell her folks what a pretty little thing she was. Even then, he gave Amy the creeps. He wore light gray from head to toe. If he stood in front of a gray cloud, all you'd be able to see would be his teeth. He smiled all the time. But it never reached his gray eyes. They were ice cold and calculating.

Now, the mention of his name brought back memories of those penetrating, dagger-like eyes appraising her. Anytime she was forced to look into those eyes, she shivered as though his intense evil could reach into her heart and drag her down into some abysmal world.

Amy shook free of the memory. She wasn't that frightened little girl any longer. And Clifford Jacobson was no different from any other preacher, looking out for number one. Listening to the conversation of the two men behind her, it became evident that Jacobson had done quite well for himself over the years.

The men mentioned Jacobson was currently living in a grand mansion in Baltimore, Maryland. A king among peasants. They laughed as they talked about the blind, trusting souls who poured out their hearts and their life savings to support his self-indulgences. The simple people had put him on a pedestal. Jacobson was no longer the mere pastor of a small flock in southern Virginia, he was now the leader of one of the most powerful religious organizations in the country.

It would have to be someone with that kind of clout, she mused, to do the unspeakable things that had happened at the abortion clinics and get away with it. Who better than a preacher, someone everybody trusted.

THE BABY SOLDIERS

Hurriedly, she gathered her jacket and library books and left the restaurant. Once she reached the safe confines of her Plymouth, she clutched her stomach, aching for the child that had once dwelled there. "Don't worry, little one," she whispered softly. "Mommy will find you. If anyone has done anything to harm you, he'll wish to God he'd been aborted himself."

CHAPTER TWELVE

David Williams noticed Lieutenant Woolard's strange behavior after returning from his so-called urgent trip to Baltimore. At first, David thought he was imagining things, but Woolard was definitely showing signs of strain. David hoped that whatever was making him edgy, wasn't going to explode all over Adele. Although Adele promised she'd call him if there were any more problems, David agreed with Danny. Adele would rather be beaten half to death than admit to anyone that there was trouble at home. He wondered what made women so damned stubborn...stubborn and such easy prey.

Horace approached David's desk. His movements quick and quiet like a panther. "I noticed the Kelsey file on your desk this morning?"

David rolled his chair back, looking at his splotchy-faced boss. "Yeah. I was going over the ballistics report again."

Horace fidgeted with the coins in his pants pockets. "Why bother? We know the bullets came from a standard thirty-eight revolver. We don't stand a chance in hell of finding it. The best thing you can do is put that file away...permanently."

David's hazel eyes bored into him, like a wolf sizing up a victim. "There really isn't much chance of forgetting that case with Kelsey calling here twice a day, mocking us because we don't have any leads on his son's murder."

"Kelsey," Horace grumbled. "He writes that we don't know how to conduct an investigation in that worthless rag of his. He thinks we're just a bunch of ignorant dickheads."

THE BABY SOLDIERS

David bit his lip. "I guess his private eye isn't having any better luck than we are."

Woolard's glacier blue eyes widened as he leaned far over David's desk. David feared he would fall on his face. "When did Kelsey hire a P I?"

"The day it happened. He told me about it when I went over to talk to him."

Horace's face contorted. "How long did you plan on keeping that information to yourself?"

David shrugged. "I didn't think much about it one way or the other. I figure he's got the bucks, so go for it. We're so damned short on man-power, we couldn't catch someone breaking into the evidence locker."

Woolard straightened up and backed away from the sergeant's desk. "What if he found something? It would make us look foolish." He reached into his pockets, fumbling with the coins once again. "I think you'd better go over there and have a little talk with Mr. Kelsey. Just a friendly chat, you understand. See how much he really knows."

"He's not holding out on us," David chortled. "If Kelsey knew anything, the whole world would know about it by now."

"Don't kid yourself," Woolard retorted. "Kelsey's one sneaky son-of-a-bitch.

He'd love to pull a fast one on me just to rub my nose in it."

David wondered why his boss was so jumpy about Kelsey hiring a private eye. He almost asked, but he didn't. He couldn't bear to hear the sound of jingling change for the next hour. "I thought you wanted to drop everything and forget about it?"

Woolard didn't reply. He nodded thoughtfully and said, "Maybe we should put a tail on him."

David slipped his jacket off the hook behind his office door. Good idea, David thought morosely. Put a tail on a harmless newspaper editor and let the kidnappers and murders run amuck.

Danny was right, he thought. His father was becoming more unhinged by the minute. It would be a relief to be out of his sight.

— 59 —

"Call me at home if you hear anything interesting," Horace said.

"Where are you going? "David asked, eyeing his boss suspiciously.

"I've got a little unfinished business I need to take care of."

David stiffened. Horace's answer sounded threatening, and left too much to the imagination. But until the lady in distress called and asked for his help, he could hardly rush to the rescue.

The deep pockets beneath James Kelsey's eyes made him look closer to sixty than forty-three. David wasn't used to seeing him without his glasses.

"What are you doing here?"James asked, rubbing the bridge of his nose. "Aren't you supposed to be out looking for criminals?"

"That's exactly what I've been doing," David replied tiredly. "Only all the streets I turn down appear to be dead ends."

"Not all of them," James answered smugly.

David arched his brow. "Have you heard something?"

"Yeah," James said, yawning. "I heard they built a new sports arena in Pittsburgh. Some shit, huh? Nothing wrong with the old one. I must have watched them play there a hundred times. Good field."

David shifted the bulky holster under his jacket. "Mind if I use the head?"

"You too good to piss in the bushes anymore?"

David chuckled. "I haven't done that here since the day I looked up and saw Sybil staring at me through the window."

"James coughed into his fist."I'm afraid I've had that experience a time or two myself."

"I'm sorry for bugging you at home," David told him. "You look like you were trying to get some sleep."

James waved him off. "Don't worry about it. I can't remember the last time I slept for more than two hours."

David nodded sympathetically. "Woolard asked me to drop by and see how you were getting along."

James smiled wryly, the way he always did when he was reading between the lines. "Is Woolard afraid to come here and talk to me himself?"

David brushed his hands over his hair, grateful it wasn't as thin and drab as the man sitting in front of him. "I don't know what to tell you, James. The man has some definite issues." Then he quickly added, "That's off the record."

James's smile widened. "You know, I wouldn't dream of saying anything derogatory about good ole Lieutenant Woolard."

"Right," David grumbled.

After David used the facilities, he found James in the den, filling two glasses with bourbon and Coca-Cola. David took the one offered and crossed the room toward the leather sofa. "

"I've been meaning to get back to you," James said. "The P I that I hired did find something interesting."

David was about to sit, but the remark brought him abruptly to his feet. "Did he find out who killed Robbie?"

James shook his head, his eyes glassy from lack of sleep and too much weeping. "Not exactly, but he thinks he knows who they are."

David sucked the drink down quickly. "What did he find out?

"It seems he's become a good friend of a girl named Amy Patterson." He eyed David suspiciously. "Ever heard of her?"

David's eyes narrowed as he shook his head. "Can't say I have. Is she from around here?"

"Somewhere around Virginia Beach or Chesapeake, I suspect. Her family moved away about a year ago. Just up and vanished. Didn't even leave a forwarding address, or so I was told."

"Your P I tell you all that?" David asked, draining the last drops of liquor from his glass.

"That's right," Kelsey said, scratching his head. "The Patterson girl disappeared last year. Now suddenly, she shows up again. Ed, that's my P I, says he talks to her on a regular basis. She told him a story I find really hard to believe."

— 61 —

David snickered. "An old news hound like you? I find that even harder to believe."

James grabbed his empty glass. "Let me fill that up for you. Have a seat, you'll want to hear this."

David sat on the plush sofa and waited.

"Ed made me swear I wouldn't repeat a word of this to anybody." Kelsey looked into David's eyes as though he were trying to make up his mind. "I trust you, David. It's just that I wouldn't want you repeating any of what I tell you to Woolard. Him, I don't trust."

David nodded understandingly. "I give you my word."

CHAPTER THIRTEEN

Kerry Trivane rubbed her swollen stomach, while staring at the small calendar tacked on the wall behind her bunk. It was the seventeenth of March. Seven months since those hateful men had kidnapped her and brought her to this horrible place. It seemed more like seven years. St. Patrick's Day. Her eyes filled with tears. It wasn't that the holiday held any special meaning for her. Kerry became weepy over a lot of things lately. The only thing she could remember about St. Patrick's Day was her mom baking cupcakes and decorating them with green icing for all the children in the neighborhood. Her dad, on the other hand, always made sure he had an ample supply of green beer in the fridge to share with their adult friends, who dropped by after the traditional parade. Kerry had never been able to understand why her folks made such a big deal out of St. Patrick's Day. They weren't even Irish.

She leaned back on the narrow cot, head pressed against the wall, waiting for the maddening attack of nausea to subside. She hadn't felt well in days. Her stomach ached all the time, and this morning, her legs were so swollen she could barely put her shoes on. No wonder she felt so awful, she mused. She had gained over thirty pounds since becoming pregnant. Margaret Hatchey had even suggested she might have twins. The thought of having twins only magnified the fear she lived with every day. If she had twins, she would lose two babies instead of one.

A squatty girl, wearing enough makeup to make a clown blush, came into the room, a smug look pasted on her chubby face. Two months ago, she had become Kerry's newest roommate. Her name was Nancy Clark, dirty blond hair and light brown eyes, and presently, the only other person who shared the ten-by-ten room with her. Nancy had adjusted to her new surroundings surprisingly quickly. She flopped onto her bunk and flipped through the pages of a new fashion magazine that one of the guards had left for her. After humming softly to herself for a few minutes, she said, "Kerry, I almost forgot, old lady Hatchey wants you to get your butt over to the galley right away. She said you still have to wash dishes whether you eat or not."

Kerry pushed a loose strand of light blond hair behind her ear and groaned. She had washed so many dishes in recent weeks, her hands looked like fish scales. She grunted as she rose from the cot and was stricken with the worst stomach cramps she'd ever had. "Oh, God," she cried, gasping for breath. "I...think the baby's coming."

Nancy looked over the top of her magazine, annoyed. "Give me a break. You're not due for another two weeks."

"Nancy, I'm serious. I never felt like..."Ohhhhh."

The second cramp was so powerful it drove her to her knees. Beads of perspiration trickled down her face as she clung to the edge of the cot. Nancy studied her quizzically, but made no move to help. Kerry tried to stand on her own, but her arms shook so badly, she decided to sit on the tile floor until the pain eased. The longer she sat, the more infuriated she became. Margaret Hatchey had instructed her to stop scrubbing the floor a few weeks earlier. Her stomach had grown so huge she was in her own way, unable to navigate under the beds anymore. From her new vantage point, she was mortified to see how much dust and debris had collected since she'd last cleaned her room.

Hatchey had told Nancy that floor scrubbing was her job now, but Nancy didn't take anything the guardian said seriously. Kerry could count the number of times Nancy had even made a bed, or washed a dish since she'd been brought in. Nancy had found her own way of beating the system. Not that Kerry would have traded places with her for anything in the world. She had too much pride to prostitute herself to the guards the way Nancy did. Glaring at her roommate, Kerry felt a confusing mixture of rage and pity well up inside her. She turned toward the bed and took one long, deep breath, pulling herself up onto her knees. Panting heavily, she leaned all her weight on her forearms and pushed as hard as she could until she was standing on her feet again. Her heart pounded frantically from the exertion. She held onto the bed frame for dear life, afraid to let go and fall again.

"Oh, no!" she gasped, feeling as though someone had shoved a hot poker inside her. A dizzying nausea engulfed her, and bloody water trickled down her legs. She watched helplessly as it formed a puddle on the floor between her feet. Her eyes grew wide, frightened by the reality of what was happening. "Get help," she cried.

When Nancy looked over and saw the pool of blood, she finally went into action.

CHAPTER FOURTEEN

Working at the glass factory was all right, but it didn't pay nearly as well as the job Bernie Trivane had left behind when he and Priscilla moved to Pittsburgh. But it wasn't the job that troubled him today. Something else was wrong. He'd felt odd since getting out of bed that morning. He didn't mention anything to Priscilla, not wanting to upset her. The past few months had been extremely difficult for her. She hated leaving their home at the beach as much as he did, but they both feared what would happen if they stayed. When the foreman came around and asked if anyone wanted to knock off early, Bernie was the first to reach the time clock. He had already tallied fifty hours for the week, and the company didn't like paying that kind of overtime to anybody, particularly a new guy.

Bernie opened the front door, thinking the house was much too quiet. But then, he didn't usually knock off early. Priscilla was working at Mercy Hospital, a job she'd found less than two weeks after moving here, and Jimmy was still in school. As far as Bernie was concerned, getting better acquainted with Priscilla's mother was the only good thing that had come out of moving north. Mert was a gutsy broad who wasn't afraid of anything. He wondered what she was like thirty years ago. He bet she wouldn't have run away at the first whiff of trouble, the way he and Priscilla had. But if they had stayed, Jimmy might have been taken away from them, too. He didn't know what he would have done if he had lost both his children. When he thought of his beautiful daughter, kidnapped by thugs and taken only God knew where, his chest ached with the kind of loneliness that only someone who'd ever lost a child could understand.

At twelve-thirty, Bernie watched the mailman scale the steps to the front porch. He went out to go through the mail, to see if he could find any gardening ads for the spring planting season. Priscilla always threw away the good junk mail before he had a chance to read it.

The mail carrier looked surprised to see Bernie home so early during the week.

"Hello, Mr. Trivane. Looks like we're going to have a chilly spring this year."

Bernie breathed deeply, filling his lungs with fresh mountain air. "It sure does. Next thing you know, we'll be complaining about cutting grass and pulling weeds."

The mail carrier laughed. "Not me. No, sir. Me and my wife moved to a condo last summer. No more yard work for me. When I get through climbing up and down steps all day, the last thing I want to do is push a lawn mower."

Bernie nodded understandingly as he thumbed through the mail. The moment he walked inside, his ears began to ring. Then everything starting going black. He grabbed for a kitchen chair and slowly sunk into it. He hadn't felt woozy like that since the time he was wounded in action. When his head cleared, he decided that if he still felt this bad tomorrow, he was going to see a doctor. He didn't know what was wrong with him, but it definitely had him worried.

Tears streamed down Kerry's face as she lay on the sturdy desk in the guardian's office, watching Margaret Hatchey pass her newborn infant to a woman standing in the doorway. She reached out, trying desperately to touch her baby, but one of the guards shoved her arm away. The sharp faced woman clutched the screaming child to her breast and disappeared. Kerry fought to sit up, begging them to bring her baby back. But her cries fell on deaf ears. She placed her hands on her stomach, which seemed more inverted than flat. She felt as though her heart had been ripped from her body as well as her child.

Margaret Hatchey busied herself beneath bright fluorescent lights, waving her arms and barking orders to the other guards. She cursed like a football player who'd just lost a championship game. Kerry had never heard the guardian swear like that before, although she had often seen her lose her temper.

"No, damn it! She can't leave right now!" She yelled at a man who whispered something in her ear. "Are you blind? Can't you see she's lost a lot of blood. She'll have to stay a few days longer, until she gets her strength back. Now get the hell out of here before I'm forced to do something you'll regret!"

The man eyed her skeptically, shrugged and then backed out of the room.

Margaret Hatchey locked the door and began gathering up the stained towels and sheets that had been used in the delivery. "You gave us an awful fright, missy," she said, looking at Kerry. Her dark eyes softened. "You're going to be just fine. You just need to get some rest. You'll be up and out of here before you know it."

Kerry rolled her tongue around the inside of her mouth, trying to work up a spit.

"I...I want my baby," she whimpered weakly.

Hatchey studied Kerry's taut face. "Funny, you should say that," she replied thoughtfully. "That's the first thing you all say."

"I do, Miss Hatchey. I really do want my baby."

The guardian shook her head solemnly from side to side. "And seven months ago, you wanted to abort it."

Kerry sobbed softly. "I never wanted the abortion."

Margaret gathered the soiled linens into her arms and left the room, leaving Kerry alone with her tears and her thoughts.

Kerry stared blankly at the rivets in the metal roof and the slivers of light that slipped in around them. She didn't even know if her baby was a boy or a girl. She supposed it would only hurt that much more if she knew. She wiped her wet face on a small towel the guardian had left behind, remembering the horrible things Amy had told her—things she never wanted to believe, even after she'd seen them happen to the other girls.

"Once your baby is born, they'll take it away from you, and you won't have anything but yourself."

Kerry shivered, feeling more frightened and alone than ever before. She wished she could wake up from this awful dream. She wanted to see Robbie and feel his arms around her. She wanted to hear his laughter. She wanted to tell him how much she loved him. She wanted to be home in her kitchen, setting the table while her mother cooked breakfast. She wanted to see her dad wink at her over the top of his newspaper. She wanted to hear little Jimmy brag, as he showed her the latest baseball cards he'd won playing flip after school.

Suddenly she shuddered, remembering something else Amy had told her. "You won't have a home or a family to go back to. By the time you get out of here, your folks will be long gone."

Kerry shook her head from side to side, her tears flowing freely. It can't be true. Her parents would never desert her, no matter what. She closed her eyes, trying to summon their presence, and drifted off to sleep.

━━

When she woke up, Kerry was back in the cubicle she shared with Nancy Clark. She didn't know how long she'd been asleep, and there was no one around to ask. She was shocked the way her stomach had shrunken to normal size. It wasn't quite as sore as it was before, and she didn't feel as weak. She glanced around the room, but didn't see any sign of Nancy or the magazine she'd been reading. Kerry figured she was probably sneaking around outside with one of the guards. It was just as well. Nancy wasn't the kind of person you could talk to about anything important. Nancy was just consumed with what was going on in her own little world.

Kerry glanced at the door, distracted by voices growing louder as they approached her room.

She heard them discussing where she would go once she was released. "Most likely a safe house or homeless shelter," one of them tittered. When Kerry realized the men were talking about her, she jumped out of bed as quickly as she could. The room felt colder than usual, and she couldn't stop shivering. She didn't want to go to any shelter, and they weren't going to make her. She wanted to go home to her mom and dad and tell them about the horrible people in this place, and the unspeakable things they had done to her and the other pregnant girls. But more than anything, she wanted to talk to Robbie's parents and tell them how sorry she was that he was dead.

The voices grew quiet. Kerry figured the men had probably moved down the hall. She glanced at the round-faced clock on the wall above the door, the one with the broken minute hand and sighed. If only she had listened to Robbie, things would have turned out so differently. When they first found out she was pregnant, he tried to talk her into having the baby. He told her their love was strong enough to survive whatever means his parents could find to keep them apart. But she had been so confused and so frightened. She didn't want to quit school and be forced to accept the first low-paying job that came along in order to support herself and her new baby. And she didn't want Robbie to marry her out of some kind of loyalty, or pity, and miss out on the college education his parents had promised him. She didn't want him to end up working himself to death for meager wages to support her and a baby and hating her for letting him do it.

"Robbie," she cried. "What have I done to us?"

The door to Kerry's room swung open and clanged against the wall. She spun around and froze. It was the same sleazy guard she'd had trouble with right after they'd brought her here. His grin was sinister as he closed the door behind him and closed the distance between them.

"You better get out of here," she stammered. "I'll...I'll scream."

THE BABY SOLDIERS

He jammed his thumbs into his belt loops and snorted. "You think you're pretty special, don't you? Well let me tell you something. You ain't nothing. Nobody around here gives a hot damn what happens to you now. They got what they wanted. You're nothing now but excess baggage."

Kerry's anger flared, turning her face crimson. She hated what he'd said, but she knew he was right. Not even the guardian who took care of her while she was pregnant cared about her. The only reason Margaret Hatchey had stopped him the last time he tried to mess with her was because it was her job to protect the unborn child. Kerry grabbed a shoe and threw it at him as he unzipped his trousers. He chuckled. The lust in his cruel eyes made her quiver. "You know, you don't look half bad without that big belly to get in the way." Then he reached out for her and pulled her close to him.

Kerry grunted and tried to push him away.

He licked his lips and grinned menacingly. "Go ahead, honey. Fight all you want. I like it better that way." Then he lunged forward, knocking her off her feet and onto the narrow bunk.

Kerry twisted frantically beneath him, struggling to get away. His fingers tightened around her neck. She couldn't utter a sound or take a breath. Darkness whirled around her, then he tore at her jeans.

"Come on, bitch," he grumbled hoarsely. "I have a real nice going away present for you. If it's good enough, we'll see you back here again, real soon."

The meaning of his words sickened her. He hoped his seed would impregnate her so the organization would have another baby to add to their growing collection. With all the strength she could muster, she managed to push him away from her and screamed as loud as she could.

His hot spittle sprayed her face as he laughed at her feeble attempt to free herself. She turned her head away to keep from looking into his demented eyes as he kneaded her heavy breasts. For a brief moment, she thought she heard a noise near the door. She wondered if one of the other guards was coming to join in the attack. There was no mistaking the sound of heavy leather boots crossing the tile floor. She closed her eyes, unable to bear the thought of another animal looming over her, waiting his turn. Then she heard a thud. When she opened her eyes, she saw the man who had been on top of her go limp and slide onto the floor. She saw blood spurting from the side of his head and gasped, remembering that awful morning when Robbie Kelsey's blood poured freely from his mouth and the hole in his chest. Then she looked up and blinked in disbelief.

"He won't be bothering you, or anyone else ever again," Margaret Hatchey muttered, dropping the bloody crowbar on top of the corpse at her feet. "Keep an eye peeled for the others," she instructed. "I'll be back as soon as I get rid of this garbage."

Kerry felt numb. Too shocked by what had just happened to say a word, she merely nodded.

Margaret Hatchey grabbed the guard by his feet and dragged him out of the room and through the back door. Kerry sat quivering on the edge of her bed, a fresh stream of liquid running down her legs. She got up slowly and grabbed a towel to wipe fresh blood away. Then she saw the wide streak of blood running from her bed to the open door. What just happened to her was finally settling in. She grabbed the sheet from her bed and got down on her hands and knees and began cleaning the bloody trail leading to the back door. She breathed heavily, moving as fast as she could. She had to hurry. Nancy might walk in at any time.

It wasn't until after the last trace of blood was gone that Kerry finally stopped what she was doing, her breathing heavy and ragged. She felt like the walls were closing in on her. She couldn't stay in this tiny box another minute. She burst into the hall, running down the length of it until she reached the front office. Then she darted inside and grabbed the back of a chair, sucking clean air into her lungs, air that didn't carry the sweet, sickly scent of fresh blood and death. She stepped up on a chair beneath the window and pulled the curtain aside. Then she unfastened the latch. Her eyes widened in horror as she watched a stretch limousine turn off the road and park in front of the building. Margaret Hatchey walked in and closed the door behind her. Her face was beet red and her uniform was soaked with perspiration and blood. She reached behind the door and grabbed a clean uniform from a hanger and changed quickly. Then she walked over to Kerry and glanced out the window. "That'll be your ride," she said, taking a deep breath.

Kerry's eyes welled with tears as she stared at the woman who had just killed a man to save her. The stone-faced guardian didn't frighten her any longer. Kerry reached out and touched Hatchey's muscular arm. "I...don't know what to say," she stammered.

Margaret stiffened. "Don't say a word about anything you saw here today. Now go," she ordered, pushing Kerry toward the door. "Go wherever life takes you. You'll be all right. The best thing you can do now is forget the past and get on with the rest of your life."

Kerry walked trancelike from the office, glancing one last time down the hall, toward the room that had been her prison for so many hideous months. She wasn't the same naive girl she had been back then. Her entire life had changed. The man she loved was dead, and she would never know the thrill of holding her firstborn child in her arms. She turned back at Margaret and said, "Forget the past? That's impossible."

CHAPTER FIFTEEN

The limo driver was tall and didn't appear much older than Kerry. He smiled shyly, but didn't look directly at her as he opened the back door. She got in slowly, hugging herself tightly. No amount of sun would ever be strong enough to warm the coldness she felt in her heart.

The limo turned onto a gravel road, which eventually lead to the main highway. Kerry stared at the back of the driver's head. He looked familiar, but that wasn't possible. It was probably her imagination playing tricks on her. She couldn't see him that well anyway. His dark glasses and the beak on his uniform cap covered most of his face. She decided to keep her mouth shut and not ask questions. His smile might be a phony come-on. Considering who he worked for, he was probably as bad as the guard who had just tried to rape her. The driver glanced in the rearview mirror too often for comfort. Kerry fidgeted with the friendship ring Robbie had given her, wondering if the driver had more on his mind than driving her to her destination. She stared out the window, pretending not to notice.

The countryside was alive with lush green grass, wildflowers and daffodils. It had rained the previous day, making the air smell fresh and clean. Kerry's thoughts drifted to the previous spring. Days like this, when she and Robbie would pack a picnic basket and drive to the beach. She smiled thinking of the way they'd shriek as they dipped their toes in the frigid water. She remembered holding his hand and walking from one dune to another. When they grew tired,

THE BABY SOLDIERS

they'd collapse onto the warm sand, and hug each other fiercely, as frothing waves washed over them.

"We did have some good times, didn't we?" she murmured softly.

"Did you say something?" the limo driver asked.

Kerry shifted uncomfortably on the leather seat as she saw the reflection of his sunglasses in the rearview mirror. "Not really," she replied nervously. "I was just thinking about something that happened a long time ago."

The young man exaggerated a sigh."That's a relief. I heard they do some pretty weird things in that place. It's good to know they didn't make you crazy enough to start talking to yourself."

"How much longer will it be before we get to where we're going?" she asked, wary of his friendly attitude.

"Not much longer. About five minutes."

She nodded, turning her attention back to the window.

"You look scared," he said.

The comment rattled her. "I…I…"

He nodded. "It's okay to be afraid. I've lived with fear most of my life. I'm an expert on the subject."

Kerry was becoming more curious about him, but refrained from starting a conversation. After the humiliating experience she'd just had, she didn't want to give him the impression she was interested in him.

"Was that your first time at the clinic?" he asked innocently.

The skin on her face prickled. "Clinic?"

He nodded. "Yeah. I heard some of the patients are regulars."

Kerry couldn't believe her ears. "Are you saying that some of the girls who leave there have been there before?"

"I know a male nurse who works there. He said some of the girls come back as many as three and four times."

Her mouth gaped open when he used the term nurse rather than criminal pig to describe the guards. "I'd rather die than go through that again."

"I heard that," he said. "Once around the track should be enough for anyone."

Kerry wondered if he had any idea what went on inside the camp. She looked down at her stomach, still unable to accept what had happened to her. "It was horrible," she muttered softly. "I'll never forget it as long as I live."

The driver stopped the limo in front of an old three-story house. The wooden sides were badly chipped and in desperate need of painting. Kerry studied the house grimly. It looked like it should have been condemned years ago.

"This is it," he said, getting out and opening the rear door for her.

Kerry climbed out slowly, staring grimly at the worn gray steps leading to an uneven front porch. Then she gazed at the splintered plywood that had been nailed over the windows on the first floor, and the iron bars crossed over the glass panels in the storm door. She sighed heavily as she walked toward the house, hoping they had a telephone she could use to call her dad to come and get her.

The young man standing at the foot of the steps called out, "Good luck in your new home."

"Fat chance," she muttered. Then she caught her breath. His voice. She recognized his voice. It had to be him. But what was he doing here? Why was he working for those horrible people who ran the camp? Kerry felt more confused than ever as she hurried up the steps.

Her breath came in short, ragged spurts as she knocked on the front door and waited for someone to respond.

When it squeaked open, she jumped back startled. Her blue eyes fixed on the olive-skinned young woman standing in front of her.

"My name is Kerry...Kerry Trivane. I...the driver just dropped me off. I'm supposed to stay here. But it won't be for long," she added hastily.

The woman was older, maybe twenty-five. Her dark eyes shifted mysteriously from left to right, checking the street traffic before drawing Kerry inside. "My name is Rebecca," she replied, flashing a smile. I'll show you to your room. It's right at the top of the stairs.

THE BABY SOLDIERS

It's not much, but it's a lot better than sleeping in the street, or staying at the camp. Besides, I figure the first thing you'll want to do is take a long hot bath."

Kerry sighed tiredly. "To tell you the truth, I'm just looking forward to going home and sleeping in my own bed."

"I heard it was pretty rough for you the first few weeks," Rebecca said, leading Kerry up the stairs.

Kerry balked on the stairs, her long fingers curled around the polished banister. "How would you know that?"

When she reached the landing, Rebecca turned around, appraising the haven's newest guest. "Let's just say a little bird told me."

Kerry frowned as she followed Rebecca down the musty hallway. She was pleasantly surprised to find the room clean, in spite of the stale odor. "Is someone staying here who was at the camp the same time I was?" she asked.

Rebecca chuckled. "Probably more than one." Her round eyes washed over Kerry sympathetically. "It's not fair to tease you," she said, her voice soft and refined. "You've been through too much already. Actually, it was Amy Patterson who told us about you."

Kerry's eyes lit up immediately. "Amy! Is Amy here?"

Rebecca crossed the room and opened the window. A gentle breeze billowed the curtains like open sails on a ship. "Amy's not here right now," she replied. Then she moved toward the narrow closet and opened the door. "I realize it doesn't look like much, but you're welcome to wear whatever you find in here that fits halfway decent."

Kerry barely glanced at the closet's contents. "I want to hear more about Amy," she said excitedly.

Rebecca walked to the open bedroom door. "Amy said she'd be contacting you real soon. She said you should get plenty of rest. You're going to need it."

Kerry glanced around quizzically. "Rebecca, do you have a telephone here? I'd really like to call my parents, now."

Rebecca touched her arm. "I'm afraid your parents aren't living in the house where you grew up anymore."

— 77 —

Kerry paled once again. "What are you saying? Where are they?"

Rebecca's eyes misted over. "I hate to be the one to tell this to everyone who comes to stay here."

"Hate to say what?" Kerry prodded.

"They moved away," Rebecca said slowly. I don't know where."

Kerry stared at her numbly. It was just like Amy had told her it would be.

The shelter was situated on a street consisting mainly of two and three-story dwellings, occupied mostly by senior citizens who had lived in the same neighborhood most of their lives. The thick foliage of the Magnolia trees, on either side, gave a comforting sense of security, as well as shading the house from the penetrating rays of the sun. Kerry glanced around the room, but didn't see any sign of an air-conditioner or a window fan. She wasn't too concerned though. She felt safe for the first time in many months. Leaning out the open window, she noticed a bud on one of the rose vines that clung to the rickety wooden trellis in the backyard. With a little hard work, she thought, this place could be fixed up real nice. She wondered where her family had gone as a single tear started down her face.

Kerry woke from a short nap startled. Her heart was racing as she recalled the nightmare. The guards were chasing her with guns, telling her she had to go back to the camp. They weren't finished with her yet. She buried her face in her pillow and wept.

When she couldn't cry any more, Kerry dried her tears and wandered from the room, down the musty hallway to the bathroom. She filled the tub with hot water as she disrobed, then stepped into the short, claw-footed tub. Settling back, she pressed the warm wash cloth onto her stinging eyes. A soft moan escaped her. It was her first leisurely bath in months. After drying and brushing her silky

THE BABY SOLDIERS

blond hair, she changed into some of the used clothing Rebecca had provided, and went downstairs to meet the others.

Twelve girls were seated in the dining room around a long wooden table. The table was covered with a vinyl cloth, on top of which were a colorful garden salad, a platter of broiled pork chops, and two large serving bowls with apple sauce in one and broccoli in the other. Kerry smiled weakly. Her folks had a table just like it. Only theirs was in the backyard for picnics.

Rebecca jumped to her feet and began introducing Kerry to the others. After Kerry was seated, Rebecca said, "Amy called. She's glad you arrived safely. She'll try to come by and see you tomorrow. Our crusade takes up most of her time these days."

The other girls grunted in unison.

"Crusade?" Kerry asked, reaching for the salad bowl.

Rebecca lowered her fork. "I was under the impression you knew about it."

Kerry lifted the tongs from the bowl, dropping a mound of fresh vegetables onto her plate. "Only if it has to do with what Amy talked about while she was at the camp."

Rebecca smiled, seemingly relieved. "It wasn't just talk, Kerry. We have a powerful little organization here. We all work together."

Kerry lowered her eyes to her plate. "I'm afraid it will take a lot more than the people here to put an end to what's going on. We're talking about major trouble. There are people involved in this thing that I never..."

Rebecca nodded understandingly. "We actually have a lot more people who support us than the ones you see here."

Kerry pursed her lips. "I think I may know one of them."

The others lowered their forks, anxiously waiting for her to continue.

"The driver who brought me here," she said. "I thought I knew him from high school, but I wasn't sure, not with the sunglasses and the cap pulled down over his eyes. When I got out of the limo, he said something. When he did, I recognized his voice. His name is Danny Woolard. He's Lieutenant Woolard's son."

Rebecca chuckled. "That's our Danny all right. Son of the infamous police Captain Horace Woolard."

"He...he's a captain now?" Kerry stammered.

"We just read about his promotion in the newspaper this morning," Rebecca told her. "I can't think of a single soul who likes him. He always seemed like a sneaky brown-noser to me."

"Do you think he's involved with the group, who started the camp where I was held prisoner?" Kerry asked.

Rebecca chewed vigorously. "I wouldn't be surprised if he were," she replied.

"Could be the reason Danny is helping us. He hates everything about his father."

Kerry frowned. "Maybe he's a spy, working for his father."

A few of the girls tittered.

"Lord, no!" Rebecca said. "If Danny thought his father was involved in all the crazy things that are happening, he'd be even more determined to help us."

Kerry shook her head from side to side. "From what I've heard about Lieutenant, I mean Captain Woolard, if anyone, including his own flesh and blood, ever went against him, he'd probably shoot him."

Rebecca sighed heavily. "If Captain Woolard is involved with that group, and he finds out that we're doing our best to expose them, we'll all be shot."

Kerry toyed with the lettuce on her plate. "I don't mind telling you, he scares me. His eyes are cold...like icicles. Sometimes it looks like he doesn't have any. He really scared me when I was a little kid."

Rebecca reached out and squeezed her hand reassuringly. "Try not to worry, Kerry. Everything is going to be all right. You'll see."

Kerry looked glum. "Danny had the radio on while he was driving me here. I heard there was a bombing at another abortion clinic last night."

One of the girls at the table snorted. "Yeah. The guardians of life are busy destroying it."

Kerry shivered. "They really are crazy, aren't they?"

"Crazy isn't nearly as upsetting as the fact that they believe they're doing the right thing," a girl named Angie replied.

"Can we do anything to stop them?" Kerry asked.

"Wait until you talk to Amy," Rebecca said. "She'll be able to answer your questions a lot better than we can."

The conversation drifted off to lighter things as the group finished eating.

CHAPTER SIXTEEN

Captain Woolard parked his Mercedes in the double driveway, leaving the windows open to let the new car smell wear off. He couldn't stand the smell of those cheap deodorizers that looked like evergreen trees. Horace had wanted a Mercedes long before he married Adele. But when she became pregnant with Danny, he had to put his dream on hold and do the right thing. Now, there were no excuses to prevent him from buying whatever he wanted.

He could hear his younger sons, Jason and Mark, upstairs, talking and laughing. He smiled smugly, figuring they were playing games on the new computer he'd bought them. He wondered if that had been a mistake. On a day like today, they should be outside playing. Adele left a message on the dining room table. She was working at the church bazaar and wouldn't be home until after nine. He wadded it up and tossed it on the floor. "Worthless bitch," he mumbled. Then he sauntered into the master bedroom and removed his uniform jacket and shirt. He stood in front of the dresser mirror frowning. The paunch around his midsection had doubled in the past five years, and the thick crop of blond hair, that once made women swoon, was disappearing fast. His pale blue eyes had all but drowned in the bloody red pools surrounding them. He touched his nose, wondering if anyone had noticed how swollen it was lately. "Christ," he muttered. "I look like a bubble-nosed drunk."

He'd been drinking more lately, not enough that anyone would notice. He bet that bastard in Baltimore had noticed. Clifford Jacobson didn't miss a thing.

THE BABY SOLDIERS

Horace sighed heavily and opened the bottom drawer of the armoire, where he kept his private stash of liquor. He poured a generous dose of brandy into a cocktail glass, and drank it slowly, savoring the burning sensation that started in his throat and intensified as it reached the inner wall of his chest. He poured a second drink, then returned the bottle, closing the golden oak door.

He turned toward Adele's dresser. It had three mirrors angled like the ones in fancy dress shops. Seeing his bloated stomach in three-dimension made him feel that much worse. He walked away quickly, his elbow catching the corner of an antique lamp. It rocked before falling onto its side. "Jesus," he muttered sharply, picking it up and inspecting it to see if it was chipped.

Adele called the lamps Heirlooms. As far as Horace was concerned, they were dust collecting junk. As he replaced the lamp, he noticed something beneath the long scarf covering the dresser. Blue envelopes? He hadn't seen them before and wondered why they were hidden under the scarf. Curious, he picked up one and flipped it over, looking for a return address. "Priscilla Trivane!" he spat. "That trouble making whore."

The house was unusually quiet when Adele got home. She was surprised the boys weren't in the den watching TV with their father. She called out, but there was no answer. That's odd, she thought. She knew Horace was home. She'd seen his car in the driveway. "Horace? Horace, are you here?"

The front door slammed shut behind her. Adele jumped, clutching her chest.

"Of course I'm here," he snapped indignantly. "Where else would I be?"

She stepped back, overpowered by the smell of liquor on his breath. "I thought you may have gone out on a case or something."

"No way," he sneered. "I'd much rather be home with my sweet, devoted wife."

— 83 —

Adele's flesh began to crawl. Something was definitely wrong, but she had no idea what.

Horace walked over to the bar and picked up the stack of blue envelopes he'd found on her dresser. He waved them in front of her face. "I thought I'd put an end to this," he bellowed. "I forbade you to have anything more to do with that slut!"

Adele's eyes widened. "Where did you find those?"

He slapped her face with the back of his hand. "You know better than to hide anything from me. What am I going to have to do with you, tie you up and leave you in the cellar whenever I go anywhere?"

His heavy ring had connected with her jaw, causing her legs to wobble like rubber. She needed to sit down, but she didn't want to give him the satisfaction of knowing how badly he'd shaken her.

"Priscilla Trivane is my best friend," she replied defiantly.

He clenched his fists. "WAS your best friend!" he screamed. "The key word is WAS! She's no better than a common murderer."

Adele deferred to her unsteadiness and sat down on the edge of the sofa. "How can you say such awful things about her?" she cried.

Horace's face turned as red as his blood-shot eyes. "Trivane and the rest of her baby killing cohorts should all be burned at the stake," he spat. "Witches, that's what they are, witches from hell!"

Adele folded her arms over her chest, hugging herself tightly. Her husband's rage frightened her more with every outburst. He had been irrational before, but nothing compared to this. She knew how Horace felt about the abortion movement and anyone who supported it. And Priscilla Trivane did support it. Adele always thought of abortion as a personal matter between a woman and her physician, although she'd never admit that to Horace. Their situation was bad enough. It tore her apart, knowing how much he hated her friends. Not only her old friends, but his own son as well. Adele wondered how much longer she would be able to stand the abuse. At times she thought she'd be better off dead than living the way she was living now.

THE BABY SOLDIERS

Horace grabbed a bottle of whiskey from behind the bar. Adele watched his contorted face beneath the bar's dim lights, and scowled. She never realized how much he looked like a bulldog. The way his nose flared and his jowls sagged, even down to the way he snorted.

"Jason and Mark are in their rooms," Horace told her. "And if you know what's good for you, you'll go to yours."

Horace was treating her like a child. "Horace, it's too early to go to bed. I just got home from the bazaar. I haven't even had dinner yet. What in the world is wrong with you?"

Before she could say another word, Horace lunged across the room and fisted her auburn hair, yanking her off the sofa. "Horace, stop!" she cried.

She clawed at his hands, trying to get him to let go of her hair before he pulled it out by the roots. "Let me go," she screamed at the top of her lungs. Horace lowered his fists jabbing her in the stomach and ribs, the way he pummeled his opponents in the boxing ring during his college days. When Adele slumped forward, he drew back and drove his right fist into her face. She staggered backward, connecting with the edge of the entertainment center and went down, losing consciousness before hitting the floor.

Mark Woolard stood in the den, staring helplessly at his mother as she tried unsuccessfully to get up. He was only nine years old, hypnotized by the blood oozing from her mouth onto the beige carpet, making a wider and wider red circle.

"Mark," Adele whispered hoarsely. "Where did your father go?"

Mark shrugged. "I don't know. He came upstairs and told us to stay put. He blinked. "But...but I couldn't. I wanted to see if you were okay."

She attempted to reach out and touch his angelic little face, and cried sharply, unable to move her arm. "Where's Jason?" she asked breathlessly.

— 85 —

"He left right after Dad," Mark replied, unable to pull his teary eyes away from her.

She tried to turn her head, but her neck hurt too badly. "Mark, I need you to listen to me very carefully. I...I can't do this myself. I want you to find my little telephone book. It's upstairs in the top drawer of my nightstand. I want you to look for Doctor Stevens' phone number and call him. Don't talk to anyone else, just Doctor Stevens. I want you to tell him what happened. He'll know what to do."

Mark stared into her frightened eyes, and nodded, his blond hair bouncing over his brow. "Right now," he said, scurrying across the room. Then he stopped and turned around. "Mom, when I get big enough, I'm going to kill him for you."

Adele burst into tears. "No, Mark. You mustn't talk like that. Your daddy is very sick. He's been under a lot of pressure lately. He doesn't mean to do the terrible things he does."

"Yes he does!" Mark retorted. "He wanted to hurt you. He did it on purpose. He wants you to be as afraid of him...as we are. That's why he made Danny move out. Danny wasn't afraid of him anymore."

Adele lay on her side, helpless to comfort him, and mortified her children had witnessed their father's brutality once again. She tried to take a deep breath and felt a stabbing pain pierce her chest. Something was broken. She didn't need a doctor to confirm that. She didn't want to go to the hospital again, but she had no choice. She knew there would be more talk. Horace had beaten her before, but she'd always been able to make up some excuse. She had seen the nurses exchange those knowing looks. After all, how many times could one person fall down the stairs, or walk into a door? She was so ashamed.

CHAPTER SEVENTEEN

David Williams paced the laminated wooden floors of Chesapeake Regional Hospital waiting to speak to Adele's doctor. The 911 operator had contacted his office the moment the call came in. The dispatcher wasn't a rookie, when it came to Mrs. Woolard's numerous accidents.

David had witnessed his superior's brutality dozens of times over the years. Mrs. Woolard wasn't involved in another accident. What happened to Adele was no accident. David clenched his fists. Horace was setting himself up to have one of his own.

An older man wearing a white jacket with a stethoscope draped around the collar walked toward David. He was writing something on a clipboard. David sucked in his breath, prepared for the worst. "How is she, Doctor Stevens?"

The doctor removed his spectacles and rubbed the bridge of his nose. "This is an extremely delicate situation," he mumbled. "Adele said she fell down the stairs."

"She said what?" David huffed loudly.

The doctor motioned for him to lower his voice. They walked down the hall to a private room and sat down. "I know," the doctor replied tiredly. "Mark was with her when the ambulance arrived, and went along with what she said."

Stevens shook his head from side to side. "Poor kid, having to live like that."

"I can't believe it," David said, the shock sharpening his rugged features.

The doctor's expression was grim. "David, the injuries I saw tonight indicate she's had one hell of a beating. She has a broken arm, several broken ribs and a cracked collarbone. Then there's the damage to her eye."

"I'd like to take that rotten bastard out and horsewhip him in front of the whole damned town," David growled.

The doctor grunted. "I'm with you, son, but trying to make a case against Captain Woolard wouldn't be easy. Most folks around here quake at the mere mention of his name."

"Yeah, " David scoffed. "Those that don't know him respect him. And those that do are scared shitless. Christ, Doc, why in the hell does she stay with him?"

The doctor returned his spectacles to his face. "You said it yourself. She's scared to death. I've been treating Adele Woolard for years. I delivered her three children, and helped her through a series of miscarriages. But she's no different from the thousands of other abuse victims you see day in and day out. She's afraid to leave for fear he'll hunt her down and kill her. Or worse, kill her children."

David shook his head in disgust.

The doctor continued. "A man in Woolard's position has a lot of friends, if you know what I mean."

David sighed. "The religious fringe, for instance."

Doctor Stevens nodded. "Among others."

"Any suggestions?" David rubbed the stubble on his chin.

"I'm afraid, there's nothing you or I can do. We'll have to leave that up to Adele. Whatever she decides, we have to abide by her wishes."

David spun around, raking his fingers through his hair. "I wish there was some way I could get through to her, before it's too late."

"Talk to her, David," the doctor replied. "If you really care about her, talk to her. Maybe if she feels she's not alone, she'll find the strength to make the right decision."

"Can I see her now?"

"Sure, they moved her to 308."

"Thanks, Doc. Thanks for everything."

THE BABY SOLDIERS

David took the elevator to the third floor. The smell of disinfectant was much stronger than downstairs. His stomach felt like someone was in there doing somersaults. A nurse balancing a tray filled with medical paraphernalia nudged the door to 308 open. She acknowledged David sympathetically. He grabbed the door and held it open until she'd cleared it. Then he followed her inside.

His stomach lurched a second time when he saw Adele's bandaged face, lying so still on the white pillow. Monitoring devices were hooked to her head and body. They clicked and hummed in a macabre rhythm. He wanted to turn and run out of there as fast as he could, but his legs wouldn't budge. He approached her slowly, looking at the bandage covering her eyes. When she moaned, he realized she was awake.

"David?" she murmured, her voice barely above a whisper.

Gently, he reached out and touched her bandaged arm. "Everything's going to be all right. I'm here now."

"How...how did you?"

"I was in the office when the 911 call came in about your...accident."

She winced. "Oh."

He leaned closer, like a priest about to hear her confession. "I want you to tell me what really happened."

Adele coughed. A sharp pain in her chest made her cry out. "I can't...I can't talk now," she answered weakly.

"Listen to me, Adele," David said anxiously. "I know what happened to you was no accident. Horace did this."

She didn't answer.

David felt so helpless, he wanted to stand there and bawl like a baby.

Adele tried to move her head, moaning in defeat. "No one will ever believe Horace did this to me. Everyone thinks he's so perfect."

"That's not true," David retorted. "They don't think he's perfect at all. They're just afraid to stand up to him."

— 89 —

She frowned. "It amounts to the same thing, doesn't it, David? Either way, I lose."

"It doesn't have to be that way, Adele. Please, let me handle this."

Though she couldn't see them, his hazel eyes filled with tears of compassion.

"He's your boss, David. He could have you fired if you cause him any trouble."

"Why don't you let me worry about that. I won't let him do this to you again. I promise you that."

"I'm so tired. Can we talk later?"

David stepped back and wiped his eyes. "I'll come back tomorrow. If you need anything, call me. I mean it."

Adele lay motionless.

As David stepped from the room, he nearly ran into another nurse on her way in.

"Are you Captain Woolard?" she asked politely.

He gawked at her, unable to believe there was a living soul in the area who didn't know Horace Woolard on sight. She continued staring, waiting for an answer. David looked into her questioning face and replied, "Not in this lifetime." Then he walked out.

CHAPTER EIGHTEEN

Kerry Trivane woke up, crying for the child she longed to hold in her arms. The breast fluids that had saturated her nightgowns since giving birth had just about dried up. What good was a mother's milk anyway…when her baby was gone? She wondered if her baby was hungry, or if the people who had it were abusing it in some way. Her grief was inconsolable. She was going to miss out on all the special things that other mothers experienced. Things like her baby saying its first words and taking its very first steps. What troubled her more than anything was knowing her child would grow up believing she never wanted it. Whoever had taken her child would tell him or her that she wanted to abort it, and how lucky it was that they had interceded. She hoped for the child's sake, it was a boy. Girls were of no value to the ultimate plans of the organization. Rebecca told her that.

Kerry had seen Amy twice in the three weeks she'd been at the safe house. Amy was busy gathering support for the crusade. She was also searching for a new shelter for the girls, since learning their adversaries had found out the whereabouts of the present one. Kerry wished there was something more she could do, but Amy wanted her to keep a low profile. She said she could learn more that way, and her anonymity would be more of an asset when she was called into action.

Kerry searched through the used clothing in her closet, looking for something suitable to wear to the job interview she had that morning. It was only a part-time job. Waitressing at a truck stop off

Independence Boulevard. But it was better than siphoning funds from the haven that could be put to far better use. She never realized how difficult it would be to find a job at sixteen with no skills. She wished she were still living at home with her mom and dad, enjoying her own room with its colored television and CD player. She missed her designer clothes and seeing her friends from school. Not that there was anything wrong with her new friends. Nothing that going back in time couldn't cure. Most of them were already bitter beyond their years, and the oldest among them was twenty-five. She wished she could close her eyes and wish away the last year. She wanted her life back the way it was before…before she got pregnant and was convinced that she and Robbie had no choice but to have an abortion.

She slipped into a faded navy, A-line skirt, which was at least a size too large for her. Then she put on the crisp white blouse Rebecca had loaned her for good luck. Staring at herself in the mirror, she burst into tears. She looked awful. If only I had known what would happen when I agreed to go to the clinic, she mused. Now, I have nothing. My baby is gone, Robbie is gone, and I look like a bag lady.

She blotted her tears on the same Kleenex she'd used to blot her lipstick.

She missed Robbie as much now as she did the last time she saw him. In her heart, she knew she'd never be able to love anyone the way she'd loved him. She thought of a future without Robbie and her baby and wondered if the emptiness would ever end.

Where had those people at the camp taken her baby? Was it still alive? She had to find out what happened. The other girls at the haven felt the same way. If they didn't learn something soon, they would all go freaking mad.

The Stop Over looked even worse than Kerry Imagined. The front windows were spattered with grease, and the tape used to hold the daily specials to the glass, was torn and ragged. Max Neely, the man she'd spoken with on the phone, looked more like an auto mechanic

THE BABY SOLDIERS

than a restaurant owner. His hands had done their share of manual labor, and his eyes carried the wisdom of the world.

Mr. Neely directed Kerry toward a small office in the rear of the diner where they could talk in private. He was a tall man, about six three, and his gait was so long, she found herself scurrying to keep up with him. Her eyes darted warily over the clutter. Neely seated himself behind a metal desk and nodded toward the only other chair. Kerry removed a stack of magazines and sat down.

Neely's dark eyes studied her face. Then he shifted his gaze to her application on his desk. "You ever work anywhere before?"

She shook her head. "No, sir. I was going to school."

He shifted a toothpick to the other side of his mouth. "Why aren't you there now?"

Kerry cleared her throat. "I...I was kidnapped last year. They let me go a few weeks ago. I'm still trying to find my family."

She watched his Adam's apple bob up and down as he swallowed whatever was in the mug on his desk. She didn't think he believed her story about being kidnapped and unable to locate her parents. But then, who would believe such an incredible story?

Mr. Neely's eyes narrowed suspiciously. "How come you can't find your folks?"

She sighed. "They moved away while I was gone."

He furrowed his brow. "Where are you staying?"

She squirmed, more embarrassed by this question than the others. "I'm...I'm staying at a shelter."

He tossed the toothpick into the trash can by his desk and lit a cigarette. "I suppose you're anxious to find a place of your own?"

"Yes, sir. As soon as I get a job and save some money," she replied earnestly.

Neely blew smoke rings into the air. "Can you start tomorrow morning?"

Her blue eyes grew wide and bright. "You mean I have the job?"

His smile was thin, but warm. "I wouldn't have asked you to come back tomorrow if I planned on giving the job to somebody else now, would I?"

"No, sir," she said. "I don't suppose you would."

"Can you be here by seven? That's our busiest time."

Seven a.m., she thought. That's when they served breakfast at the shelter. Tomorrow, she'd just have to skip breakfast. "Yes, sir. I'll be here."

He stood up and extended his right hand.

Her stomach flipped as she shook it.

"By the way," he said. "There's one more thing."

Her smile faded. She knew it was too good to be true.

"The girls here wear uniforms. Nothing for you to worry about. I'm sure we have something around that'll fit you."

"I...I think I wear a seven," she said. "At least that's the size I used to wear."

When he cocked his head to one side, Kerry bit her tongue, thinking she may have volunteered too much information.

He fished another toothpick from his shirt pocket, rolling it between his fingers.

"Well then, you're in luck. The girl who just quit wore a seven."

"Good," she said relieved. Then she thanked him and walked out.

Rebecca waited for her in an old Chevette that had been donated to the shelter by an anonymous benefactor.

"Well?" she asked, as soon as Kerry climbed inside. "How did it go?"

Kerry reached over and hugged her, squealing with delight. "I got the job!"

"That's great," Rebecca said. "Once you get a little experience under your belt, you'll be able to write your own ticket."

Kerry didn't understand what Rebecca meant by writing tickets, but it didn't matter. She had a job, and soon she'd be able to start supporting herself.

The Stop Over didn't cater exclusively to truckers. Most mornings, the diner's L-shaped counter and the booths that ran alongside it were filled with businessmen and teachers, who gulped gallons of coffee while perusing their newspapers. Kerry was quickly learning that being a good waitress was a lot more complicated than she thought. There was so much to remember. She had to memorize all the items on the daily special along with the prices. She had a certain number of customers to serve and had to remember what they'd ordered. Mr. Neely frowned on writing orders down on pads. He said they didn't have the same personal touch as a good memory. Besides, the customers were inclined to leave better tips if they saw your smiling face, instead of having it buried behind some confounded notebook.

By eleven-thirty, Kerry's legs ached so badly she thought for sure they were going to fall off. It was time for her lunch break, so she ordered and headed for a vacant stool at the counter. A low moan escaping her lips. Then she heard a muffled chuckle coming from the stool next to her. "Amy!" she exclaimed. "What are you doing way out here?"

Amy laughed. "I might ask you the same thing. I do like your outfit though," she said, appraising the short pink uniform. "I bet you didn't find that in any closet at the shelter."

Kerry blushed. "The diner supplies our uniforms. You don't think it looks too...too..."

Amy shook her head. "It looks just fine."

An older waitress approached them, placing a grilled cheese sandwich and a glass of chocolate milk in front of her.

"Sorry I haven't been around much lately. I've been really busy."

Kerry sipped her milk. "Rebecca told me you're looking for another safe house."

Amy sighed heavily. "As if we didn't have enough to worry about."

"Amy," Kerry said softly. "There are so many things I need to find out. No one at the shelter can help me. I think most of them know even less than I do—and that's not saying much. I get the feeling we're in as much danger now as we were back at the prison camp."

Amy nodded thoughtfully. "Kerry, I need your help."

"Sure...sure," Kerry stammered. "Anything, you know that."

"I have an idea I want to run by you. You're a few years younger than me. I think the school kids will take our message more seriously if they hear it coming from somebody closer to their own age."

Kerry frowned. "I...I don't understand?"

"We have to concentrate on kids your age, and younger. We have to warn them of the dangers they're up against if they try to have an abortion."

Kerry studied Amy's face, surprised by the dark shadows beneath her green eyes. She wondered if something was wrong, something more serious than worrying about finding a safe place for the girls. She couldn't remember Amy looking so weary, not even when she was nine months pregnant.

"I'll do anything I can to help," Kerry said. "If abortion is legal, how come people are getting away with kidnapping and murder? Doesn't anyone care what's going on?"

Amy finished her tea and pushed the empty glass across the counter. "Fanatics push the buttons that make the world go round," she replied sullenly.

Kerry swallowed a bite of her sandwich. "I used to think Robbie's folks were fanatics."

Amy grunted. "Probably still are. Hard to believe they could be responsible for their own son's murder though."

Kerry gasped. "I never thought of it that way before."

Amy shrugged. "If they believe the same things their leaders do, they're just as guilty."

Kerry looked at the half-eaten grilled-cheese and pushed her plate away.

"I'm having a meeting at the shelter tomorrow night," Amy said. "Since you work days, you shouldn't have any conflict. I want you

THE BABY SOLDIERS

to meet some of the other people who are working for our cause. They'll be happy to know you're going to help us."

Kerry looked puzzled. "How can my help make such a big difference. I'm nobody."

Amy arched a brow. "On the contrary, my young friend. You know the right people, and you know where they live. Your knowledge can be extremely important to our cause."

Kerry still didn't understand. "What people?"

"Well, for starters, you know the Woolards and the Kelseys."

Kerry shifted her eyes. "I've been in their homes at one time or other. I even babysat Mark Woolard on occasion."

Amy nodded. "I remember you telling me that when we were at the camp. That's what makes you such a valuable asset."

Kerry gulped hard. "They all have something to do with the camp where we were taken, don't they?"

Amy exhaled slowly. "You're going to have a tough time with this, but those are some of the fine folks, who came up with the idea of starting a camp like the one we were in. I just don't think they planned for things to get carried away like they did. I'm not sure they're really aware of everything that goes on there."

Kerry rubbed the goose flesh rising on her arms. "Mrs. Kelsey was trying to pressure me into keeping my baby. Do you suppose she knew what would happen if I tried to have an abortion?"

Amy chortled. "Could be."

"That…that's horrible!" Kerry stammered.

"It's a lot worse than that," Amy replied, sliding off the stool. "Listen, kid, I gotta run. I'll see you tomorrow night."

"Okay," Kerry said, picking up their plates. "I'll be there."

Rebecca called Kerry at the diner at two-thirty and told her she'd be late picking her up. She asked Kerry if she could walk over to the mall and she'd meet her in front of Target. Kerry agreed, although she was afraid that after standing on her feet all day, her legs wouldn't carry her that far.

Before she left for the day, Mr. Neely called her into his office and told her he was pleased by her performance her first day on the job. Then he handed her a bulging envelope.

"What's this?" she asked, staring at it curiously.

"That's your share of the tips."

"But I didn't see anyone leave a tip?" she replied, confused.

He snickered. "They don't leave them on the counter anymore. We had too many people coming in here with sticky fingers, who would slip the tips into their own pockets before the waitresses could get them. Now, we collect them at the register when the customers pay their checks."

"Oh." she replied hollowly, her eyes glued to the envelope.

"You be careful going home. I'll see you tomorrow. Seven a.m. sharp."

She bobbed her head up and down. "Seven a.m. I'll be here."

She walked outside, feeling the warmth of the sun penetrating the short, nylon uniform. The temperature felt like it was in the high eighties, but she knew it couldn't be more than seventy. As she made her way down the narrow walkway, she choked on the exhaust fumes from passing vehicles, and wondered why she'd agreed to meet Rebecca at the mall. Although she could see the cluster of buildings, they seemed a hundred miles away. Eighteen wheelers whizzed by, their horns blaring. Men wearing hard hats and plaid shirts hung out pickup windows, howling like starving hounds as they passed by. Kerry didn't wave back, or giggle the way she had when she was just a kid. Instead, she lowered her head and hastened her stride. She was afraid to be friendly to anyone anymore.

She turned right, leading to the mall's spacious parking area. Suddenly, the hairs on the back of her neck prickled. She knew someone was watching her. But when she turned around, all she saw were some teenagers laughing and passing a joint around. She continued walking, but couldn't shake that eerie feeling.

An automobile slowed down beside her, its engine puttering loudly. Her heart pounded so hard she could barely breathe. She thought of the men who had forced her into a car and taken her to the prison camp. It couldn't be happening again, she thought. No one would want to kidnap her now. She wasn't pregnant anymore. Kerry pretended not to notice the car.

"Hey, stuck-up!" a male voice called out. "Hey, pink lady!"

She thought she recognized the voice, but couldn't bring herself to turn and look.

"Kerry! Kerry Trivane, are you deaf?"

She stopped walking and turned toward the voice. Danny Woolard stood half in and half out of the driver's side of his VW.

"Danny?" she said, puzzled."What are you doing out here?"

"Becca called me. She said she was going to be later than she thought. She asked me if I'd track you down and drive you back to the shelter."

Kerry was so grateful. She didn't think she could walk another step. Danny climbed back inside and pushed the passenger door open. "Climb aboard," he said, smiling. "It's nice and cool in here."

After taking several deep breaths, Kerry said, "I didn't think these older models had air conditioning?"

Danny laughed. "I'm a mechanic of sorts. I took care of that little problem shortly after I bought it."

She nodded. "Thanks for picking me up. I don't know if I would have made it all the way to Target."

"I bet Becca never walked that far in her whole life," he replied.

Kerry looked out the window. "Danny, can we stop somewhere so I can call her and let her know you found me?"

"I can do better than that," he said, reaching in the glove compartment. "You can call her on my cell phone."

Kerry punched in the number for the shelter. After leaving a message, she hung up. "She didn't answer."

"Are you hungry?" he asked.

Kerry clutched her stomach and groaned. "I've been smelling food all day. I feel like hamburgers and hot-dogs are coming out my ears."

He laughed. "I'll bet you don't smell pizza? They don't sell that at the diner."

Kerry smiled. "I haven't had pizza since...since God knows when."

"Great," he said, giving her a satisfied grin. "You look like you could use a good meal on those bones of yours."

Kerry stared down at herself self-consciously. She was thinner now than when she'd left the camp. She hadn't really noticed until Danny mentioned it. But the size seven uniform she wore fit more like a ten.

The Pizza Barn was located on the boulevard between a hardware store and an auto dealership. The parking lot was crowded when they arrived. "Do you think we'll be able to find a seat?" Kerry asked.

"No problem," Danny said. "The owner is a personal friend of mine."

The tantalizing aroma of tomatoes, cheese, pepperoni and sausage made Kerry's mouth water, in spite of the fact she'd smelled food all day. She couldn't believe how much she had missed this simple treat. After gorging on three pieces, fixed all the way, Danny looked at her in awe. "Shall I order another?"

She looked at him and laughed. "No, thank you. I couldn't eat another bite."

He whistled. "For a minute there, you had me worried. I was afraid you took my remark about your boney self too seriously."

"Well, I admit I don't feel as skinny now as I did when we walked in."

After paying the check, Danny and Kerry headed for the shelter. They rode in silence most of the way. Kerry felt a strange sense of déjà vu, remembering the day Danny had driven her to the shelter in the limousine. All she wanted to do was hold her baby in her arms

THE BABY SOLDIERS

and tell it how much she loved it and missed it. She closed her eyes, wondering if that day would ever come.

"Kerry," Danny said softly. "I've been thinking about you ever since the day I dropped you off at the shelter."

She listened quietly.

"I was…I was wondering if…if maybe you'd like to go to a movie with me sometime?"

The question made the blood drain from her face. "I'm not ready for anything like that, Danny," she snapped defensively. "Besides, I doubt your father would approve of you going out with someone who almost aborted her baby?"

She watched his fingers tighten on the steering wheel. "I'm not like my father," he said, almost hissing the words.

She shook her head, fighting back a tear. "I'm sorry, Danny. It's just that I've been through so much, I don't think I could enjoy going out with anyone right now…maybe never."

"Don't say never," he replied. "My old man uses that word all the time. I hate that word."

CHAPTER NINETEEN

Detective Williams walked into Adele's hospital room, surprised to see Jason and Mark there so early in the afternoon. Jason was kneeling on one knee tying his shoelaces, while Mark gazed absently out the window at the Burger King across the street.

"Hi, David," Jason said, jumping to his feet. "Mom' s not here right now."

David nodded toward Mark, who had turned away from the window. "I see that. More tests I suppose."

Mark nodded grimly.

"I'm a little surprised to see you fellows here so early. Shouldn't you be in school?"

"Easter vacation," Jason explained. "We don't have to go back until next Tuesday."

With all the commotion, David had completely forgotten about the holiday. He knew Adele was in no condition to shop for the boys and wondered if she'd object if he brought them a little something from the Easter Bunny.

He glanced at the freshly made bed, almost relieved that Adele wasn't in it. He was having a hard time coping with the way she looked since Horace had remodeled her features. "How long has your mom been gone?" he asked, turning back to the boys.

Mark looked over at Jason and then shrugged his shoulders. "They took her down for more X-rays. I think it was about an hour ago."

THE BABY SOLDIERS

David placed the vase of flowers he'd bought at the gift shop downstairs on the stand by Adele's bed.

"They're real nice, David," Jason said. "Whenever Mom gets flowers, it always makes her feel better."

David nodded grimly. "Remember that when you get older, Jason. Women love flowers, even when there's no special reason for getting them."

"Did Miss Ann like flowers?" Mark asked.

David reached out and ruffled the youngster's blond hair. "She sure did," he said. "Carnations were her favorite. She said they lasted longer than all the others, and they smelled better, too."

Adele's wheelchair rolled into the room. Her auburn hair hung limply over her shoulders. Her face was as white as the bed sheets. "Mrs. Woolard, would you like to sit up for awhile?" the nurse holding the chair asked.

Adele forced a smile. "Thanks, Betsy. I'll buzz you when I'm ready to get back in bed."

The perky nurse smiled at David and the boys, closing the door behind her.

Mark hurried to his mother's side. "Mom, did you know that Miss Ann liked carnations? David said they were her favorites."

Adele looked at the beautiful bouquet of red roses in the vase on her table and smiled. "Yes, Mark. Mr. Williams used to have them sprayed in different colors for her, too."

The small boy wrinkled his nose as he leaned back against the wall. "Sprayed them different colors? How do you spray flowers?"

David laughed. "I think I may have gotten into something I don't know how to get out of." Then he looked into Mark's questioning blue eyes and said, "You know, Mark, that's a real good question. I don't know how they spray them, or what they use. I never thought to ask."

"All Mark ever does is ask stupid questions," Jason grumbled.

David walked over to Adele's chair, touching the arm without a cast. "How are you feeling today?"

She smiled weakly. "Better than yesterday, I think."

— 103 —

David felt himself being drawn into her green eyes. Beneath the fluorescent lights, they seemed to sparkle more than usual. For a moment, he felt as though he was looking into the ocean's tropical waters.

Jason grabbed Mark by the arm. "Let's ride down to the main floor. I want to show you the fish tank in the lobby."

Mark watched the way his mother and Sergeant Williams were staring at each other and exaggerated a sigh. "Jason, couldn't you just say they wanted to talk without us being in the room?"

Jason yanked his brother's arm, pulling him toward the door. "Let's go, runt."

Mark chuckled. "I'm going to ask the lady in the gift shop how they spray flowers different colors."

"That's a great idea, sport," David replied, his eyes never leaving Adele.

"You never know when that kind of information will come in handy."

After the boys were gone, David studied Adele face more seriously. The ice pack they'd been keeping on her jaw had reduced the swelling considerably, although her cheek remained puffy and hideously discolored. "The boys said you had more tests done today. Was that to see how your ribs were mending?"

She lowered her head. "My ribs will be fine, eventually," she replied tiredly. "But it seems I have some kidney damage."

"That's it!" David said clenching his fists tightly. "You're not going back to that house ever again."

Adele looked up at him; her eyes shimmered with tears. "Where would I go, David? It's the only home I know. I haven't had a real job since before Danny was born. It's best that I stay where I am."

David wanted to grab her right out of the chair and shake some sense into her, but she was already frightened, and he didn't want to add to her grief. He hadn't seen Horace since the "accident" happened, which he considered smart on Horace's part. Maybe if he kept out of sight long enough, he'd forget about wanting to kill him with his bare hands.

"I appreciate the flowers," Adele said weakly. "That was very thoughtful of you."

"Yeah," he muttered. "Next time, you may not be able to smell them."

"Please don't start that again, David. I have too much on my mind right now to have you angry with me, too."

David lowered his eyes, feeling like a heel. He hadn't come here today to make her feel worse. He hoped his visit would help her find the strength to settle things with Horace once and for all.

The first few days after Adele was admitted, David hadn't been able to see her for more than a few minutes at a time. He thought Doc Stevens was an okay guy, but he would have felt better if she'd been taken to Norfolk General instead. At first, the doctor said Adele had a cracked jaw, some broken ribs and a busted left arm. It wasn't until a week later, when she passed out on the floor of her room, that more tests were ordered, and they discovered she had a punctured lung. Now, she had kidney damage on top of everything else. Christ, he thought angrily, her nine-year-old kid could have done a better job diagnosing her injuries. If Horace Woolard didn't finish her off, the staff at Chesapeake Memorial probably would.

"I'm sorry, Adele." he said, rubbing the deep crevices in his forehead. "I wasn't thinking. I'm just worried, that's all."

She nodded, accepting his apology.

"Does anyone know how long you're going to be in here?"

She cleared her throat. "I thought I'd be getting out next week, but with this new setback, I...I just don't know. If something is wrong with my kidneys," she said, her voice faltering. "I could be here for months."

When he thought of Adele being chained to a dialyses machine for the rest of her life because of that coward she married, he fumed. "Maybe they're just badly bruised," he said, hoping with all his heart that were true.

Adele wiped her eyes. "I'm praying that's all it is," she said. "I don't think I'd want to live as an invalid."

"Has Danny been by to see you?" he asked, changing the subject before he started punching holes in the walls.

"The nurses told me he came by late last night, but I was asleep." She looked distant. "I haven't had a chance to talk to him since... since it happened."

David wondered if she was planning to tell Danny she'd fallen down the steps, too. She wasn't aware that Jason had confirmed what really happened to her that night. Danny had already threatened his father once. Seeing his mother like this could send him off the deep end. He doubted Jason would have told him, or Adele, either. She wouldn't want her oldest son going to prison for killing his father... no matter how much he deserved it.

Adele pushed a button on the wheelchair. It hummed as it moved toward the window. "David, do you have a few minutes? I have something I need to talk to you about."

He grabbed a metal chair and sat down facing the wheelchair. "I'm all ears," he said, folding his arms over his chest.

Adele ran the fingers of her free hand lightly over the cast on her broken arm. "Horace was here last night."

David leapt to his feet. "Horace was here? He had the nerve to show up here at the hospital?"

Her eyes shifted nervously. "David, listen to me, please. This is important."

His wide shoulders slouched as he sat back down.

"Horace feels terrible about what he did."

David sat rigidly, feeling like his toes were going to come up through the tops of his leather shoes.

"I...I never saw him cry before," she said, closing her eyes at the thought. "He promised me he was going to change." She looked directly at David and said, "I believe him. I really do. I think everything is going to be different from now on."

— 106 —

THE BABY SOLDIERS

David sat there staring at her, but not really seeing her. He felt numb. Everything Adele said to him after that moment was completely lost. All he could think about was what Doctor Stevens had said the night the ambulance brought her in. "She's no different from the thousands of other abuse victims you see day in and day out." But David didn't want to believe that was true. In his heart, he wanted Adele to be different.

She was his friend. One of the best he'd ever had. And no matter what she thought, he wasn't going to sit by and wait for Horace Woolard to beat her to death.

He stood up slowly, leaning forward, he kissed her lightly on the forehead. It was the only part of her face that wasn't purple. "I have to go," he said hollowly. "I have some business I need to take care of."

Adele's misty eyes followed him as he crossed the room and walked out. "Don't be angry with me, David," she whispered. "Everything will be all right. You'll see."

CHAPTER TWENTY

The house looked like an ante-bellum mansion with wide white pillars standing like soldiers along the edge of the front porch. The grounds were landscaped and sloped gradually toward the main road. The house was located mid-way between Chesapeake and Suffolk, Virginia. It was a lot farther from the beach than Amy had hoped for, but the house itself was perfect. It offered a certain amount of seclusion, and was large enough to accommodate all the girls at the shelter. She wanted Rebecca and Angie to see it before she made a final decision. She knew they would both be pleased with the rent. Amy thought it was uncanny the way real estate prices dropped the farther you got from the beach. If the low rent didn't convince the others that they were in love with the place, nothing would.

CHAPTER TWENTY-ONE

Jason and Mark were shocked when they came home and saw their father's Mercedes in the driveway. "What's he doing here?" Mark whispered.

Jason pushed his younger brother off the walk. "He lives here. Remember?"

"Yeah, but he's been gone for so long that..."

Jason snorted, reading his brother's mind. "We're not that lucky. He was probably in Baltimore, kissing his preacher friend's ass."

"Did Mom know he was coming home today?" Mark asked warily.

Jason shrugged. "Beats me. Nobody ever tells us what's going on. I hope they don't start fighting again."

"If they do, I'm going to run away."

Jason stopped walking and studied his brother. "Yeah. Right. And where do you think you'll go?"

Mark rolled his eyes toward the clouds. "Maybe I'll go and live with David."

Jason pretended he was choking. "What makes you think he'd want a runt like you following him around all day asking stupid questions?"

Mark pantomimed zipping his lips. "I'd be very quiet. He wouldn't even know I was around."

Jason placed his arm on Mark's shoulder. "You sound like you got it all figured out, squirt."

Mark nodded again. "If I do move out, you can have my bicycle."

Jason's mouth dropped open. "Why would I want that old thing? It doesn't even work."

"Maybe Danny could fix it for you."

Jason sighed. "If you're going to run anywhere, how come you don't just move in with Danny? After all, he is our brother."

The book bag slipped off Mark's shoulder. He bent down to pick it up. "Danny wouldn't have any time for me. He likes girls."

Jason laughed. "What makes you think David doesn't?"

"I never saw him with one after Miss Ann went away," Mark answered.

Jason tussled his hair. "Yeah. And I never saw him with any runts either."

"Be quiet," Mark warned. "Dad's standing at the door watching us."

Jason lowered his head as both boys walked inside.

"How was school today?" Horace asked, appraising his sons.

Jason looked puzzled. Their father didn't usually ask about their day. And he couldn't remember the last time he'd seen his dad smile. "It was okay," he replied.

"And yours?" Horace said, turning to Mark.

Mark looked at Jason and shrugged. "It was okay, I guess. Where's Mom?"

"She's upstairs," Horace said.

Mark's eyes widened fearfully.

"Don't worry," Horace said. "She's getting dressed. I'm taking her out to dinner this evening to celebrate her homecoming."

"Where are you going?" Mark asked.

Jason tried to pull Mark away before his dad got mad at him for asking so many questions.

"We're going to a nice restaurant out of town. You remember me telling you about Reverend Jacobson, don't you?"

Mark rolled his eyes. "Only about a million times," he replied innocently.

THE BABY SOLDIERS

Horace frowned. "Well, Reverend Jacobson bought an old building at the beach, that used to be a steak house, and he renovated it. I hear the food is excellent."

"Did Reverend Jacobson tell you that?" Mark asked suspiciously.

"Come on, Mark," Jason prodded. "We have homework to do."

"I don't want you kids to worry. We'll be home early," Horace said.

Jason couldn't get up the stairs fast enough. He raced down the hall to his parents' bedroom and pushed the door open. His mother was standing in front of the mirror draping a shawl over her cast. It looked to Jason like she was trying to hide it. She was wearing her hair down instead of up the way she usually did. He figured she was trying to hide the ugly bruises on her face and neck. "Is everything okay, Mom?" he asked, his voice shaky.

Adele spun around. "Oh, Jason. You startled me. Is Mark with you?"

"He's in the bathroom. Do you want him for something?"

"No. That's all right. I'll talk to him later, when we get back."

Jason watched her sit on the bed and put on her shoes. The pained expression on her face didn't escape him. "Dad said you were going out to eat. Are you sure you feel like going out?"

She sighed heavily. "Your father is trying very hard to make things better, Jason. I think it's only fair that I meet him halfway."

Jason backed out of his parents' bedroom and walked down the hall to his own. He tossed his books on the bed. Meet him halfway, he thought miserably. The only time she meets him halfway is when her face meets his fists. He didn't understand grown-ups at all.

CHAPTER TWENTY-TWO

The Intracoastal Waterway runs through the heart of the City of Chesapeake. On the Northern side lies a small community park; a quiet place to while away the hours, or watch the endless procession of yachts, tugs, and colorful sailing vessels that run both north and south. It was a warm morning in early June. The park was nearly deserted, save for a young woman sitting beneath a maple tree reading a book, while her children played on the swings near the water fountain. An older man sat on a bench near the water's edge, making charcoal sketches of sail boats as they passed him by.

A gray Honda Civic turned off Route 168 and inched along the pine cushioned road, then rattled to a stop beneath an expansive cover of Poplar trees. The driver lowered his window and turned off the ignition. He was surprised that only a few people were here, enjoying the park. Since it was June, he figured most folks had taken to the beach instead, fighting tourists over plots of sand and wearing T-shirts that boasted, "Virginia Is For Lovers."

He glanced at his watch and hoped that nothing had gone wrong. Although he wouldn't be surprised if it had. In his business, waiting for a calamity to strike was like waiting for the other shoe to drop. You knew it was going to happen, you just didn't know exactly when.

A few minutes later, a shiny silver Buick bounced along the same tree-lined road and parked next to him. David climbed from the Honda and walked toward the driver's side of the Buick. His smile was pleasant as he leaned against the door. "I was beginning to worry that something had happened to you."

THE BABY SOLDIERS

Adele Woolard glanced in the rearview mirror; her emerald eyes fixed on the highway behind her. Then she looked up at him and shook her head. "I had the strangest feeling someone was following me. I think I'm becoming paranoid."

David Williams opened the door, offering his hand. "After what you've been through, you've earned the right. Let's walk around a little. The fresh air will do us both good."

Adele slid from behind the steering wheel, steadying herself on his arm. They walked along the wide path that led to the boat ramps.

"I've been doing a lot of thinking about what you said when I was in the hospital—about helping me."

"I meant every word," he replied softly. "I can't bear the thought of you living with that animal. I knew he had a real problem with that temper of his. I just never realized how far he would go."

She lowered her head. "Horace wasn't always like that."

David grimaced. "It's amazing how people change over the years. When I first joined the department, I heard Horace was one of the nicest guys you'd ever want to meet. Funny though, I never saw that side of him."

Adele reached down and picked up a penny. "Since Horace got involved with that radical religious group, he…he's become a stranger… to all of us."

David took a roll of Lifesavers from his pocket and offered one to Adele.

She declined.

"I can't imagine Horace getting mixed up with a bunch like that," he said, popping a green one into his mouth. "He has so many fanatical ideas of his own, I don't see him sitting on the sidelines, heeding anyone else's."

Adele pushed a wisp of auburn hair behind her ear. "I think it has more to do with politics than anything. Horace thinks he's going to become the Chief of Police someday."

David grunted. "A lot of us were stunned when he made Captain."

Adele snapped a leaf from a tree. "Just goes to show you, personal charm has nothing to do with promotions, regardless of what the books say."

He sighed heavily. "I've talked to the boys since you were released from the hospital."

She crumpled the leaf and let the fragments fall between her fingers. "What did they tell you that you didn't already know?"

"Not much. I was actually trying to get a feel for what they thought of their father now that things have begun to settle down some."

"It hasn't been easy for them. It's as though they expect him to turn into Mr. Hyde anytime at all."

David shoved his hands in his pockets. "That's understandable, considering."

"When I was admitted to the hospital, I made them promise not to tell anyone what Horace had done to me, I never dreamed that everyone in town already knew. I thought you were the only one who suspected the truth."

"Yeah," he muttered. "The doctor and the entire nursing staff at Chesapeake Regional had seen it all before. Contrary to the fine print on their job contracts, they don't keep those little details to themselves." He pulled a handkerchief out of his pocket and wiped the sweat forming on his brow. "I will say though, Doctor Stevens is a real piece of work."

"What makes you say that?" she asked.

"Right after your little accident, I tried to get him to put his findings in writing. He didn't mind telling me face to face what had happened to you, but he refused to document what happened for the record. I guess he didn't want to step on any toes either."

Adele's mouth gaped open. "What did you expect him to do? Everyone in this town knows who Horace is. He was probably worried about getting sued for slander."

"I know a little something about people, too," he said. "And I know how they behave when they're scared out of their wits."

THE BABY SOLDIERS

Adele paled. "You...you think Doctor Stevens was afraid to tell the truth for...for fear of his own personal safety?"

David rubbed the mole on his right cheek. The question made him uneasy. "Horace scares a lot of people, Adele. The rest, he just pisses off."

She nodded grimly.

"Speaking of the latter group, I had a long talk with Danny a couple weeks ago. I can relate to him. Your husband is definitely not on his list of favorite people."

Adele sat on the split-rail fence, separating the park from the waterway. The thick foliage of an elm tree shaded her face, making the dark circles under her eyes less conspicuous. "I didn't want Danny to know anything about the last episode. He's been working out of town a lot the past few weeks. I was hoping everything would be back to normal before he found out about it. I hadn't counted on Jason calling him. Danny's seen more of Horace's anger than the younger two. Horace usually held his temper in front of them. I don't believe they feel quite as strongly as Danny does about their father."

"Give them time," he chortled. "He hasn't started knocking them around yet."

Her eyes grew wide and fearful. "I remember one time, when Horace was having one of his crazy spells, I was so afraid he'd start in on the boys...after he'd finished with me." She rubbed her arms. "David, I couldn't live with myself if he ever hurt them."

David put his muscular arms around her, holding her gently, like a lost kitten. He hadn't realized how badly she was trembling.

"Adele, I'm going to see if I can find a place for you and the boys to stay where you'll be safe."

She squeezed her eyes shut, shaking her head. "David, I can't leave Horace. If he found out I was even considering such a thing, he'd...he'd kill me."

"He's not going to find out, at least not until after you've gone." He stepped back, holding her at arm's length, peering into her eyes. "Adele, you have to trust me. I can't help you if you won't let me."

— 115 —

"Her slender body began to weave. "I'm so afraid of what could happen."

David's arms dropped slowly from around her. He turned to stare at the water.

Adele sighed heavily. "Let me think about it, okay?"

David looked at the trees beyond the hazy waterway, thinking of the women he'd tried to help over the years and couldn't. The ones who'd wound up in the morgue. He didn't want that to happen to Adele. "It's your neck," he said, blinking away a tear. "I just don't want to see it get broken."

She studied him intently. "David, why are you doing this?"

He looked at her face and could still see the bruises. Her left arm was pale and the skin dry and flaky from wearing a cast for so long. But he supposed she was lucky. She didn't have kidney damage after all. It was just an infection from one of the drugs she'd been given at the hospital. He turned to watch a motor boat skimming toward the mouth of the Chesapeake Bay, wishing he were on it. "I hate bullies," he said. "Especially the kind who fool people into believing they're decent men, while they're tormenting the hell out of the people closest to them."

She lowered her head. "Is that what you and Danny talked about?"

He didn't answer.

"David, you said you could relate to Danny. Was your father a bully, too?"

He closed his eyes, as if trying to block out the first fifteen years of his life, but it never worked. The darkness only made the horror that much harder to forget. "He was worse than an ordinary bully," David told her. "He was a judge. A bully of the highest degree."

"I think I remember that." Adele replied.

"The people where we lived treated him like he was Buddha and Christ all wrapped up in one. But his family knew better. Not one of them had the guts to cross him."

She moved away from the fence, deep in thought, and walked slowly toward a thick patch of trees. David followed.

THE BABY SOLDIERS

"I wonder what happens inside a man's head that makes him want to strike out and hurt others?" She shivered. "It's such an awful sickness."

David shook his head. "The trouble is you can't convince them they need help. Have you ever seen a certified loon volunteer to go to a shrink?"

Adele coughed, holding her ribcage. "It's always the other person's fault," she said. "That was the way it started with us. Little things escalated into big things. You know, I actually cringe whenever I hear him opening the front door. He's not drinking like he was before. He promised to quit altogether, but I never expected him to keep that promise. He still criticizes everything I do, the same way he did before. Even if he hasn't had a particularly rough day, he still finds something to complain about. I can't seem to please him, no matter what I do." She bit her lower lip. "But at least, he doesn't hit me anymore."

"How long had it been like that between you two?" David asked.

"It started around the time I got pregnant with Jason."

"Jesus, Adele, that was almost seventeen years ago!"

She nodded. "I kept thinking things would get better."

"Do you remember exactly what started it?"

"It was right after Congressmen Dewey invited Horace to go on a retreat with a bunch of fellows who worked for the city. Most of them belonged to the same organizations, you know. I remember how excited Horace was the evening before he left. That was the last night I remember seeing the man I fell in love with."

"What do you suppose happened on that retreat?" David asked, more curious about the radical group than ever.

"I don't know. When Horace came back, he acted like a complete stranger. He started barking orders at Danny like a frustrated drill sergeant. He was only four then."

"You're never too young to be affected by that shit," David told her.

— 117 —

Adele winced. "After awhile, he stopped playing games and watching cartoons with them on Saturday mornings. He changed and they didn't know why. Whenever they asked me, I didn't know what to tell them. I didn't understand what was happening myself. It wasn't long after that, he started drinking heavily and becoming physically abusive. If something got spilled on the carpet, or if the tub wasn't immaculate after the boys finished bathing, he'd rail at me. Sometimes, he'd grab me so hard, I had to wear long sleeved blouses, even on hot days, to hide the bruises."

David scowled, shocked by the revelation."You should have left him a long time ago."

"David, you say you know what fear is, but you never experienced that kind of fear. Where would I have gone? By then, I had three children, one of them an infant. The only real friend I had was Priscilla Trivane, and she was in no position to help. She'd just lost a baby, and Bernie was bouncing from job to job after his discharge from the service. So, I did the only thing I could. I stayed put and tried to make the best of a bad situation."

"I'm not trying to change the subject," he said. "But don't you think that's odd?"

Adele looked at him puzzled. "Odd? What are you talking about?"

"Bernie and Priscilla Trivane. Where in the hell did they go after Kerry was kidnapped? And why?"

Adele lowered her head, gazing at the fallen pine needles. "They moved shortly after Kerry was kidnapped. At first, I thought they moved because of Sybil."

"Sybil Kelsey?" he mumbled. "What in the world does Sybil have to do with anything?"

Adele leaned back against a pine tree, and sighed raggedly. "Sybil was telling anyone who would listen that the Trivanes were responsible for Robbie's death.

She said if Bernie and Priscilla hadn't forced Kerry to have an abortion, her son would still be alive."

"For God's sake," he growled.

THE BABY SOLDIERS

David rubbed his chin. "I remember James saying something to that effect when I stopped by their place the day Robbie was killed. I let it go over my head. I figured he was in shock—losing his boy like that." He paused thoughtfully and added, "I know what losing a child can to do a man."

Adele reached out and touched his arm, her gaze sympathetic. "I'm sorry, David. What happened to Kerry and Robbie must have been devastating for you, too. It hasn't been that long since Ann and Ginny disappeared."

He rolled up his sleeves, wishing he'd worn something lighter. "It's been four years. Sometimes it feels as though it happened yesterday." He forced a smile. "But I'm learning to cope with it."

She forced a smile. "You still believe you'll find them someday, don't you?"

He sat on a wooden bench and crossed his legs. "I don't know, Adele. I'm afraid they're dead."

She grimaced. "I thought the same, but I was afraid to say so."

"I've considered the probability they might be dead a hundred times. But you'd think that one way or other, I would have heard something by now." He nodded toward the bottom of the tree directly in front of them. A squirrel was busily picking a pecan shell apart.

Adele smiled at the small animal. "It never made any sense, them leaving without saying a word to anyone. The way Ann raved about you, I naturally assumed you were the most perfect man in the whole world."

"Oh, please," he chortled.

"Who knows," she said thoughtfully. "Maybe they're safe and sound, like Priscilla and Bernie."

His brow rose. "What do you know that I don't?"

"I know where Bernie and Priscilla are. Pricilla writes to me when she can. As a matter of fact, that's what led to my most recent stay in the hospital."

David raised his hands defensively. "Whoa. You want to roll that footage back a little?"

— 119 —

Adele took a deep breath and let it out slowly. "After the Trivanes got settled in their new home, Priscilla and I began corresponding… against Horace's wishes, of course." She cupped her hands over her knees. "My mistake was keeping her letters. When Horace found them, he went ballistic. He told me I couldn't be Priscilla's friend anymore, because she talked her daughter into having an abortion. He said awful things about her, and Bernie, too."

David groaned. "He's even nuttier than I thought. What makes him think he has the right to pick and choose your friends? What does he think you are, a child?"

"No," she replied flatly. "A beleaguered servant."

He frowned. "Can you tell me where the Trivanes are? I'd love to drop them a line."

"They're living high on a mountain in Pittsburgh, Pennsylvania."

"That reminds me, I forgot to mention that I saw Kerry a couple of weeks ago."

Adele's eyes widened. "Kerry Trivane? Really? How is she? How did she look? I'll have to tell Priscilla right away. She's been so worried that Kerry was dead." She stopped abruptly.

"It's okay," he murmured. "Kerry is okay. She looks a little older though. That kid used to have a real sparkle in those baby blues of hers."

"Did she tell you what happened to her? My God, David, she's been gone since Robbie died. That was what…more than a year ago."

He nodded. "I asked her, but she didn't want to talk about it, so I didn't push. She did ask me if I knew where her folks were. I told her I hadn't heard from them since they left town." He lowered his head. "I don't think she believed me. That's the part that really hurts. Bernie and I were really close at one time. You'd think he would have confided in me if he had a problem."

"The way I did," Adele replied hollowly.

"Yeah," he snorted. "Seems like none of my friends trust me."

She clucked her tongue on the roof of her mouth. "It could have something to do with the people you work with."

"I can remedy that," he said.

"When Priscilla wrote, she made me swear on a stack of bibles that I would never tell Horace where they'd moved."

"I knew they had no use for Horace, but why was she being so secretive?"

Adele bit her lip. "It was more the things Priscilla didn't say... the things written between the lines." Adele looked grim. "Priscilla believes Horace had something to do with what happened to Robbie and Kerry."

"I don't think he would have tried very hard to prevent it," he quipped. "But I'm still puzzled as to why they moved so far away."

"Priscilla told me that shortly after Kerry and Robbie were attacked outside the Nelson Clinic, she got an anonymous telephone call. A man told her that if either she or Bernie attempted to find the girl, or go public, something awful would happen to them."

"What more could happen to them?" David muttered. "Somebody had already kidnapped their daughter."

Adele shifted her eyes thoughtfully. "Well, they still have Jimmy... and each other, of course."

"Lord, I wish Bernie had told me." David said, shaking his head from side to side. "I think I'll have a serious talk with Horace and see if I can get to the bottom of this."

Adele clutched his arm tightly. "David, please don't. I don't want you putting yourself in danger. I don't know what I'd do if anything happened to you."

He glanced from her troubled eyes to the pale hand resting on his arm, wondering what he was going to have to do to convince her that he wasn't afraid of her old man.

Adele blushed. "I mean..." she stammered. "You've been so kind to me and the boys, that I...."

He nodded. "Adele, nothing is going to happen to me. I guarantee you that. Will you give me the Trivanes' address? I think Kerry has the right to know where her folks are, and why they moved away. I hate to think of that poor kid, all alone in the world, without the foggiest idea of whatever happened to the only security she'd ever known."

David couldn't keep his mind off Adele the rest of the day. He wanted to pound Horace Woolard so badly he'd never be able to harm anyone ever again. He never hated anyone that much in his life before, not even the judge. He wished he could get rid of Horace without drawing any suspicion. It wouldn't be all that difficult, he thought. Woolard had a lot of enemies, and he was a detective. He could investigate the case at his leisure, or until he retired.

He remembered a story his grandfather had told him when he was a boy. There was a mean old fart by the name of Nate Custer, who didn't get along with any of the regular folks in the county. When anyone caused trouble for Nate, he'd invite them to go hunting with him. Strange thing was old Nate was always alone when he returned from those hunting trips. The locals did their share of speculating, and the law did their share of investigating, but they could never prove anything. Hunting accidents happened all the time.

David thought about the Remington shotgun in his bedroom closet. It hadn't been fired since he was fourteen. He wondered if he could interest Horace in a little hunting trip—just the two of them.

CHAPTER TWENTY-THREE

At nineteen, Danny Woolard had a steady job, a car, his own apartment, and was totally responsible for his own fate. No longer did he have to live under his father's roof, or bear the brunt of his obsessive scrutiny. His only regret being he hadn't been there to protect his mother when she needed him.

The last time he saw her, she was still carrying the purple bruises of her last encounter with his father. He couldn't take his eyes off the hideous marks, while she repeated, over and over, how his father was making a real effort to change. His father had been lying for so long, he couldn't believe anything he said. He didn't think his mother did either—not really. Horace Woolard didn't have the capacity for change, unless it was for the worst. Danny hadn't expected his mother to tell him that his father was living at home again. Just like nothing ever happened, he thought morosely. The last time he'd talked to David Williams, David said Horace had taken a leave of absence. Danny smirked, remembering how David said he hoped the absence was permanent.

Danny was on the road so much; he began to wonder why he was paying rent on an apartment at all. Amy Patterson kept him so busy fixing up a place to house the stolen children once they were found, he barely had time to flip on a TV or scan the evening newspaper.

At times, he wished he was still behind the wheel of that cushy limo he used to drive. At least, he didn't have sore muscles and blisters that never seemed to heal. But he had to give Amy credit, she didn't ask him to do anything she wouldn't do herself. He never saw anyone work the way she did, man or woman. But she was extremely careful. She didn't want the wrong people getting wind of her plans, before she was ready to spread the word herself. And so far, her plans were right on schedule. Last month, she'd even felt confident enough to tell him it was okay to give Jason a number where he could be reached in case of emergency. But by then, an emergency had already happened. Even so, Danny was reluctant to share information with anyone. He had become as obsessed over protecting Amy's scheme as she was.

Danny hadn't seen Kerry Trivane in some time. The traffic leaving Morehead City, North Carolina, ran fairly smooth until he reached Elizabeth City. Between local truck drivers hogging the road to shoot the breeze with each other, the twenty-five mile an hour speed limit, and stop lights placed every thirty feet, he was afraid it would be another month before he arrived in Chesapeake. He hoped enough time had elapsed for Kerry to come to grips with her loss. If so, maybe he had a chance of changing her mind about going out with him.

Motorists smiled at Danny as they drove by. His lips were moving. They probably figured he was just some crazy fool talking to himself. But he wasn't. And he wasn't singing along with the radio either. He was rehearsing the speech he planned to give Kerry when he arrived at the shelter. No matter how sincere his words were, he knew they would mean nothing if he couldn't win her trust. He thought about everything she'd endured this past year and wondered if he'd have been as brave if anything that awful had happened to him. Amy had confided that one of the guards had hurt Kerry badly while she was at the camp. The guard's name was Evan Polk. Danny knew Polk by sight but had never met him. He tried tracking him down, just to have a man to man talk with him, but he couldn't find any sign of him. It was as though he'd disappeared from the face of the earth. He'd even gone so far as to ask David Williams if he could check out Polk's home address. After David checked Polk out, he told Danny that Polk's possessions were still at his apartment, but his landlady hadn't seen or heard from him in months. Danny wondered if Evan Polk had moved away. But that didn't make sense. He wouldn't have left his clothes and computer behind. When things calmed down, if they ever did, Danny decided he'd do a little investigating on his own. Too many people were disappearing.

CHAPTER TWENTY-FOUR

Most of the houses in the old, settled neighborhood south of Chesapeake were sturdy two and three-story wood frames with box shaped front porches. The only change making each house unique was the color of the front door.

Danny slammed on the brakes, gripping the wheel hard to keep from swerving. The house where the girls were living now looked so good, he nearly zipped right past it. The front steps had been rebuilt and painted a warm gray along with the rest of the porch. Strips of lattice had been added to the sides with colorful rose vines clinging to them. What really got his attention were the shiny glass windows along the first floor. He smiled appreciatively. Someone must have made a sizable donation to the shelter to pay for all the work that had been done.

Rebecca peered out the narrow opening in the front door, watching Danny as he unfolded from the old VW. Her beady dark eyes darted from side to side, wary of everyone who approached the door, including the postman. She had become overly cautious answering the door and the phone in recent weeks. She worried that every passerby was a potential threat to the residents. When they bought this house in Chesapeake, she thought she'd be on cloud nine. But life never worked out the way Rebecca thought it should. The residents in the nearby houses had threatened several of the girls for coming and going at odd hours. There was nothing they could do about their job schedules.

When Danny approached, Rebecca flashed a welcome grin and let him in.

"Danny," she said exasperated, her hands planted firmly on her hips. "What in the world are you doing wearing a mustache?"

He chuckled as he smoothed the short brush with his fingers. "It was Amy's idea. She thought it would make me look older. That way the police wouldn't be so eager to stop my car just for the hell of it."

"Hmmm," Rebecca replied thoughtfully. "As if driving a VW with duel mufflers isn't enough of a red flag."

Danny clutched his chest, as though he'd been stabbed in the heart. "Rebecca Corbitt, how can you say such horrible things about my favorite girl?"

Rebecca laughed. "I'm sorry, Danny. I wouldn't insult Josephine for all the money in the world." She rubbed her rough hands nervously down her jeans. "I'm afraid I've got an awful lot on my mind."

He followed her into the kitchen, breathing in the heavenly aroma of homemade spaghetti sauce. He removed the lid from the steaming pot and inhaled hungrily. "I wish I lived here. This stuff smells great!"

"Very funny," she said, tossing an oven mitt at him.

"You have this place looking so fantastic. I almost didn't recognize it."

Rebecca's thin lips parted. "It does look good, all spruced up, doesn't it?"

"What happened?" Danny asked. "Did some millionaire die and leave you guys a bundle?"

"Not hardly," she answered, nudging him away from the stove. "Just some fresh paint and a lot of hard work."

He put his hands in his pockets and sauntered across the room, gazing down the hall. "Is Kerry around? This is her day off, isn't it?" He looked back puzzled.

Rebecca slipped her small right hand into the oven mitt. "I don't think Kerry knows the meaning of a day off."

Steam poured from the oven as she opened the door and basted two plump chickens inside. The aroma wafted across the room, making Danny moan.

"Kerry and Angie went to the hardware store. They should be back any time now. You're welcome to stick around and wait if you like. You won't be bothering me, as long as you keep your nose away from the food."

Danny pulled out a kitchen chair and sat down, breathing in the succulent odor of baked chicken mingled with spaghetti sauce. "What are they doing at the hardware store?"

Rebecca nodded toward the front of the house. "All that work you saw outside was Kerry's idea. She said if we ever have to move from here, we'll be able to sell this place for a nice profit."

Danny gawked at Rebecca. "Kerry Trivane helped rebuild the porch and paint everything?"

"The one and only," Rebecca said proudly. "That girl is a bundle of untapped talent."

"So I see," he said admiringly. "I wonder where she learned how to do all that stuff?"

Rebecca washed her hands. "Kerry said her father was a carpenter of sorts. He decided that she was the closest thing to a boy he was ever going to have, considering her brother, Jimmy, was more interested in music, so he taught her what he knew."

Danny twisted the ends of his trim mustache. "Maybe you should convince her to quit working at the diner and look for another job. A good carpenter is a rare find."

Rebecca laughed. "If the powers that be don't want women having abortions, I hardly think they'd cozy up to the idea of putting them on scaffolds where they'd really have some clout."

"That power machine will soon be changing."

"Oh, my," Rebecca said, placing a glass of iced tea in front of him. "Sounds like Amy Patterson has been brainwashing you."

THE BABY SOLDIERS

Danny picked up the glass and gulped quickly. "I've never met anyone quite like Amy before. She moves faster than a ball shot from a cannon. And she never gets tired."

Rebecca folded her arms over her chest. That description fits our Amy to a T. And speaking of Amy, how is everything going south of the border?"

Danny looked puzzled for an instant and then grinned. "Oh, you mean down in Carolina."

Rebecca feigned a cough. "A geography whiz you ain't."

Danny folded a paper towel and placed it under the sweating tea glass. "Whenever anyone mentions border, I think of Mexico, not Carolina."

She nodded. "You're forgiven."

"Actually," he said thoughtfully. "We're making decent headway. There are still a million things to do. Amy will tell you all about it next weekend."

"I'm glad you told me she was coming," Rebecca said. "That'll give me time to round up the others. I'm sure she'll want to have a group meeting."

"No doubt," he replied. "Amy told me that she asked Kerry to help with some special project."

Rebecca nodded. "Yes. In addition to her carpentry skills, Kerry could make a fairly skilled architect. Did you know she can draw floor plans for a house, right down to the number of square feet in the closets?"

He squirmed uncomfortably, making the wooden chair squeak. "You really know how to make a guy feel inferior."

"No reason for that," Rebecca said, once again smoothing her short, curly hair. "We all have things we're especially good at and others we're not so good at."

"Yeah," he muttered. "Keep talking. Maybe someday, I'll start believing you."

"You know what your problem is, Danny?"

He looked up questioningly. "What?"

— 129 —

"That miserable father of yours harped on you for so long, he'd just about convinced you that you're worthless."

"He was a good convincer."

Rebecca rubbed her palms together. "Well, we're going to have to do something to change that. I guess we'll have to spend the next nineteen years telling you how wonderful you are."

Danny laughed so hard he didn't hear the front door open.

It closed with a thud. Kerry and Angie suddenly appeared in the doorway, arms loaded with plastic bags filled with tools, sandpaper and paint. Danny grabbed the largest of the bags and carried them into the dining room, placing them in an empty corner on the hardwood floor.

Angie's inquisitive eyes stared after him as he followed Kerry back outside. Then she turned to Rebecca, who was busy unpacking the new merchandise and stacking it neatly against the wall.

"What makes Danny so wonderful?" Angie asked her.

Rebecca laughed. "You must have caught the tail end of our conversation. I was just practicing a little child psychology on him."

"Funny?" Angie muttered wryly. "I thought child psychology had been outlawed."

Kerry entered the dining area, Danny close on her heels. They dropped more bags on the floor at Rebecca's feet. "What's this about child psychology?" Kerry asked. "I heard the latest strategy was basically whips and chains."

Danny clutched his hands at his sides. "Funny my dad never thought of that. He tried everything else."

Rebecca waved her hands defensively. "You know Danny, putting you back together again may be a lot tougher than I thought."

Kerry unpacked the paint and brushes, seemingly oblivious to those around her. Danny's watchful eyes never left her. Rebecca smiled, taking her dark-skinned friend by the arm and steering her toward the kitchen. "Come on, Angie. You can help me make the salad."

THE BABY SOLDIERS

Angie protested. "How can I think about food after walking five miles through toilet seats, paint cans and carpet swatches?"

Rebecca rolled her eyes. "You certainly do exaggerate. How could you possibly walk for miles inside a hardware store?"

Angie stopped abruptly. "You've never gone shopping with Kerry, have you?"

Rebecca giggled. "Come on. It can't be all that bad."

Angie sighed heavily. "Next time, you go. I'll stay home and stir spaghetti sauce and watch the soaps on TV."

"Well, if it's soaps you want," Rebecca said, nudging Angie ahead of her. "You can watch Days of Our Lives while chopping the vegetables."

"You hate me," Angie whined.

"I don't hate you, Angie. I think you're very talented. You're the best darn cucumber peeler in the whole world."

Kerry glanced at Danny and smiled. "Rebecca sure has a way with words, doesn't she?"

Danny coughed nervously. "Yeah. I wish I did."

Kerry looked confused. "You seem awfully edgy today? Is something wrong?"

"I just...I just wanted to...to talk to you," he stammered. "If that's okay?"

She smiled as she rose to her feet. "Well, I thought that's what we were doing." She stuffed the small plastic bags into a larger one. "Let's go out to the backyard. I want to show you the benches I fixed up that I found in the shed. You can actually sit down on them without falling through the slats, or having a permanent case of grunge on your butt."

Danny worked his fingers slowly through his thick hair. "Becky was telling me you're a whiz with a hammer and nails."

She snickered. "You should see me use a paint brush. I'm a regular Picasso."

Danny took her laughter as a good omen. The last time they'd parted company, she couldn't manage more than a thin smile.

— 131 —

The backyard was filled with shrubs and flowers, secluded within the walls of a high privacy fence. "Didn't there used to be a chain link fence back here?" he asked, puzzled.

"It was nothing but a rusty mess. One of the local churches donated some wood, and viola! Now we have a privacy fence."

Danny groaned. "Don't tell me you built that, too?"

"Thanks for the vote of confidence. But I'm afraid that job required a lot more muscle power than this frail girl has."

He cocked his head appraisingly. "I wouldn't exactly call you frail. Those shopping bags you carried in weren't exactly light."

Shyly, she turned away. "I guess Angie and I got a little carried away. We just went to pick up a few things and before we knew it, our carts were overflowing."

They sat on a freshly painted bench in front of a small rock garden. "How's your new job working out?" he asked.

"Well, it's not as new as it once was," she replied tiredly. "I was afraid I'd never get the hang of it. Now, I can balance a loaded tray on one hand while counting out change with the other."

"I thought the cashiers were the only ones who touched the money?"

Kerry laughed. "Mr. Neely thought I was doing such a good job that he agreed to let me operate the cash register, too."

David frowned. "I'll bet he didn't double your salary."

"Oh, it's not so bad," she replied. Mr. Neely is a peach once you get to know him. He doesn't wear a suit, or a special uniform, but he's a lot nicer than men who do."

Danny nodded. "In that case, it sounds okay."

Kerry studied his somber face. He appeared thinner and older than he had the last time she'd seen him. She couldn't decide whether or not she liked the mustache. It didn't look real. She looked away for fear she'd start laughing. "Danny, was there something in particular you wanted to talk to me about?"

He ran his palms over his knees. "I was thinking about the last time I saw you."

THE BABY SOLDIERS

She leaned her head back and laughed. "I must have been a sight, trudging down the main highway in my little pink uniform. By the time you came to my rescue, I was soaking wet. I must have smelled like a goat."

"I thought you smelled wonderful," he said, then quickly blushed. "I...I felt really bad after I dropped you off. I didn't mean to upset you by saying the things I said. I wasn't trying to pressure you into going out with me, or anything. With you just getting out of that... that place and starting a new job, I shouldn't have said anything at all."

"It was a bad time for me," she replied.

He took a deep breath and let it out slowly. "I hope I'm not putting my foot in my mouth again, but I was thinking..."

She watched the way his thick eyebrows dipped to a peak in the middle of his forehead, almost touching.

"There's a good movie playing at the mall this weekend. I was wondering if you'd like to go?"

Kerry nibbled her thumbnail thoughtfully. "After the work I've been doing around here lately, I could probably use a break. Sitting in an air-conditioned building, watching a movie sounds like heaven."

His pale green eyes grew wide and excited, like a deer hearing human footsteps nearby. "Then...then you'll go?"

"Yes," she said, bobbing her head. "If Amy trusts you enough to go all the way to Carolina with you, I guess it will be okay for me to spend a couple hours in a crowded movie theater."

He leapt to his feet. "That's great!" he said. "You won't be sorry."

Kerry rose and took his hand, noticing how damp it was as she led him through the house to the front door.

Danny said goodbye To Rebecca and Angie, and then walked toward the VW ecstatic, and yet disappointed. No one had invited him to stay for dinner.

When Kerry went to bed that night, she reflected on the plans she'd made to go to the movies with Danny Woolard. She closed her eyes

— 133 —

and said a prayer for Robbie and her baby. Then she talked to Robbie, as was her nightly ritual, telling him that Danny was just a friend, and assured him that she could never love anyone the way she'd loved him.

Although Kerry couldn't remember being more exhausted in her life, she couldn't sleep. She tossed and turned, thinking about her baby. And thinking about her missing child only made her heart ache for her parents that much stronger. She wondered where they were, and feared she would never see them again. She got up and opened the window, letting the cool night air dry the tears on her face. Someone had to know something. It didn't seem right that her dad would just quit his job and move away without anyone knowing where he'd gone. Maybe she wasn't asking the right people. Maybe Danny could find out for her. He probably knew something about tracking people down. After all, his father was an expert.

"Why didn't I think of it before?" Kerry whispered. "Mrs. Woolard and Mom used to be best friends. Danny's mother would definitely know where they were."

After taking a shower, Kerry slipped into her new robe and knotted the sash. She was going to call Mrs. Woolard right now. As her fingers tightened on the phone, she stopped. She knew Danny's father hated her folks because they stood up for women's rights. Suddenly, she wasn't so sure her parents would have confided in Adele Woolard after all. They may have decided it was too dangerous to tell her. Everyone knew how terrified Mrs. Woolard was of her husband. Whatever had happened, Kerry was certain her folks didn't move away because they wanted to. Amy had been right when she told her they wouldn't be home waiting for her when she got out. In the beginning, she thought Amy was just being spiteful. But after getting to know her better, Kerry believed everything Amy told her. When she was released from the camp, her darkest fears were realized. With no family or relatives to turn to, she'd been forced to stay at the shelter. Each day that passed, she waited for Amy to tell her they were ready. Ready to do unto others the way others had done unto them.

CHAPTER TWENTY-FIVE

Amy Patterson's new group was called Revelation. She looked over the faces of some two hundred members, who had come to the fellowship hall of the Baptist church to hear her news of what had been accomplished in Morehead City, North Carolina.

"We have worked on the old hospital building day and night," she told them. "But we still have a lot more to do before it will be ready for our children."

"Our Children?" someone in the back blurted out. "How much longer is it going to take before we find our children?"

Amy raised a hand to quiet the crowd. "I know a lot of time has passed since this project began." She smiled faintly. "For most of us, it seems like forever. But from the beginning, we were aware of the challenges we would face. And personally, I feel that we've accomplished a great deal, considering the odds against us." She turned to Kerry Trivane, seated at a long folding table on her left. "Most of you don't know Kerry. I've been reluctant to bring her into the open before now, because of the circumstances involved in her own kidnapping."

All eyes were focused on Kerry. The murmuring had stopped.

"Kerry's boyfriend was killed when the men kidnapped her in front of the Nelson Clinic."

A cacophony of gasps erupted.

Amy shouted to be heard above them. "We were afraid that when Kerry was released from the prison camp, she'd be under more scrutiny than the rest of us. Kerry's boyfriend was the son of newspaper editor James Kelsey. And if you read the newspapers at all, you know that Kelsey has been on a personal vendetta to track down whoever killed his son ever since it happened. No doubt, we figured Kerry was being watched ever single minute—not by Kelsey's private detectives, but the cops."

Amy took a deep breath. "And, since we have good reason to be wary of certain members of the police department, we thought it best to communicate with Kerry as little as possible until the time was right. We didn't want to give the powers that be any excuse to start thinking she was a threat to them in any way." She turned to Kerry and smiled proudly. "Kerry, I'd like you to tell the crowd what you've been up to."

Kerry rose to her feet, shaking the contents from a paper bag. Videotapes fell onto the table. She looked at the stunned faces and said, "Principal Robinson's house was easy to get inside. For years, they'd kept an extra key under a geranium pot on the front porch. Their study is on the second floor, directly off the master bedroom." Her grin was sinister."I always figured he was hiding something. If you want to look at the tapes, you will see that he's been hiding plenty."

Amy grimaced. "Just give them a summary of what you found. If anyone wants the complete shock treatment, they're welcome to view the tapes after the meeting."

Kerry gazed down at the tapes and then looked into the expectant faces before her. "For those of you who aren't familiar with Scott Robinson, he was the principal of the Justice Academy; a private school that supports just about everything that goes on in the community. As I look around the room, I recognize several of you who know Mr. Robinson quite well." She lowered her eyes and blushed. "I'm only saying that because he took the liberty of taping you while you were having sex with him. And now, I have the tapes."

A flurry of gasps followed.

"Calm down everyone!" Amy shouted.

THE BABY SOLDIERS

When the noise level dropped, Kerry continued. "For ten years, perhaps longer, Scott Robinson had been seducing young girls at the school and getting them pregnant."

Amy leaned toward Kerry and whispered. "Kerry, if you're not completely sure, I don't want you putting yourself out on a limb."

"It's all right, Amy. Everything I say can be proven by the tapes. He even had the balls to put the dates and the names of his conquests on each one."

"That's awful," Rebecca muttered, clutching her stomach.

"It gets worse," Kerry replied grimly. "I believe Robinson is working with the people who kidnapped us and stole our babies."

After the angry crowd calmed down, Amy asked, "Have you had any luck identifying their leader?"

"Not yet, but we're getting closer."

Kerry turned from Amy to the faces in the crowded auditorium. "Would you be interested in knowing what happened to the babies after they were taken from the camp?"

A dreaded silence followed.

Kerry held up a spiral notebook. "Mr. Robinson's job was to find homes for the female babies…making a lucrative commission on each sale, I might add."

Rebecca paled. "You…you mean he sold them?"

Kerry nodded toward the notebook. "There were some records mixed in with the sex tapes. I didn't know what the notebooks contained, but once I had time to go through everything, the books were self-explanatory. Robinson gave each child a number rather than a name. I guess he figured it would be harder to trace them that way. And next to each number was a dollar sign and an amount."

"Oh God!" Angie cried.

Amy looked from one horror-stricken face to another. "What about the boys?" she asked, a tremor in her voice. "Did you find out where the boy babies were taken?"

Kerry looked at the ashen faces of her friends. "Those rumors we heard at the camp turned out to be true."

— 137 —

Amy staggered back as though she'd been struck. "I was afraid of that," she murmured.

"From what I've been able to gather, it's just scraps and pieces of information at this point," Kerry explained. "The boys were taken to a secret location to be trained as soldiers for the same people who stole them from us."

"But, they're only children!" one of the girls cried.

"Some of them may be as old as ten or eleven by now," Kerry replied thoughtfully. "As I said before, this operation has been going on for quite some time.

The older children probably believe the guardians are their parents. After all, they are the only families they've ever known." She bowed her head so the others couldn't see the tears welling in her eyes.

"We need to locate their training camp," Amy said. "We've got to find those kids and get them out of there as soon as possible."

Kerry nodded. "I'm sure that the older ones have already been brainwashed. It may be too late to save them."

An eruption of nervous chatter followed.

"That's the reason we're hustling to get the place in Carolina ready," Amy explained. "There will be too many children involved to harbor them anywhere closer. They'll be needing medical and psychological care…for only God knows how long."

Angie stood up. Kerry cringed, remembering seeing her friend on one of Robinson's tapes. "What about the female babies, the ones that were sold?" she asked anxiously.

"I've made an appointment to give social services all the information I have. They won't be very happy when they find out we've uncovered a black market for babies in Tidewater, right under their noses."

Amy snorted. "Say your prayers the people at social services aren't in cahoots with the organization behind this whole nightmare."

"Yeah," someone yelled. "Maybe they get a cut, too."

THE BABY SOLDIERS

The large group who had come to mistrust everyone was out of control.

Amy waved her arms wildly. "Please, everyone, please quiet down! We have a lot of work ahead of us. And keep in mind that everything you heard today must go no further than these walls. Does everyone understand that? We have to be very careful what information gets to the general public."

The loud voices simmered down.

"The tapes and other documents which Kerry located are invaluable. This is the first serious break we've had. Once we start putting pressure on Robinson, it's only a matter of time before we have all the rats involved in this abduction ring turning on each other."

"Just how do we go about doing that?" Angie asked skeptically.

Amy picked up one of the tapes and held it high for everyone to see. "Anybody here know a TV personality, who'd like the scoop on the sordid life of Scott Robinson?"

The applause was deafening. Rebecca chortled, "They all would."

Amy nodded. So why don't we make some copies of these things and start mailing them out?"

"What about the girls who are on the tapes?" Angie asked, lowering her dark eyes knowingly.

Amy looked at her with compassion."Can anything be worse than the loss of your babies and the fear that they are in grave danger?"

Angie fidgeted with the silver ring on her pinkie finger. The ring belonged to her grandmother. She planned to give it to her own child one day. The little girl she'd only glimpsed before she'd been taken away. Angie lifted her troubled face, staring intently at Amy. "You're right. At this point, the best thing that could happen would be for Scott Robinson to kill himself over the notoriety."

The room rocked with intoxicating laughter.

Amy turned to Kerry. "Kerry, do you want to be the head of the Robinson demolition committee?"

Kerry shook her head. "Let some of the others handle that. I want to find out who the actual leader of the organization is. My bet was on Robinson himself. He's perverted and greedy, but I have my doubts he's smart enough to pull off something of this magnitude. Besides," she added, "I need to find out where the baby soldier camp is located."

Amy nodded her approval.

Rebecca rose to her feet. She was so short it was difficult to tell she was standing until she spoke up. "Amy, I'd like to tag along with Kerry. I have a personal interest."

Angie clutched the back of the chair in front of her. "And I have a personal interest, as well, seeing sleazy Robinson get exactly what's coming to him."

"Okay," Amy said. "Do I have some other volunteers out there? Maybe some of you who unwittingly posed for Robinson's videos? Wouldn't you like to play a part in making his shiny star disintegrate?"

Four girls in the rear of the room looked at each other sheepishly and slowly rose to their feet. "Count us in, too," they said.

A thunderous applause followed.

CHAPTER TWENTY-SIX

Scott Robinson walked into the living room scratching his head. He was wearing the same dark suit he'd worn to the academy earlier that day. Dandruff flakes speckled the shoulders of the jacket. His slacks were rumpled. Darlene, his wife of twenty-five years, looked at him puzzled. "Scott, what is it?"

"I'm...I'm...not sure," he stammered. "I was going to do some work in my study, but some of my records seem to be missing."

"They have to be in there somewhere," she replied matter-of-factly. "No one goes in that room but you."

His thin red hair had receded in recent years, exposing dark age spots on his head. His eyelids flickered involuntarily. "Darlene, have you been home all day?"

She scowled. "Well, no. I went out early this morning to deliver food baskets to the shut-ins. After that, I drove over to Edna Griffith's house to play bridge. Scott, you don't think someone broke in while I was gone, do you?"

He walked through the arch separating the living room from the dining room and then retraced his steps, rubbing his chin thoughtfully. "I don't know what I think. It doesn't appear as though anything else has been disturbed. But I'm sure some of my things are missing." His eyes shifted from side to side. "Darlene, would you mind taking a good look around down here to make sure that everything is where it's supposed to be?"

She got up and fluffed the sofa cushions. "Of course not," she said annoyed. "But I don't think it will accomplish anything."

He frowned, somewhat ticked by her response. "Just humor me, okay? Then he turned around and retreated back upstairs to his study.

After once again checking the cabinet where he usually kept his videotapes, Robinson spun around wildly, his arms knocking some classic books from a shelf. He cursed lowly and lumbered across the room to his desk. He tore through every drawer but found not a single tape. He had already gone through the cabinet twice, but he gave it another go. He stared blankly at the old CD's he'd been storing for his son, while serving his hitch in the navy. The tapes and the ledgers where he kept his personal business records were nowhere to be found.

His stomach was on fire. His ulcers didn't need the tension he was feeling. If someone stole those tapes, he'd be ruined. Darlene knew nothing about the secret tapes, or his involvement with young students, or the sale of infants. Beads of perspiration formed in groves and trickled down his face. If those tapes ever became public, he'd lose her too. Robinson sat down hard. Everything he'd ever worked for would be gone. And he could forget about inheriting Darlene's family fortune.

Darlene called from the foot of the stairs. "Scott, I've looked everywhere. I didn't find a single thing out of place."

"Thanks," he muttered hollowly.

He leaned back in the swivel chair and closed his eyes. Why would anyone steal a bunch of old tapes and ledgers? They weren't important to anyone but him. Besides, no one else even knew they existed. He looked around the room at the silver and gold figurines he'd collected, and the oil paintings he'd purchased on various trips to Europe and the Orient. If someone was intent on robbing him, why didn't they take something that was obviously valuable...something that could be easily sold. A chill of foreboding raced through his veins. He felt as though a legion of dead spirits had just breezed through him.

"That whore," he muttered angrily. "What was her name?" He remembered the way she swore she'd get even when the guards took

— 142 —

THE BABY SOLDIERS

her to the camp last year. Although she was just one of the many girls he'd bedded over the years, she worried him. He was concerned that she'd call Darlene and tell her about their little tryst.

He exhaled smugly. No worry there. Darlene wouldn't believe her. Darlene believed only him. That little bitch. She'd be out of the camp by now, he thought, counting back the months. He wondered if she could have broken into his study and stolen the tapes. Of course not, he decided. She didn't even know he'd been taping her. The tapes were strictly for his own amusement. It had to be someone who had been in his house recently. The window washers? The floor finishers? He sighed despairingly. It could be anyone.

Reluctantly, Robinson picked up the telephone and punched in the familiar number. Then he waited, strumming his fingers on his desk. When the voice on the other end answered, he said, "Horace, it's me. We have a problem."

""We?" Horace chuffed. "We don't have a problem. You may have a problem. I take care of my problems."

"Smart Bastard," Robinson mumbled.

"I hate to bust your bubble," Robinson retorted. "But someone broke into my study and stole my tapes along with the record books I'd been keeping."

"Books?" Horace asked confused. "What books?"

Robinson sighed impatiently. "You know…The records of all the fine folks who benefitted from the baby sales. And that makes it your problem, too."

Horace clutched the phone so hard he cracked the plastic receiver."Who stole them?"

"I don't know, you damned fool! But if whoever it was turns that information over to the wrong people, we're in deep shit! And I do mean WE!"

"Listen, Robinson, I'm not on any of your stupid video sex tapes. I don't even know what you're talking about. I'm afraid you're on your own."

— 143 —

"Nice try, cop. You may not be on the tapes, but your name sure as hell pops up in those ledgers. I kept track of all the sluts who were taken from the Tidewater area and from Maryland. I also have the names of everyone who delivered the infants to their happy new homes. What's more, I put a dollar amount next to the initials of the people who made those deliveries. I don't have to remind you that you made over twenty of those deliveries yourself. At quite a sizeable profit, too."

Horace's throat was as dry as an empty bottle lying on hot sand. "How could you be so damned stupid?"

"Stupid!" Robinson shouted. "If I remember correctly, it was you who said we'd be smart to keep records of everything we did, so the boss couldn't cheat us out of our share of the profits."

Horace's heart pounded. He feared he was having a heart attack. Then he wondered if dying wouldn't be preferable to being exposed for corruption and losing his prestigious title of Captain. "Look," he said, his voice mellowing. "What if I come over to your place and have a look around myself? If we don't turn up anything, we'll put our heads together and come up with a plan to straighten out this mess."

"You can't come here," Robinson replied hoarsely. "I don't want Darlene to suspect anything is going on. If she sees you here, she'll know something is screwy. Meet me tomorrow night at the academy. We'll talk there."

Horace hung up, noticing the crack in the receiver for the first time.

CHAPTER TWENTY-SEVEN

It was dark when Horace drove his Mercedes to the rear parking lot of the academy, his eyes ever watchful of his surroundings. The spotlights mounted on the corners of the building covered the entire lot, making it appear as bright as the middle of the day. He watched Robinson climb from the red Jeep he had squeezed between two school buses.

Emerging from the Mercedes, Horace called out, "I'm over here."

Robertson was greedily sucking air by the time his bulky frame reached Horace. "This is the biggest mess in the world," he said, wiping the sweat from his brow. "I could lose everything if those tapes get into the wrong hands. What happens if the girls we sent to the camp recognize themselves and decide to come forward?"

"We never sent any girls from the academy to the camp," Horace said.

Robinson hung his head, coughing to clear his throat. "That's not exactly true."

Horace glared at him. "What are you saying?"

"Well...some of the girls were taken from abortion clinics, but others..."

"What others!" Horace yelled.

"The ones I er...how shall I say it? The ones I was intimate with."

Horace's face turned crimson. "I don't believe this. Are you saying you were fucking some of those girls who wound up at the camp?"

— 145 —

Robinson nodded grimly.

"I knew that goddamn dick of yours was going to get you in trouble one day," Horace clenched his fists. "Any chance one of them might be out to get a little revenge?"

"I never told them I was taping our sessions," Robinson said defiantly. "I'm not that stupid."

"No. Just stupid enough to knock them up and have them towed to the camp." Horace mumbled wryly.

"They wouldn't know I had anything to do with that."

"Well, you can bet your ass somebody knows," Horace spat. "You shouldn't take things for granted. What do you know about this new group that's making waves lately? I heard rumors that some of those sluts who left the camp have been warning kids of what will happen if they choose to have abortions."

Robinson frowned. "I heard some kids talking about that outside my office here one afternoon. They call themselves Revelation. What do you know about them?"

"Next to nothing," Horace admitted. "But I've got my ears to the ground."

"Maybe you could find out who they are and put a real scare into them," Robinson said.

"And just how would I go about doing that?" Horace asked belligerently.

Robinson's eyelids flickered wildly. "You got kids in school. Could be they have contact with this group. Wouldn't hurt to ask. You might solve the whole mystery right in your own backyard."

"Fat chance," Horace mumbled.

Robinson nodded thoughtfully. "You know, I thought I saw your oldest boy with one of those girls who was released from the camp… when I was attending a conference in North Carolina."

Horace looked dumbfounded. "You must be mistaken. My boys have no reason to be in Carolina. They stay right here at the beach, where they belong."

THE BABY SOLDIERS

Robinson chuffed. "Yeah. We're always the last ones to know what our kids are up to."

"I'm telling you, you're wrong."

Robinson scratched his freckled chin. "I'm sure it was Danny. He got tall, didn't he? He was as close to me as you are now. He didn't say anything, but I'm sure it was him."

Horace frowned, realizing he'd lost control of his oldest son."Who was this girl?" he snapped.

Robinson raised his light brown eyes toward the sky, as though the stars could aid his memory. "Not sure. I think her name is Halverson…Patterson. Christ, there were so many of them, who can keep track?"

Horace turned gray as stone. "Danny's been real full of himself lately, but I can't believe he'd be keeping company with a common whore."

"They looked pretty friendly to me." Robinson edged, sprinkling salt on the wound. "They were talking to a real estate agent." He cocked an eye. "You don't think they're planning on buying a cozy little getaway, do you?"

Horace folded his arms over his chest. "I think you enjoy being an asshole."

Robinson smiled tersely. "You know, your boy might be drawn toward that type. After all…there were rumors of your wife hanging around with that Trivane bitch."

"What kind of rumors?" Horace asked threateningly.

The academy principal raised his hands defensively. "No need to get rattled. Everyone knows your wife was a good friend of that Trivane woman. And everyone knows for a fact the Trivane clan supports abortion." He shrugged. "If your old lady doesn't think there's anything wrong with killing babies, maybe your boy doesn't either."

"Adele doesn't have anything to do with her anymore. I forbid it!"

Robinson raised a brow. "You what? Are you her husband or her father?"

— 147 —

"Don't get me pissed, Robinson. I've broken men a lot bigger than you. What you're talking about is just rumor. If truth were known, that damned Sybil Kelsey is probably behind it. She never did like Adele...the jealous bitch. We should have dumped her years ago."

"Well, we couldn't do that unless the big man said so," Robinson reminded him. "She has supported the movement from the beginning. Sybil Kelsey is the biggest anti-abortionist the organization has. Her old man running the newspaper hasn't hurt us...well...not until recently. Seems he's got his own issues since his boy was killed."

"If Sybil were my wife, I'd clobber her good."

"Yes," Robinson said. "We all know how good you are at clobbering women."

Horace grabbed Robinson's shirt and pulled him up close, until their noses were almost touching. "And just what is that supposed to mean?"

Robinson snorted. "What I mean is, you'd better lay off your old lady. People at the hospital are getting tired of gluing her back together. The word is out on you. If it gets to the boss, you can say goodbye to your cushy career. Even he doesn't believe in smacking women around."

"No," Horace muttered grimly. "He just hires people to kill them."

"Well, I'm just warning you, that's all."

Horace laughed until he began to choke. "Aren't you the perfect one to be giving advice? At least no one has me on tape fucking teenagers!"

"Let's stop fencing," Robinson told him. "We've got to find a way to stop whoever has that information." Then he nodded thoughtfully. "You know it could very well be someone from that Revelation group. Maybe you ought to lean on them a little and see what turns up."

"Lean on them? I don't even know who they are."

Robinson smiled. "But you can find out. You're a cop, remember?"

"Yeah, I'm a cop," Horace replied smugly. "If I run them in, they'll crack...eventually."

THE BABY SOLDIERS

Robinson chuckled nervously. "Woolard, you give new meaning to the term police brutality."

Horace glared at him. "And if it weren't for dumb fucks like you, I wouldn't have to be so damned brutal."

Robinson shrugged. "Well, I suppose brutality is okay, as long as it gets the job done."

"If you come up with a better idea, I'm listening," Horace said, sauntering back to the Mercedes.

Scott Robinson watched the sand spray from the Mercedes' tires as Woolard fish-tailed out of the parking lot. He hoped the captain would be able to solve his problem before it was too late. Slowly, he walked back to his own vehicle, fearful it already was.

CHAPTER TWENTY-EIGHT

Horace Woolard seethed over the blunder that made it necessary to drive to Baltimore again so soon after his last visit, but he found the scenery flawless. Colorful wildflowers sprinkled the countryside north of Fredericksburg, and the grass cascading down the mountain slopes appeared more blue than green. The stately antebellum homes, sitting back from the road, reminded him of a simpler time, before the country became so damned liberal. Though the highways were just as crowded as those in Tidewater, the drivers here weren't as blatantly determined to run over you. If he weren't so bogged down, dealing with the incompetence of others, he could relax and enjoy the trip.

For the past week, he couldn't sleep, unable to shake free of the unpardonable dilemma Scott Robinson had put him in. If the fool had to keep records of their activities, surely he could have stored them in a safer place than his home study. Horace wouldn't be caught dead hiding anything important in his home where Adele and the boys could find it. And to think Clifford Jacobson had actually put Scott Robinson in charge of The Justice Academy, knowing full well what a fuck-up he was. No wonder today's kids were growing up without principles. Look at their numb-nuts leaders.

Horace figured the miserable bastard had been overreacting when he said somebody had stolen his secret records. He'd probably misplaced them, the way his kind often did. Over the years, Horace had observed most people with high IQ's had very little common sense. But then, rumors of the missing tapes began to circulate. A radio personality in Chesapeake claimed he had received an interesting tape of a prominent figure in Virginia Beach doing the nasty with young schoolgirls. He said he was waiting to hear from said individual before going public. He refused to announce the person's name over the radio.

Horace knew what the radio jock was up to. He was planning to squeeze the principal for every dollar he could get. Even Scott Robinson should be bright enough to figure that one out. Robinson had called and begged him to find the thief and end the gossip before all hell broke loose. Now, it was too late.

Horace's head throbbed. He shouldn't have hit the Scotch so hard last night. But there were times when it was the only thing that mellowed him. Robinson wasn't the only thorn in his side. He still wasn't able to come to grips with the way his own son had turned against him. None of them had any respect for him. You do everything you can to raise them right, and they spit in your eye. He blamed Adele for that. She was as sorry a mother as she was a wife.

His stomach lurched as he approached the exit for Glen Burnie. He had to tell Jacobson about the tapes and the records Robinson had kept. If those records were found by the wrong people, Horace could forget about his career. Robinson's written words would destroy the whole organization.

He turned up the air conditioner and unfastened the top button on his shirt. He wished he could blame everything that happened on Robinson, but those sluts were as much to blame as he was. Dumb little whores. He was grateful he never had girls. Boys were bad enough. He didn't know what he'd have done if Adele had told him she was having a girl. He snickered. He might have considered making her have an abortion. Females, he snorted, were nothing but trouble.

Horace whizzed by a maze of shopping centers, self-service gas stations, and fast-food joints. Once they faded from his rear-view mirror, he entered the well-heeled part of Baltimore.

Jacobson's triple-decker estate sat on the crest of the hill. Woolard couldn't even imagine how much the believers had contributed to fashion the great one's golden calf.

It was a mansion, all right, built with a combination of gray stone and Italian marble. The windows that overlooked the rolling hills towered from floor to ceiling. Some two hundred white pines lined the driveway. Six white pillars stood like stalwart soldiers along the perimeter of the front porch, giving the impression that the people who lived there were well-bred as well as well-heeled.

Horace sighed heavily as he climbed from of the Mercedes. When he reached the enclosed porch at the top of the stone steps, he noticed a fresh coat of varnish had been applied to the hard wood floor, and colorful cushions covered the wrought iron sofa and chairs. He figured Clifford Jacobson spent more money on maintenance in one year than he made in twenty.

The preacher once told him he had designed the place after becoming fascinated by a southern plantation he'd visited in Savannah. He smirked, wondering if that old plantation in Savannah had an eighteen-hole golf course, like this one.

Horace rang the bell and waited impatiently. A chorus of barking Dobermans echoed from the other side of the door. It was a full minute before a solid-built man wearing an immaculate white suit answered the door. He held it open and nodded curtly.

"Good afternoon, Captain Woolard. Reverend Jacobson is expecting you. He's in his study."

"Thank you, Spears," he mumbled, following the broad-shouldered man down a chandelier lighted hallway.

Clifford Jacobson stood at the study window; his cool gray eyes scoured the grassy countryside as though he were looking for a sniper. He spun around when the two men entered.

"Captain Woolard," he said, patronizingly. "I'm so pleased to see you, again."

Horace glanced at the diamond rings the preacher flaunted rather than facing him directly as he shook his hand. The phony grin unnerved him to no end.

"This is quite a surprise," the preacher said, raising a brow. "I've been trying to reach you since yesterday. I've heard some troubling rumors."

Horace could feel those steely eyes examining every pore on his face. He was unable to explain the sudden chill and wished he hadn't left his jacket in the car.

"Forgive my manners," Jacobson said. "Please sit down."

Horace sunk into the soft leather chair as though it were goose down. He could feel the preacher's hard eyes on him and crossed his legs, giving the impression he was completely at ease.

"Clifford, you were trying to reach me? Is there a problem?"

"As a matter of fact, there is." Jacobson replied, gliding toward his desk. "Something has come up that will require your particular expertise."

Horace leaned forward, giving the preacher his undivided attention. He decided he would put off telling him about Robinson's fiasco until later.

"Horace, it seems our Mr. Robinson has created a serious dilemma that the organization cannot tolerate."

Horace's heart leapt into his throat. How did he find out? He wished Spears had offered him something to drink before he'd conveniently disappeared.

"Scott Robinson?" Horace asked, knowing damned well which Robinson he meant.

Jacobson reached into the top drawer of his desk and removed a videotape. Horace blinked, dumbfounded as the preacher held it between his manicured fingers.

"One of our local radio stations received this tape in the mail yesterday. The reporter happens to be a member of our organization and was kind enough to bring it directly to me."

Horace swallowed hard.

"Carl, said the package had a Chesapeake post mark on it." He tapped the side of the cassette on the edge of his desk. Which leads me to believe that copies of this are already circulating in your vicinity."

Horace didn't move a muscle, although his mind was racing at warp speed.

"I played the tape," Jacobson told him, a distasteful sneer spreading over his colorless face. "Not all of it, mind you, just enough to get the gist of what was on it."

Horace attempted to swallow, but couldn't summon up the saliva.

Jacobson's gaze grew hostile. "I'd play it for you, but it's so evil." He grimaced, shaking his head from side to side. "I think it best if I destroy it."

Horace felt like his face was on fire, and yet chilled to the bone at the same time. His worried eyes shifted anxiously from Jacobson to the door. Where was Spears? He sure could use something to drink. He coughed nervously. "Are you going to keep me in suspense?" he asked.

"Vile sex!" the preacher spat, slamming the tape down on his desk. "The tape is a mockery. Robinson having sex with young girls - - - girls from our academy for crissake! It's disgusting."

Though his insides were shaking, Horace tried to remain calm. "That's horrible," he replied. "Do you think Scott knew he was being taped?"

The preacher's eyes widened for a split second, then narrowed. "Of course he knew. I have no doubt he recorded the tape himself. He's a very sick man," the preacher muttered sadly.

Horace lowered his eyes, having nothing to add.

"I had Spears do some checking for me. It seems that the young woman on the tape is from Virginia Beach." He lowered his head. "And she was a registered student at our academy."

Horace nodded, continuing his silence.

Jacobson pounded his clenched fist on the desk. "This is partly my fault. I chose him for that position. In a way, I rolled out a red carpet, condoning his wanton behavior."

Drops of sweat rolled down Horace's face and neck. "You couldn't know," he lied. "Robinson has always put on a good front."

Jacobson leapt to his feet. "Robinson must be eliminated at once!"

Horace's face turned ashen. Now he knew why he felt so cold inside.

"Robinson has gone too far this time," he spat."I looked the other way when I heard about his indiscretions over the years. He was such a large contributor to the organization. But this," he said, scowling at the tape. "I don't know who got a hold of this tape and sent it to the radio station, but whoever it is, he's got to be stopped, too."

Horace's shoulders slumped. He felt as though the weight of the world had been dropped on him.

Jacobson's icy eyes glared like storm clouds. "We have no idea how many tapes are out there. God knows how many radio stations may already have them."

"God," Horace mumbled. "There must be a hundred radio stations between here and Tidewater alone. That's a lot of ground to cover."

Jacobson nodded grimly. "I've already got my people working at the post offices here, destroying anything that even remotely looks like a video cassette. I've also sent some of our most trusted men to keep a lookout at the radio stations, ready to intercept any tapes that arrive."

Spears knocked lightly on the door. "Reverend Jacobson, would you and Captain Woolard care for refreshments?"

Jacobson turned to the man dressed in white linen. "Yes, Byron," he replied thoughtfully. "I'll have my usual, tea with a squirt of lemon, and bring Captain Woolard whatever he wishes."

Horace turned to Spears, a thin smile twisting his lips. He was grateful for the interruption. "I'll have the same," he replied, wishing Scotch were an option.

Spears backed out and closed the door, leaving them alone once more. Jacobson turned to Horace. "I've been so wrapped up with this Robinson business, I never asked you the reason for your visit?"

Horace knew there was no point in lying. The preacher had an uncanny way of sniffing out the truth. "My visit was prompted by rumors of those tapes," he said, nodding toward the cassette lying on Jacobson's desk.

Jacobson exhaled heavily as he appraised the diamonds glittering on his fingers. "I'm afraid Mr. Robinson has become a terrible liability," he mumbled. Then he looked across the room. "Horace, I've always admired your dedication. You've never failed me."

Horace sat rigidly, feeling the blade of the ax about to strike.

"I have two very important assignments I want you to handle personally."

Horace replied weakly. "I'll do whatever you deem necessary."

"First," he said, running his manicured fingertips over his thin lips. "I want you to find out who is responsible for making those tapes accessible to the media."

Horace nodded agreeably. He was already working on that very thing.

"Secondly," Jacobson said, his eyes drawn to his bejeweled hands once more. "I want you to eliminate Scott Robinson as quickly as possible."

Horace didn't know whether to jump up and run or sit there like a lump without a brain in his head. Hating himself for his own weakness, he chose the latter.

The preacher stared at him coldly. "I don't want you to have someone else do it this time, the way you have before."

Horace squirmed in his chair. He had paid someone four thousand dollars to kill Fritz and Pauly, the guards who had murdered Robbie Kelsey and kidnapped the Trivane girl. He wondered, how in the world Jacobson knew he didn't kill them himself.

"I understand," Horace replied meekly.

Jacobson stood up and stretched his arms high above him. "As long as I have men like you in charge, Horace, I'm confident our ministry will survive any storm."

THE BABY SOLDIERS

Horace still felt numb after leaving Jacobson's study. The aroma of freshly cut roses that decorated the hallway made him think of mortuaries and silk-lined caskets.

Byron Spears caught up to him before he reached the front door and gave him a manila envelope.

Horace noted it was sealed.

"Reverend Jacobson said this should cover any expenses you incur while carrying out your assignments."

Horace looked at the envelope as though it were a coiled snake. But he knew it wasn't the envelope that was dirty, it was the money inside. He walked out into the drizzling rain, in no particular hurry to reach his car or his home. It never dawned on him until now, he was nothing more than a paid hit man.

Jason Woolard crawled from beneath the window ledge, looking both ways to make sure no one had seen him. Then he began to run. His breath came in sharp, heavy gasps as he jumped over a high hedge and snaked between jagged rose thorns. When he reached the area where he'd parked his old jalopy, he clutched his chest wishing it didn't hurt so bad. He bent over, holding his knees, and took a series of slow, deep breaths. When the pain in his chest subsided, he crossed the street and disappeared into the thick foliage of overgrown shrubs and maple trees.

Mark waited nervously for his brother in the rusty Chevy. He turned the radio dial from station to station, looking for something besides country music. Finally, he settled on a station playing the kind of music his mother listened to at home. She called it Oldies but Goodies. The beat was okay, but the words sounded pretty lame. *I shot the sheriff, but I didn't shoot the deputy.* Mark couldn't imagine that song had ever been a big hit, even way back then. He jumped when the door sprung open and Jason jumped inside. His mouth opened in awe, seeing Jason's sandy, wet hair plastered to his red face.

"Jason, what happened?" he asked fearfully.

— 157 —

Jason pressed his forehead to the steering wheel, waiting for the air-conditioner to do its magic. "Mark," he said, nearly choking. "We've got to get home right away."

Mark couldn't tear his eyes from his older brother. "Did you see dad?"

Jason's head bobbed up and down. "I saw him. I heard him talking, too."

"How could you hear him talking? I thought you were going to stay outside?"

"I did." Jason replied testily. "I heard him talking to Reverend Jacobson through the window."

"What were they talking about?" Mark asked.

"Dad...Dad's going to kill Mr. Robinson!"

Mark could tell Jason wasn't teasing him this time. Jason whipped onto the main highway, driving faster than he'd ever driven before. Mark wanted to know why his dad was going to kill the academy school principal, but Jason's driving scared him too much to ask. All he could do was sit there and listen to the crazy words of that stupid song. *I shot the sheriff, but I didn't shoot the deputy.*

CHAPTER TWENTY-NINE

Danny Woolard whistled along with the radio as he drove home from his date with Kerry Trivane. He thought about how much they had in common: chocolate covered raisins, Pepsi Cola, popcorn with lots of butter, and mystery novels. He really did like her. She was sweet and sincere, nothing at all like the selfish slut his father said she was. Not that his father's opinion meant anything. Horace Woolard was the biggest hypocrite in the whole world.

The farther Danny drove, the more excited he became at the prospect that he and Kerry could become more than friends one day. After all, she had agreed to see him again. He couldn't keep his newfound happiness to himself. He'd burst if he didn't share it with somebody. He drove over to his parents' home, and parked in his father's empty space in the driveway. He was relieved he wouldn't have to face that demon tonight. It had been such a perfect evening. He didn't want to spoil it now.

When Danny walked in, Adele was reading in the den. She noticed the smile on his face, which spread from ear to ear. "Danny," she said, standing up to hug him. "I wasn't expecting you tonight."

"I know, Mom," he replied. "I just had the greatest time of my life and wanted to tell you all about it."

"Would you like something to drink? There are some cookies in the kitchen."

"No, I'm okay," he answered, perching on the edge of the sofa.

"Well, you look like you just won the lottery?"

"I did in a way. I just went out with Kerry Trivane."

Adele didn't appear shocked, or even surprised. What did shock her was learning that Kerry was still living in the area. She thought she would have moved to Pittsburgh to be with her folks. The last time she'd talked to David Williams, she was sure he had mentioned something about Kerry leaving town. She studied her tall, handsome son, thinking that someday he'd be married and have a family of his own. She just prayed the home he'd grown up in hadn't warped his mind so badly that he wouldn't know what a real marriage was supposed to be like.

"Kerry is a lovely girl," she said softly. "I'm happy to see that she's adjusting so well…after everything she's been through. That poor girl."

Danny touched his mother's arm. "Kerry's doing fine, Mom. She's got a job she likes, and she's fixing up the old house she lives in." He lowered his head and grimaced. "She'll be even happier once she gets her baby back."

Adele narrowed her eyes, concerned. "David told me she had a child, although he doesn't know anything about the circumstances. Since you're seeing her, I suppose you know more about what's going on than the rest of us?"

Danny arched his thick eyebrows. "I'm sorry, Mom. Kerry asked me not to talk about it. I gave her my word."

Tears filled Adele's eyes. "Be careful, Danny. Don't mention anything about Kerry in front of your father."

Danny put his arms around her. "Yeah, Kerry's been through enough. She doesn't need to have him or his goon squad hassling her. He's done enough damage to the people I care about."

While driving home, Danny remembered what good friends his mother and Mrs. Trivane used to be. His dad had managed to put an end to that, too. He'd never forget, his father screaming at the top of his lungs, calling the Trivanes and everyone like them baby killers.

Danny turned into the parking lot outside his apartment complex and frowned. He recognized the old beat-up Chevy his folks had given Jason for his sixteenth birthday. It was parked on an angle,

— 160 —

THE BABY SOLDIERS

under the bright lights of the community swimming pool. He unfolded his legs and climbed out of the VW, wondering what Jason was doing out this late. When he stopped by to see his mom, he had naturally assumed that Jason and Mark were already in bed asleep.

Jason's eyes, a warm brownish green, shifted anxiously as Danny approached. "Danny, we need to talk?" he asked, rubbing his hands up and down the front of his jeans.

"Sure, Jas. What are you doing here so late?"

"Can we talk inside?" Jason asked, his voice quivering. "I don't want anyone to hear what I have to say."

Danny scowled. "You didn't have an argument with Dad, did you?"

Jason shook his head vehemently. "Danny, this is important."

Danny pulled out the key to his apartment and unlocked the door. Then he walked across the hardwood floor, his brother on his heels.

"Want a Pepsi? There's some in the fridge."

Jason plopped down on the sofa. "Not right now. We gotta talk!"

Danny frowned as he sat in the worn recliner across from his brother. "You're starting to worry me, little bro."

Jason sighed.

Danny untied his shoes. "Talk. I'm listening."

"It is about Dad," Jason said.

Danny puffed out his cheeks and blew. "What's he done now?"

Jason leapt to his feet, running his fingers through sandy, windblown hair. "He hasn't done it yet, but...it's what he's going to do."

Danny pulled off his shoes and placed them beside the chair. "Did he tell you that?"

Jason shook his head. "No. But I know what I'm talking about. You have to believe me."

Danny squinted as he looked at the lamp near his chair. It only had a fifty-watt bulb in it. "Let's go out to the kitchen. It's too dark in here."

— 161 —

Jason followed his older brother into the other room and pulled out a chair. He ran his fingers lightly over a scar in the center of the maple table and said, "You're going to think I'm crazy when I tell you what I did."

Danny opened the refrigerator. "We all do crazy things sometimes. Like driving that old jalopy outside before you got your license."

"I wanted to find out what Dad did when he went on his trips to Baltimore."

Danny's face paled. "What! You drove all the way to Baltimore?"

"Well, I found out," Jason replied, staring up at him.

Jason pushed his chair back and stood. "Mom was going to a meeting and asked me to look after Mark, so I took him with me."

"Holy Shit!" Danny said."I can't believe you drove that far, and in all that traffic. You could have been killed!"

"Well, I wasn't," Jason said, tears welling in his eyes. "Sometimes, I wish I was dead. Then everyone would stop treating me like I was a dumb little kid."

Danny laid a hand on Jason's shoulder. "I didn't mean to yell at you, Jas. It's just that…I worry about you guys…especially now that I'm not living there anymore."

Jason sniffed, rubbing his nose on his shirtsleeve. "Do you want to hear about my trip, or not?"

"Yeah. I do," Danny said, removing two cans of Pepsi from the refrigerator and putting them on the table.

Jason wandered aimlessly around the kitchen as though he were having a hard time figuring out just how to tell Danny what he'd come to say. He picked up one of Danny's softball trophies sitting on the microwave. Danny had always been good at sports. And his younger brother, Mark, was showing a lot of potential, too. Jason didn't feel like he was good at anything. Even when he thought he might be good at something, his father always made it a point to tell him he didn't measure up. It wasn't until the night Danny threatened

THE BABY SOLDIERS

to kill his dad that Horace quit throwing Danny's accomplishments in his face.

"You'd better drink that before it gets warm," Danny said, nodding toward the can on the table. Jason looked at it absently and then ambled toward the table.

"So, what happened in Baltimore?"

Jason took a long sip, emptying half the can. Then he took a deep breath. "I followed him to a big mansion on a hill in a rich part of town. I let a few cars get between us, so he wouldn't see me."

Danny smiled impressed. "Just like the TV detectives."

Jason nodded woodenly. "After I saw him go inside, I drove around looking for a place to stash my car where no one would see it. I parked by a grove of trees a couple blocks away. I told Mark to wait in the car until I came back."

Danny nodded. "I hope he did."

Jason nodded. "Yeah. He didn't want to, but he did."

"Unlike some people I know," Danny murmured.

Jason ignored the remark. "Danny, I never saw a house that big before. It had a monster swimming pool, tennis courts, and even a golf course out back."

"Hmmm." Danny uttered. "And Dad always told us we were rich."

"Not like those people," Jason replied hollowly.

"Did you find out who lived there?"

Jason bobbed his head excitedly. "You know that preacher that's on television all the time? I know you've seen him a million times. He always wears gray clothes. Gray suits, gray ties, gray shirts. He even has gray hair."

Danny eyed his brother curiously. "Are you talking about Clifford Jacobson, the guy who used to be the preacher at the church we went to a long time ago?"

Jason shrugged. "I don't remember. But his name was Jacobson. I heard Dad call him that."

"I wonder why Dad drove all the way to Baltimore to talk to him?"

— 163 —

"I saw them through a window," Jason explained, his eyes fixed on the scarred table. "The room had a huge desk, some regular furniture and all kinds of bookcases built into the walls."

"A study," Danny said.

"Yeah, a study. It looked like Dad's study, only it was twenty times bigger. The window was cracked open, so I was able to hear everything they said."

"What did you hear?" Danny asked, prodding his brother to go on.

Jason looked across the table at his brother and began to cry. "That man...Jacobson...he told Dad that he had to kill somebody."

Danny's eyes narrowed suspiciously. "Jason, are you sure that's what you heard?"

Jason nodded while rubbing his eyes. "I'm sure. I even heard who he's supposed to kill."

"Who?" Danny asked, scraping his chair away from the table.

"Scott Robinson."

Danny shook his head as though he were trying to wake from a bad dream. "Mr. Robinson? The principal of The Justice Academy?"

Jason nodded.

"Geez. This is some real heavy stuff you're laying on me. Reverend Jacobson lives in Baltimore, and Mr. Robinson lives down here."

"They were talking about some secret organization they belong to."

The hair on the back of Danny's neck began to rise."

"Secret organization," he repeated.

Jason snorted. "The way they were talking, it sounded like the Mafia. Everything they do is hush-hush. The preacher even talked about people Dad had killed for them before."

Danny's mouth dropped open. "What?"

Jason crossed his heart. "I swear it's true. Mr. Jacobson was talking about the time he ordered Dad to kill the people who shot Robbie Kelsey and kidnapped Kerry Trivane."

"Oh, no," Danny groaned. "She was right."

Jason gawked at him. "Who are you talking about, Danny?"

— 164 —

THE BABY SOLDIERS

Danny shook his head. "That's not important now." He remembered hearing his father brag about what a great man Reverend Jacobson was, and how he was going to put an end to the sickness spreading through society. Only back then, Danny hadn't paid much attention to him. He thought it was just the booze talking.

"Jason, did you actually hear Reverend Jacobson telling Dad he had to kill Mr. Robinson?"

"Yes. I heard him. I was looking right at Dad when Jacobson told him. Dad looked kind of funny, you know, the way he looks when he's hung over. He wasn't happy. I don't think he wants to do it."

"Did Jacobson say why he wanted Dad to kill Mr. Robinson?"

Jason gulped down the last of his drink. "He had some video tape Mr. Robinson made. He was having sex with some girl from the school. Reverend Jacobson told Dad that the girl on the tape was a slut and a student at the academy. He said she'd been in the camp."

Jason shrugged his shoulders."I don't know what camp he was talking about. He didn't say. The preacher said one of the radio stations got a copy of the tape in the mail and showed it to him. Jacobson told Dad he was afraid there were a lot more of those tapes floating around. He told Dad he wanted Robinson dead and whoever was responsible for mailing the tapes to the media. He said he didn't want anyone tracing Robinson's sick behavior back to him, or the organization."

Jason stared at nothing in particular while Danny digested the information his brother had given him. Then Jason rubbed his eyes. "The only thing the preacher seemed sad about was the fact that Mr. Robinson had donated a lot of money to the organization, and killing him would put a sizable dent in their bank account."

Danny's hands began to tremble. He thought about Kerry and Amy. They had both been at the camp Jason was talking about. He knew for a fact that Robinson wasn't the one who got Kerry pregnant. It was Robbie Kelsey. He didn't know about Amy's baby. She never talked about it…not to anyone.

— 165 —

Danny shook his head in awe. "Who would have thought old man Robinson was a sex pervert?"

"*Was* is right," Jason quipped. "When Dad gets through with him."

"I wonder what made Jacobson pick Dad?"

"He said it was Dad's duty to preserve the integrity of the cause… whatever that means," Jason quipped.

Danny snorted. "It's hard to preach about sins of the flesh, when one of your chief supporters is screwing young girls and getting them pregnant…not to mention taping it, too. Jesus!"

Jason looked helplessly at his brother. "What are we going to do?"

Danny spun his drink can, making circular watermarks on the table. "You know the worst part?" he said, looking at Jason."Dad is a police captain. He can kill anybody he wants and get away with it."

"Yeah," Jason retorted. "We've known Mr. Robinson since we were kids."

Danny hated that school. But his father had insisted, saying it was the best school in town. Everybody had to wear geeky uniforms. He hated that most of all. It made everyone look alike, regardless of sex. It probably wasn't that bad when the school first opened, he thought. Back when it was just a boys' school. He heard Robinson had been totally against the school going coed. He'd relented under pressure from his superiors. Danny's face contorted. He probably used those poor girls to get even. And that definitely made him a criminal.

"So, what are we going to do?" Jason asked him.

Danny looked across the table. Jason looked older somehow. As though he'd become a man since the last time Danny had seen him.

"Well?" Jason asked, standing up.

"I don't know what to tell you."

"I'm still thirsty. Mind if I have another drink?"

"No. Help yourself."

Jason stopped at the refrigerator door and turned around. "I almost forgot. Dad is supposed to kill Mr. Robinson this week. I'm not sure what day. But we've got to find some way to stop him."

THE BABY SOLDIERS

Danny crushed the empty drink can in his hand. "Let me sleep on it, okay? I'm having a tough time swallowing all this."

Jason tossed the cold Pepsi into the air and grabbed it on the way down. "Well, at least I don't feel like I'm alone anymore. I'll drink this on the way home. If Mom checks my room and finds me missing, she might think somebody kidnapped me, too."

Danny glanced up at him and frowned. "Just drive careful."

The phone rang about the time Danny was getting ready to turn in for the night. He thought it was Jason calling back, but it was Amy Patterson. She laughed giddily, as though she'd been drinking.

"Amy? Are you alright?" he asked.

"Danny, you have no idea how alright I am. We just finished sending tapes of Mr. Robinson's sex-capades to every radio station between Carolina and Maryland. Some were even dropped off in Washington DC, where all the super media stars are located. What do you have to say about that?"

Danny slumped onto the sofa. "I think you're in way over your head. You have no idea what kind of people you're dealing with."

"I...I don't understand?" she stammered. "No one knows who did it. We were very careful."

He rubbed the bridge of his nose. "Listen carefully," he said. Then he proceeded to tell her about Jason's trip to Baltimore, and the horrible things he'd overheard between Horace Woolard and Reverend Jacobson. When he finished there was a long silence.

"Your father?" she muttered. "We always thought he was a little crazy, but we never thought he went around killing people."

Danny had a headache for the first time in years. And to think that earlier in the evening he was the happiest guy in the world. He had a date with the most fantastic girl he'd ever known, and for the first time in ages, he thought things were going to get better. Now this.

"Amy, do you want me to come over?"

— 167 —

"No, that's okay," she answered hesitantly. "I don't think I'm in any real danger. Not for right now anyway. I'll call the others though, and warn them to keep their eyes and ears open, just in case they hear anything."

"Are you really sure you'll be all right?" he asked, knowing Amy led everyone to believe she was tough enough to handle any crises, although at times she wasn't.

"Honest, Danny. I'd tell you if I wasn't."

"Okay," he relented. "I'll see you first thing tomorrow morning."

He stood up and stretched. There was no point in trying to go to bed now. He knew he'd never be able to get to sleep. He needed someone older and wiser to talk to about this mess. He grabbed his car keys and turned off the lights.

CHAPTER THIRTY

Amy Patterson opened the cedar chest at the foot of her bed, pushing aside the linens her grandmother had embroidered for the hopeful day when she would marry.

When Amy learned her folks had moved to Nevada, she thought she'd never see any of her personal belongings again. Seven months after her release from the camp, a large package had mysteriously appeared at the Haven with her name on it. She was moved to tears, seeing all the things her late grandmother had taken years to make for her. She couldn't remember if she'd ever thanked her grandmother for all her hard work. Now it was too late. She'd also found her prized collection of Barbie Dolls, which had been carefully packed along with childhood photos, and paintings she had done in junior high, when she was going through her creative period.

They know I'm alive, she thought, even if they don't call me. Amy wondered if they had been frightened into moving, the way the Trivanes had, or if they'd moved away because they couldn't cope with the embarrassment of their daughter becoming pregnant as a result of an affair with a foreigner.

On the one occasion she'd taken Oshar home to meet them, her father had taken her aside and mumbled, "His skin's a might dark, isn't it?"

Her challenging reply had been, "What did you expect? He was born in Egypt. Isn't that part of Africa?"

You'd have thought she'd stabbed him right through his Scandinavian heart. What great Christians they were. She wondered if anyone ever bothered to tell them that their God had also been born in Africa.

When Amy's parents learned she was pregnant, she agreed to go to the clinic to keep peace in the family. But not once did she ever agree to have an abortion. She was merely going to ask some questions...stalling, until she could find a better way to handle the situation. Unfortunately, Oshar was pressured into returning to his homeland to fight in some futile war that had been going on since before Christ was born. Although he promised Amy he'd return, she knew in her heart she'd never see him again. Oshar had gone home to die.

Amy remembered how nervous she'd been the day she'd gone to the clinic. It was an old building in a former industrial/business zone. A friend told her the neighborhood looked a whole lot worse than it was. She remembered seeing homeless people leaning against barred store windows and how hesitant she'd been to get out of her car.

After weighing her personal safely against the endless criticism she'd have to endure when she went home, she threw caution to the wind and got out of the car.

Amy was surprised to find the clinic had a regular medical staff, credentials and all. The nurse she spoke with had braided blond hair, tall and extremely thin, but friendly. She talked about her other job, working as an emergency room nurse at a hospital in Virginia Beach. The nurse introduced herself as Julie Newman and explained how working in the emergency room absolved some of the guilt she carried from working at an abortion clinic. When Amy asked her why she worked there at all if she didn't feel like it was right. Julie simply replied, "It's like being drafted in the army. You don't want to kill anybody in a war, or be killed yourself, but you have to do your part to keep the country free.

Amy stiffened visibly when a young doctor appeared in the doorway. He had long sandy hair and a rangy beard. He looked more like a sixties-hippie than a doctor. The only thing that gave him away was the stethoscope draped around his neck. Julie smiled up at him and then turned to Amy. "Don't let him scare you. He's not a heavy, he's my brother."

The doctor reached over and playfully tweaked his sister's nose.

Amy envied their relationship. It was obvious they cared a lot about each other. She explained to them that she really didn't want to have an abortion, she'd only come to keep her parents off her back until she could come up with a better solution than living at home with them. After explaining her predicament to Julie and her brother, Amy sat there sullenly, expecting them to tell her abortion was her only option, but instead, they encouraged her to keep her child.

Amy left the clinic, feeling a lilt in her step she hadn't felt in weeks. She would have her baby and raise it herself. Julie's brother had given her the name of someone who would help her with a job and a place to stay until her baby arrived. She wished she could get in touch with Oshar to tell him about the baby, but the letters she'd sent him had been returned, address unknown.

As Amy crossed the street in front of the clinic, a car approached at a high rate of speed, nearly knocking her down. The car swerved sideways, the passenger door ajar. Then a hideously scarred man pointed a gun in her face and forced her to get inside.

The next thing she remembered was waking up in a tiny room that smelled like ammonia, and Margaret Hatchey staring down at her.

She shivered now, just thinking about it.

A Smith and Wesson 357 revolver lay on the bottom of the cedar chest. Amy picked it up, marveling at how right it felt. She had bought the gun right after Rebecca told her about the strange cars cruising the Haven in recent days. Amy made a promise to herself the day she left the camp; she'd never be unprepared to defend herself again. She insisted Rebecca and Angie buy weapons, too. It wasn't difficult to convince them after what they'd already been through. Amy checked to make sure the revolver was fully loaded before slipping it under her pillow. If anyone tried breaking in, they were in for an unwelcome surprise.

At one-thirty a.m., Amy heard a light tapping on her door. Her heart jumped, thinking about her earlier conversation with Danny. She slid from the bed and wrapped herself in a terry cloth robe. She glanced at her clock again, wondering if she'd only dreamed that someone had been knocking at the door. Then she heard the sound again. It was louder this time. She tried to keep her hand steady as she removed the gun and stalked down the hall toward the door.

"Who is it?" Amy asked, her face pressed against the wooden door.

"Amy, it's Margaret Hatchey," came the firm response."I have to talk to you."

Amy's heart hammered as she slid the gun behind her back. If she didn't know better, she'd swear she was dreaming. The guardian from the camp couldn't possibly be standing on the other side of her door. She remembered Danny telling her to be very careful. Reverend Jacobson had instructed his father, Captain Woolard, to destroy whoever had mailed Scott Robinson's tapes to the media. She wondered if Hatchey had been summoned to finish the job?

"What do you want?" Amy asked, trying to exude a courage she didn't feel.

"Let me in, Amy. Please. It's urgent."

Amy slid the dead bolt back and cracked open the door, still fortified by a brass chain. She stared curiously at the solid framed woman in the dim light of the hall, thinking how different she looked. She was wearing regular street clothes instead of her sexless uniform. Hatchey looked just like any other forty-something woman and not as intimidating as she'd appeared at the camp. Amy gave her a quick once-over, noticing she wasn't carrying a handbag of any kind, leading her to believe the woman didn't have a weapon.

Against her better judgment, Amy took a labored breath and unfastened the chain.

THE BABY SOLDIERS

Margaret Hatchey glanced at the gun in Amy's right hand and cocked a brow as she stepped inside the apartment.

Amy glared at the formidable woman for a long time before speaking. "I'd be lying if I told you I ever expected to see you again."

Margaret glanced coolly from the gun in Amy's hand to her pale face. "If you're not going to shoot me, would you mind putting that thing away. I didn't come to harm you."

Amy nodded, remembering Hatchey had been an evil bitch at times, but she had never lied to her. She crossed the room and put the gun in a kitchen cabinet.

Hatchey followed her into the kitchen where Amy turned on the overhead light. "I've been hearing a lot about you since you left the camp."

Amy's eyes narrowed, wondering who'd been jacking their jaws. "News travels fast," she said. "Is that why you're here?"

"You could say that," Margaret replied, pulling out a chair and sitting down as though she were a regular visitor. "Would it make you feel more comfortable if I told you who suggested I talk to you?"

Amy shrugged, in keeping with the cool attitude she'd developed. "I guess it couldn't hurt."

"It was your friend, Kerry. Kerry Trivane."

"Kerry? Why would she…"

"Let's just say I helped her out of a difficult situation, and she trusts me."

Amy pursed her lips. "Kerry mentioned you weren't really as tough as you wanted everyone to believe."

Margaret smiled at that. "I don't suppose Kerry's mentioned that I stop by the diner on occasion to see how she's getting along?"

"How nice," Amy muttered wryly. "What does that have to do with coming here to see me?"

"Amy, I want to help you."

Hatchey's response hit her as though someone had kicked her right behind the knees.

— 173 —

Amy rubbed her bleary eyes, trying to convince herself she was actually awake. She didn't want Hatchey to get the impression she was excited, but someone like Margaret Hatchey working for their cause could make a real difference. She was already on the inside. And Hatchey was a trusted member of the organization responsible for kidnapping her and the other girls and stealing their children. She could get her hands on information they desperately needed. Yes, she thought. Oh, yes!

"Margaret," she said, continuing to play it cool. "May I offer you something to drink?"

She had never seen the prune-faced guardian relax before. "If a cup of hot tea wouldn't be too much trouble?" She replied, smiling warmly.

CHAPTER THIRTY-ONE

When Danny Woolard arrived at David Williams' home, he didn't see the Honda in the driveway, or parked along Prescott Street. He checked his watch. It was one-forty a.m. He decided to wait.

At two-thirty, the Honda clattered into the driveway. David got out and locked the door. He swung his keys, humming as he walked toward the front door. Then he stopped abruptly, hearing footsteps behind him. Slowly, he slipped his revolver out of his jacket and spun around. "Stop right there!" he ordered.

"Whoa!" Danny yelled, raising his hands in the air. "David, it's me, Danny."

David lowered the gun, trembling. "You shouldn't sneak up on people like that. It could get you dead."

"Yeah," Danny said, taking a deep breath. "I'll be more careful next time."

"What brings you here in the middle of the night?" David asked, unlocking the door.

"I've got a problem," Danny said, stuffing his fists in his jeans. "I thought maybe talking it out might help."

David flipped on the lights, concerned by the worried look on Danny's unshaven face. "Well, you know I'm a good listener." Then he cocked his head quizzically. "Does this have anything to do with your old man?"

Danny shuffled his feet. "In a way," he answered. Then added quickly. "But it's not what you think."

— 175 —

David nodded. "Well, that's a relief. You want something to drink?"

"No thanks," Danny replied, sitting on the brick by the fireplace. "I think I should start at the beginning."

And so he did. He opened his heart to David, telling him all about Jason's trip to Baltimore and the string of unbelievable things that followed. After he finished, he looked up and said, "Hard to believe, isn't it?"

"Jesus," David muttered. "So that's who's behind all the damned shit that's been going on around here. And Horace, that sly bastard, pretended not to know a thing about it. He sent me to investigate Robbie Kelsey's homicide, knowing full well who'd killed him. What a rare bastard he is." He eased into his recliner. "You know, it all makes sense when you think about it. Who better than a demented preacher to head up a ring of kidnappers and murderers. I'll bet every one of those self-righteous assholes thought they were doing the Lord's work. Damn them! Damn them! Damn them to hell!"

Danny shook his head. "A few months ago, Amy Patterson told me she had a feeling Reverend Jacobson was behind the organization called The New Order, but she didn't know for sure. She called it a gut feeling. But she said even if she was right, it would take a lot more than guts to stop him."

"And I call myself a detective," David lamented. "I should have guessed long before now. When Sybil Kelsey and the rest of that nutty crowd were talking about what a wonderful man preacher Jacobson was. I should have known then something was wrong with him. Jacobson was their leader…even back when he had his little church right here." David lowered his head. "I wonder how he managed to get away with killing her son without her raising a stink about it?"

Danny cleared his throat. "I don't think Mrs. Kelsey suspects Reverend Jacobson had anything to do with that. She still blames Kerry and her folks for Robbie's death. Mom told me that."

"I must be slipping," David said sadly. "Why didn't I think of him?"

THE BABY SOLDIERS

"Don't blame yourself, David. You couldn't know. Jacobson doesn't even live around here anymore. We all figured whoever was giving the orders to bomb the clinics was someone local."

David coughed into his fist. "This might shock you, but for a long time, I had my suspicions your old man was behind the clinic bombings. He's was always ranting about hanging the doctors and nurses who work at those places."

Danny chortled. "He is responsible, for a lot of things."

David frowned. "God knows how many people Jacobson has on his payroll. If Horace is in his pocket, there must be a thousand more."

"I don't know," Danny told him. "All I know is Dad is in so deep, he'll never be able to dig his way out. It's as though Reverend Jacobson has him on a leash. He jerks it and Dad jumps."

David sat there feeling his hair turning gray. "I suppose you came over here thinking I can figure out a way to stop your dad from killing Mr. Robinson?"

Danny blinked. "Can you?"

David chuffed. "You have a lot of faith in me, son."

"I figured if anyone could figure out a way to stop him, you could."

David nodded. "I appreciate the vote of confidence. You know, after everything Scott Robinson's done, killing the bastard might not be such a bad option."

Danny stood up, shifting his weight from one foot to the other. "I know me and dad don't get along, but I wouldn't want to see him go to prison for killing anyone - - - not even Mr. Robinson."

David pursed his lips. He wondered how a crumb like Horace Woolard managed to elicit such devotion from the family he treated so badly. "Okay, Danny. Let me mull it over for awhile. I'll try to come up with something."

He stood and put an arm around his young visitor. "Try not to worry. You'd better get some sleep. I don't think your boss would appreciate you showing up for work in the morning with your eyes bleeding down your face."

"I don't have to worry about that anymore," Danny assured him. "My boss knows that whatever I do, day or night, I'm doing it strictly to help the group."

"The group?" David asked.

Danny wished he hadn't mentioned the group. Now he was facing a man he had never lied to in his whole life. He nodded. "I'm working with Amy Patterson and her friends. They're trying to find their babies and get them back."

David grunted. "They have balls, I'll say that for them." He cocked a brow as he studied his nocturnal visitor. "You'd better do what you can to keep them under wraps. If Horace finds them, Robinson will have to stand in line to get wasted."

Danny shuddered. "Yeah. I know. Especially now that I know Amy and her friends are responsible for sending those tapes Robinson made."

"Sounds like your new friends have a death wish. Tell Amy and the rest of her crowd to be extremely careful. They're not dealing with amateurs, or anyone in their right minds, for that matter."

"I don't have to remind them," Danny replied sullenly. "They already know what those people are capable of doing."

David watched the VW until it disappeared down the street. He and Ann never had a son. He wondered if Horace Woolard knew how precious the gifts were, he was tossing aside. No, he thought sadly. Men like Horace were too busy with their own selfish ambitions to care about the truly important things…things men like him would give anything to have.

CHAPTER THIRTY-TWO

Priscilla Trivane dropped the telephone receiver and burst into tears. Her heart-wrenching sobs lifted Bernie right out of his easy chair. "What is it, Babe?" He tossed the morning newspaper aside. "Is it Kerry?"

Priscilla shook her head violently from side to side, unable to answer.

"Cilla?" he coaxed. "Please, tell me what happened?" He knelt by the sofa, holding her trembling hands in his.

"Bernie...I..." she gasped. "That was Adele Woolard on the phone. She...she called to let us know that Ann and Ginny Williams have been found." A painful wail escaped her lips."Oh, Bernie, they were found dead."

"Good suffering Christ," he said, stumbling to his feet. "Poor David."

Priscilla nodded. "He must be going through hell right now."

"When were they found?" Bernie asked.

Priscilla blinked back tears as she looked up at him. "Some hunters found them off a country road west of Suffolk. Adele said they were so badly decomposed they had to be identified through dental records."

Bernie rubbed the back of his neck, trying to make sense of this latest tragedy.

"How long has it been since they disappeared?" he asked.

"Over four years," she replied reflectively. "Bernie, do you remember how wonderful Ginny was with Kerry and Jimmy when she used to baby-sit for us?"

He crossed his arms over his chest, tightly, as though he were trying to hold himself together.

"The last time we saw Ginny was when we had that party for Kerry's eleventh birthday. Do you remember, Bernie?"

Bernie hung his head. He remembered that day very well. The clown they had hired to entertain the kids had called at six that morning, saying he had the flu and couldn't make it. He remembered wanting to pull the guys short hairs out one by one. He didn't want anything to spoil his little girl's special day. David and Ginny had stopped by that morning on their way home from the roller rink. David had asked if he and Ginny could do anything to help, such as blowing up balloons, or stringing crepe paper in the backyard. When Bernie pulled David aside and told him the clown couldn't come, David had shocked him by volunteering to substitute. David Williams had been a pal, as well as an old navy buddy. But after that day, he became Bernie's brother.

Bernie sat on the sofa, shifting the telephone from the table to his lap. "I'll call Adele back and see if the funeral arrangements have been made. Then I'll call David to see if there's anything we can do."

Priscilla wiped her eyes as she stumbled to her feet. "Where did I put David's phone number?" she asked, seemingly dazed.

"I think it's in your little address book," Bernie offered.

She nodded. "Yes, you're right. I put it in the dresser."

Bernie gazed at the telephone and then sighed helplessly. He felt terrible about what had happened to Ann and Ginny, but at the same time, he was relieved it hadn't been a call from Virginia telling them Kerry was dead. The mixture of relief and guilt made him physically sick.

Priscilla skimmed through the pages, her eyes anxiously scouring each line. "Here's David's number," she said, handing him the book. "You do the talking. I'm afraid I'll start crying again."

— 180 —

THE BABY SOLDIERS

He nodded understandingly and placed the call. He listened while the phone rang and rang. "I thought David had an answering machine?" Bernie said, narrowing his eyes.

Priscilla looked startled. "With his job, you'd think he'd have one."

Bernie cradled the receiver. "Maybe he turned it off. I'm sure by now, everybody and their brother has heard about Ann and Ginny. They're probably pestering him to death. We'll try calling him later."

Priscilla removed the phone from Bernie's lap and put it back on the end table.

"I asked Adele if they knew how Ann and Ginny died."

Priscilla's fingers automatically went to her stomach. "Adele said they'd been shot."

Bernie rubbed his knees and added. "Shot like Robbie Kelsey."

Priscilla covered her face and sobbed.

"What a tragic way for this to end," Bernie said. "David always said he wanted closure, but somehow, I don't think this was what he had in mind."

Priscilla gnawed her lip

"Adele said the autopsy report revealed Ginny was pregnant. David never mentioned anything about Ginny being pregnant when she disappeared, did he?"

Priscilla rubbed her arms. "Maybe David didn't know."

"Yeah," Bernie said. "I guess that's possible."

Priscilla reached out for Bernie's arm. "I just had a horrible thought. Do you suppose Ann could have been taking Ginny to an abortion clinic when they disappeared...like Kerry?"

Bernie gawked at his wife in disbelief. "Do you think whoever kidnapped Kerry and killed the Kelsey boy is responsible for killing Ann and Ginny, too?"

"I...I don't know what to think anymore," she stammered. "Ann and Ginny were the dearest people I've ever known."

Bernie rubbed his chin thoughtfully. "I wonder if David has thought about the connection?"

— 181 —

"I don't know," Priscilla replied hollowly. "But if he even thinks that the same people are involved, he might start looking at his boss a lot closer. Adele confides in David. And if she told us she was worried about what Horace and his friends were up to, you know she told David the same thing." She shuddered. "I don't want to think about what David would do to Horace if he found out that he had anything to do with killing Ann and Ginny."

"I know what I'd like to do to him," Bernie grumbled as veins bulged on his arms.

"Priscilla cupped her small hands over his clenched fists. "We don't have any real proof that Horace has done anything, Bernie—not really."

He studied his wife, confused. "But you said that Adele as much as admitted that Horace had something to do with the trouble at the abortion clinics?"

"Well..." she stammered.

"You know, Cilla, the world would be a lot better place without the likes of Horace Woolard and his kind screwing it up."

Priscilla's blue eyes wandered from one side of the room to the other. "I wonder if David had a chance to talk to Kerry since the last time we spoke with him?"

"We'll find out as soon as we get through to him," Bernie replied, drumming his fingers on his knees. "Right now, I'd feel a lot better if she was here, instead of working at some cheap diner where she's open game for any nut who comes along."

Priscilla paled. "Do you think Kerry may still be in danger?"

Bernie's face sagged noticeably. "The way things are going, I don't think anyone is safe anymore."

———

Dusk hung over the modest house on Prescott Street, reflecting the dismal mood of its single inhabitant. David Williams sat in his recliner, completely unaware the room around him had fallen into darkness. He hadn't slept since Lieutenant Hanks called from the

THE BABY SOLDIERS

Suffolk Police Department to tell him the bodies of two woman, suspected to be his wife and daughter had been found in an abandoned field. That was a week ago. After dental records had finally confirmed their identities, a deluge of questions followed. He closed his eyes, trying to erase the sight of what was left of them. About the only thing vaguely familiar had been their shreds of clothing. The coroner said they'd been shot twice at close range with a pistol bearing thirty-eight caliber slugs. A thirty-eight, he thought morosely, the most common of weapons had ended the lives of two special people. The weapon used to kill Robbie Kelsey had also been a thirty-eight. His fingers tightened on the arms of the chair. And how many countless others, he mused. He pushed himself out of the chair and walked listlessly to the refrigerator where he removed a cold Bud. He wondered how long it would take for the lab boys to match the slugs taken from his wife and daughter to the ones taken from the Kelsey boy. He was almost certain they were killed with the same weapon.

He wandered upstairs to the bedroom and opened the armoire near the window overlooking the dark street below. Ann and Ginny smiled sweetly from the 8 x 10 photos sitting on the shelf. Bile rose in the back of his throat as he carefully removed each photo from its silver frame. Earlier, when he'd called the mortuary to make arrangements, Mr. James had requested a current photo of his wife and daughter. The pictures would be placed on top of the closed caskets during the viewing.

"Viewing," David muttered, choking back sobs. "What was the point of having a viewing when there was nothing left to see?"

After David had digested the tragic news about his family, he called Adele and asked if she would mind getting in touch with everyone who knew Ann and Ginny to let them know what happened. He couldn't bear the thought of talking to one more person and hearing the same questions repeated over and over again. He held the beer can to his lips and drank until it was empty. He'd rather do anything than face tomorrow. He hadn't seen anyone in Ann's family in nearly four years. After she'd disappeared, her kin seemed to follow suit. Not that he minded their absence. Ann and Ginny were the only things they'd ever had in common. And now, that common bond would bring them together one last time.

As David thought about Ginny, tears trickled down his face. Her school friends, still living in the area, would most likely show up tomorrow to pay their last respects, too. Many of them had gone away to college, he mused. He wondered if Ginny would have gone to college, if she had lived? He'd been shocked by the revelation that Ginny had been pregnant at the time of her death. He wondered who was responsible for getting her that way. He didn't even know she had a steady boyfriend. She was so young. Ann would have known, he thought. She and Ginny were as close as sisters.

David hadn't been as much a part of their lives as he should have been. First it was the navy and the long cruises which had taken him away from them. Then, it was the police department and its constant demands on his time. Ann and Ginny had taken a back seat more and more frequently. How he wished he could bring back the years and live them over again. But he couldn't do that. No one could.

He remembered when Ginny was a little girl. One day, she climbed on his lap and told him she wanted to be a doctor when she grew up. He didn't know why he thought of that now—now that she was gone. There were no doctors in their family, never had been. They didn't even know any doctors on anything but a professional basis. But that didn't matter to Ginny.

"I want to save lives, Daddy." That's what she'd told him. He carried the glossy pictures downstairs and reverently placed them on the kitchen table, so he wouldn't forget them in the morning. He stared down at Ginny's freshly scrubbed face and that confident smile she always wore. He wondered how many people would die, because his little girl never got to fulfill her dream of becoming a doctor?

He grabbed another beer and glared at the telephone. It hadn't stopped ringing in days. He had two choices; he could either yank it out of the wall, or answer it. He didn't feel up to doing either, but whoever was calling was determined not to give up.

He picked up the receiver and growled, "Hello."

"David?" Adele said startled. "How did everything go with the funeral home?"

If the caller had been anyone but her, he would have said something vulgar and hung up. But Adele was the one person in the world he could never do that to. "The undertaker didn't ask many questions. He was courteous to the point of nausea. He said the viewing would be tomorrow. Then the curious interlopers can parade through and gawk at nothing but a couple of sealed boxes."

"David, I...I don't know what to say," she stammered. "I called everyone, like you asked. Almost everyone I spoke with plans to attend the service."

He frowned. "Yeah. I figured that."

"Is there anything else I can do?" she asked, her voice quivering across the line.

"I can't even think straight right now," he replied, rubbing his brow. "Maybe tomorrow. I need to get some sleep. These past few days have been like a nightmare that won't end."

A brief pause followed. "I'm so sorry, David. I know how awful this is for you," she said sympathetically.

"Adele, did Horace say anything to you after you told him what happened to Ann and Ginny?" he asked, trying his best to sound casual.

"I told him everything the moment he returned from his latest conference. He seemed surprised? Like he couldn't believe they'd been found way out in the country like that. I suppose he thought they had run off, or something."

David disagreed with her interpretation of her husband's comments, but he was far too tired to get into it. "Or something. What about Bernie and Priscilla?"

"They plan on coming for the service."

He sighed helplessly. "I appreciate them wanting to be here, but I don't think they should come. If whoever threatened them finds out they're going to be here...They'd be a lot better off if they just stayed put."

"I tried to tell Priscilla you didn't expect them to come, but Bernie called back shortly after I talked to her. He said you needed the support of your friends, and hopefully, he was still one of them."

David wiped at a tear leaking down his face. "They're about the only people I won't mind seeing," he said, his voice trailing off.

Adele sighed. "David. I know what a strain this is on you."

"I won't deny it," he replied flatly.

"David, I'm afraid I have more bad news for you."

He tossed the empty beer can toward the trashcan. It bounced off the lip and rolled across the floor. "Go ahead," he said, I'm listening."

"A shelter for young women burned down early this afternoon. The firemen on the scene said it looked like arson."

"Where was the shelter?" he asked, seeming to shake free of his trance.

"The shelter was set up in a house in one of the older, more settled neighborhoods. It's not far from Chesapeake."

"Was anyone hurt?" he asked, picking up the can and placing it in the trash.

"Three of the young women who were staying there died, and two are in intensive care. They wouldn't give the names of the deceased because they haven't been able to contact their families. The two women in intensive care have been identified though. I wish I could remember their last names. One of them was named Rebecca something. Her last name may have been Corbitt. I'm not sure. A witness at the scene said the name of the other girl was Angelina. Her friends called her Angie. Do you know anything about the shelter, David?"

"No," he said. "But I think I know someone who might."

"Someone on the police force?" she asked.

THE BABY SOLDIERS

"I'd rather not go into it right now," he said, his mind racing. "We'll leave that for another time. Thanks for everything you've done, Adele. I'll talk to you tomorrow."

"If you need anything, David, just call. Now try to get some sleep."

"I will," he replied. Then he hung up.

The telephone rang the instant the receiver hit the cradle. He figured it wasn't Adele calling this time, so he scooped up the receiver, and bellowed, "Who is this?"

"David, it's me, Bernie. We've been trying to get through for hours."

"Sorry, Bernie. I've been pretty much avoiding the phone. I just finished talking to Adele. She says you plan on coming for the funeral, or should I say funerals."

"We were devastated to hear about Ann and Ginny," Bernie said consolingly."Is there anything we can do...anything at all?"

"I can't think of anything right now. Thanks. Maybe once things calm down."

"David," Bernie said slowly. "This may not be a good time to bring this up, but Priscilla was wondering if you had given any thought to the possibility that whoever killed Ann and Ginny had something to do with killing Rob Kelsey and kidnapping our Kerry?"

David sighed heavily, pushing a shock of dark hair back from his brow. "That thought has crossed my mind—more than once."

"I know you got a million things going on right now, and I shouldn't even be bothering you, but have you talked to Kerry since the last time we spoke with you?"

"She hasn't been at the diner the last few times I stopped by. A friend of hers told me she's working on some special project. I left word for her to get in touch with me."

"After Adele told us what happened to Ann and Ginny, we started worrying about Kerry all over again. I don't like what's been going on down there."

"I like it even less," David muttered wryly. "I doubt if Kerry will show up for the funeral tomorrow. Too many memories to contend with."

"I suppose you're right," Bernie said. "She loved Ann and Ginny as though they were family. I'm so sorry, David. I wish things could have turned out differently."

David nodded grimly. "Look, I've got to get off this thing. I'll see you guys tomorrow."

After he hung up, he opened another beer. He wondered if he could drink enough to sleep straight through tomorrow. He kicked off his shoes and started up the stairs, the telephone clamored incessantly behind him.

CHAPTER THIRTY-THREE

It was nearly noon when Bernie and Priscilla Trivane arrived at McBride's Funeral Home in Virginia Beach. A somber faced man greeted them and led them to the floral scented room containing the remains of Ann and Ginny Williams.

David was sitting in one of the red velvet chairs, chatting to someone they didn't recognize. The moment he saw them, he leapt to his feet and hurried toward them. Priscilla reached out to embrace him, shocked by his gaunt appearance.

"I'm glad you could come," David said, embracing Pricilla and then Bernie. "There are so many people here I don't know."

While Bernie and David reminisced, Priscilla wandered through the crowd, hoping to catch a glimpse of her daughter. Although she'd been told Kerry probably would not attend the services, she hoped with all her heart she would see her.

Priscilla drew little attention as she strolled through the sitting rooms, indistinguishable from the other women present, who wore basic black dresses and little or no jewelry. Her ash-blond hair was longer than it had been when she left the beach, but she'd swept it back away from her face, making it less noticeable.

David navigated through the crowd until he eventually caught up with her. "You look so much like Kerry," he told her.

Priscilla was relieved that David had seen Kerry and thought she was doing well. Bernie was across the crowded room, a massive pillar of strength, who evoked little more than a passing nod from the people he knew, as well as those he didn't. The sleeves of his dark blue suit gathered uncomfortably at his muscular biceps. He didn't have an occasion to wear a suit in recent years, and when Priscilla suggested he buy a new one for the funeral, he told her his old one was good enough.

While Priscilla and David discussed Kerry, Bernie perused the parlor, wondering if Horace Woolard had been responsible for the threatening phone calls they'd received. The threats that had driven them to leave their home at the beach and seek refuge in the hills of Pittsburgh, Pennsylvania. If it hadn't been for Priscilla's mounting fear that one of them would be killed if they stayed, he was sure he would have gotten to the bottom of things…one way or the other. But at that time, he thought Kerry was dead, and he couldn't risk having Jimmy or Priscilla taken from him, too.

By two o'clock, the rooms reserved for those who'd come to pay their last respects to the Williams' family were packed to capacity. David looked over his shoulder, expecting Adele to arrive at any moment. Danny, Jason and Mark had stopped by before going to the hospital to see if Rebecca and Angie were still in intensive care. Before leaving, Danny had pulled David aside and whispered he had something important to discuss with him. David assumed it had something to do with their conversation about Horace killing the principal and had assured Danny they'd discuss it after everyone had gone home.

At two-thirty, Adele Woolard arrived. She and Priscilla embraced amid a flurry of anguished sobs. Bernie tensed, waiting for Horace to make his grand entrance. He seemed disappointed when Adele told them she had come alone. He was about to ask where Horace was when she suddenly disappeared into the adjoining room where David was talking to some junior members of the police force. They stepped back when they saw her. She nodded, recognizing them from less formal occasions, and moved close to David, touching his arm. He held onto her hand like a lifeline tossed to a drowning sailor.

Her misty green eyes caressed his furrowed brow, his swollen eyes, and the bumpy ridge of his nose, which he'd broken playing

THE BABY SOLDIERS

football in high school. She wanted to put her arms around him and tell him that everything would be all right, but she didn't dare. Too many people would take the gesture the wrong way. The wordless intensity between them was broken only when a new wave of mourners gushed into the room.

Adele smiled thinly and backed away to join Bernie and Priscilla in the other room. As the three of them perused cards attached to floral arrangements, a tall, rather stunning redhead approached them. She smiled, first at Bernie and then Priscilla. "Mr. and Mrs. Trivane," she said warmly. They appeared bewildered, never having seen her before, but managed to return her greeting. Then the young woman turned to Adele. "Are you Mrs. Woolard?" she asked.

Adele smiled uncomfortably. "Why, yes."

Amy extended her hand. "My name is Amy Patterson. I'm a friend of Danny."

Adele glanced around, realizing for the first time that her sons weren't there. "I'm afraid you missed him. He came by earlier with his brothers. He mentioned having an important errand to run."

Amy nodded, not bothering to explain that she knew where Danny was. She glanced at the door expectantly. "Is Captain Woolard here with you?"

Bernie stiffened at the mention of the name.

"I...no," Adele stammered. "Some urgent business came up last night. He said he wouldn't be able to attend the service."

Amy nodded. Bernie relaxed.

"Well," Amy said, more confidently. "I just wanted to introduce myself, since I'd heard so much about all of you."

Bernie put his arm around Adele's tiny waist. "We're going to David's place later for refreshments. Are you coming, Adele?"

"Ohhhh...I took a covered dish by earlier and left it with Ann's cousin, Paula. Poor Ann," she said shaking her head sadly. "It's still hard to belief she's gone. I mean really gone."

Priscilla leaned close to her old friend and whispered. "David said Kerry will meet us there."

Adele smiled knowingly. "It's been a long time since either of you saw her. Just knowing she's back seems like a miracle. How long has it been...a year?"

Bernie coughed into his fist. "More like a lifetime," he quipped.

Adele eyes shifted from Bernie to Priscilla."This has been a horrible time for everyone...all the mysteries."

Amy glared at Adele in disbelief, wondering how she could pretend to know nothing about her husband's involvement in what was happening all around her. "No one is going to have to worry about them much longer." Amy's words sounded more like a cold prediction than a casual comment.

Adele had no idea what Amy was talking about.

Bernie took Priscilla by the arm. "I want to go back to the hotel and change before we go over to David's."

Priscilla smiled knowingly. "I told you to buy a suit that fit you, dear."

"To wear to a funeral for thirty minutes," he snipped, rolling his eyes. "My wife thinks we're loaded."

As mourners filed from the chapel, Adele studied Amy's strong features, thinking she was perhaps the most stunning young woman she'd ever met. "Will you be going by David's house, too?" she asked hesitantly.

Amy nodded. "Yes, I will. But first, I have to swing by my place and pick up Kerry. She didn't want to show up here—for obvious reasons."

Adele frowned. She decided it best not to expand on the conversation. She had a chilling feeling she already knew why Kerry hadn't come.

Danny talked Jason into tagging along to the hospital with him. If anything had happened to Rebecca or Angie, he didn't want to be

THE BABY SOLDIERS

alone when he heard the news. A prudish woman with gray hair and wire-rimmed glasses balanced on the edge of her nose met them in the lobby and told them the girls were still on the critical list. There had been no change. Danny sighed helplessly and thanked her.

He had just turned on the ignition when the announcement came over the radio. Danny and Jason exchanged a look of sheer panic, then drove straight to David's house.

David had just stepped outside when he saw the VW rattle to a stop in front of the house. Danny and Jason looked so grim, he feared the worst had happened to the young women in the hospital. He whispered something to his sister-in-law before joining the boys.

"Danny? Jason? What is it?" he asked, drawing them aside, so none of his guests could hear. "You fellows look like you're ready to jump out of your socks."

Danny glanced fearfully at his younger brother then turned to David. "We just heard the news on the radio."

David grabbed each of them by an arm and steered them toward the front porch where they could sit down. "Exactly what did you hear?" he asked impatiently.

"Mr. Robinson is dead," Jason answered startled. "His body was discovered on the floor of his office at Justice Academy."

The color drained from David's face. "Did they say what happened to him?"

Jason shifted nervously from one foot to the other as though he had to pee awful. Danny buried his fists in his pockets. "He was shot in the back of the head. They believe he was killed sometime last night."

David narrowed his eyes coldly. "Do they have any idea who did it?"

"No," Jason said quickly. "One of the detectives at the scene told a reporter you had more pressing business today. He said they could use your help investigating this one."

"Believe me," David chortled. "I'd rather be there than here."

"I...I can't believe he actually did it." Jason mumbled, trembling all over. His long hair swayed from side to side as though his neck were broken.

David touched Jason's arm. "Don't jump to conclusions, son, not yet. I know what you're thinking, but someone else may have beaten him to it. Ever since those tapes were circulated, Scott Robinson's name was probably on a lot of hit lists."

"Maybe Dad paid someone else to do it," Jason said, looking tearfully from David to his older brother. "Reverend Jacobson said he'd done that before."

David stood up abruptly."Whatever you heard, or thought you heard at Jacobson's place, I strongly advise you to keep it to yourself...for the time being anyway. We don't want anyone going off all half-cocked."

"You mean like forming a lynch mob?" Jason said, his eyes wide and anxious.

David stared into the young lad's face, wondering if Jason would be all that broken up if someone actually did lynch his father. Right now, he needed to take his own advice. He needed to find out if Horace Woolard was guilty of anything, before he did something rash. He wasn't thinking about Scott Robinson anymore. He was thinking about Ann and Ginny, and wondering if Horace had paid someone to take care of them, too. But no matter how he juggled the pieces and tried to make his boss accountable. He had a stickler of a problem. There was no motive.

***

The next afternoon, David said goodbye to the last of his house guests. He closed the door just as the phone started ringing. He spoke to the caller briefly, then hurried upstairs to change clothes. It took forty minutes to drive from Prescott Street to Battlefield Boulevard. As he wound in and out of traffic, he watched the sun give way to a purple hue that spread languidly over the horizon. It was enough to make him want to believe in God again. He steered the Honda onto a deserted road leading to the park and came to a stop near a grove of pine tree. He climbed out and walked toward the waterway, hoping the strong breeze would clear the sickly scent of floral wreaths from his nostrils. As he sat watching fishing boats and small yachts sail through the locks, he imagined himself high on a plateau surrounded by spirits. The spirits were telling him something important, but he couldn't hear them. He rubbed the moisture from his eyes. Oh, Christ, he thought, what next?

He jumped when he heard the sound of a car door closing, followed by soft footsteps heading his direction.

Her auburn hair bounced lightly on the shoulders of the beige suit she had worn to visit Scott Robinson's wife. "David," she cried softly, placing her arms around him. "Will the horror never end?"

He held her close, unable to answer her agonizing question. Yesterday Scott Robinson had been murdered and Horace had vanished into thin air. David figured he had high-tailed it to Baltimore after killing Robinson—that is, if he was the one who actually did kill the principal. David figured Jacobson would probably keep Horace under wraps until the media lost interest. Or maybe, Jacobson would kill Horace himself, thinking he'd become too much of a liability, like Robinson. He felt the heat of Adele's body trembling against him. "I wish I knew the answer," he said somberly.

Suddenly, Adele wrenched from his embrace. "I hate to say it," she said, rubbing her arms, "but I wish he was dead!"

David studied her features. Her expression showed no grief, but rather sheer hatred that glared in her eyes. He knew she had reason, probably more than anyone. After being used as a punching bag for so many years, it would be a stretch to say she still cared for Horace.

David took her hand. "Let's walk a little?"

She nodded as they started down a narrow path brightened only by the glistening sun reflecting off passing watercraft.

"The boys are handling this much better than I expected."

He bit his lip to keep from saying what he was thinking. Why wouldn't the boys be taking their father's disappearance in stride?

They knew what he was. It wasn't like they feared he'd been kidnapped, the way Kerry Trivane had been, or murdered the way Ann and Ginny and young Robbie Kelsey had been. If it hadn't already happened, he hoped one day he could make Adele's wish come true. He'd love to make Horace Woolard go away—permanently.

"David," she said gazing pleadingly into his eyes. "Will you spend the night with me?"

He sighed heavily and took her in his arms. Her eyes were moist, like the leaves of a precious orchid after a rainfall. He felt the longing for her burning deep into his soul. He brushed his lips against her cheek, her silky neck. It was then he caught a whiff of her perfume. It was intoxicating, spurring him with unbridled desire. His arms tightened around her, holding her, caressing her back, drawing her nearer and nearer until she was almost part of him. His lips met hers gently, pressing down. Then more urgently, hungrily.

Adele clung to him fiercely, returning his kisses and wanting more, so much more. She was aware this moment would come one day, if not today, then tomorrow. The signs had been there for so long. Perhaps as long as seven years. By then, she realized her love for Horace was nothing but a distant memory. David had always been there for her. So strong, so dependable. His quiet manner and inner strength had always been a comfort to her, during the most trying of times. He seemed to know what she wanted to say before she said it. The way she shivered whenever she brushed against him at a cookout, or sitting next to him in the bleachers, watching the boys play softball. All those years were preparing her for now.

David wanted her more than he had ever wanted anyone in his entire life before. Many a night, he'd dreamed she was in his arms, holding him like this. So many times, he had pictured his arms around her, kissing her, feeling her body quivering. He wanted to possess her completely. To bury himself deep inside her. All the years since Ann and Ginny had disappeared seemed a blur. Now, this was all that mattered, all that would ever matter. He loved her so much. Before today, he had let his imagination run free, pretending, play-

THE BABY SOLDIERS

ing the what if game. Now, it was real. Adele was in his arms, and he would never let her go.

After what seemed like an eternity, they managed to pull themselves apart. David gazed at the full moon blinking through the rustling trees. Yes, he wanted to spend the night with her more than anything in the world. But they couldn't stay at her place. That was definitely out of the question. His place wasn't much better, not with Danny and Jason popping in unexpectedly at all hours of the day and night. He considered driving out of town to a motel where no one would recognize them. But that didn't appeal to him either. He loved this woman and refused to cheapen what was between them by a few stolen moments in a seedy motel room.

David took a long-labored breath, his eyes intent on hers."Soon," he said, an anguished sigh making him hoarse. "We'll be together, soon. I promise you."

Adele nodded tearfully. She understood. She wanted so much to spend the night with him. Not only this night, but all the nights to come. But she knew David was right. Their time would come. Surely their love would survive however long it took until they could safely and legitimately be together.

"Hold me, David," she whispered, nuzzling closer to him.

He wrapped his strong arms around her and pressed her close. "I love you," he murmured.

She lay her head against his chest, listening to the steady beat of his heart. All she could think of were the years she'd wasted on a man she no longer loved or respected.

"Promise me we'll be happy, David. I need for you to promise me that."

His lips came crushing down on hers. Their silhouettes casting a single shadow in the moonlight. He could promise her he'd love her forever, but he couldn't promise her they'd be happy. He had no control over the future. Yesterday, he had witnessed the caskets of his wife and daughter lowered into the ground. He became more aware than ever that no man had control over his destiny, no matter how badly he wanted to believe he did.

CHAPTER THIRTY-FOUR

Rebecca moaned as she lay on the hospital bed. The heat. The pain. The insane itch she couldn't reach. Darkness hovered over her. She remembered carrying an armload of fresh linens to the third floor of the Haven. The space, formerly used for storage, had been converted into two additional bedrooms to make room for the overflow in recent days. She remembered hearing a loud crash. Then she heard screams.

She remembered racing to the top of the stairwell and calling, "What's going on down there?"

"Fire!" someone screamed. "We're on fire!"

Rebecca raced down the stairwell, already spiraling with smoke, and ran toward the bedrooms at the far end of the second floor. Brenda Riley and Wendy Gibson were in the last room. She could hear them screaming for help. Halfway down the hall, she was struck with a wave of heat so intense she felt her skin shrivel. She ran back to the linen closet and grabbed a blanket. In the bathroom, she soaked it with water. Then she covered herself with the blanket and tried once again to reach the girls at the end of the hall. She couldn't believe how quickly the fire had spread. She moaned in frustration, unable to get as close to the door as she had before. "Brenda?" she cried out. "Wendy?"

There was no reply.

Rebecca staggered back toward the stairs leading down to the first floor and caught a glimpse of Angie fighting her way through the perilous smoke. She was clutching the hot banister and sobbing bitterly.

"Wendy and Brenda are gone," Rebecca said, starting down the stairs. "I couldn't reach them in time." Soot filled her mouth and nose, making it nearly impossible to breathe.

Angie's small frame sagged despondently on the stairs."Someone threw a fire ball through the dining room window," she said choking. "Lisa…Lisa was in there. She…she was on fire. I…I tried to put it out…"

Rebecca watched fearfully as giant flames licked at the wallpaper and the plaster beneath them turning it to ash. She grabbed Angie's arm. "We have to go up," she said urgently.

She placed her right arm around Angie's waist and helped her to her feet. Then she grabbed the mahogany banister, using it for leverage to climb the stairs. Flames were everywhere and the smoke was so thick she couldn't see the next step in front of her. The heat from the banister scorched her palm; reluctantly, she let it go. She wished she had thought to count the stairs, so she'd know how many she had left to climb.

"Are we going to die?" Angie whispered hoarsely. "I don't want to die."

Rebecca drew the blanket around Angie and herself the best she could, attempting to keep them safe. The flames were already biting at their arms and legs. Just as they reached the second-floor landing, a splintering crash resounded behind them. Rebecca spun around; horrified to see the stairs they had just climbed had vanished into the inferno on the first floor. The putrid odor of burnt hair and flesh invaded her senses. She realized she was on fire. Angie's screams spurred her on, in spite of the fear that her own lungs were about to explode. Rebecca had never been more terrified in her life. If she didn't do something quick, they would die like the others. With every ounce of strength she had left, she pulled Angie to the window overlooking the garden Kerry had planted alongside the house. The smoke burning her eyes and throat was the worst pain she had ever

THE BABY SOLDIERS

known. She dared not breathe too deeply for fear the onslaught of smoke would kill her faster than the fire itself. Angie moaned incoherently and dropped onto the floor beside her. Rebecca knew there wouldn't be another chance. She leaned back, using Angie's crumpled body for support, and kicked at the glass as hard as she could. She kicked and kicked until the entire pane broke into shards at her feet. Then she wrapped her arms around Angie as tightly as she could and dove through the window. She couldn't feel Angie in her arms anymore, or the searing pain spreading through her body. She was falling...falling.

CHAPTER THIRTY-FIVE

Julie Newman had the radio tuned to her favorite local station as she packed for her vacation. When the music stopped abruptly, she stopped what she was doing and listened. A news bulletin announced the follow up to a previous report that the fire that had burned a large house in southern Chesapeake, leaving three young women dead, was under investigation. The two women who'd survived the fire remain in critical condition at Chesapeake Regional Hospital.

Julie dropped the jeans she was folding and grabbed her car keys. Then she raced to the hospital as quickly as she could.

———

Julie spent nearly every waking moment at the hospital, doing whatever she could to make the burn victims more comfortable. She had known Rebecca Corbitt since high school in Baltimore. Funny how they both ended up here in Virginia. Even back then, she remembered Rebecca begging her classmates for spare change so she could give it to the poor kids who couldn't afford to go on field trips with the rest of the class. Tears filled her eyes. It only seemed natural that Rebecca would end up running a shelter for people needing help. She remembered Angie from the meetings Amy held. Sitting with them, wondering if they would ever wake up again, was unbearable. She often fell asleep in the stuffed chair beside Rebecca's bed, unable to stay awake any longer.

Suddenly, Rebecca's body jolted. "Angie," she whispered hoarsely. "Angie."

THE BABY SOLDIERS

Julie's heart raced wildly as she reached Rebecca's bandaged arm. Mucus and blood continued to ooze from beneath the bandages covering her eyes, in spite of the fact they were bathed as often as the doctor permitted. Rebecca felt the light touch on her arm. "Angie? Is it you?"

"Rebecca, it's Julie."

Rebecca tried to move her head, but couldn't. The cast on her neck prevented her from moving even a fraction of an inch. "Angie," she cried helplessly.

"It's alright, Becky. Angie is going to be fine. You both are."

Rebecca closed her eyes and fell into a deep sleep.

Julie reached in her bag and found the card Amy had given her the day Rebecca was admitted. She promised Amy she'd call and let her know of any change, one way or the other. She felt hope was not lost for the first time since the afternoon she'd sat in a critical care room, just like this, and watched her brother die, the victim of a senseless drive by shooting.

The police were still looking for whoever had set fire to the Haven, but as yet they had no leads or eyewitnesses. Angie regained consciousness later, that same day. Her first thought had been for Rebecca. Although her legs were burned so badly the doctor feared amputation, her upper torso had been spared, thanks to Rebecca wrapping her in the wet blanket. After alerting the resident on duty, Julie called Amy. The sheer relief in Amy's voice was all she could hope for.

Julie promised she would stay close by and do everything she could to help. Her vacation plans would have to wait.

CHAPTER THIRTY-SIX

When Ann and Ginny Williams disappeared, James Kelsey told his wife, the idea that Ann had run off with another man was ludicrous. But his valiant defense of Ann did nothing but infuriate Sybil all the more. He supposed he had himself to blame for the way she felt about Ann. He should never have told her that he and Ann had dated in high school. But he was high on pot and Coors when he'd made the revelation. Unfortunately, Sybil had never forgotten. She had done everything she could to ruin Ann's good name, even to the point of spreading vicious lies to anyone who would listen. Attacking the innocent while at the same time professing her own morality. What a hypocrite she was, he mused.

But then, he was no better. He never contradicted her or tried to stop her. That made him even worse, he thought bitterly.

He gazed solemnly at Robbie's monument, wishing there were some way he could make amends for the mistakes he'd made over the years. Maybe if he had more backbone and had stood up for the things he actually believed, he wouldn't be standing here today, weeping over his son's engraved stone.

James Kelsey was so absorbed in self-pity he didn't see the car stop on top of the hill, or realize that anyone had entered the cemetery. Then he looked up and saw a young woman walking slowly toward him. He removed his glasses and wiped the tears from his eyes, thinking the girl was another visitor like himself, here to mourn the loss of someone she, too, had loved. He closed his eyes, thinking, why do we find solace in this desolate place, where no one greets you with an out-stretched hand, or even a kind word?

He didn't look directly at her for fear he'd embarrass her. But in truth, he was more concerned with embarrassing himself. She didn't look anything like the bright-eyed teenager he remembered. Her long blond tresses were pinned up on top of her head and her blue eyes looked like funnel clouds over a gloomy ocean.

She nodded silently.

James swallowed the lump in his throat and nodded back, so ashamed for the way he and his wife had talked about her. He hung his head, wondering how he could have blamed that poor, frightened child for what happened to his son. He had no excuses. There was no one to blame for his arrogance and self-righteous behavior but himself. Thinking about it now made him want to puke.

"I heard you were back in town," he said hesitantly.

Kerry placed a single rose on the marble headstone. "I'm sorry about what happened to Robbie, Mr. Kelsey," she said, her eyes fixed on the gray stone. Then she turned and looked at him, her eyes filled with tears.

James couldn't bare the tortured expression on her face. "Oh, my dear," he muttered, placing his trembling arms around her. "It's not your fault. The maniac who shot Robbie is to blame, not you."

"I should have been stronger and refused to go when they wanted me to have the abortion," she replied sniffing.

He shook his head. "No need for that, now," he assured her. "You were very young and very afraid. You both were." He looked at the grave, searching for the right words. "Maybe, if we all had been the right kind of parents, none of this would have happened."

Kerry blinked back tears as she studied him. Mr. Kelsey had aged drastically in the last year. Back then, he didn't have gray hair at all. Now, his hair appeared lifeless with far more salt than pepper. He was thinner, too—not that he had ever been a large or muscular man. The circles beneath his eyes were so dark, like someone suffering with a terminal disease. She knew Robbie's death had caused the change. His death had changed all of them.

"Kerry, would it be all right if I asked you to lunch, or to just go somewhere for a cup of coffee so we could talk?" James asked timidly, hoping she wouldn't turn him down.

She nodded. "I don't have to be at work until two o'clock today."

"Where are you working?" he asked, although he already knew.

She forced a smile. "I'm sure it's no place you've ever been," she replied, knowing the Kelseys generally frequented the most expensive restaurants. "It's a small diner off Independence."

James convinced Kerry to go with him in his Lincoln, so they could talk on the way. He assured her that he'd bring her back to pick up her car later on. As he sped along the boulevard, he remembered that Kerry had once expressed a desire to go to college. What was it she wanted to become? He tortured himself, trying to remember. At last, he did. An architect. That was it.

"Have you gotten back to your studies?" he asked, feeling like a typical reporter rather than someone truly interested in her welfare.

Kerry shook her head. "The day I was kidnapped killed any plans I had for a real future."

James glanced at her, instantly sorry for bringing up her future. "If you're not going to school now, you could still go back," he said gently.

"Maybe someday. Right now, I have more important things to do."

He smiled ruefully, remembering Robbie making similar statements.

"Sounds pretty serious," he replied. "What could be more important than finishing your education?"

She clasped and unclasped her hands and then took an anxious breath. "Things like finding out who the animals were who killed Robbie, kidnapped me and took my baby."

James startled as though he'd been struck by lightning. He jammed the brakes so hard that they were both thrown forward,

— 206 —

THE BABY SOLDIERS

straining their seat belts. "Baby?" he muttered softly. "We thought you had an...You had a baby?"

She pushed back and adjusted her seat belt. Then she looked at him in disbelief. "You didn't know?" Then she shook her head. "No, of course not," she said, answering her own question. "How could you?"

"Kerry, I want you to tell me everything," he said, easing his foot onto the gas pedal.

She stared straight ahead for a long time before replying.

"The men who kidnapped me...and killed Robbie...took me to a place they called a camp. There were about twenty other girls there. All of them ended up the same as me. We were all kidnapped on our way to abortion clinics." She stopped to catch her breath. "Those men knew we were pregnant. That was the reason we were kidnapped. They made us stay at this horrible place until our babies were born."

"That's inhuman," he said, his voice brittle.

She closed her eyes, moving her head slowly from side to side. "They gave me some kind of shot after they forced me into their car. When I woke up, I was blindfolded. They didn't remove the blindfold until after they'd taken me to the camp. I was so afraid. I thought they were going to kill me...the way they killed Robbie."

"You poor child," he said sympathetically, squeezing her hand.

"We were treated like prisoners. We ate, we slept and we exercised. After my baby was born, they let me go."

"Your baby?" he asked anxiously. "Was it a boy? Where is he?"

"I don't know," she replied hollowly. "They wouldn't let me see it before it was taken away."

Her entire body trembled as tears spilled down her cheeks. "They took my baby away from me. I never got to see it, or hold it, or tell it how much I loved it."

"Who are they?" James asked, his voice cracking from the mixture of rage and indignation swarming inside.

"I only knew the names of the people who were watching over us. I don't know who was in charge."

Kerry inhaled raggedly, wondering if she'd already said too much. Amy had warned her not to be too trusting. But something told her it would be safe to tell him. She wondered if it was Robbie's spirit, reaching out to let her know everything was going to be all right.

"I've been working with some of the other girls who lost their babies. We're almost positive Captain Woolard is involved." She gulped hard. "So was Mr. Robinson from the academy."

"God, no," he muttered, pulling into a parking place outside Cracker Barrel. He turned off the ignition, his grim expression more pronounced than before.

"Kerry, do you know what you're insinuating? Are…are you certain?"

She hugged herself fiercely. "I have proof."

His shoulders slumped. "Of all the people to be messed up in something like that. It's unbelievable."

"Yeah," she replied bitterly. "A police captain and a school principal. The other girls and I have been gathering evidence. We knew that no one would believe us without it."

After they were seated, he nodded for her to continue.

"It hasn't been easy. We managed to find some tapes that Mr. Robinson had made of himself…having sex with some of the girls."

James gasped loudly. "That was you?"

She nodded. "We sent copies of the tapes to all the radio stations, but even that didn't work out the way we'd intended. Some of the people who saw the tapes claim the girls probably had sex with the principal for kicks. How they were trying to destroy his reputation in order to assuage their own guilt." She shrugged helplessly. "It's just their word against ours. And now that Mr. Robinson is dead, it makes him look even more like a martyr."

James nudged his eyeglasses into place. "It sounds like you're trying to swim up Niagara Falls."

"I think that would be a lot simpler," she quipped.

"Kerry, did you get a chance to visit with your mother and father when they came down for the Ann and Ginny's funeral. I was in Washington on business, but I heard they were in town."

She nibbled her lip. "They wanted me to move back with them, to where they're living now, but I have to stay here until I find out what happened to my baby."

Kerry was hesitant to tell him exactly where her parents were living. She wasn't entirely certain he could be trusted. He sounded like he didn't believe her when she told him Captain Woolard was involved in her kidnapping and the theft of her baby.

After James and Kerry placed their order, he gazed into her swollen eyes and said, "Kerry, I want to help. I want to help you find your baby."

She blinked, somewhat stunned by his words. "Wh...what?"

His eyes appeared cold as anthracite, and completely fastened on hers. "I said, I want to help you find your baby."

After the waitress brought their club sandwiches and iced tea, Kerry nibbled slowly, while telling James Kelsey everything she knew about the place where she'd been taken, and the guards who had watched over her and the other girls. "I don't know what they did with our babies once they took them away," she said, pushing her plate aside. "For all I know, my baby may have been sold."

James reached across the table and squeezed her hand. "We're going to find out."

Kerry winced silently.

He pulled away immediately. "I'm sorry. I didn't mean to hurt you. I guess I got carried away." His eyes wandered slowly over her face. "Why would you think they sold your baby?"

"Supposedly, they took the boy babies to some secret location, where they would be trained as soldiers. The girl babies were to be sold, because they were of no value to the organization. I don't know if my baby was a boy or a girl."

"This sounds like a nightmare straight out of a cheap novel." he mumbled. "If there's an organization out there that powerful, I'm surprised I haven't heard of it before now."

She blinked, wondering if he was telling her the truth. The waitress came and refilled their tea glasses.

James studied Kerry's creamy face, thinking how lovely she was. He was beginning to understand why Robbie had fallen in love with her.

"Mr. Kelsey, surely you've heard of a group called The New Order?"

The color drained from his face. He reached for his tea and gulped it down quickly. "The...The New Order," he stammered.

The spin-off group that screwball preacher, Clifford Jacobson, dreamed up. Sybil was always throwing Jacobson's name in his face, talking about how smart he was, or how handsome he was. And most obnoxious of all, how divinely rich he was. A wave of nausea overcame him. He thought about the horrors Kerry had endured, and he thought about losing his son. He wondered why Sybil wouldn't discuss the incident; other than to say what had happened was the Trivanes' fault.

In the beginning, he had blamed them, too. But then reality set in. He figured Sybil's insistence on blaming the Trivanes for what happened to Robbie was a reflection of her own grief. Now he wondered what she really knew about that day. More to the point, he wondered what she wasn't telling him.

James pushed his empty glass aside."I'd like to do some digging on my own. I know some people who are quite good at finding the impossible."

Kerry let go of the crumpled napkin she'd been squeezing. "If they're so clever," she said, "how come they never found the men who killed Robbie?"

The question stunned James so badly; he didn't know which way to turn. He felt completely helpless as he looked into her haunted eyes. She had asked the one question he couldn't answer.

THE BABY SOLDIERS

Sybil stood in the dimly lit foyer, drumming her fingers on the antique table she'd picked up at an auction. When James walked in, she glared at him accusingly.

"Well. Where on earth have you been all day? We were supposed to go with the Morgans to pick out shrubbery for landscaping around the church. I finally had to call and tell them we wouldn't be able to make it. Honestly, James, I was never so embarrassed. I hate to give my word and then break it."

He removed his glasses and wiped them on the tail of his shirt. "I went to the cemetery today to visit Robbie."

Sybil's tongue clucked the roof of her mouth. "What in the world for? Robbie isn't there, James. He's gone. He's dead. You can't bring him back by talking to a stone!"

"You don't know what you're talking about," he mumbled angrily. Then he pushed her aside and retreated to the den.

Sybil followed him, and stood there tapping her foot on the hardwood floor. "You weren't at the cemetery all this time. You went somewhere else, didn't you? You don't have to lie to me, James. I smell whiskey on your breath."

He chuffed. "It's heartening to know your sense of smell is so accurate."

She picked up a small cushion from the sofa and hurled it at him. "Why do you talk to me like that? I do everything I can to please you, and all you do is humiliate me."

He poured three fingers of bourbon into a glass and followed it with a handful of ice cubes. "I wouldn't dream of humiliating you, my dear," he said, sipping his drink. "You do such a fine job of that all by yourself."

Sybil crossed her arms over her chest and eyed him like a raptor. "I want you to tell me where you've been all day."

He grunted, wishing he had never married her. No man should be so damned cursed. When he first met her, she had bragged about

— 211 —

how rich her family was—said her father was some big shot in the publishing business. James was young and impressionable. He figured life with Sybil would put him on the fast track with the right people. It wasn't until after they were married that he found out her father was a has-been reporter. He owed money to half the people in the mid-western town where he lived.

Now, some twenty years later, he and Sybil were little more than strangers, who happened to share the same living quarters. Once upon a time they had a son. But he was gone. Now, they had nothing. James had no intention of telling Sybil how he'd spent his day. For all he knew, she could be one of the people responsible for killing his son and kidnapping his grandchild. No, he planned to keep that information to himself. He had made a promise to help Kerry find her baby. He owed her that much. He knew that Robbie would want him to help her anyway he could.

He looked at Sybil through the bottom of his cocktail glass. The picture was distorted, as distorted as the woman standing in front of him. She had absolutely nothing going for her, he thought. The only thing people ever commented on was her loose tongue, and it was far from complimentary. His father believed that whatever choices you made in life, you had to live with them. And he had chosen Sybil for better or for worse. James would regret that choice until the day he died. He thought of Ann Williams once more. She had everything a man could possibly want. But he had let her slip away in favor of fame and fortune. Now she too was dead. And she had never hurt a living soul. He raised his glass as though he were making a toast. "To Ann and Ginny and Robbie," he whispered. "May you all rest in peace."

CHAPTER THIRTY-SEVEN

Byron Spears crossed Jacobson's study and placed the silver coffee service on the marble table. He turned to his employer of many years; his smile permanently fixed. "Will there be anything else, Reverend?"

Jacobson dismissed him with the wave of a hand. He was in no mood to be gracious, or civil for that matter. Captain Woolard had become more and more belligerent in recent days, and he could think of nothing that would achieve absolute order more than his unwelcome house guest's permanent disposal. He rose from his desk and rubbed the small of his back. He had accomplished little more than mulling over Woolard's fate most of the morning. He sincerely regretted dealing with Woolard the same way he had dealt with others who'd become so wretchedly careless over the years. But the call he'd taken the night before left him little choice.

Jacobson wondered who had reported seeing the captain near the academy the night Scott Robinson was murdered. His men in Virginia Beach, hadn't been able to confirm or deny it. He poured a cup of coffee and carried it back to his desk. Perhaps he should eliminate them as well, he mused. They were all worthless.

He folded his hands on the edge of the desk as though he were about to pray. Regardless of the current dilemma he was facing, he was relieved that Robinson was out of the way. His tawdry sex scandal could have proven disastrous to the organization. And there was no way he could silence every radio jock within five hundred square miles without going broke. Women, he thought morosely. He

— 213 —

wondered what had possessed the good lord to create the first one. They'd caused nothing but trouble ever since.

Spears knocked lightly before opening the study door. "Captain Woolard says he needs to have a word with you."

Jacobson shifted his eyes from his manservant back to his coffee cup. "Show him in, Byron."

Horace Woolard waltzed into the spacious room exuding the arrogance of ownership. He flopped down on the plush sofa, casually lacing his fingers behind his balding head. "They're still chasing their tails in Tidewater," he announced. "No one has come up with any leads in the Robinson shooting. Just like I expected."

Jacobson's steely gray eyes fixed on the hulk lounging on his sofa. Apparently, Woolard didn't know about the eyewitness.

"I suppose you have something to tell me other than old news?"

"Yes. The naughty vixens," Horace replied, breaking into a grin. "I haven't forgotten about them." He tugged the crease in his slacks before crossing his legs. "I've been doing a lot of thinking about the risk involved. This will be more complicated than arranging a simple house fire." He cocked a brow. "I need to be duly compensated."

Jacobson flicked an infinitesimal speck of lint from his gray lapel. His contempt for the policeman had grown exponentially during the past few days. "You've already been compensated—more than adequately," he snapped.

Woolard's face contorted as though he were chewing a lemon. "You must be joking. If you're referring to the pittance you gave me the last time I was here, you'd better start looking for someone else to do your dirty work. I've dropped more than that in the Sunday collection plate."

Jacobson sipped the tepid coffee, staring at the stubborn ox over the rim. "I don't pay for service unless I get it."

Woolard unlaced his fingers and shifted his weight. "That's unacceptable. As I said before, there is a lot of risk to consider. We're talking about more than one person. And to tell you the truth, killing women is out of my field of expertise."

THE BABY SOLDIERS

"Really?" Jacobson replied, raising a silvery brow. "What about Ann Williams? I doubt you lost any sleep when you killed her, and her daughter."

Woolard's face flushed. "I...I don't know what you're talking about," he stammered. "I had nothing to do with what happened to them."

Jacobson enjoyed toying with people who thought they were smarter than he was. He was as close to losing his composure as he'd ever been. He pushed his empty cup aside. "I don't recall anyone giving you permission to kill the Williams' women. As far as I know, they posed no threat to anyone."

Horace's chest deflated as he fought to inhale.

Jacobson straightened the cuffs on his white shirt. "I understand your reluctance to admit killing them...but you drink too much. You were overheard talking about it."

Horace glared at the preacher. His icy gaze intimidated most men, but Clifford Jacobson wasn't in that group. "I don't know why you're bringing that up now," Horace replied sullenly. "Are you looking for some sordid confession?"

"An explanation would be sufficient," Jacobson replied curtly. "I probably wouldn't have mentioned it if their innocent faces hadn't been gracing the front page of every newspaper I've picked up in recent days."

Horace sighed despondently. "What happened in the past had nothing to do with you or the organization. It was strictly a personal matter."

Jacobson reached into his desk and extracted a silver nail file. "I'm listening."

Horace rose to his feet, rubbing his sweaty palms together. "That bitch thought she was too good for me."

Jacobson ran the file lightly over his manicured nails. Of all the weaknesses he'd attributed to Horace Woolard, lechery had not been one of them. "After all the vile things you said about Principal Robinson, I assumed you were above indulgences of the libido."

— 215 —

Woolard's jowls trembled. "At least I'm not a child molester, or some queer pervert!"

Jacobson put down the file and ran his fingertips lightly over his silk tie. The touch of silk calming him. "Are you insinuating that those of us who manage to control our sexual desires are queer?"

Horace exhaled a cough, staring uncomfortably at his adversary. "That's not what I meant. It's just that people with blood flowing through their veins need an occasional stimulant. It's only healthy."

"I see," Jacobson replied smugly. "And I suppose Ann Williams was to be that stimulant? Did you think that since you were Sergeant Williams' superior officer, that put his wife automatically at your disposal?"

Horace wiped the saliva dripping from his mouth as he teetered dangerously close to the coffee service. "She was a snotty bitch. She needed to be taught a lesson."

Jacobson raised a hand to silence him. "I imagine rejection must be very difficult for someone with your ambitions, he said thoughtfully. "But how does that justify killing the girl?"

"She was nothing but a slut!" Horace bellowed.

Jacobson nodded. "I heard she was pregnant."

"I told you she was a slut."

"Who was responsible for the girl's pregnancy? Were you?"

"Me?" Horace said, clutching his chest like a guiltless martyr. "I would never touch a child. They know nothing about pleasing a man."

Jacobson's smile was sinister. "I hear they can be taught."

"I didn't have the time. I'm a busy man. I just wanted to mix it up with her mother."

"You haven't answered my question," Jacobson said, interrupting him.

"How in the hell should I know who got her pregnant? I didn't know anything about that…until last week…when the autopsy report came back."

"Well then," Jacobson said, trying to trap him. "How did you come to the conclusion that she was a slut?"

— 216 —

"They're all sluts," Woolard spat hatefully. "They bleach their hair, paint their faces, and wear clothes so tight they leave nothing to the imagination. Then they wiggle their tight little asses in your face, begging you to fuck them. When you do, they scream rape. They're all sluts!"

Jacobson sat back; Woolard was out of control. "Let's drop the subject for now. I need to know when do you plan on completing the assignment that I've given you?"

Horace eyed the preacher as though he had lost his mind. "I need more money. If I have to make it any clearer, I'll draw you a blueprint."

"Money," Jacobson drawled slowly. "The root of all evil. How much do you think you'll need to cover your expenses?"

Woolard returned to the sofa, trying to calculate the best he could without a calculator. "Five thousand should do it."

Jacobson rose to his feet and walked to the coffee service. "That's preposterous."

He slowly poured a cup of coffee, stirring in two cubes of sugar, and returned to his desk.

"You know," Woolard taunted. "It would be a real shame if those girls weren't stopped, and those ugly rumors about Robinson started up again." He shook his head. "It would be really awful if someone connected you to your squirrelly followers. A New Order, indeed. You could lose a lot of valuable supporters with a cloud like that hanging over you?"

The coffee cup rattled in the saucer. Jacobson managed to quell it without spilling a drop.

Woolard smiled with complacency. "You understand, of course, I'd do the job for nothing if I could. But I'm afraid my whereabouts this past week may have aroused a little suspicion." He stared directly into Jacobson's taut face. "That's your fault, you know. You shouldn't have insisted that I come directly here to report on Robinson's death. Those girls would have been history by now."

Jacobson could not tolerate anyone insinuating he was in error. In particular someone as offensively sloppy as Horace Woolard.

Weary of the mindless game he'd been playing, he pushed a button under his desk.

Spears walked in. "Reverend?"

Horace looked at Spears, surprised by his sudden appearance.

"Mr. Spears, would you please open the safe and bring me three thousand dollars."

"Very good, Reverend," Spears said, bowing as he left.

Woolard shook his head in disbelief. "Your servant knows the combination to the safe?"

"Only Mr. Spears," Jacobson assured him. "He's been with me for many years. I trust him implicitly."

"I wouldn't trust anyone that much," Horace said, eyeing him curiously. "And I believe the amount I requested was five thousand."

Jacobson studied him ruefully. "Let's just call this an incentive."

Woolard pursed his lips as he rose to his feet. "Since there are no other pressing matters, I think I'll pack my things and go home."

"Give my regards to the wife and kiddies," Jacobson said coldly.

Horace Woolard met Byron Spears in the hall outside the study. He opened the envelope and counted the money twice before leaving.

***

Margaret Hatchey's second floor apartment offered a spectacular view of the Chesapeake Bay. Unfortunately, that was its only redeeming quality. The apartment itself was compact, with one bedroom barely large enough for a standard bed and a small dresser. The kitchen was a mockery, even for someone as unfamiliar with culinary skills as she was. And the cluttered living room was only adequate. Margaret had furnished it with a sofa bed and an easy chair from a local thrift store. The table where she ate most of her meals was fairly new, as was the three-tier bookcase stacked with paperback mystery novels. A wooden framed picture of Margaret's late parents sat on top of the portable television in the corner of the room. In the twenty years that she'd worked for Clifford Jacobson, the cheap objects that surrounded her were the only material things she'd managed to accumulate.

The organization was growing in size and strength. Margaret wondered how it were possible, when the people in charge of running it. She's supposed changing the name to The New Order had been a last-ditch effort on Jacobson's part to inspire his followers to participate more fully in his plan to obliterate the evils of society. She snorted. The most dangerous evil facing society was Clifford Jacobson himself.

Margaret glanced around the stifling apartment, unable to arouse the least amount of pride. If she had been more like that girl, Amy Patterson, when she was younger, how differently her life would be today. Amy had such fire and conviction, even though it was fueled by hate. The children of Margaret's generation weren't permitted to nurture such foolishness. They were trained to be respectful to everyone, to serve their masters, and above all, to keep their mouths shut unless instructed differently. Amy would die laughing at that, she thought.

Margaret wondered when everything began to fall apart. What had happened to cause the family structure to become so disorganized and weak that no one objected when the organization began enforcing its own rules on everyone? It hadn't been a military coup, she thought. But it had been a coup just the same.

Margaret could remember a time when abortion was neither a public or a political issue. She only remembered one girl becoming pregnant when she was in high school. Regina was too afraid to tell her parents she was pregnant, so she had attempted to abort the child herself by using a coat hanger. Margaret closed her eyes tightly, thinking back to that dreadful time. Regina had bled to death, and her shameful secret had made front-page news. But that was long ago, she thought, rubbing her eyes. Way before everyone became so liberated.

Liberated, she mused wryly. Just another word for selfishness. Whatever the name of the seed, the fruit was just as poisonous. The tidal wave of liberation had crippled the family and society as a whole. No wonder Jacobson and other madmen like him were able to lead the masses around by their noses. Drug abuse and unwanted pregnancy had virtually destroyed the family structure and made it easy for fanatics like the preacher to beguile the helpless with false promises of making everything rosy.

The old established rules had been abandoned, lost forever, like the extinct civilization that had created them. A generation raised on the golden rule gave way to a generation of spoiled children, who grew into self-serving adults. And each generation that followed became more and more watered down in character and morals, until the final outcome was a generation that had no more common sense than chickens running around with their heads cut off. And that mindlessness had become the lifeblood of the organization.

The people were desperate for leaders who would tell them what to do and when to do it. And Clifford Jacobson, the self-professed knight in shining armor, had come to the rescue.

The first few years the organization was in power, Margaret thought Jacobson's plan was actually succeeding in solving society's massive problems. Gang violence ended abruptly, and not a whiff of cocaine or marijuana could be found anywhere. The masses had turned back to attending church on Sunday, rather than sleeping in, or shopping at the malls.

Margaret and her siblings had become swept up in the frenzy along with everyone else. They had become so bedazzled by righteous intentions that they willingly volunteered to serve the organization in whatever capacity they could. Her poor sister, Peggy, had become so obsessed by Jacobson and his plan to redeem society that she began attending church services three and four times a week. It wasn't long before the preacher noticed the pretty young girl sitting in the front row, ogling him with obvious worship. Peggy was so lovely and so naïve, Margaret thought. She giggled when she told her family what a perfect preacher's mate she would be. Margaret could still see that

THE BABY SOLDIERS

sparkle in Peggy's eyes the day she announced that Clifford Jacobson had asked her to marry him.

In the ten years that followed, Margaret heard the most unbelievable horror stories about the man whom she had sworn to follow—through the pits of hell, if that was his intention. Peggy spoke of secret plots to strip away human rights and make people no more than mechanical robots. Peggy confided that her husband had hired a flood of scientists from all over the world to built clones in the event humans failed to live up to his supernatural expectations. She told Margaret about a bevy of unsavory characters he had hired to keep order. The way Peggy described her husband, Margaret thought he sounded a lot like another man, who once had the same vision. A man who had destroyed millions in his quest to form a perfect society.

"Dear, sweet Peggy," she muttered softly. Peggy had always dreamed of having a house filled with children. But Clifford Jacobson had denied her every woman's dream. When Peggy asked him why, he explained that the fruit from her womb would be inferior, too inferior to help him rule his perfect world. Peggy had been crushed. Her depression became more and more severe until Jacobson, embarrassed by her irrational behavior, had taken it upon himself to have her committed to a facility for the mentally ill.

When Margaret visited her, she couldn't believe how much Peggy had changed. The once vital young woman had grown old beyond her years. She told Margaret that she had begged her husband to give her another chance to prove she could be a loyal wife to him, but he had brushed her off. Margaret had found her sister's groveling too painful to endure.

Reverend Jacobson saw to it that Margaret's duties took up most of her time. After awhile, she figured that he was trying to prevent her from having any contact with her sister.

It surprised everyone, including Peggy's doctors, when the preacher walked into the medical facility one day and checked his wife out. He explained that her health would return much more quickly at home, under his personal supervision.

Margaret remembered the last time she had visited her sister in Jacobson's would-be temple. It was shortly after the preacher had moved to Baltimore to supervise a much larger congregation. He bragged that it was a major step toward fulfilling his ultimate destiny.

Peggy would sit huddled on the sofa, wide-eyed, like a cornered rat. She jumped up each time he walked into the room. When he finally left the two of them alone, Peggy told Margaret about the beatings. She showed Margaret the bruises on her breasts and stomach, caused by the rings on his fingers. She told Margaret she had to find a way to escape before he killed her.

Although Margaret was shocked by her sister's accusations, she was skeptical. For years, Clifford had been the godly figure she'd looked up to. Peggy was on so much medication, she thought Peggy was imagining things, although the bruises were quite real. But it was difficult to determine whether the bruises had been inflicted by the preacher, or by her sister's own flagellation. She couldn't believe the stories about the hired gunmen, or the mad scientists. Everyone respected Clifford Jacobson. Surely, he wasn't the monster her sister had portrayed.

Six months later, Byron Spears had called to tell her Peggy, had disappeared. Margaret was beyond consolation, wondering if she had been wrong. If Jacobson really was the venomous monster her sister had professed, she hoped with all her heart that Peggy had somehow escaped.

Not long after that, Margaret heard that her infamous brother-in-law was involved with some powerful men from around the country. Men who planned to build an empire and had appointed Jacobson as their public face. Margaret thought it was a bunch of nonsense. Until her transfer came through. No longer was she a nursemaid for the school children at the academy. Her new role was guardian—guardian of pregnant young women living in a pit of abomination.

When she'd first arrived at the camp, Margaret learned that this was the place where unwed girls came to have the babies they

THE BABY SOLDIERS

planned to abort. Margaret was stunned, but decided that this was a worthy attempt to save innocent lives. But once she learned that the babies were taken from their mothers and given to strangers, she was horrified.

All those years, she thought Clifford Jacobson had been doing something honorable to protect and enhance the lives of the common people. It took her a long time to learn that Jacobson and the organization, which she served so valiantly, were sucking the very souls right out of their ignorant supporters. In the end, no one had been saved from the evils of society. The evil had become widespread and consumed it.

Little more than two years ago, Margaret learned the female babies born at the camp were sold like vegetables at a farmers' market. Last year, she learned the male babies were shipped to a secret location, which formerly housed the most notorious prisoners. That was after Jacobson determined those wretched criminals were too besotted by sin to waste another dime on their rehabilitation. The children taken to the former prison were groomed to become soldiers to defend the rigid policies of The New Order.

Margaret shivered. It was like witnessing the horrors of Hitler's armies up close and personal. Only this wasn't reliving a portion of history that no one wanted to remember. This tragedy was taking place here and now, on American soil.

When Margaret heard about the fate of the children, she concluded her sister had been telling the truth all along. And that eventual acceptance made her feel like a fool who had wasted her whole life.

Margaret Hatchey, the guardian, had seen hundreds of girls pass through the doors of the camp in the seven years she'd worked there. Some never survived the trauma of having their babies stripped from their wombs. Over the years, she'd been grateful the good Lord had seen fit to make her unattractive in men's eyes. She was never regarded as anything but a dedicated guard. She had never been raped like some of the others, whose beauty was no more than a curse. And she had never been forced to carry a child that would be sold to strangers or taught to kill.

Of all the humiliating indignities that had been inflicted on the girls at the camp, Margaret never saw one who reacted quite as stalwart as Amy Patterson. In the beginning, Margaret assumed that Amy was just like the others. She was tall and pretty with aqua eyes and wild, red hair that flowed down to her tailbone. Girls like her were a dime a dozen, or so Margaret thought. In spite of the degradation she suffered, Amy had somehow found the strength to rise above it. She served her time in the camp well. She hadn't cried out, not one time, throughout her entire labor. And Margaret was mindful that Amy's labor had been an extremely difficult one. The day Amy left the camp; she swore she would find her baby and get it back. The hatred Margaret had witnessed in the young woman's eyes made her shiver. But that same hatred had done something more. It made her ashamed for playing any part in such unforgivable inhumanity. The final straw had been witnessing Kerry Trivane's rape by that putrid animal that considered himself a redeemer of society. Margaret wrinkled her nose. She counted his demise as her first act of redemption.

Margaret finished her tea and rinsed the cup out in the sink. Then she walked to the bedroom closet and removed one of the two civilian outfits she owned. Her other clothing consisted entirely of uniforms provided by The New Order. She didn't mind wearing uniforms, not really. In a way, she felt they had protected her, making her appear even more homely than the good Lord had intended.

Today, she wore a pearl-gray blouse and a black pleated skirt, allowing her the anonymity to blend in with any crowd. She slipped the trusty 357 revolver that she'd been allotted when she became a guard into her handbag. She never carried the weapon when she wasn't on duty before. But today, she figured she might need it.

The latest atrocity had been reported by a female guard at the camp, who had become disenchanted with the way human life was so blatantly scourged. The guard had confided that an abortion clinic was going to be bombed that very afternoon. A host of unsuspecting nurses, doctors and various technicians would surely be killed in the explosion. After hearing the news, Margaret called the emergency department at Chesapeake Regional Hospital to warn her new friend, Julie Newman. But she learned that Julie was on vacation. She had hoped she could count on Julie to be a lookout, but now, she realized she was on her own.

She removed a white poster-board sign from the back of the closet. It was painted with blood red letters, protesting the killing of innocent babies. She had carried the same sign in countless demonstrations since joining the organization. Today would be the last.

Today, she planned to defend the lives of God's adult children. Today, she would stop the men who carried the bombs.

Margaret remembered her father preaching that two wrongs did not make a right. She thought about that as she walked down the apartment stairs. She didn't know who had committed the first offense; the parents for failing to instill morals into their children, or the children for becoming victims of their own fleeting passions, and ultimately becoming pawns in Jacobson's perverted game of chess. In a liberated society where no one accepted responsibility, it was impossible to judge a child for his impulsive actions. Margaret didn't blame any of them, not anymore.

"Until you walk in another man's shoes." Another of her father's favorite sayings.

Margaret had concluded that the time had come to eliminate the worst of two evils. And the organization that made millions, preying on frightened young women was by far the worst evil she could ever imagine.

Twenty minutes later, she reached her destination. She parked the two-door Ford beneath a weeping willow not far from the targeted clinic's entrance. She removed the sign from the back seat. She didn't

GERRY R. LEWIS

remove her sunglasses on the remote possibility that she might be recognized. She stationed herself on the sidewalk, near the curb, in front of the Nelson Clinic. While she gazed up and down the street, waiting for a sedan that would bring the bombers, she formed a plan.

A small group of protesters were forming a line behind her. Margaret didn't acknowledge them, or engage in frivolous chitchat. It wasn't unusual for demonstrators to march without speaking to one another. Outside of their noble cause, they had little else in common. Margaret reached into her jacket pocket, comforted by the cool barrel of the 357. The silencer was in place. She raised the red lettered sign, and waited.

CHAPTER THIRTY-EIGHT

When filled to capacity, the auditorium of Justice Academy comfortably seats six hundred people. The renovation of the building had been one of Clifford Jacobson's pet projects before his move to Baltimore. Only on rare occasion did he return to the beach to use the auditorium for conducting Sunday services. This was one of those times.

As he stood on the raised stage rehearsing the speech he would deliver this coming Sunday; Byron Spears stood attentively in the rear of the empty hall, checking the acoustics to be sure Jacobson's voice would not fade-out during the sermon and lose its conviction. Suddenly, the preacher slammed the loose papers he was holding down on the pulpit and stormed out. The pages floated from the wobbling stand like leaves swaying listlessly on an autumn breeze.

Spears ran toward the nearest exit to find out what had happened to anger him. In his frantic attempt to catch up with Jacobson, Spears cursed the ankle he'd sprained playing tennis for slowing his sprint. When he finally reached the preacher, he was out of breath and limping painfully. "I thought your speech was going very well. I could hear every word distinctly."

Jacobson bit his lip. "Thank you, Spears. But I want this sermon to be better than good. It must be perfect."

"Of course," Spears replied patronizingly. "Would you like me to drive you somewhere?"

Jacobson rubbed his furrowed brow. "I…I don't think so. I'd better go back inside." His gray eyes appraised his trusted employee.

Finally, he smiled. "It'll never be perfect if I waste time lolling around out here, will it?"

Jacobson began the speech again and again, always stopping before he reached the halfway point. No matter how hard he concentrated, Horace Woolard continued to muddle his thoughts. "Damn him to hell!" he muttered.

Concentrate on the sermon. He took a long, raspy breath before starting over again. The delivery and acceptance of his message were critical. His words had to be convincing enough to assure his followers that The New Order had nothing to do with Scott Robinson's tragic death, or the bombings at the abortion clinics—in spite of accusations to the contrary. His followers must believe that although he did not condone abortion, he would never harm anyone in order to make them see the wickedness of their ways. He closed his eyes, saying a silent prayer to the almighty. Above all else, he must make them believe that.

Those women were still causing problems. First, distributing those horrible sex tapes, and now this. He knew they had something to do with the travesty that had happened at the Nelson Clinic. He also knew they couldn't have managed that feat without advance warning. There was a leak in the organization, and he had to find out who it was.

When the preacher woke up, he couldn't quite put his finger on it, but he had sensed danger lurking in the shadows at the brink of dawn. Then the call came from the beach, dashing all hope of making it through the week without a single calamity.

The Stone brothers, two of his best men, were dead. Shot by an unknown assailant, while parked in front of the Nelson Clinic. He mused bitterly. The same place his men had botched a simple kidnapping assignment more than a year ago. For a brief moment, he wondered if Horace Woolard was the leak. He had been behaving mighty peculiar lately. But that was foolish, he reasoned. Horace

THE BABY SOLDIERS

wouldn't have killed Robinson if he weren't completed dedicated to the cause. The preacher sighed tiredly. If Woolard had done his job, like he was supposed to, the Stone brothers would still be alive. He should have been at the clinic watching for trouble. "The man was a disgrace to his uniform and the organization," he muttered angrily. "As soon as he finishes this assignment, he'll be eliminated."

"Did you say something?" Spears asked, entering the room.

"It was nothing, Spears. Just thinking out loud."

CHAPTER THIRTY-NINE

Pittsburgh, Pennsylvania. "I can be a lot more helpful to you in Carolina." Bernie Trivane said, staring earnestly into Amy Patterson's aqua eyes.

Kerry smiled, clutching his hand tightly.

Amy took a sip from the carbonated drink she'd been offered. "I appreciate the fact you want to help, Mr. Trivane. But you would have to uproot your family and start your life all over again." She glanced around the spacious room admiringly."If I were you, I'd give it a lot of thought."

Priscilla stood directly behind her husband and put her arms around his thick neck. "Amy, whatever Bernie wants to do is fine with me." Then she came around the sofa and sat down.

"Besides," Bernie added. "If we move to Carolina, we'll be able to see Kerry more often...and our grandchild...when we find him."

Amy looked from one Trivane to the other. "What about the people who threatened Jimmy? Aren't you afraid they'll try something else if they find out you're moving to Carolina?"

Bernie's mouth twisted as he rubbed the stubble on his chin. "Amy, we're through running." He turned to Priscilla and winked. "All of us. We want to help, but we certainly can't do it long distance. Besides, listening to the way you girls have been talking since you arrived, it sounds as though the problems you're having in Virginia may soon be ending."

Kerry chuckled. "We sure hope so."

"We can be there in two weeks," Bernie said. "We'll work around your little hospital, or wherever we're needed, just so we can be close to Kerry. Kerry did mention my wife is a nurse, didn't she?"

Kerry grinned. "See, Amy, I told you we could count on them."

Amy crossed the room to where the Trivanes were sitting, taking each of them by the hand. "What can I say?" she said teary-eyed. "We're glad to have you aboard."

Priscilla went to the kitchen and returned minutes later with more soft drinks and snacks. "Now," she said, smiling at Amy. "Tell us exactly what it is we're volunteering to do."

Amy sped along the Pennsylvania Turnpike, while Kerry sat quietly, making a list of things to do once they got home.

"How come your parents moved to Pittsburgh? I can't say that would have been my first choice. I still can't believe how cold it gets up there."

Kerry grinned. "Mom grew up there. My grandmother used to live right down the street from where we were today. Mom used to tell me about all the fun I missed living in the south all my life."

Amy frowned. 'What kind of fun?"

"Sled-riding, for one. She said they used to ride sleds down the mountain and then ride back up the hill on the incline."

Amy shook her head. "The view from Mount Washington was pretty terrific. I never realized how much we missed, living in the flatlands." She paused. "But I don't think I'd miss the freezing temperatures or the snow."

Kerry laughed. "Mom and dad used to bring us up here to visit during summer vacation. It was awesome watching the Pirates play baseball at the stadium."

Amy smiled reflectively. "I had a friend who was nuts about baseball."

Kerry nodded. "Dad used to take us fishing on the Monongehelia River, too. I don't remember catching any fish though."

Amy snorted. "What did you catch?"

"We caught old shoes and inner-tubes from bicycle tires. I even caught an empty wallet once."

Amy chuckled. "It figures it would be empty."

Kerry frowned suddenly.

Amy noticed the change. "Why so glum?"

"I was thinking of something else we caught one time."

"What was it?" Amy prodded.

"It…it was a hand. At first we thought it came off one of those department store mannequins, but my dad took a good look at it and said it was a real hand."

Amy paled. What did he do with it?"

Kerry shrugged. "He threw it back in the river."

"Don't you think he should have told somebody?" Amy asked.

Kerry shook her head. "He said if he called the cops, they'd probably accuse him of taking it away from whoever owned it."

"Those boys in blue sound like bad news," Amy replied.

Kerry pursed her lips. "That's probably one of the reasons the crime rate was so low there. Grandma never mentioned anyone getting mugged or robbed when she went shopping."

"Sounds like a place you'd find in a fairy tale," Amy said dreamily. "Maybe when we get our kids back, we should all move to Pittsburgh. Let them grow up where they won't have to worry about getting shot, or kidnapped whenever they leave the house."

Kerry gawked at her. "Amy, it's not like that anymore. I was talking about a hundred years ago…when I was a kid. Bad things happen everywhere now. You can't get away from it, no matter where you go."

Amy's shoulders slouched. "Maybe we should make that our next project."

"Sure," Kerry snorted. "Next thing you know, we'll be running around like that crazy old guy on the boulevard, holding a bible in one hand and a whiskey bottle in the other, screaming repent to passing motorists."

Amy smacked her lips."We could do a lot worse."

THE BABY SOLDIERS

Kerry nodded. "Like bombing abortion clinics."

"And stealing babies," Amy added bitterly.

Kerry worked the four to twelve shift at the diner. She was so tired from the drive back from Pittsburgh she was afraid she would fall asleep standing up. The place was loud and crowded with kids, socializing over burgers and cokes. Danny Woolard walked in and slipped into the only available booth. She placed a tray of burgers and fries on a table across from the counter, then walked toward the front door. A hand reached out and grabbed her arm. An alarming cry escaped her lips.

"I'm sorry, Kerry," Danny said. "I didn't mean to scare you."

She clutched her chest. "You almost scared me to death."

He lowered his eyes, like a puppy who'd been swatted with a newspaper.

"I got the message you left on my answering machine."

She glanced warily over her shoulder. "You need to see Amy right away."

He frowned. "Do you know what it's about?" he wondered if it had something to do with his father's whereabouts. No one had heard from him in a week.

"I think she wants you to go back to Morehead City."

"I wish she'd make up her mind," he mumbled.

"Danny, the greatest thing has happened!"

He stared at her attentively. "I'm listening."

"My folks are going to move to Morehead City. Amy and I just returned from seeing them in Pittsburgh."

He looked puzzled. "That's good news, I think. But what does that have to do with me going back down there?"

Kerry noticed Mr. Neely standing at the end of the counter with his arms folded, watching her. She took the damp towel draped over her arm and started wiping breadcrumbs from Danny's table. "I can't talk now. We're too busy. Amy will explain everything when she sees you."

"He shrugged. "Okay. Since I'm here, any chance of getting a soda?"

"Sure," she replied brightly, watching Mr. Neely walk away. "What flavor?"

CHAPTER FORTY

Clifford Jacobson stood at his study window, gazing over the distant horizon. It had taken two days, but he had finally finished his sermon. It was going to be perfect, just the way he wanted. There wouldn't be a dry eye in the house when he was finished.

The preacher loved Sunday. Not only was it the Lord's day, but it was his as well. A day to reflect over the previous week. A day to target your mistakes and conceive of ways to keep from repeating them. As for himself, he rarely made mistakes. Lately, however, he had made two. The first had been selecting Horace Woolard to run the beach police department. The second had been giving him the task of killing Scott Robinson. Woolard was a fool. He didn't seem to notice he'd been seen leaving the scene. He should have chosen someone more careful. The sheep were the only ones, who were to make mistakes, not the shepherd.

He glanced furtively when Spears opened the study door.

"Reverend, Captain Woolard is on the telephone. He'd like to speak with you."

Jacobson thanked Spears and waited until he closed the door before lifting the receiver. "What now, Horace?"

"Jacobson," Horace replied agitated. "What in the hell is going on around here? I just heard the Stone brothers were blown away."

Jacobson's face pruned. "Where in the name of God have you been? The Stones were killed days ago."

Horace hesitated. "When I left your place, I was going to come straight back here, but I decided to do a little site-seeing along the way. Who in the hell ordered that hit?"

"No one ordered that hit," Jacobson said, seething. "If you had been where you were supposed to be and did your job, the way you were supposed to do it, the Stones would still be alive!"

"What are you crawing about?" Horace asked. "What do the Stones have to do with..."

The words died in his throat.

"I suppose you've just had a revelation?" Jacobson replied sarcastically.

"If you had taken care of those girls, the way you were told, they wouldn't have been around to throw a monkey wrench into my plans."

Horace nodded, then realized how ridiculous the gesture was. Jacobson couldn't see his head moving, or could he?

"Look," Horace said nervously."I've got to have more money. It's too dangerous for me to be seen right now. I just got back in town and picked up the local rag. Kelsey is making my life miserable. He has me pegged as the chief suspect in Robinson's murder."

Jacobson closed his eyes and shook his head from side to side. "Imagine that," he muttered wryly.

"I'm serious, damn it! If I don't get the money I need right now, I'm calling the whole thing off."

"You'll call nothing off," Jacobson said flatly."You will do exactly as you're told. If you don't, you'll have more than James Kelsey nipping at your heels. There won't be a place on earth you'll be able to hide."

Woolard's hands were sweating so badly, he could barely hold the receiver. "I...I need more money," he stammered. "I have to figure out a way to disguise myself so no one will recognize me. I won't be able to get anywhere near those sluts unless I look like a complete stranger."

"Try the Union Mission," Jacobson replied harshly. "Surely you'll be able to find something suitable there for a man of your caliber."

Horace threw his phone across the car. "Rotten bastard!" he growled. "A man of my caliber. Who does that phony son-of-a-bitch think he is anyway? I made him what he is today. Now he thinks he's God Almighty. I'll show him," he spat hatefully. "I'll show them all."

CHAPTER FORTY-ONE

Jason Woolard dropped his schoolbooks on the dining room table and called out, "Mom, I'm home." Hearing no reply, he shrugged nonchalantly and went into the kitchen to find something to eat.

He used to worry when he came home from school and the house was quiet, especially when he knew his father was there. Jason worried about his mother a lot back then. He was always afraid that one day he'd come home from school and find her lying somewhere dead. He didn't have any idea what had happened to his dad, but whatever it was, he wished he were gone for good, like Mr. Robinson.

Jason had just finished his second chocolate chip cookie when the phone rang. He shuffled across the kitchen floor and picked it up. "Hello...Hello?" he said, waiting impatiently for a reply. He didn't hear a thing, not even deep breathing on the other end. "Hello," he repeated, raising his voice. "Is someone there?"

A click followed and then a dial tone.

He hung up, grumbling and returned to his snack.

Mark walked in and sat at the table across from his older brother.

Jason studied him curiously, wondering how long he'd been home."Do you know where Mom is?" he asked.

Mark twisted his index finger into the dimple on his cheek. Then he gazed at the ceiling.

"Mark!" Jason yelled. "I asked you a question."

Mark's shoulders nuzzled close to his neck as his thin body shriveled down in the chair.

— 238 —

THE BABY SOLDIERS

Jason groaned as he stood up, realizing he sounded just like his father. He knelt down beside Mark's chair."I'm sorry, squirt. I didn't mean to yell at you."

Mark bobbed his head mechanically. "Mom went out."

"Jason sighed heavily. "I figured that. Did she say where she was going?"

Mark reached for the bag of cookies. "She said she had some errands to run. She told me she'd be back in a little while."

The phone rang again. Mark's head spun toward the ringing. He stared at it warily. "Don't answer it, Jason. Whoever it is won't say anything."

Jason frowned. "How many times has it happened?"

Mark started counting on his fingers; his eyes fixed on the telephone. "I don't remember," he replied frustrated.

Jason snatched the receiver from its cradle, but didn't say anything.

After about ten seconds, he heard someone whisper, "Jason, is that you?"

Jason's heart sank, recognizing his father's voice. "Yes," he answered reluctantly. "It's me."

"Jason, I need you to do something for me," Horace said anxiously.

"Where are you?" Jason asked.

"Never mind that now," Horace snapped. "I need you to gather up some things and bring them to me."

"Okay," Jason answered. "Where should I bring them?"

"You have to promise you won't tell anybody else were I am. Do you promise?"

Jason leaned against the wall. "Yeah. Okay. I promise."

"Good," Horace replied, coughing so loud Jason winced, pulling the phone from his ear.

"Listen carefully. I want you to bring me a couple changes of clothes, my sunglasses, and the jacket and cap hanging in the back of my closet. You know the ones I mean. The ones I wore when I was in the Army."

— 239 —

"You want me to bring your rifle, too?" Jason asked, wondering why his dad was acting so weird.

"That's not a bad idea," Horace replied. "Yeah, bring it along. I'm staying at the Crescent Motel down past the mall. You know where that is, don't you?"

Jason nodded his head. "Yeah. It's where those people from New York got shot a couple weeks ago."

"That's right," Horace answered. "We're still trying to solve that case."

Jason pushed his long hair back from his face. "When do you want me to come?"

"Right now!" his father yelled. "I want you to come right now!"

Jason hung up.

"What did he want?" Mark asked fearfully.

"He wants me to take him some clothes and other stuff."

Mark chuckled. "Why doesn't he just come home and get them?"

Jason stared at his brother, wondering if he was really as dumb as he sounded. "Dad's in trouble, Mark. Lots of people are looking for him."

"Who's looking for him?" Mark asked, his eyes wide with innocence.

Jason picked up his milk and gulped it down. "Never mind. You wouldn't understand."

Mark rolled a cookie across the table, pretending it was a wheel. "Are the police looking for Dad because he killed Mr. Robinson? The kids at school were picking on me. They said my dad killed an icon." He looked at Jason, his small nose wrinkled.

Jason was upset to hear the other kids were laughing at Mark. He thought he was the only one the kids were giving a hard time. He hurried toward the stairs. "I don't know, squirt. Ask Mom when she comes home."

Mark picked up another cookie. Now he had two wheels.

THE BABY SOLDIERS

Danny rang the bell outside Amy's apartment. Then plopped into a wrought iron chair next to a small patio table. The seat felt cold on his rump. Amy answered the door before he had time to get it warm.

"Hi, Danny, come on in," she said brightly.

He got up, rubbing his cold tail, and followed her inside.

"Are you hungry?"

"What are you having?" he asked skeptically.

"Spaghetti and meatballs."

"Then I'm hungry," he replied, licking his lips.

She motioned toward a chair by the table. "Want a Pepsi?"

"Yeah, thanks."

"Look, Danny, I know you just got back, but I need you to go to Morehead City again next week. I'll need you to be down there for at least another month." Her eyes shifted thoughtfully. "That should do it."

"What am I supposed to do this time?"

"I want you to help Mr. and Mrs. Trivane get settled. Show them around the place. Explain what we've done so far. I want them to know everything that's going on by the time we find the children and take them there."

His dark eyes narrowed. "Are you sure you want them to know everything?"

After the things Danny had learned about his own father, he suspected everyone was bad news.

"I trust them," Amy said, looking directly into his eyes. "They're going to help us, Danny. That's the important thing."

He chortled. "We could use more of that."

"Now that the Trivanes know they have a grandchild somewhere, I expect they'll be a valuable asset to our cause."

"When do you want me to leave?" he asked, shifting his gaze toward the bubbling sauce.

"Next Friday will be soon enough. That will give you plenty of time to tie up any loose ends you have here."

"Will Kerry be going, too?" he asked, trying not to sound goofy.

— 241 —

Amy pinched his cheek until it turned red. "No, lover boy," she laughed. "Kerry will be staying here, for the time being. We need her at the diner. I never realized how much you could learn by listening to kids talking to each other."

"Yeah," he replied wryly. "It's a good place to find out who's pregnant and who isn't."

"Exactly." She smiled. "If we can find out who they are, we can warn them before the baby snatchers get a hold of them."

Danny cocked his head to one side and stared at her admiringly. "Now I know why the group picked you to be their leader."

She scooped some sauce onto a wooden spoon and let him taste it. "I just wish there would have been someone around to warn me."

***

Horace Woolard polished off the fifth of Dewar's scotch that was standing on the scarred dresser. Then he sat listlessly on the edge of the bed staring at the blank television screen. He had just showered and wore a paper-thin towel around his bloated mid-section. He glanced at his reflection in the mirror above the dresser and winced. His hair stood on end, making him look like a circus clown. He ran his shaky fingers along the rumpled bedspread, feeling for his comb. Then he cursed. It was probably outside in the rental car. Right now, he needed another drink. Where in the hell was that boy?

Someone rapped lightly at the door.

"Just a minute," Horace slurred, looking for something to cover himself besides the towel. Finding nothing but the dirty clothes he'd taken off before his shower, he called out, "Jason, is that you?"

"Yeah, Dad. It's me."

He flung the door open, his bleary eyes danced left and right before grabbing Jason's arm and pulling him inside the room. "Hurry up," he snapped. "I don't want anyone to see you standing out there. You may have been followed."

THE BABY SOLDIERS

Jason looked at his father disapprovingly. He could smell the rancid odor of liquor on his breath. He placed the shopping bag on the bed. "Here's the stuff you wanted."

Horace swayed idly as his son stepped away from the bed. Then he bent down and rummaged through the bag as though he was a crazed shopper in a bargain basement. "Thank Christ, you finally got here," he mumbled. "Now I can get dressed and get the hell out of this dump."

Jason watched his father groping through his things. "Where are you going to go?" He asked innocently.

Horace spun around and glared at him. Hate pierced his blood-shot eyes. A couple of years ago, he would have whacked Jason good for asking questions that were none of his business. But Jason was a lot bigger now. Horace wondered when the boy had grown so tall. He must be six-foot; he mused—just like that trouble-making brother of his. "Don't you worry where I'm going," he snapped, staggering back and falling onto the bed. "I'm on a secret mission."

"Oh," Jason said hollowly. "Like when you killed Mr. Robinson?"

Horace grunted, forcing himself to his feet. His glacier blue eyes fixed on his son. "What do you know about that?"

Jason stared at his father, thinking how pathetic he looked; a far cry from the way he looked in his wedding pictures. "The newspapers say you shot him in the back of the head while he was working in his office at the academy."

Horace sat on the edge of the bed, placing his head between his knees. Then he giggled eerily. "His fat head exploded like fireworks on the fourth of July. A big old watermelon falling off the back of a pickup truck. Splat!"

Jason turned away. He knew his father did it, but hearing him admit it sickened him. "When are you leaving?" he asked.

Horace balanced precariously against the edge of the bed. Then he grabbed Jason by the arm and thrust him toward the door. Jason backed into the parking lot toward his car.

"You get the hell out of here, now!" Horace yelled. "Ya hear what I'm telling ya, boy?"

Jason backed away, his shaky fingers prying the car door open.

"And don't say a word to anyone about seeing me. You understand?"

Jason gunned the engine and the old Chevy squealed out of the lot.

Horace slammed the motel door shut and started getting dressed.

Adele Woolard walked briskly into the kitchen, a full bag of groceries under each arm. Mark was still sitting at the table. He was up to four wheels now, all spinning across the table at the same time.

"Mark, where's Jason?" she asked, dropping the bags on the counter. "I didn't see his car outside."

"He had to take some clothes and stuff over to Dad."

Her fingers froze on the quart of milk she held. "He what?"

"Vroom." Mark answered, racing the cookies to the other side of the table. "Dad called. Said he wanted Jason to bring him some stuff."

"Where was he?"

Mark shrugged. "Jason wouldn't tell me. I think it's a secret. Vroom."

Adele frowned as she turned back to the grocery bags.

"Mom?" Mark asked.

"Yes," she replied, lining soup cans up in individual rows in the pantry.

"Why did Dad kill Mr. Robinson? I thought he was nice."

Adele blinked as she tried to digest the question. Reporters, she mused. She was about to tell him that Horace had merely been accused of the crime; he hadn't been convicted of anything. Then the telephone rang. She reached for it quickly.

"Hello," she replied.

"Adele, it's David. Have you heard anything?"

— 244 —

THE BABY SOLDIERS

"David," she said, her voice strained. "I think you'd better come over here."

"I'll be right there," he said.

Just as she hung up, Jason walked in. "Hi, Mom. I'm not hungry. I already ate."

Adele gave him a furtive glance. "Jason, where have you been?"

"I saw Dad. Man, was he drunk. He could hardly stand up."

"Where was he?" she asked, her emerald eyes wide with terror.

Jason recognized the look. It was always worse when she knew his dad was drinking. "He was at a motel by the mall."

She clutched her chest. "What's he doing there?"

Jason was about to answer when he heard the doorbell. "I'll get it," he said. "I invited Tommy over to play my new computer game."

He strolled to the front door and pulled it open. He looked surprised. "Hi, David. Mom's in the kitchen. She's grilling me."

David scowled as he followed Jason inside the house. "What's she grilling you about?"

Jason snickered. "I saw Dad a little while ago. I think she's afraid he might be coming home."

David swallowed hard. Considering Horace was on the run, he hadn't given any thought to the idea he might go home. You're slipping, detective, he chided himself. Going home was so obvious.

CHAPTER FORTY-TWO

Danny opened the front door of his parents' home and heard loud voices coming from the kitchen. He cocked his head to one side, listening attentively. He furrowed his brow, wondering why David Williams was asking Jason questions about their father. When he reached the kitchen, he crossed his arms over his chest. Everyone stopped talking and stared at him.

"What's going on?" Danny asked.

Adele wiped her hands on a dishtowel she'd taken from the counter. "Danny, I'm glad you're here."

"I just got back a little while ago," he explained. "I wanted to see if you heard anything from Dad."

David looked up from the table. "Danny, you may as well sit down. You need to hear this, too."

Danny frowned, looking from one somber face to the next. Jason and Mark were staring at the floor. "Did something happen?"

David slid the pencil he was holding behind his ear. "Jason saw your father after school this afternoon. He's staying at a motel by the mall."

Danny sat down and turned from the sergeant to his brother. "How did you find out where he was?"

"Your dad called and asked Jason to bring him some clothes and a few other things," David replied.

"Yeah," Jason mumbled. "Like his old army jacket and rifle."

THE BABY SOLDIERS

David nodded grimly. "I sent a patrol car over there, but he'd already checked out." He looked at Danny. "Do you have any idea where he might go?"

Danny looked out the window behind the counter where his mother stood trembling. The sun melted below the horizon, leaving the sky a blotched pink and purple.

"What else did you take to the motel?" he asked Jason.

Jason scraped the chair back and got up. "His old army cap, the furry one." He scratched his head. "And he wanted some regular clothes, too. You know, pants, shirts, that kind of stuff."

Danny frowned. "His old army jacket and hat."

Jason nodded.

"Sounds like he's trying to disguise himself," Danny replied thoughtfully.

The others looked alarmed.

Danny shrugged. "Why else would he want that old moth-eaten rag?"

David snorted. "I'm more concerned about him taking the rifle."

Danny's eyes narrowed. "Sounds to me like he's not finished." He turned to Jason. "When you followed Dad to Baltimore that day…"

"What?" Adele cried, looking from one son to the other. "When did you go to Baltimore?" she asked, her eyes fixed on Jason.

"A while back," he murmured. "I followed him to Reverend Jacobson's house." Then he shot his older brother a look that said, thanks for nothing, big mouth.

David raised a hand to calm her."It's all right, Adele." Then he turned to the boy. "Jason, did Jacobson say anything to your dad besides telling him he had to get rid of Mr. Robinson?"

Adele covered her mouth in shock. "You knew about it!" Then she burst into tears and ran from the room.

Jason's eyes followed her. After she was gone, he turned to David. "He told Dad about some girls who had tapes of Mr. Robinson having sex. He said the girls mailed the tapes to a bunch of radio stations.

Jacobson said if they weren't stopped, he could get in a lot of trouble. I think he wanted Dad to kill them, too."

"Holy shit!" Danny said, leaping from his chair. He looked at David, his eyes wide with fright. "David, can't you see? That's why he needs a disguise. Dad's gonna try to kill Kerry and Amy!"

The others sat dumbfounded as Danny raced from the house.

David ran after him. He caught him gunning the VW's engine. David put his hands through the open driver's window, resting them on the door. "Where are you going, Danny?"

"I'm going to the diner. Kerry's working late tonight. See you later, David," he said. "I've got to hurry."

David nodded. "What's Amy's address?"

Danny rattled it off.

"Meet me there," David told him. "As soon as you check on Kerry."

Danny floored the gas, sending a funnel of black smoke into the air behind him.

———

Danny wheeled the small car onto the macadam, veering to the right, around the drive-thru window. He looked toward the back of the parking lot where the employees parked. It was empty. Mr. Neely's pickup truck was gone, too. He wondered if Amy had already come by to pick up Kerry. Then his thoughts strayed to something more sinister. What if his father had shown up unexpectedly and taken Kerry off somewhere to put a bullet in her head? "Please, God, let her be all right," he muttered frantically.

Danny mind was going a hundred directions at once. Maybe Kerry's at Amy's place right now, he thought. Ever since the fire at the shelter, Kerry had been staying with Amy. He made a U-turn in the parking lot and sped away from the diner, turning west on Route 64.

CHAPTER FORTY-THREE

Sybil Kelsey left Beamon's Book Emporium just as David Williams sped by in his Honda. Her long neck bobbed between the horde of vehicles in the parking lot to see where he was parking. Then she leaned forward, like a bull zeroing in on a red flag, and charged in that direction. Her plastic shopping bags clapped loudly against her legs as she scampered down aisle K.

"David!" she yelled. "David, wait up. I need to talk to you."

David cursed under his breath. He didn't have to turn around to see who was calling him. He'd recognize that miserable screeching voice if he were standing under Niagara Falls. He thought of darting in the opposite direction as though he hadn't heard her. But it was too late. She was already blocking his retreat.

"David," she said, gasping for breath. "I wanted to tell you how sorry I was to hear about your family. Being found dead like that, must have been awful for you. I'm sorry I couldn't make it to the funeral. I heard a lot of our old friends were there. I had to attend a church conference in another state. It's something I'd been planning for months. And, you know how it is. I just couldn't stay away, knowing how much it would let the others in the group down."

David stared at her blankly, having absolutely nothing to say to her.

"I just wanted to tell you how devastated we were to hear the news. It's like I always say, it does pay to stay close to the Lord in case the inevitable happens."

David muttered as he brushed past her. "I don't have time to talk right now. I'm in a hurry."

Her beady eyes followed him as he jogged between rows of parked cars. Then he disappeared through a glass door in front of the mall.

"Well, I never!' she exclaimed. Then she spun around as though she were lost and ventured through the lot, trying to remember just where she'd parked her car.

Sybil couldn't understand why everyone was behaving so rudely. She remembered when people used to have time to stop and chat, or drop by the house for coffee and homemade cakes fresh from the oven. She wondered what had happened to make everyone change so much.

David's face was flushed when he reached the section where the movie theaters were located. Someone had called the precinct and reported seeing a man carrying what appeared to be a rifle into the theater. His gut instinct told him it was Horace, so he took the call. "Jesus," he muttered, staring at the marquis, "six movies under one roof. And this time of day, they'll all be packed."

He nudged his way through the crowd until he reached the ticket taker's booth. The pimply faced boy behind the shatterproof glass stood rigid, like a Marine at attention.

David flashed his badge. "I need some information, son,"

He didn't want to alarm the people standing in line behind him, so he spoke softly.

"Did a man come through here carrying something wrapped in a coat that looked like it could have been a baseball bat or a rifle?"

The boy's eyes brightened like lighthouse beacons. "Yeah. A slimy looking dude. He bought a ticket for the Armageddon flick. It started about twenty minutes ago."

David reached for a ten spot and shoved it through the small opening. "Thanks. You'd better give me a ticket."

THE BABY SOLDIERS

The boy took David's money and gave him one adult ticket and two dollars change.

David stared grimly at the two bills as he walked toward the dark blue door with the number four blinking brightly above it. He heard a group of people tittering behind him. He turned to see them doing a bizarre imitation of Horace Woolard shooting Scott Robinson in the back. He shook his head, wondering what Horace would have thought had he seen the parody. Those kids should thank their lucky stars "The Dirty Rat" was already inside.

The theater was completely dark, except for huge gray monsters with red eyes that glared down from the wide screen. Once David's eyes became accustomed to the darkness, he found an empty seat on the right side near the back of the theater. He sat down amid the low grumbling of the people seated directly behind him. A loud explosion resounded through the cramped theater, catching him off guard. He jumped, startled. Two fellows seated a few rows behind him snickered. It wasn't until then that David realized the noise had come from the movie. He sighed restlessly. It was going to be a long wait.

While everyone appeared engrossed in the sci-fi flick, David scanned the heads of the people seated in the rows in front of him. He guessed most of the moviegoers were between eighteen and twenty-five. If Horace was in here, he shouldn't be hard to find.

David's eyes wandered over the various sized heads in the audience, still trying to digest his unexpected encounter with Sybil Kelsey in the parking lot. She hadn't sounded all that convincing when she told him she was sorry to hear about Ann and Ginny. He figured the only thing Sybil regretted was being unable to convince them to join her and her fanatic friends in that church of hers. His late wife had been Catholic. Ann used to tell him she had enough brain-washing when she was growing up. She didn't need more of the same. David peeled the wrapper from a stick of gum and popped it in his mouth, remembering James used to be just about as bad as Sybil. They used to drop in unexpectedly about once a week. Sybil was always preaching the holy word, according to Reverend Jacob-

— 251 —

son. After Ann and Ginny disappeared, the Kelseys seemed to lose all interest in his salvation.

David was aware that Sybil was still actively participating in every real and unreal cause that crossed her path. Last year, James seemed to wean away from that group altogether. Come to think of it, he couldn't remember the last time he'd seen one of those boldly printed ads warning of approaching damnation blazoned across the pages of the daily newspaper. Not since Robbie died, he mused. David wondered if James had put two and two together and figured out the same fine people, he was rubbing elbows with on a social level, could have had something to do with his own son's murder.

As he scoured the front section of the theater, David sucked in his breath. Horace was sitting in the second row on the left side. The flickering light from the big screen made his thinning blond hair look like freshly spun cotton candy. He squinted to make sure it was really him. Then he felt a chill, seeing an object protruding above the middle of Horace's right shoulder. David shifted uncomfortably in the narrow seat. The people on either side of him had laid claim to the armrests, leaving him at a loss for what to do with his own floundering limbs.

He toyed with the twist-a-flex band on his wristwatch, resigned to the fact he was going to have to sit through the entire film before confronting Horace. He'd have to wait and catch him outside. There was no safe way he could draw him out before then—not as long as he was cradling that rifle. If Horace killed Scott Robinson, he would have no qualms about wasting half the people in the theater. David knew the juries in Virginia Beach were among the toughest in the country. If Horace were convicted of Scott's murder, he'd be tossed into the general prison population where his execution would surely be handled by those he'd sent there. If David confronted him now, it would make little difference to Horace if he died for killing fifty people, or one. You only died once.

David checked his Timex. He had another hour before the movie ended.

CHAPTER FORTY-FOUR

Jacobson asked Byron Spears to close the door on his way out. Certain he was now alone, he picked up the telephone on his desk.

He cordially greeted the person on the other end of the line, then listened impatiently to the endless stream of banter that followed.

Finally, he said, "Yes. I was as devastated to hear about Scott Robinson's shameful activities as you were. All those years we worked together. Yes. Yes. It was a terrible shock. Imagine the arrogance… filming his own…Of course, you were. A lot of people were disappointed by his behavior. Yes, who would think that a school principal could…."

He tapped the Mont Blanc on the gray ink blotter on his desk. "You know," he said, selecting his words wisely. "Ordinarily, I wouldn't make such a request. But something urgent has come up that requires our immediate attention."

A bolt of lightning flashed through the window, illuminating his gray eyes. They glinted like sharpened daggers. "Yes, I'm thankful. I can always count on you. You've always been a worthy supporter. That's exactly why I chose to call you today."

"I'll do anything…anything at all," was the zealous reply.

Jacobson licked his lips. "Since you happen to be a personal friend of our police captain, I feel that you will be able to carry out this assignment without arousing the slightest suspicion." His lips pressed into a tight smile as the chattering continued. "I'll call you back with instructions. Goodbye, now."

After the preacher hung up, he sat back in his swivel chair, admiring the three-carat diamond ring on the third finger of his left hand. The finger where his wedding band had been. There was no point in continuing his pretense of grief over that crazy woman any longer. No one had mentioned Helen in years. They all assumed her mental collapse had led to her disappearance. That she had simply run off. They had no way of knowing his crazy wife had been dead for years.

Horace Woolard sat in the noisy movie theater, not daring to turn around. He sensed he was being watched. He hadn't seen anyone follow him inside the theater, but he'd been a cop long enough to know when someone was stalking him. He frowned as he thought about Clifford Jacobson and the nutty plot that had driven him here. If it weren't for that fool of a preacher, he'd be sitting in his big office, where he belonged. He shifted as he tried to relax. In spite of his growing paranoia, he couldn't fathom what had possessed him to bring the rifle into the theater. Even though he had it wrapped in an army jacket; it wouldn't take much imagination to figure out what it was. He should have hidden the weapon outside somewhere. He was surprised no one had called the cops to report him when he walked in with it. He glanced warily from side to side. Maybe someone did.

Two weeks ago, no one would have given him a second look if they'd seen him with a rifle slung over his shoulder. But that was before the unfortunate incident that occurred at the academy. Leave it to a jogger to get in the path of his escape, he thought ruefully. Ever since that health freak spilled his guts, he'd been afraid to be seen in public for fear someone would recognize him from the pictures Kelsey had generously plastered all over his newspaper.

Horace wondered why nothing ever went the way it should. He'd been working on the right side of the law long enough to know how to murder someone and get away with it. If things had gone without a hitch, he'd have popped Robinson and been back home long before anyone realized what had happened. It was always the unexpected

THE BABY SOLDIERS

things that tripped you up. How many times had he heard hard-core lifers tell him that same thing?

Whoever was watching him would probably wait for the crowd to thin out before approaching him. He surveyed his options. His tail most likely expected him to leave the theater through the main doors in the back like everyone else. He glanced at the side exit, no more than twenty feet from his seat and smiled wryly. Getting out of the theater would not be a problem. His fingers closed around the rifle barrel, like a small child groping a security blanket. No problem getting out, he thought. But where would he go from there?

Danny Woolard pulled up to the curb in front of Amy Patterson's place. The Trivanes had changed their mind about waiting a couple weeks before going to Morehead City. They were already on their way. He wanted to make sure he had everything he needed before leaving to meet them. It had finally stopped raining around four that afternoon. Not that a heavy rainfall normally bothered him. It was just that he hated driving through one particular section of Route 17 whenever it was dark, or raining. Mosquito-infested ditches, abandoned cars, and miles of dying trees and rotted stumps bordered the winding road. Local folks called it the Dismal Swamp. As far as Danny was concerned, it should have been called the Twilight Zone. It was one of the last single lane highways left in the state. Virginia and Carolina had been fighting over widening it for years. Carolina didn't want to spend its money improving property that belonged to Virginia, and Virginia didn't want to spend the money to widen a highway that would make it easier for tourists to spend their vacation dollars in Carolina. A catch twenty-two, he mused, one that would never be resolved—not in his lifetime.

Kerry opened Amy's front door, her blue eyes wide with surprise. "Danny, what are you doing here? I thought you left for Carolina hours ago."

— 255 —

"I stopped to see if Amy had anything else she wanted me to take along."

"Just a sec," Kerry replied. "I'll go upstairs and get her."

Danny ambled into the living room and sat down on the worn, but comfortable sofa. He thumbed through a stack of magazines spread over the coffee table until he found a current issue of Field and Stream. He thought it odd that Amy would subscribe to Field and Stream. But, then again, he'd been around Amy long enough to know she was no ordinary girl. Amy was full of surprises.

When Amy walked in, he closed the magazine. "Field and Stream, huh?"

She smiled, "I've been known to bait a hook a time or two. Dad used to take me to the lake every summer. He always wanted a boy."

Danny nodded. "I'm sure you didn't disappoint him."

"Just that time I fell in love with a foreigner and got knocked up," she replied ruefully.

"Yeah, that would do it," Danny replied, turning his head, so she wouldn't see how embarrassed he was.

Amy shrugged nonchalantly. "I suppose my sordid experience did have one positive outcome."

Amy had never discussed her past with him before, and he wasn't sure he wanted to hear about it now.

"While I was confined at the camp, my folks disappeared, just like Kerry's. Only difference was they did a more thorough job of it."

He studied her curiously. "Are you thinking about trying to find them?"

"Not really," she answered, her voice trailing off. "They were the ones who pressured me into going to the clinic to begin with. I never wanted an abortion. Then, as luck would have it, I was kidnapped. I hope they go to their graves feeling guilty as hell."

"I doubt if they will," he replied sullenly. "Those that should, never do."

Amy groaned loudly. "Why do I get the feeling that we're not talking about my folks anymore?"

— 256 —

Danny stood up abruptly. "Now you sound like Becca. My personal analyst."

Amy smiled.

He studied her expressive face. "By the way, how are Rebecca and Angie? I won't be in town long enough to check on them myself."

Amy winced. "They're doing as well as can be expected. Now that we have a new place with everything on one level, Angie manages to get around fairly well in the wheelchair." She shook her head slowly. "But I'm afraid Rebecca doesn't want anyone to see her since the last of the bandages came off. She said she looks like a freak."

Danny frowned. "I can't imagine Becca saying that. She was always so upbeat."

Amy closed her eyes. "The insurance we had on the Haven won't be enough to cover the re-constructive surgery she'll need to feel whole again."

His eyes brightened. "I have money."

Amy laughed. "What? A couple hundred dollars?"

Danny shook his head. "No. I promised my grandfather I wouldn't tell anyone, but grandma left me a small fortune in her will."

"You never told us you were rich," Amy replied.

He chuckled. "Grandfather said I had to keep it a secret until I turned twenty-one, so my dad wouldn't figure out a way to get his greedy mitts on it."

"Ah," she replied. "Now I understand."

"I'm serious, Amy. If Becca needs anything that the insurance won't cover, tell her I'll take care of it."

Amy nodded appreciatively. "I'll pass it on. Knowing there's a good chance she'll have a real face again someday will give her a reason to want to live again."

He shoved his hands deep into his pockets. "I sure hope so. Becca was always there when I needed somebody. It's the least I can do."

Amy studied his somber face. "You know, Danny. You're a good person."

His face reddened. "Before we get completely off track, I just stopped by to see if there was anything else I can take to Carolina, or anything special you want me to do once I get there."

Amy's pensive green eyes shifted from Danny to the kitchen, where Kerry was busy fixing dinner. She tapped her index finger against her lips. "I made reservations for the Trivanes at the Comfort Inn on Bridges Street. I figured that would put them close enough to our building they can drop in anytime. I didn't want them to have to drive any more than necessary. Just make them as comfortable as you can. Answer their questions and be sure to show them the town."

He grunted. "Show them the town. That should kill about ten or fifteen minutes."

She shot him a furtive glance. "Drive slow. It'll take at least twenty. And tell the Trivanes I'll be down to join you in about a week or so."

He looked longingly toward the kitchen; the fragrant aroma wafting by his nose made his mouth water. He sighed longingly."Will Kerry be coming down with you?"

Amy chuckled. "We've got to find something for you to do to keep that one-track mind of yours occupied."

Danny blushed.

"Would you like to have dinner with us before you leave?" Amy asked.

Danny bobbed his head excitedly.

CHAPTER FORTY-FIVE

By the time David realized Horace had left through the side door, the mass exodus through the main door of the theater was moving slowly. No way he could break through the line to chase after him. When he finally reached the parking lot, he looked around anxiously, but didn't see Horace anywhere. He cursed himself while walking back to his car.

David wondered if Horace suspected he was being followed. Then he shook his head. No, of course not. He had entered the theater long after Horace was seated. Horace probably figured that a lot of people would be leaving the theater at the same time, so he left by the side door, not wanting the rifle he carried to draw any unwanted attention. Considering the likelihood that Horace had seen his pictures plastered all over the newspaper, David decided, the last thing Horace wanted to do was anything that would draw more attention to himself.

Horace clutched the rifle close to his chest as he darted between the parked cars surrounding the mall. He slowed down when he reached a line of trees beyond the range of the mall's security lights. Then he spotted a dumpster outside an apartment complex on the far side of the trees and dropped the rifle into it. It struck the bottom with a palpable thud. The noise startled him. He didn't think they ever emptied those things. He shivered as he slipped on his old army jacket. Panting, he tried to zip it, but the forty pounds he'd gained since the last time he'd worn it got in the way. He folded his arms over his chest, holding the jacket closed. The temperature must have dropped twenty degrees since he'd gone inside the theater. He pulled the beak of the furry cap down over his eyes, protecting them from the stinging wind, and tried to figure out what to do next.

Moviegoers and shoppers rushed from the mall and hurried to their cars in the parking lot. Moments later a flood of headlights bobbed along the macadam, and then darkness. Horace was growing more desperate by the minute. A gust of wind sent disposable drink containers skipping across the road. The wind cut through his wool slacks as though they were made of paper. He had to make a move. He couldn't continue walking out on the streets the way he looked. Eventually, some cop would come along and roust him for vagrancy and haul him down to the station. If he weren't so damned cold, he'd have laughed at the irony. He needed to get out of the area and get out quick. Too many people in Tidewater knew him. He suspected a few of the people who were in the theater would have recognized him right off the bat, if he hadn't looked like a down and out bum. He wondered who was tailing him. It didn't matter, now, he thought. He had out-foxed whoever it was.

Horace wished he hadn't left his car in the shipyard parking lot, but at the time, he figured that was as good a place as any. Half the cars there were abandoned, or broken- down relics no one wanted to repair. If an APB went out on his car, it would take months to find it at the shipyard. By then, this mess would be all cleared up. He shivered, wishing he were inside that beautiful Mercedes right now. At least he'd be warm. What he needed was someone he could trust.

Developing lasting friendships hadn't been one of Horace Woolard's strong suits over the years, but he could think of at least a dozen people who owed him favors. Considering his present circumstances, those people would be the last ones he could count on to help him. They'd just as soon see him freeze to death—and be out of their lives for good.

THE BABY SOLDIERS

He walked beneath a cluster of low hanging apple and pear tree branches until he came to a crossing in the road. Bright lights flooded the macadam of the gas station diagonally across the intersection. He darted across the street, careful not to get sideswiped by some driver, who didn't think he looked respectable enough to drive around. Then he headed straight for the telephone bank along the outside wall.

The plexi-glass shields along the sides of the phone booth barely protected his face from the howling wind. How he longed for the kind of telephone booths you could walk into and close the door behind you. They didn't have those anymore, thanks to Jacobson and the organization. Too many people, living in the moment, had started using them for sex, rather than paying the price of a cheap hotel room. His fingers were so numb it was difficult to hold onto the coins, let alone drop them into the right slot. He punched in the numbers and waited.

"Hello," she answered groggily.

She sounded hoarse, like she just woke up. He wondered why she'd be sleeping this early in the day.

"Hello?" she repeated, seemingly annoyed. "Is someone there?"

"Sybil, it's me, Horace Woolard."

He waited impatiently while she coughed up phlegm.

"I'm sorry, Horace," she explained. "I must have picked up a bug or something. I was just taking a nap. Horace?" she asked startled. "Is that really you?"

He sighed as he tightened his numb fingers around the receiver. "Sybil, I'm in a real jam. I need you to do me a favor."

Sybil forced herself to sit up, and wiped sleep from her eyes. "Horace, you wouldn't believe the horrible things people have been saying about you. I can't imagine where they get their ideas. I just want you to know that I don't believe any of that mean gossip, not a single word of it."

So far so good, he thought. "I appreciate that, Sybil, really I do. You've always been a good friend."

She spat into a tissue. "What's this about a favor?"

— 261 —

"I know it's a bad time, considering you're not feeling well and all. I know what a busy lady you are…"

She tittered like a silly schoolgirl, just the way he'd expected.

"My car…my car broke down," he stammered. "I can't get it repaired until Monday…and I need to get someplace right away. Do you think you could drive me there?"

"Why, of course," she said, pushing herself from the sunken mattress. She pulled a dresser drawer open and tugged out panties and a bra. "Where shall I pick you up?"

"I'm at a Texaco Station on Military Highway, not far from the mall."

"I know exactly where that is," she replied quickly. "I had a flat tire near there one time. And would you believe it, no one knew how to change it? I promised myself I'd never go back there again."

Horace rubbed his furrowed brow. The last thing he wanted to do was listen to one of Sybil's endless spiels."I know exactly how you feel," he said patronizingly.

"Look, Sybil, I need you to come as fast as you can. It's colder than a country graveyard on New Year's Eve, and I'm about to freeze to death."

She giggled. "Oh, Horace, what would you possibly know about a country grave- yards?"

He sighed loudly.

"Forgive me for jabbering. It's just that no one seems to have the time to talk to me anymore. Let me finish dressing and splash some water on my face, and I'll be right there."

Horace hung up and once again tried unsuccessfully to zip the old army jacket.

CHAPTER FORTY-SIX

David wished Danny Woolard hadn't left town this week. It was becoming more and more difficult to cover all the bases himself. He never was much good at being in two places at one time. When he promised Danny that he'd look after Amy and Kerry, he had no idea he'd also be tracking down Danny's father, who could have written a best seller on the perfect escape.

David turned down Rodgers Street, glancing at the stalwart brick homes, which had once symbolized an affluent community. In the past twenty years, the neighborhood had deteriorated from upper middle-class to borderline slum. The elderly homeowners had given up landscaping yards and painting unreachable window frames, opting for the fellowship and security of more modern senior communities.

He removed his foot from the accelerator. Amy's apartment was in the next block.

Kerry Trivane met him at the door. He thought she seemed a bit on edge.

"Have you heard any news about Captain Woolard?" she asked.

David scratched the back of his head. "I should have him in custody right now. But unfortunately, he outsmarted me."

Her blue eyes narrowed like a gas flame crushed by an iron skillet.

"What happened?" she stammered.

"We got a call at the station late this afternoon. Someone said they thought they saw a man carrying a rifle near the movie theater at the mall. The moment I heard the word rifle, I went over there to see if it was Horace. Even if it turned out it wasn't, I was afraid it could turn into a hostage situation." He sighed heavily."Too many damned nuts to contend with anymore. I'll be glad when I can retire."

"Would you like a cup of coffee?" she asked, wringing her hands.

David nodded and followed her into the kitchen.

He sat with a loud groan, as though he were seventy instead of forty-two. "When I got to the mall and realized the man with the rifle was actually Horace, I sat through the worst movie I've ever seen in my entire life, just waiting for him to get up and leave." David rested his elbows on the table and shook his head in disbelief. "When the movie ended, he shot out the side door and disappeared."

Kerry's pale hands trembled as she filled the cup and placed the pot back on the stove. "Then, he's still out there somewhere?"

David nodded. "I'm afraid so. I came here as soon as I could to warn you and Amy not to go anywhere by yourselves until he is apprehended."

Amy walked through the open doorway, having caught the end of the conversation. "That's impossible, David," she said abruptly. "We can't stay cooped up in here like prisoners. We have work to do. Besides, if Woolard really wanted to harm us, this would be the first place he'd look."

Kerry glanced from Amy to David and frowned. "She's right, David. We're not safe here."

He thought about the situation, while stirring too much sugar in his coffee. "Is there somewhere you could go for a few days…until we wrap this up?"

Amy thought for a moment and then nodded. "I think so. Kerry and I will pack a few things. It will only take a few minutes." She turned to leave the kitchen and then turned back facing him. "It might be better to leave my car here. That way, he'll think I'm still here."

"That's good," David said, cocking an eye, impressed. "I'll have a couple of men set up a stake out. If he shows up, we'll nab him."

THE BABY SOLDIERS

Sybil Kelsey beamed when she saw Horace waiting behind the Texaco station. She parked the sleek-lined white Mercury close to the rest rooms. Horace climbed in awkwardly and took a deep breath. "I'm glad you finally got here," he said hoarsely. "It's colder now than it was ten minutes ago. I would have waited in the rest room, but wouldn't you know it, they keep 'em locked."

"I'm sorry I couldn't get here sooner. I had a phone call right before I left." She glanced at him and smiled demurely. "But, I'm here now. That's all that matters."

"You have no idea how much this means to me."

Sybil laughed with her mouth open, exposing her big teeth. "Just knowing I can be of service to someone makes me feel tingly all over." She patted his leg lightly. "You know what I mean."

He nodded. "I think we'd better get moving. I don't know how much time I have before the bloodhounds close in."

"Very well," she said, putting the car in gear. "Where to?"

"I have a cabin," he answered, rubbing his hands to warm them. "I guess that's as good a place as any."

Sybil eyed him curiously. He wasn't dressed the way he usually was. As a matter of fact, he looked downright shoddy. He looked nothing like the dapper man she and James had seen that night at the Grecian Horse Restaurant. When he spoke, she was shocked to see how yellow his teeth were. The tobacco stains on the enamel not only looked bad; they smelled bad, too. She was glad James didn't smoke. His drinking was bad enough.

"How do we get to this cabin?" she asked, turning her attention back to the road.

"Go west on Route 58. It's out past Suffolk."

Sybil gasped. "Isn't that a coincidence? My grandparents used to live out that way. They raised hogs in Sussex County. I'm sure I told you about them. Granddaddy McCloskey came from County

— 265 —

Cork, Ireland. He said living in the country here made him feel right at home."

"No, you didn't tell me." He replied, irritated by her constant chatter. It would take another hour or more to reach his destination. He'd almost forgotten how Sybil's constant talking could drive a body mad.

Sybil drove the next thirty miles quietly humming to herself. He thought the melody sounded like the Old Rugged Cross, but he wasn't sure. He didn't want to risk asking for fear she'd start to sing.

"You know, Horace, I haven't been out in this area in years. James and I used to talk about moving up this way after he retired from the newspaper. But he's busier now than he was when he took over. That was fifteen years ago."

She sighed heavily. "After Robbie died, James didn't want to retire at all. If he didn't have his precious newspaper to keep him occupied, he'd just have more time to dwell on Robbie being taken away from us. I suppose it's just as well. He spends too much time at the cemetery as it is. I can't imagine what he'd do if he didn't have a job to go to each day."

Horace squirmed uncomfortably. There could be another reason James was reluctant to retire, he mused. Then he'd have to listen to Sybil run her mouth twenty-four hours a day.

"Do you want me to stop somewhere and get something to drink?" she asked. "Or, how about something to eat? You must be famished."

The last thing he'd eaten was a Snickers Bar at the movie-theater, but he wasn't hungry. "I would like something to drink," he said. "Now that I've gotten warmed up, I am a little thirsty."

Sybil nodded understandingly and then pulled into an Exxon station near Suffolk. Horace started to get out. "Don't," she said, grabbing his arm. "Someone might recognize you. I can get whatever you want. Do you prefer Pepsi or Coke?"

"Make it Diet Dr. Pepper," he replied. "I'm watching my weight."

Her beady eyes fixed on his protruding stomach. Then she snorted.

Horace drummed his fingers on his knees waiting for Sybil to return with their drinks. When she did, she handed him one and popped the cap on the other.

After putting hers in the caddie between them, she reached into her coat pocket. "Look!" she said excitedly. "I bought a lottery ticket. If I win, I'm going to travel all over the world. It's always been a secret dream of mine."

He stared at the ticket, remembering how Sybil had always denounced people who played the lottery, or indulged in any type of gambling. He wondered how she'd feel if she knew she was aiding and abetting a murderer.

"There's a lot to see right here in the United States," he replied hollowly.

"This is truly amazing," she said. "All the years I've know you, and I never knew you had a cabin out in the country."

He sighed. He should have called Adele and made her bring him out here. She was his wife. She owed him that much. "I never mentioned the cabin to anyone outside the family. It's no big deal. It's just a quiet place to go whenever things get me down."

Sybil began to laugh, then stopped abruptly. "Well, you certainly have a load of problems on your plate this time. What you're going through would be enough to get anyone down."

He bit his lower lip. "Sybil, you know they're all lies. All those things you've heard about what I did to Scott Robinson are lies. I wouldn't dream of hurting Scott. We were closer than brothers."

She nodded grimly. "I was telling James that same exact thing. You and Scott were like brothers. It must have been a terrible shock when you heard he'd been killed that way…shot in the back of the head of all things." She shuddered.

"Not only that he'd been killed," Horace replied. "But knowing the people I swore to protect thought I was the one who killed him." He dropped his head sadly. "That was the worst part of all. I can't begin to tell you how badly that tormented me."

Sybil reached over and squeezed his hand. "You poor dear man," she said sympathetically. "I know it's been awful for you…and poor Adele, too. She has to bear the brunt of all that horrific gossip."

Horace frowned, knowing he was sitting beside the most notorious gossip on the east coast. "You can turn right at the next road," he instructed. "Better slow down. The road is gravel."

She slowed as directed and made the turn without either of them straining their seat belts. The road was riddled with potholes; some covered with pine needles, some deeper and filled with mud. "Maybe I should get out and walk the rest of the way," he mumbled. "This is putting your car through an awful lot of unnecessary torture."

"Nonsense," she replied quickly. "I'm doing a favor for a friend. Don't you worry one iota about my car; it will be just fine."

Horace pointed to a narrow opening between a cluster of pine trees. "Turn left here," he said. "The cabin's up ahead."

She followed his instructions as the car dipped and grunted.

"That's it," he said proudly, pointing straight ahead. "We made it."

Sybil looked at the small cabin and frowned. No wonder he hadn't bragged about it, she thought. It looked like an old-time shanty.

Horace climbed out quickly and stretched. "I'd invite you inside," he said facetiously. "But the place is a wreck. I haven't been up here in a long time." He forced a smile. "The place lacks a woman's touch."

He thanked her once again and closed the door. Then he started walking toward the cabin. He stopped suddenly, hearing the unmistakable sound of a rifle being cocked. The familiar sound made the hairs on the back of his neck prickle. When he turned around, Sybil was standing outside her car, pointing it right between his eyes.

"Sybil?" he asked, sounding more confused than frightened. "What are you doing with that rifle?"

Sybil's face twitched as she answered. "This is such a perfect, quiet place. You know, I was wondering how I was going to do this, but you've made my assignment so much easier."

He scowled at her use of the word assignment. It was one of the preacher's favorites.

THE BABY SOLDIERS

She chortled loudly. "You actually didn't believe Clifford was going to forgive and forget the way you bungled the Robinson murder, did you?"

Horace didn't move a muscle. He knew that whatever he did, he must remain calm at all costs. He'd always thought Sybil was a little nutty when it came to her zealousness over the preacher. But now he realized she was quite insane. He decided it best to play along with her. "Sybil, I think you should know the truth. Reverend Jacobson was the one who ordered me to kill Scott Robinson. I had no choice. I was merely following orders."

"I talked to Clifford about that," she said smugly. "We're very close, you know. He explained he had good reasons for wanting Robinson out of the organization. He was a dirty, little man."

Horace moved a little closer. If he could get within range of the gun, he'd be able to take it away from her. But the way her hands was shaking, he didn't want to make any sudden move that would alarm her. He figured he'd hold off until he'd calmed her down some more.

"Clifford thought you would have had enough common sense to take Scott somewhere besides his own office to kill him. Really, Horace! Can you imagine those darling children walking into that office Monday morning and seeing their principal's brains and blood spattered all over the walls? You should have been more discreet."

His mouth gaped open in disbelief. He couldn't believe any of this was happening. Did Jacobson really think Sybil Kelsey was clever enough to take him out? If the preacher was planning on killing him, the least he could have done was hire one of his professional goons, not some fruitcake who couldn't do anything right if her life depended on it. What in the hell was that fool thinking?

Horace would never learn the answers to his questions. The last thing he heard was a cracking explosion inside his head.

— 269 —

CHAPTER FORTY-SEVEN

After shooting Horace Woolard, Sybil Kelsey thought the toughest part of her assignment was over. No one ever told her how difficult it was to move a dead body. By the time she finished dragging Horace into the densely wooded area behind his cabin, with nothing to guide her plight but the lights from her car, she was so exhausted she could have bawled her eyes out. She rolled him into an unused irrigation ditch and covered him with twigs, fallen branches and dried leaves that were scattered about. When she finished, she stood over his grave and muttered a quick prayer for his poor soul.

She brushed her hands down the front of her slacks and staggered back toward her car, hoping she wouldn't die of a heart attack out here, in the middle of this desolate wilderness. The moment she opened the car door, the heat blowing through the open vents stung her face and hands, making them feel like they were on fire.

"Oh, sweet Jesus," she cried softly, looking down at her soiled clothing. Traces of fresh blood, grass stains and clay from the ground behind the cabin were everywhere. She hadn't thought to bring along a change of clothing. Raking her fingers down her face, she trembled. She would have to wear the filthy outfit and pray her car didn't get stuck in the mud, or have a flat tire before she got home.

By the time Sybil passed Suffolk on her way east to Virginia Beach, she had calmed considerably. She had reenacted Horace Woolard's demise a thousand times as the miles rolled by. When Reverend Jacobson told her it was her duty to kill Horace Woolard, she didn't actually believe she could go through with it. But it hadn't been all that difficult. She was talking to him one minute, and then, pop, he was gone. She had never killed anything in her life before. She couldn't get over how simple it was. Then she frowned, wondering if the man who killed Robbie had felt the same way.

Sybil pulled into the driveway, noticing a light burning in James' study window. She padded inside and went directly to the laundry room. There, she peeled off every bit of clothing and stuffed everything into the washing machine. She inhaled raggedly. Now, all she had to do was make it to the bathroom without James seeing her. She leaned against the laundry room door, listening for footsteps. Hearing none, she opened the door and scampered down the hall to the bathroom. Once inside, she locked the door behind her.

The steaming water spraying over her felt wonderful, even though Sybil doubted she'd ever feel completely clean again. She stood motionless for the longest time, letting the water sooth her taut muscles. As long as James remained in his study, she'd have time to dispose of her unsightly shoes and ruined clothing. She knew she'd never be able to wear the outfit again, and burning it in the fireplace could be risky. She decided the best thing to do would be to scrub it the best she could, then take it to the thrift store on the boulevard. Some poor woman who didn't know the history behind it, would consider it a wonderful bargain.

Sybil climbed from the shower stall and wrapped a long towel around her body, absorbing the excess moisture. Then she grabbed a smaller one and wrapped it around her dripping hair. After slipping into a bathrobe, which she was grateful she'd forgotten to put away, she opened the bathroom door and gasped. James stood in the center of the hallway, staring down at the newspaper he was holding.

"What in the world are you doing, standing out here?" she asked accusingly. "You nearly scared me to death."

James's expression didn't change as he continued to read. Then he looked up from the paper and blinked. "I received the strangest phone call," he said as though he were in a trance.

Sybil's guilty heart skipped a beat. She recovered quickly. "Considering the horrid things you write about, I'm surprised you don't get more of those than you do."

"Hmmm," he replied curiously.

She lowered her arms to her sides. "All right, James. Tell me about it."

"It was from that preacher friend of yours."

Sybil's mouth gaped open. "Reverend Jacobson?"

He nodded.

"I wonder why on earth he would want to talk to me?"

James shook his head from side to side. "I haven't the foggiest. When he asked to speak to you, I told him your aunt was ill and you'd gone to check on her. Whatever he wanted, he sounded like it was really important."

"That is odd, isn't it?" she said, drying her hair. "I wonder what in the world he wanted?"

James shrugged. "I told him I'd be sure to give you the message. He said to have you call him back as soon as you returned." James rolled the newspaper up and chuckled. "Maybe he wants you to play the Virgin Mary in the Christmas play this year."

She eyed him hatefully. "That's not very funny."

He shrugged unconcerned. "You know, Sybil, once you get involved with radical people like him, you never know what he's going to expect from you."

Sybil pursed her lips, her mind reeling. "Well, I did fill out a form at church a few weeks ago, volunteering to do whatever I could to organize a new anti-abortion demonstration down here." She fluttered her lashes pretentiously. "Do you think that could be why he called?"

James cleared his throat. "Maybe it's time you got away from that group. It probably wouldn't hurt if you developed some other interests."

Her dark eyes narrowed. "I'm very happy with the interests I already have, thank you very much. I only wish you were more active...the way you used to be."

He snorted. "That was when I was young and foolish. The last thing I need is one of your preacher friends calling me up and asking me to picket something or other. Count me out."

"Are you hungry?" she asked, attempting to change the subject. "I could fix you a snack before you go back to the study."

"I wouldn't want you to exert yourself," he quipped.

Sybil arched her back. "James, are you trying to make me feel guilty?"

He groaned. "Whatever would give you a crazy idea like that?"

She removed the towel from her hair, clutching it in her right hand. "I don't know. Sometimes I get the feeling you don't think I'm a very good wife."

He eyed her skeptically. "Maybe you don't need another interest to fill your time. Maybe you need a shrink."

Sybil pushed him out of the way and marched across the master bedroom. "I suppose you'll be late coming to bed again?" she said argumentatively.

James stood at the bedroom door, watching her search through her underwear drawer like a dog, digging for a bone. "I have a lot to do. I'll see you later."

"Yes. You be sure to do that," she replied huffily.

CHAPTER FORTY-EIGHT

James Kelsey drove the big Chrysler slowly down the tree-lined street. The lights were on early in a number of the homes he passed. Real families, seated around the table, passing toast and jelly, discussing their plans for the day. How long had it been since he'd enjoyed little things like having breakfast with a family? His eyes began to seep. The last time he remembered sitting around a table having any kind of civilized discussion was before Robbie died. An immeasurable loss seized him, an ache that pierced all the way to his soul. He didn't have a family anymore. From the time James was eighteen, he dreamed that one day, he'd have a family to provide for and be proud of. That dream ended the day Robbie was murdered in front of the Nelson Clinic. He stopped at a traffic light and rested his furrowed brow on the steering wheel. "Oh, Robbie," he muttered softly. "I miss you so much."

———

Clifford Jacobson slammed the newspaper down on his desk, and bellowed, "What in the hell does that stupid fool think he's doing?"

Byron Spears set a fresh pot of coffee on the table across the room, his face grim. He had already read the article about the president's decision to eliminate churches from their coveted tax-free status.

"That ungrateful bastard! Do you have any idea how much money we've donated to him over the past six years?"

Spears knew exactly how much, since he wrote the checks. "What do you suppose possessed him to do a thing like that?" he asked.

THE BABY SOLDIERS

"Well, I can promise you one thing," Jacobson spat. "He'll never get another dime from me! And I know for a fact the other church leaders will agree with me. That man has just committed political suicide!"

Spears nodded thoughtfully. "The president is acting quite brazen all of a sudden. He can't run for another term, so he thinks he doesn't need his old friends anymore."

Jacobson leapt from his chair and began to pace. "I'll show him what he needs," he hissed. "By the time I get through cutting his perks, he won't be able to hail a cab to Burger King."

Spears bowed as he departed. The preacher had the power to back up his threats all right. He owned the companies that fueled and serviced the president's aircraft and his motorcade. He held mortgages on the homes of his drivers, his housekeeping staff, and half of the members of his cabinet. He even held notes on the gambling debts of the vice president, the secretary of state, and the attorney general. And last but not least, he had those incriminating pictures of the first daughter, which were taken in Europe the previous year. Pictures Scott Robinson had paid someone two thousand dollars for of the two of them, coupled in the most peculiar position. Spears was certain that President Carlson wouldn't want those pictures to turn up in the tabloids. His own sex-capades had become infamous enough. What a shame it would be to see his daughter's life ruined before it ever really began.

Spears touched the intercom. "Reverend, I have President Carlson on the line."

"Good," Jacobson muttered. "It's time we set him straight."

After Jacobson had completed his conversation with the President, Spears buzzed him a second time. "Sybil Kelsey wishes to speak with you," he said.

Clifford Jacobson smiled glibly as he picked up the receiver. "Good morning, Sybil," he said brightly. "I tried to call you at home last night, but James said you were off taking care of a sick rela-

— 275 —

tive—you foxy devil. I was concerned when I didn't hear from you right away."

"No need to be concerned," she assured him. "The assignment was completed per your instructions. It took longer than expected."

A surge of relief spread through him. His eyes sparkled like silver coins. "Tell me all the details," he said excitedly.

When Sybil finished telling him about the place where she'd killed Horace, and how she'd covered the grave with twigs and dried leaves, so it wouldn't look any different from the rest of the area, she waited expectantly for his response.

"You have proven yourself a devoted servant," he replied smugly.

She stood stunned, holding the dead receiver in her hand. He hung up? There were no accolades, no mention of a reward, or promise of a lucrative position in the New Order. "He...he called me a servant," she muttered bitterly. Then she dropped the receiver into its cradle and began to cry.

Sybil was still blubbering when the phone rang again. She drank some water to clear her throat before answering. "Hello?" she replied hoarsely.

"Sybil, it's Clifford."

She sat ram rod straight, thinking that he'd called back to give her the praise she so richly deserved. Perhaps he had to cut their earlier conversation short due to some interruption.

"Yes, Clifford" she said, her mood brightening.

"Mr. Woolard was supposed to take care of an urgent matter for us. But he had been dragging his feet in recent weeks. After your performance last night, I know we can count on you to complete the assignment he left unfinished."

"Wh...what is it?" she stammered.

"Get some paper and a pen," he ordered. "I want you to write this down."

"I have it," she replied, an uneasy feeling spread through her.

"I'm going to give you a list of names of people who must be eliminated...for the good of the organization," he added quickly.

— 276 —

"Since you are aware how urgent this is, I'm sure you'll want to get started right away." Then he rattled off a list of names.

An icy fear raced through her veins. "K....Kerry Trivane?" She muttered, not recognizing the other names. "Why her?"

"No questions, now," he said, admonishing her. "The less you know the better, for your sake as well as all concerned. I merely expect you to do as you're told. A servant's job is to carry out his master's commands."

Sybil's hands trembled violently as she hung up the telephone. "Oh, God," she moaned. "What have I done?"

CHAPTER FORTY-NINE

Morehead City, North Carolina. The brick structure of the old hospital building had two entrances facing Bridges Street. One had been for walk-ins, the other for emergencies. Nothing about the old building suggested it had been constructed for any other purpose than housing the sick and the angels of mercy intent on healing them. For generations, the hospital had served the community well. But in recent years, the city had expanded to accommodate an influx of diversified businesses and cash wielding tourists. High-priced restaurants and condominiums staked their claims along the oceanfront, where lovers had once strolled on hot summer nights, and avid fishermen had captured their bounty beneath the waking sun. The curse of progress soon found the old hospital inadequate. A new building twice its size had been erected to appease a more sophisticated cliental and a medical staff from across the country.

Amy Patterson had spent nearly all the money she'd raised for the down payment on the old hospital building. She was grateful that donations continued to come in from people brave enough to risk taking part in her venture. Many of the donations were from the family and friends of girls, who'd joined the cause after leaving the camp in search of their babies.

Bernie and Priscilla Trivane followed Danny Woolard down the brightly lit main corridor, listening attentively as he explained the various services which would be provided once the child care facility was in full operation. Half the rooms on the main floor had been refurbished and designated as offices. They were currently

— 278 —

THE BABY SOLDIERS

overflowing with stacks of files, containing confidential information on the girls forcibly detained at the camp, including blood types and other pertinent information that Margaret Hatchey had graciously obtained.

Priscilla's sapphire eyes twinkled brightly beneath fluorescent lights. "There must be hundreds of files here," she whispered in disbelief.

Danny nodded grimly. "We sure have our work cut out for us."

"How in the world do you plan on finding all those children?" Bernie asked skeptically.

Danny grabbed a metal chair and spun it around, straddling it backwards. "When Amy and some of the other girls at the shelter first came up with this idea, no one took them very seriously...including myself." He looked at the Trivanes and smiled self-consciously. "I think my reaction was based mainly on fear. A lot of people were afraid to get involved. So much had already happened to them. Abortion clinics were being bombed on a regular basis. And every time you turned around, a family with established roots mysteriously disappeared."

Bernie pursed his lips. "Like ours."

"We know what it's like to be afraid," Priscilla replied glumly.

Danny searched her face thoughtfully. "You were afraid, but you're not anymore. Look at you," he smiled. "You're both here, ready and willing to do anything you can to help us find the children and bring them here to be taken care of until their parents are located."

"Are there many more like us?" Bernie asked mindfully.

"Yes, but not nearly enough," Danny replied. "But the numbers are growing every day. Having Margaret Hatchey join us was a big shock, as well as a needed boost to our morale."

Priscilla asked, confused. "Just who is this Margaret Hatchey?"

Danny smoothed his hand over his dark hair. "Margaret Hatchey was one of the guards at the camp," he explained. "She was privy to a lot of stuff none of the rest of them knew anything about."

Bernie studied him warily. "You seem to know an awful lot about this camp?"

Danny's shoulders shriveled. "I guess you could say I was involved, too. Although, I didn't know anything that was going on inside the place."

"How so?" Bernie asked.

Danny folded his arms over the back of the chair. "I used to be one of the drivers who took the girls out of there after they had their babies." He chuffed. "I thought I was working for some swanky limo service, until I started talking to some of the guys on the inside who hung out at the local video arcade. They told me the camp wasn't an exclusive fat farm."

Priscilla's eyes narrowed. "Fat farm?"

Danny sighed. "I was so naive. You know," he explained."You go in fat and then you come out skinny.' He mused miserably. "Of course, my father may have led me to believe that. He sighed heavily. "Problem was, none of the girls would talk about it. I'd just pick them up and drop them off at the bus station, or wherever address they gave me."

"Unbelievable," Bernie muttered.

"The day I was sent to pick up Rebecca Corbitt, changed everything for me."

"How so?" Priscilla asked.

"When I tried to drop her off at the bus station, she started yelling and screaming like a drill sergeant." He laughed. "Rebecca is only five foot tall, but she sounds a lot bigger than that. Anyway, she insisted I take her to some bank at the beach."

"What did you do?" Priscilla asked.

"I took her of course. She told me she'd make it worth my while."

"Hmmm," Bernie replied skeptically.

"After we left the bank, she made me take her to a real estate office."

Priscilla scowled. "Real estate office. What in the world for?"

THE BABY SOLDIERS

Danny grinned. "She told me she was going to buy a house. Just like that."

"And I assume she did," Bernie said.

Danny expanded his chest proudly. "She did. Although she admitted she had a lot of help. She called it The Haven. Rebecca told me everything. She said I had an honest face. She trusted me." He blushed. "No one ever said they trusted me before."

"Rebecca never went to the authorities to tell them what had happened to her?" Priscilla asked incredulously.

Danny gawked at her. "Who was she going to tell, my father? Besides, Rebecca said we had to be careful. We couldn't trust anyone."

Bernie shook his head. "Damn. That really put you right in the middle, didn't it? Knowing Horace, he was probably responsible for starting the camp to begin with. His way of dealing with the damned abortion phenomena."

"You really think he was responsible for Kerry's kidnapping, don't you?" Danny asked.

"And Robbie Kelsey's murder," Priscilla replied, her voice wavering.

Danny lowered his head. "There was a time when I thought my dad was a hero. I used to get all hyped up every time he talked about this new organization he belonged to. He claimed they were going to solve all the problems of the world. They were going to stamp out crime and cure disease. Jesus," he muttered. "I was such a dumb little shit."

Bernie gripped Danny's shoulder. "There's no way you could have known what they were doing."

Danny took two folding chairs off the stack by the door and opened them. Bernie and Priscilla sat down.

"I remember when the Kelseys were involved with that group," Bernie said.

"Me, too," Priscilla said, rolling her eyes. "Once Horace and Scott Robinson started bragging about all the good they were going to do, Sybil and James became like clones. They couldn't think or talk for themselves anymore. It was frightening." She said, shivering from the memory.

Bernie nodded grimly. "I remember the day Kerry told us she was..."

Danny shifted uncomfortably.

"Pregnant," Priscilla said, finishing for him. "When the Kelseys found out Kerry was pregnant, they were beside themselves. Naturally, we expected Robbie and Kerry would get married. But James put his foot down. His son wasn't going to get married and ruin his whole life. So...we assumed they would go along with our decision to have Kerry get an abortion."

"The children were much too young to be faced with that kind of responsibility," Priscilla explained. "Besides, we wanted Kerry to finish her education before starting a family."

Bernie took out a roll of Lifesavers and passed it around. "Sybil hit the roof when we mentioned abortion. She started yapping about how abortion was the same as murder, and we were no better than murderers ourselves, forcing our daughter to kill an innocent baby."

Priscilla paled. "She actually sounded possessed."

Danny leaned forward. "Did Mrs. Kelsey say Robbie would help Kerry raise the baby if she didn't go through with the abortion?"

Bernie snorted. "Surely you jest? They didn't want their precious son tied down with some little whore and her bastard child." His face was crimson as he glanced from Danny to Priscilla."That's what they called her when they found out she was pregnant."

Priscilla's lips tightened, remembering that day. "The way they carried on, you'd have thought Kerry got pregnant just so she could ruin Robbie's life."

Danny nodded. "My dad's the same way. He goes around preaching about the evils of abortion, but he doesn't care what happens to all those kids who get born that nobody wants." He stared off into space. "Dad should know better than anyone what happens to kids that no one wants. He's seen enough burned and mangled bodies over the years."

THE BABY SOLDIERS

Bernie stood up, adjusting the belt on his jeans. "I bet you never heard one of them anti-abortionists agree to adopt one of the precious little darlings, did you?"

"Fat chance," Danny said. "Besides, I'd feel kind of sorry for any baby who got dropped into one of their laps. They'd have to grow up listening to the same crap I had to listen to."

Priscilla stared at him sympathetically. "Your mother wasn't like that, Danny."

He sighed. "No, she wasn't. But you saw what happened to her, because she wouldn't conform?"

Priscilla closed her eyes and nodded.

"What do you think happened to all the children who were born at that camp, Danny?" Bernie asked.

Danny scowled, remembering what Amy had told him. "The boys were taken to a secret place where they'll grow up to be soldiers. The girls were sold to anyone who had enough money to buy them. I guess if you bought a baby, you could raise it to be anything you wanted, like having your own personal slave."

"That's disgusting!" Priscilla shivered.

Danny shrugged. "Not as far as the organization is concerned. The way those fanatics see it, everyone benefits."

"Everyone benefits," Bernie repeated the words slowly. "What about the girls like Kerry, who were kidnapped and taken to the camp against their wills? How did they benefit from being forced to have children and then cast out to survive anyway they could?"

Danny's shoulders slumped. "Don't get angry with me, Mr. Trivane. I didn't have a thing to do with any of that."

"I know, Danny," Bernie muttered. "I just don't know who I'm supposed to be angry with. What makes it even worse is I'm to blame, too."

Danny nodded understandingly. "When I found out that group Dad was meeting with was responsible for the camp where the girls were taken, I didn't know what to do. I guess I figured everybody who was anybody was involved somehow. I even thought of leaving

— 283 —

the country, just to get away from them. But I figured it would make it that much tougher on Mom and my brothers."

"Horace took all his frustration out on your mother," Priscilla said sadly. "I remember her showing me the bruises. I begged her to get away from him, but she was too afraid. 'He's a policeman,' she'd tell me. 'The rest of them know what he's like. They don't care what happens to me. No one would take my word against his.'"

Priscilla rubbed her arms. "I felt so helpless."

Danny shifted uncomfortably. "I think it made him feel like a real man when he made people afraid of him."

Priscilla nodded.

"Kerry told me you moved away after she was kidnapped." Danny said, turning from Priscilla to Bernie. "Did you think she was dead, like Robbie?"

Bernie got up slowly and peered out the window. He blamed their sudden exodus on Horace, too. "I figured Kerry probably told you all about that."

Danny shrugged. "She told me a little."

Bernie pursed his lips."Did she tell you about the threatening phone calls in the middle of the night, or about Jimmy being attacked on his way home from school?"

Danny's eyes widened. "No. Really?"

Priscilla squirmed in her chair. "We had our suspicions, of course, but no proof. At first, I thought Jimmy had gotten into a fight over something that happened at school. But Jimmy didn't know who stabbed him. He said the person was a lot older. Then I started thinking about the phone calls warning us to get out of Virginia. I figured Sybil Kelsey was behind it somehow." She paused. "And your father."

Danny frowned. "Jimmy was stabbed?"

Bernie nodded. "Thank God it wasn't that serious. Like Priscilla said, there just wasn't any proof." He stared directly into Danny's eyes. "We didn't want the same thing that happened to Robbie to happen to our boy. We didn't want him dead, too. So, we cleared out."

THE BABY SOLDIERS

Danny's eyes shifted thoughtfully. "Couldn't you have told someone about the calls and who you thought was responsible for stabbing Jimmy? What about David Williams?"

Bernie snorted. "We didn't want to get David involved. Your father was his boss. Besides, what could David do, march up to him and say, I know some people who think you're behind the kidnappings at the abortion clinic and the Kelsey boy's murder?"

Danny shook his head. "Yeah. And David's family was missing, too."

Priscilla rubbed her chapped lips. "Right after Robbie's funeral, the phone calls started. We were told to get out of town, or the same thing that happened to Robbie could happen again."

"I guess the Kelsey's were pretty shook up when Robbie got killed," Danny said. "Maybe it was them, blaming you for what happened."

"In the beginning," Bernie told him. "I was pissed. I was determined to find out who was calling and put an end to it."

Priscilla paled. "Then my brakes went out while I was visiting my sister in Richmond. The mechanic said the brake line had been cut."

Bernie's face contorted. "Not long after that, somebody threw a torch through my office window. Thank God, my men were able to clear the area without anyone getting hurt."

The trembling in Priscilla's hands was more noticeable. "Bernie, tell him about the mailbox."

Danny's eyes widened as he stared at Bernie.

"It was a few days later, when I came home from work. I was about to check the mailbox, as was my usual routine, when one of the neighborhood kids rode up on his bike and told me he saw a scary looking man put something in my mail box. I called the cops. When they came out to take a look, they found a homemade bomb inside."

Priscilla inhaled sharply. Bernie rubbed her shoulders.

"After the police left, I went inside and checked the answering machine. There was a message saying, "You won't be so lucky next time."

— 285 —

Danny shook his head in disbelief. "I had no idea. I wonder if the other families that left town unexpectedly had experienced the same things you did?"

Bernie's face was ashen. "I think whoever was behind it was afraid we might all band together and fight back."

"Strength in numbers," Danny mumbled.

Bernie nodded. "As long as we were scattered and running scared, those animals were safe."

Danny nodded.

"We even hired a private detective."

Danny blinked. "Was he a local guy?"

Bernie frowned, trying to remember his name. "Jenkins...or was it Jennings?"

Priscilla clicked her fingers. "It was Fred...Fred Jenson."

"Oh, brother," Danny mumbled wryly.

The Trivanes gawked at him. "Do you know him?" Bernie asked.

Danny sighed heavily. "He was one of the guards at the camp. He probably told whoever was in charge that you were still poking around."

Priscilla reached out, grabbing Bernie's arm. "Oh, God, Bernie! It was right after we hired him when Jimmy was stabbed!"

Bernie rubbed the stubble on his chin. "It seems like everyone is involved in the corruption somehow. None of it makes any sense."

Danny stood quickly. "What makes sense is that you're here right now. Tomorrow, you'll meet with some of the others who've come to help. They'll be able to tell you what they've been doing to find where the babies were taken."

Bernie looked into his wife's haggard face. "Kerry wants to find her baby very much, Danny."

Priscilla's eyes misted. "And so do we."

Danny nodded. "Kerry told me that she never really wanted to go through with the abortion."

Bernie grimaced. "I know. I've beaten myself up a thousand times over that. If I had just stayed out of it, everything would have worked out okay…Robbie Kelsey would still be alive…and Kerry would have her baby."

Danny forced a smile. "Sounds like Sybil Kelsey knew what she was talking about."

Bernie looked at him, dazed. "Well, if we committed a sin, we've certainly paid a hell of a price for it."

"Mom says there's a reason for everything that happens, good or bad." Danny said.

Bernie blinked. "Maybe she's right."

Pricilla rose to her feet. "I think it's time we got to work."

CHAPTER FIFTY

Margaret Hatchey carried her tea cup into the living room and turned on the television set. She hoped to catch a few minutes of the local news before leaving to join the others in Carolina. When the squiggly lines and the snow finally cleared from the screen, she was startled to see the somber reflection of Clifford Jacobson, his arms extended like Christ crucified. Margaret had seen the imposing portrayal a million times during the course of her brother-in-law's career. It never ceased to unnerve her. He actually did believe he was God. She'd been so busy helping Amy Patterson; she hadn't kept abreast of his current agenda. She studied his posture grimly, wondering if he was on another phony crusade to lure more members into the organization. Whatever his objective, she thought, he certainly appeared abnormally distraught. She wasn't used to seeing dark crescents beneath his eyes, or his silvery hair disheveled. He was a proud, arrogant man, who'd always insisted on having his hair professionally coifed, and his face made up to conceal any signs of aging. She considered changing the channel, but her curiosity got the best of her. She turned up the volume.

"Beloved friends in God," he started. "Today, I have some disturbing news to share with you." He winced, prolonging the effect of the words to follow. "Last night, Sybil Kelsey, wife of news editor, James Kelsey, called my home in Baltimore." He clutched his chest dramatically. "Sybil confessed that she had committed a grievous sin. She said she had murdered Captain Horace Woolard at his country cabin west of Suffolk."

— 288 —

Margaret dropped her teacup. It hit the hardwood floor and shattered, splaying tea in all directions.

The preacher closed his eyes and remained silent for a long time. Margaret thought he looked as though he'd fallen asleep.

"This terrible news is particularly devastating, because Sybil Kelsey and Captain Woolard have both been dedicated members of our church family for many years. Those of you who know Sybil can attest to what a fine, giving person she was."

He walked across the stage slowly, gathering his thoughts. "In recent weeks, Sybil had been very distraught over the tragic death of her close friend, Scott Robinson, the principal of Justice Academy. There had been rumors that Captain Woolard was responsible for taking his life."

Margaret groaned.

Jacobson's shoulders slumped like a man beleaguered by the inhuman behavior of his fellow man. Then his steely eyes stared straight into the camera. "Sybil Kelsey is no stranger to tragedy. Last year, her only son was shot down like a dog outside an abortion clinic in Virginia Beach."

Margaret's ears were ringing as she lowered herself onto the sofa.

"Early this morning," Jacobson continued, "deputies of the Greensville County Sheriff's Department found Captain Woolard's body, right where Sybil said she had buried it. Sybil is undergoing a great deal of emotional turmoil and believes that justice has been done because of her actions."

He raised his hands once again. "Please, do not judge our sister too harshly. Let us pray for her and the souls of the misguided who live among us."

Margaret shook her head from side to side as she knelt down to pick up fragments of the broken cup. She had never seen Clifford give a more compassionate or convincing performance. She didn't know Sybil Kelsey well, having spoken to her only briefly during the rallies, but she seriously doubted the hawk-faced woman would take it upon herself to kill Captain Woolard.

Margaret stayed within the sixty-mile speed limit from the time she left Virginia Beach until she reached the North Carolina State line. Then she stepped it up to seventy.

She thought about Clifford Jacobson, Scott Robinson, Captain Woolard, and finally Sybil Kelsey, and she wondered if the whole world had gone completely mad.

After crossing the bridge over the Neuse River, she turned east on Route 70, which would take her all the way to Morehead City. She estimated she'd arrive at her destination within the hour. One more hour before she saw the others. She wondered if Danny knew his father was dead. If not, she hoped the Trivanes had heard the news and had passed it onto him. She hated to be the bearer of bad news.

Trucks and vans bearing construction logos were parked near the emergency entrance of the old hospital building. The deafening whine of electric saws, and pounding hammers greeted Margaret as she parked her car. She smiled. Amy's list of volunteers continued to grow. She opened the trunk to remove three boxes filled with documents, which she had copied from confidential files at the camp. As she carried one of them toward the building, she realized just how heavy they were. She decided to send one of the volunteers back to bring in the rest of the boxes.

Danny's infectious laughter gave Margaret a start. She followed it down the long corridor, past the elevators, thinking of the unpleasant task that lay ahead. It was evident no one had as yet told him about his father's death.

Priscilla Trivane stood on a metal chair painting window trim a cheery yellow. Her husband, Bernie, crawled along the floor across the room, sanding old paint from the woodwork. Danny was perched atop a ladder in the center of the room, rolling white paint onto the ceiling. Margaret walked in and dropped the box unceremoniously on the floor. Priscilla and Bernie jumped, then spun around and

THE BABY SOLDIERS

glared at the intruder. Danny grinned as he jumped off the ladder, wiping paint smudges from his fingers.

"Margaret," he said brightly. "I was wondering if you were going to be able to make it." Glancing over his shoulder, he said, "These are Kerry's folks, Bernie and Priscilla Trivane."

Margaret crossed the room, extending her right hand. "I'm glad you're here. Kerry's told me so much about you."

Priscilla's face reddened. "We didn't mean to stare at you the way we did when you first walked in. We thought…"

"I understand," Margaret replied, waving her off. "For all you know, I could have been the enemy."

Danny howled. "It wasn't that long ago when you were."

"Behave yourself, Danny," Margaret chided.

Bernie found a chair that wasn't spattered with paint and carried it over to Margaret. "Take a load off. I'm sure you must be tired after your trip."

She thanked the brawny man and sat down, folding her arms over her chest. "It wasn't too bad," she replied."The drive is a lot worse during the summer months."

Bernie chuckled. "I remember it well, bumper to bumper all the way."

"Any good news from the beach?" Danny asked cheerfully.

Margaret studied his handsome, intelligent features. He seemed to get better looking every time she saw him. She thought it was a lucky thing for him that he hadn't inherited his father's pasty complexion or miserable disposition. "Danny," she said thoughtfully. "Can you sit down for a minute?"

"Sure," he answered. His eyes narrowed quizzically as he reached for a chair. "You look so serious. Is something wrong?"

Margaret's heart ached as she stared into his questioning eyes. The Trivanes stood motionless; their eyes fixated on the portly woman seated in front of them. Margaret glanced from Danny to the Trivanes and then coughed nervously.

— 291 —

"Danny, I hate to be the one to tell you." She took a deep breath, unable to find a way to put it off any longer. "Danny, your father is dead. I heard it on the TV right before I left home. He was murdered."

"Wh…what?" Danny said, sinking heavily into the chair.

Although neither of the Trivanes gave a rat's ass about Horace Woolard, they gasped in surprise.

"How? How did it happen?" Danny stammered.

"I don't know all the details," Margaret replied. "Jacobson held a news conference on CBS. He claims Sybil Kelsey confessed to killing your father. Apparently, she killed him at his cabin in the country."

"Sybil Kelsey?" Priscilla said, frowning. "Why that's insane."

"What cabin?" Danny asked, looking more confused by the minute.

Margaret gazed over their stunned faces. "There are still a lot of unanswered questions. But I tend to agree with Mrs. Trivane. I can't imagine Sybil Kelsey killing anyone, unless she did it with that acid tongue of hers."

"Jacobson made her do it," Danny replied matter-of-factly. "After all those people started accusing Dad of killing Mr. Robinson, the preacher probably figured…"

He ran his hands through his dark hair, blinking rapidly. "Why would he say Mrs. Kelsey did it? Everybody knows she's a witch, but I don't believe she killed Dad either. If she did, she didn't do it by herself."

Margaret cradled her over-sized handbag. "Clifford said Sybil was despondent over what had happened to Scott Robinson. He gave the impression that Sybil and Scott were the best of friends. He said she's under observation in a hospital right now. They'll probably have her talk to a shrink and that will be the end of it. The way Clifford was talking, it sounded as though Sybil couldn't wait for the Lord to dole out Horace's punishment for killing Robinson, so she took the matter into her own hands."

— 292 —

THE BABY SOLDIERS

Bernie placed his foot on one of the chairs, rubbing his leg. "I don't know why you all find it hard to believe Sybil Kelsey could kill someone? I don't doubt it for a second."

Priscilla gawked at him in disbelief. "Bernie, what are you saying?"

"Remember the way she used to get all worked up whenever she was talking about the girls who had abortions? Those beady little eyes of hers were like poison darts, ready to stick into anyone who didn't think the same way she did."

"Really, Bernie," Priscilla said exasperated. "If looks could kill, Sybil would have killed just about everyone in town."

Danny sat thoughtfully between them.

Margaret touched his arm gently. "Danny, I'm sorry."

"Don't be," he said, shaking his head. "You're probably going to think it's awful for me to say, but I'm glad he's dead. If I had the guts, I would have killed him myself."

Priscilla nodded understandingly. "Because of what he put your mom through?"

"Yeah," he replied. "Now she can start living like a human being again."

Bernie poured some turpentine into an empty can and dunked the paintbrushes they'd been using into it. "Well, folks, I think we've done enough work for one day. "What do you say we go back to the hotel and get cleaned up? I'll spring for dinner."

"I haven't done anything, yet," Margaret told him. "But I'm always ready to eat."

"I know a terrific place on Atlantic Beach," Danny said. "Amy took me there the last time we came here."

"If it was good enough to satisfy Miss Amy," Margaret chuckled. "I'm sure it will be good enough for the rest of us."

———

Jason shifted nervously as he glanced at the different colored caskets in the basement of the mortuary. Adele had suggested he stay home with Mark, but he told her he'd be okay to go with her. He didn't think making funeral arrangements for his father was something she should do alone.

A tall, painfully thin man, dressed in a traditional black suit and white shirt, approached them. He introduced himself as Michael Smith and shook Jason's hand. He looked somberly at Adele and nodded. Mr. Smith then began to explain the differences between the caskets. When he stated the more elite models contained thick innerspring mattresses, for the comfort of the beloved family member, Adele burst out laughing.

The man's charcoal eyes narrowed. "I don't understand what you find so amusing about that?" he said haughtily.

Adele clung onto Jason's arm, unable to stop laughing. After a few moments, she regained her composure. "I'm sorry," she said, fanning herself with her hand. "But just the thought of a dead person knowing whether he's lying on a firm innerspring mattress or a bed of nails strikes me as totally preposterous."

Jason looked down at his shoes and nodded.

Mr. Smith shifted his attention to the caskets. "It's my job to assist the bereaved in choosing the best possible resting places we have to offer. Most of the people we do business with want the very best for their loved ones—after all, this will be their last opportunity to show the departed how loved and respected they were."

He forced a smile. "We also offer a wonderful display of monuments."

Adele's face was somber. "We don't want a monument either. All we want is a basic coffin—the cheaper the better."

The undertaker stepped back aghast. "But Captain Woolard was such a respected member of our community; I was certain you would want..."

"Look," Adele said, annoyed. "If all those people who respected him so much want to give him an elaborate funeral, let them. My husband left a token life insurance policy. He was afraid that if he left a sizable amount of insurance, the children and I would be able

THE BABY SOLDIERS

to live in reasonable comfort. And he certainly didn't want that. He wanted us to be just as miserable after he died as we were while he was living. Now, if our business down here is finished, I have more important things to do."

The man spun quickly on his heels. "If you will follow me to my office, we'll do the paperwork."

Adele turned to Jason and winked. "Thanks for coming along," she whispered. "I couldn't have gotten through this without you."

Jason smiled as he followed her up the padded stairs. It felt good, hearing her say she needed him.

CHAPTER FIFTY-ONE

President Carlson agreed with Clifford Jacobson on most issues, but he had a real problem with the amendment to ban abortion. Most of his constituents had voted to legalize it years ago, and banning it now, seemed like stepping back in time, rather than forward. The deciding factor in his ultimate decision had been his controversial wife, Allie. Whenever Allie made up her mind to either defend or denounce an issue, the most powerful forces on heaven and earth couldn't sway her.

The President remembered the day he told Allie he was considering siding with the anti-abortionists. He didn't want to, but he owed Clifford Jacobson a lot, quite probably his success in winning the presidency...a fact Jacobson never let him forget.

Allie was livid. She said men had no right interfering in a woman's personal business, be it physical, mental, or otherwise. He wondered if her convictions would have been as rigid had she not aborted a fetus her first year at college. Before they married, Allie had told him all about the abortion, and the man who had made it necessary. She had shared all the grim details, including the fact that she was marrying him on the rebound. He sighed raggedly. There were times he wished he'd never heard of Allie Dawson or Clifford Jacobson.

Clifford Jacobson's face turned purple as he watched President Carlson's news conference from the television built into the study wall. He pounded his fists in rage, cracking the edge of a delicate China

THE BABY SOLDIERS

saucer. The gold rimmed cup on top bucked and clattered, spewing hot coffee over his desk. Carlson was singing a different tune from the one he'd sung when Jacobson presented him with five hundred thousand dollars toward his campaign fund.

"That lily-livered scum!" the preacher bellowed. "He can't do this to me. When I get finished with him, he'll curse his mother for giving him birth!"

He lunged angrily for the phone.

———

Cal Winslow had made his services available to Clifford Jacobson on a number of occasions over the past ten years. He was experienced in producing the necessary results when simple words failed to do the trick. In the early years, Cal's job had been checking the backgrounds of men Jacobson considered hiring. Cal Winslow had proven himself one hundred percent trustworthy. As a result, Jacobson had promised him that his status would rise to Lieutenant in The New Order one day. That promise had made Winslow's desire to carry out his assignments much sweeter. And now, he had been ordered to make the President tow the line.

Jessie Thorpe stood like a mythological goddess at five foot ten. Her long, auburn tresses glowed like a forest fire. Although she had the form and face of an angel, her cold gray eyes brightened at the sight of only one object, and that object happened to be cold, green cash.

Cal Winslow had seen Jessie make a series of bad career moves in the time he'd known her. But her current job as photographer for the Horton Hotel chain, seemed to have changed her luck as well as her finances. Along the way, she'd learned the proper way to apply makeup, so she no longer looked like a circus clown, and she'd discovered an elegant hair style that gave her real class. For the pleasure of her personal company, several of the hotel's more affluent guests had provided Jessie with a fabulous wardrobe, including expensive jewelry and enough furs to warm the population of Vancouver. Winslow decided Jessie was the perfect choice for his plan. His only problem had been convincing Jacobson that Jessie was worth the hundred-thousand-dollar fee she currently commanded.

The arrangement of a liaison between President Carlson and Jessie Thorpe would not be easy. Ever since the president's wife caught him in the Lincoln Bedroom with a young starlet, and threatened to ruin both their careers, he'd kept a low profile. But, as fate would have it, Allie Carlson was off on another relentless crusade for women's rights, and the President was sleeping alone.

———

Clifford Jacobson attended the state publicized fund-raiser for Senator John Waters, finding it a perfect opportunity to circulate among hopeful candidates and express his sentiments on a number of issues. It never ceased to amaze him the way the puppets followed him, bobbing their heads in agreement to every suggestion he made. He felt like a fisherman, waving a hypnotic lure to a sea of hungry fish.

Jessie Thorpe stood near the bar, wearing a floor length Versace that was cut enticingly low on top and slit open along the sides. Winslow introduced her to the prominent players as his cousin, a magazine photographer from Boston. As she shook Senator Waters hand, Jessie smiled demurely and told him she'd been a fan of his for some time. She particularly favored his goal of intensifying American military forces throughout the world. The senator appeared smitten by her beauty as well as her interest in politics. He took her by the arm and led her across the room where President Carlson stood cornered by the imposing preacher from Baltimore.

Jessie played the perfect lady, polite and well mannered. She listened intently as the President discussed his ideas for the coming year, smiling on cue at his meager attempts at humor.

Jacobson had insisted the woman Winslow hire for the assignment act shy rather than aggressive. Jacobson didn't like aggressive women. Now, observing her in action, the preacher gave Winslow an appreciative wink. Jessie Thorpe was simply perfect.

THE BABY SOLDIERS

Three weeks after Senator Waters' fund-raiser, Clifford Jacobson had all the damaging evidence against President Carlson he needed. Motel receipts, eye witnesses who would swear to the President's shenanigans with the sexy redhead, and last but not least, photos of Carlson and Jessie Thorpe that would have rivaled any of Scott Robinson's. The preacher was very pleased and instructed Cal Winslow to deliver a copy of the photos to President Carlson the day Allie was due to arrive home from China.

The President strolled leisurely through the rose garden, wondering how he would ever be able to give this all up when his term was over. He thought longingly of Jessie Thorpe. She excited him more than any woman had since...He couldn't even remember her name anymore. Jessie so enamored him, he ached to be with her even now. How would he find time for her now that Allie was back?

The sound of heavy footsteps startled him. He spun around and looked questioningly at the short, stocky man walking toward him. The man handed him a large manila envelope and nodded curtly.

Carlson looked at the man puzzled. He had never seen him before. "You shouldn't have brought this here," he said, glancing nervously at his watch. It was after eight. He held the envelope out to the placid faced stranger. "You can give this to one of the staff on duty inside."

Winslow's dark eyes never wavered. "You don't really want me to do that," he replied warily. "That information is for your eyes only."

Carlson held the envelope limply as he watched the man disappear. He was alarmed by how easy it had been for the stranger to approach him. When he first saw him, he thought he was Secret Service. It wasn't until he was dangerously close, Carlson realized he was wrong. He decided to meet with his security people right away. If a messenger could slip past them without being detected, so could an assassin.

— 299 —

He held the envelope in both hands, thinking of the stranger's words, "For your eyes-only." He wondered who'd sent it, and if it were as important as the man indicated. He ripped the flap open and watched helplessly as the contents slid out and scattered on the ground at his feet. When he bent down to pick them up, he froze. "What the.... "

A middle-aged woman, wearing a navy suit with white piping, opened the door leading to the rose garden. "Mr. President, Reverend Jacobson is on the telephone. He says it's urgent."

Carlson scooped up the pictures and shoved them back inside the envelope.

"Tell him I'll be right there."

His heart beat so rapidly, he feared it would rupture. How could someone have gotten close enough to take those pictures? His mind was reeling. No one knew he was seeing Jessie. He had been extremely careful about that. They always went to out-of-the-way places. He mouth was suddenly very dry. What would happen if Allie saw the pictures? He had to make sure that didn't happen. But how could he keep them away from her? He could burn them, but he wasn't naive enough to believe they were the originals. They were copies, and who knew how many other copies had been made? Once Allie saw them, there wouldn't be any more second chances. She'd destroy him. Sullenly, he walked to the closest house phone. "Hello," he said, struggling to swallow.

"Good morning, Mr. President," Clifford Jacobson replied flippantly. "I assume you received your surprise package?"

"You!" Carlson shrieked. "What is the meaning of this, Jacobson? Are you insane?"

Jacobson laughed heartily. "Insane? I think not. I was merely... how do they say...putting my ducks in a row."

"Ducks? What in the hell are you talking about?" Carlson shouted, perspiration beading his face.

Jacobson's laughter fringed on hysteria. "Your latest discussions with the press sound as though you're trying to renege on our agreement. That wouldn't be very smart, Mr. President. I didn't contribute so heavily to your last election to have you turn around and stab me in the back."

Carlson reached for a nearby chair and eased his trembling body into it. "I've done a lot of soul searching on the abortion issue," he explained. "I don't think it's something I should get involved with."

"Well, in that case," the preacher replied huffily. "I suggest you search your soul a little more thoroughly."

Carlson's stomach lurched as he stared at the photos.

"After the anti-abortion amendment is passed, all those nasty pictures of you and whatever-her-name is will disappear forever. If you don't comply, those pictures will find their way into the greedy hands of every bloodhound from here to the moon. What's more, I'll have that pretty slut go on a personal appearance tour that will make Allie's little jaunts to the mid-east look like vacations to Disney World! Do you get the picture?" Jacobson said coldly. Then quickly added, "Excuse the pun."

The line went dead.

Henry Carlson closed his eyes tightly, thinking how easily he'd been duped. Were all middle-aged men this addle-brained? Did they really believe it was possible for a beautiful, vibrant woman to fall madly in love with them? He rubbed the bridge of his nose and closed his eyes tightly.

"Oh, Jessie," he muttered softly. "I wanted so much to believe it was real."

Amy Patterson stuffed jeans and sweaters into one suitcase and reached for another. She dropped it on the bed when the telephone rang. "Yes," she said abruptly.

She listened in horrified silence as the voice on the other end informed her that Clifford Jacobson had found a sure-proof way to blackmail President Carlson, and he would no longer be endorsing free choice.

She hung up the phone, running her trembling fingers through her long hair. "Jacobson!" she spat. "That rotten son of Satan won't get away with this."

Amy tossed makeup and underwear into the second suitcase and spun around. "Think, Amy," she muttered. "Use your head. Calm down and think."

Her face flushed as she dialed the old hospital in Morehead City and waited impatiently for someone to answer. She was relieved when she heard Margaret Hatchey's crisp voice. "Margaret," she said hoarsely," we've got a real problem. Remember that ace in the hole you told me about? I'm afraid we're going to have to play it now."

Margaret succeeded in calming Amy enough to find out what had upset her so badly. After Amy explained how Clifford Jacobson had expunged another liberty by blackmailing the President, Margaret replied, "Listen to me, Amy. I don't want you to worry yourself over any of this. You've got more important things to do. I'll make the arrangements to see that our randy-assed President gets off the hook. Men," she grumbled disgustedly. "No wonder the world is so fucked up."

"What about the woman, Jessie Thorpe?" Amy asked anxiously.

Margaret sighed heavily."Whatever they paid for her services won't last long. Her kind doesn't think of the future. Don't worry, Miss Thorpe will behave predictably. We'll convince her that she'll never get a job, of any kind, if she doesn't."

Amy clutched the receiver tightly, listening to Margaret's response. Sometimes she wondered if the frightful guardian from the camp was gone forever, or had merely changed her alliances.

"Thanks, Margaret," she muttered weakly. I don't know what we'd do..."

Margaret interrupted. "No thanks necessary. We'll take care of them, honey. Every last one of them."

Amy hung up the telephone and shuddered. She knew full well what Margaret Hatchey was capable of doing. It wasn't the first time she was grateful that Margaret was on her side.

CHAPTER FIFTY-TWO

Byron Spears thoughtfully gathered the leather-bound journals. The preacher was going to be furious when he learned that donations for the past quarter had dropped so drastically. Financial support for the organization had dwindled sixty percent since the Scott Robinson business, and the murder of Horace Woolard by one of the organizations most dedicated followers. The converts who had joined the organization had expected moral conditions to get better, not worse.

Yesterday's newspaper from Virginia Beach divulged all the gory details of Clifford Robinson's other side. James Kelsey had included several quotes taken directly from Robinson's former speeches to back up his report. Today, Kelsey had outdone himself. He insinuated the late Captain Woolard was far from the dedicated, incorruptible public servant everyone had assumed he was. With Robbie dead and Sybil in a loony bin, James probably figured he had nothing to lose by exposing anyone he pleased. Byron hoped Kelsey wouldn't lose his shirt when the lawsuits started rolling in. But all in all, he admired Kelsey for the gutsy move.

Jacobson peered out the window overlooking the golf course. Why had his supporters suddenly become so interested in his personal finances? He'd had several inquiries wanting to know why he was paying outside agencies to conduct business he termed miscellaneous. His jaw line grew more rigid the longer he brooded. They should have more faith, he thought. Everything he did, he did for them. He had to protect them...protect them from all the evil gossip Kelsey printed in that tawdry newspaper of his.

Over the past few weeks, Jacobson wondered if he had disclosed Sybil's involvement in Woolard's murder too soon. But when he ordered her to kill the others who stood in his way, she balked. He knew then her usefulness to him and the new order was over. He couldn't trust her to keep what she'd done a secret. Sybil had never been able to keep her mouth shut about anything in her entire life. He sneered smugly. How shrewd of him to claim that she had been distraught to the point of madness when she killed Horace Woolard. Now, even if she told anyone that he had put her up to it, no one would believe her. She actually was insane.

Jacobson scowled as Byron Spears entered the study. "I certainly hope you have good news to report today. To say the past few weeks have been troublesome would be a gross understatement."

Byron walked briskly across the lengthy room and placed the ledgers on the preacher's desk. Then he perched himself on a wing-backed chair, bracing for the fall out.

Jacobson opened the first ledger containing computer-generated printouts of all the contributions made during the past quarter. His stormy gray eyes flickered over the pages. "You must have made an error in these calculations," he muttered. "According to these figures, our income is down sixty percent from what it was last year at this time. Byron," he added, not looking up. "You'd better find out what's wrong and fix it immediately."

Byron figured Jacobson would try to shift the blame onto him, rather than his hand chosen leaders for the waning financial status of the organization.

"I've checked the figures very carefully, more than a dozen times," Byron told him. "They're quite accurate. I've even taken the liberty of discussing the lack of income with our associates in Carolina and Virginia. Their losses are more staggering than our own." He stood and moved toward the window. "I'm afraid the demise of Captain

THE BABY SOLDIERS

Woolard, so soon after Robertson's fiasco raised more than a few hackles."

Jacobson opened the top desk drawer, quickly extracting his nail file. "I'm well aware of the publicity Scott Robinson's secret lifestyle and his murder caused. We can't be blamed for that." He sighed heavily. "Captain Woolard had to be stopped. Even Sybil Kelsey knew that much. It's just a tragedy. I assumed she was stronger."

Byron stared intently at Jacobson. "The people don't know what to think, or who to believe in anymore. Robinson and Woolard were both heroes in their eyes."

Jacobson dropped the nail file into the drawer and slammed it shut. "These past few weeks, we've had a lower attendance at worship service than ever before! I blame Kelsey for this. I blame him for all of it! The man is totally irresponsible."

Byron returned to his chair. "Speaking of James Kelsey, I read that he doesn't believe his wife killed Woolard...for some lame reason."

Jacobson glared at him coldly. "I don't care what he believes. She called here and admitted it to me the day after it happened. You should remember Byron. You took the call."

"Oh, I'm not questioning you. But there seems to be some doubt that she killed Woolard because he murdered Scott Robinson. He said there had to be a better reason." Byron cleared his throat. "According to James Kelsey."

Jacobson turned ashen, the blue veins at his temples bulging.

"He's not only a liar, he's a traitor as well! And to think, he used to be one of us."

Byron nodded tiredly.

"The man is a mockery to serious journalism. I'll wager that by next year at this time, James Kelsey will have lost everything he owns."

Byron turned away from him. "He's already lost his family."

Jacobson closed the ledger and leapt to his feet. "I'm not discussing this any further." Then he turned to Byron. "Come to think of

— 305 —

it, you're a rather creative fellow. Why don't you draft a letter to our supporters and tell them the stories they've been reading are nothing but cheap sensationalism? None of those accusations are true. I would sue Kelsey myself, but I'm afraid that would only add more fuel to the fire."

Byron crossed the room and picked up the ledgers. "In all the excitement, I almost forgot to tell you. One of President Carlson's people called earlier, while you were out."

Jacobson exhaled heavily. "Was there a message?"

"Yes. He said to tell you the President would be announcing his decision on the abortion amendment at a special news conference at six o'clock this evening."

The deep furrows in Jacobson's brow appeared to melt, smoothing his pale skin. "Now that sounds like good news for a change. It's certainly is about time."

Byron opened the door, then turned back to the preacher. "One more thing. Calvin Winslow called, too. He sounded rather ominous. He said he'd be on the road most of the day, and he'd try to call you back later this evening. Sounds like bad news."

Jacobson dropped his head into his hands and groaned.

———

After stacking the ledgers back on their respective shelves in a separate office, Byron went directly to his quarters.

He had left word for his sister to be near her phone at precisely two p.m.

"Hello, Margaret," he said. "Mission accomplished."

Margaret giggled with the enthusiasm of a young girl. The girl he remembered before the world turned their lives upside down.

"Byron, I can't tell you how much your help means to me and the girls. We appreciate everything you're trying to do for us."

"I'm enjoying it immensely. Your brother-in-law is more nervous than a sitting hen with a fox on the loose."

Margaret laughed openly. "I'd love to be there to see it. What do you think he'll do tonight when he hears the President veto the abortion amendment?"

"Tell you what," Byron said. "I'll tape his reaction and send it to you. I'm sure you and your pals would enjoy it immensely."

"I'm curious, Byron. How did you manage to get Carlson off the hook?"

"Destroying the incriminating photos was no major problem. Winslow brought the negatives here for safekeeping. Let's just say they had a little accident."

"That's a hoot," she replied. "Tell me about the Thorpe woman? How did you handle her?"

"I merely convinced her that staying in the country at the present time was not in her best interests. At first she balked, but I reminded her how poorly Jacobson treats his faithful servants—particularly when they are no longer of any use to him."

"She didn't give you any trouble?"

"No. I really wasn't expecting any. Miss Thorpe is just an average working girl, making a living the best way she knows how. She sure was pretty. I could see why the President came onto her the way he did."

Margaret chortled. "Be serious, Byron. Carlson would have come onto her if she had won a global ugly contest."

"He does enjoy living dangerously," Byron replied. "You know, Margaret, if I had a wife like Allie, I wouldn't be looking for anything on the side."

"Oh?" Margaret replied teasingly. "And when did you become so interested in women all of a sudden?"

He chuckled. "Reverend Jacobson's opinion on gays is no secret. So, every once in a while, I manage to be seen in public with a woman on my arm—so he won't get suspicious."

"You are a sly one," Margaret said approvingly.

"I am that," Byron replied proudly. "Be sure to give your friends my best. If you need anything else, don't hesitate to call."

GERRY R. LEWIS

"Was that your brother you were talking to?" Danny asked.

Margaret closed her eyes and smiled. "My guardian angel is more like it."

"You never mentioned him before. I didn't think you had any relatives?"

"He's the only one I have left," her voice faded. "Peggy's been gone a long time, now."

"Peggy?" he asked. "Who was Peggy?"

"Peggy was my sister. She was also Clifford Jacobson's faithful wife."

"Now that's scary," he muttered. "What happened to her?"

A frown froze on Margaret's face. "Clifford Jacobson happened to her," she replied flatly.

"Did he know you two were sisters?"

Margaret nodded. "He knew all right. In those days, we thought he was something special. We would have followed him to the ends of the earth. After Peggy married him, she started telling me incredible stories about him...stories I couldn't believe."

Danny finished the candy bar he'd been eating and tossed the wrapper into a trash bin. "What kind of stories?"

"She told me he hired people to kill anyone who disagreed with him."

Danny's bright green eyes bulged from their sockets. "You mean Reverend Jacobson was doing that kind of stuff even before my dad went to work for him?"

She sighed tiredly. "Long before that, I'm afraid."

"You know what I can't figure out," Danny said, gazing at the floor. "How come the preacher never did anything bad to Mr. Kelsey? He's always saying terrible things about the preacher in his newspaper."

"Who's to say Clifford didn't get even?" she replied thoughtfully.

Danny blinked. "You mean what happened to Robbie?"

— 308 —

Margaret raised her hands defensively. "I'm not saying he's responsible. The jury is still out on that. What I'm saying is his people kidnapped Kerry Trivane and killed that boy, with or without his knowledge. And killing that boy hurt James Kelsey more than anything else in the world."

Danny shrugged. "Mr. Kelsey's stories about the preacher and his organization are getting worse than before."

Her smile waned. "I guess he feels he has nothing left to lose."

Margaret brightened, shifting her mood. "And then we have people like the Trivanes."

"What about them?" he asked.

"I'm certain Clifford was behind that fright campaign to get them out of Dodge. Now they're more of a threat to him than ever before."

Danny nodded. "I see what you mean. Does he, I mean Reverend Jacobson, know that Mr. Spears is your brother?"

She chuckled. "Not hardly."

"But what about the background checks? I was a lot younger, but I remember my dad talking about having one before he went to work for the preacher."

"Byron is a computer genius," Margaret said proudly. "He was able to swap his information with a friend who had been killed when they served in the military."

Danny looked puzzled. "But if you all believed in Jacobson back then, why would your brother choose to keep his identity a secret?"

"He was overseas on active duty when Peggy and I got caught up in the Jacobson frenzy. By the time he came home, Jacobson's true colors were beginning to emerge. Byron thought it would be better if he went incognito. He did it for Peggy's sake. He felt that was the only way he could be close to her without arousing Jacobson's suspicions."

"Do you really believe Jacobson could have killed her?"

"For years, I thought she ran away. Peggy was always talking about it. But Byron thinks she's dead. They were very close. Before she disappeared, Clifford sent Byron to England on a special mission. I don't think my brother has ever forgiven himself for not being there to protect her when she really needed him."

Danny shook his head sullenly. "I wonder how many people the preacher has had killed over the years?"

Margaret shuddered. "I wouldn't even hazard a guess."

"It's amazing that Jacobson never figured out who Mr. Spears really was. From listening to your end of the conversation, it didn't sound to me like your brother is that fond of him."

"Byron can be quite convincing when he has to be. He pretended to be chummy with Clifford to gain his trust—which he has done quite well for a very long time."

"Do you think Jacobson ever made your brother kill anybody?"

"I never asked him," Margaret replied, shuddering at the thought. "If he ever did, I don't want to know about it."

Danny nodded understandingly. "Then your brother would be just like my dad."

Margaret's face contorted at the comparison.

"I'll bet Amy was thrilled when you told her you wanted to join our group?"

Danny said, abruptly changing the subject.

"Well, she didn't try to talk me out of it," Margaret replied. "I've done my best to do everything I can to help out. What surprises me is that you couldn't be more help."

"Me?" Danny said in disbelief. "How could I be any more help than I am right now?"

"The place the guards take the babies after they're born," Margaret said reflectively. "I figured since your father was who he was, and knew the people involved in the whole process, you probably knew where they were keeping the babies."

"Danny cleared his throat. "There were never any lines of communication open between us. I knew less than nothing about his secret life. I didn't even know he had a cabin in the woods. I probably never would have found out about it if Mrs. Kelsey hadn't admitted killing him there."

THE BABY SOLDIERS

Margaret nodded grimly. "I suppose the family is always the last to know your secrets."

"Oh, I always knew my father had a bad side," Danny grumbled.

"You just didn't know how bad," she replied.

Danny studied her intently. "Don't worry, Margaret" he said. "We'll find the babies. It's just a matter of time."

"The way people are dying off," she said, "I wonder if we're running out of time."

"Mr. Kelsey believes Dad and Mr. Robinson were involved in some kind of conspiracy to sell the babies."

"You know something," she muttered softly. "It wouldn't surprise me if Mr. Kelsey is the one who discovers where they are."

"Could be," Danny said, his dark hair bobbing up and down. "Once Mr. Kelsey sinks his teeth in something, look out."

"How is your mother doing these days, Danny?" Margaret asked concerned.

He grinned impishly."Thanks for asking. She's like a new person. If you saw her now, you wouldn't believe she was the same woman she was before Dad died. She looks more like my sister than my mother."

"It must have been hell for her, living with someone like Horace all those years."

"It was hell for all of us," Danny retorted.

"I'm sure it was. Perhaps someday, she'll find somebody who can make her happy. She certainly deserves it."

Danny grinned. "I can think of someone," he replied, his thoughts drifting. Then he wrinkled his nose. "Naw, they're just good friends."

Margaret's dark eyes twinkled brightly. "And who might that be?"

"Sergeant David Williams," he replied."Do you know him?"

"I've seen him around," she replied sadly. "I heard about his wife and little girl."

"Ginny?" Danny said, more interested than ever. "How did you come to know Ginny?"

"It was a long time ago," Margaret said. "Ginny used to accompany her mother whenever she came to the academy."

— 311 —

Danny looked puzzled. "Why was Mrs. Williams at the academy?"

Margaret rubbed her temples, remembering. "Ann used to work at the library. About twice a week, she would bring books over to the academy. She thought the students might enjoy reading about things that weren't available to them there."

Danny nodded. "Ginny would have been about my age. But I don't remember her from school."

"Ann didn't send Ginny to the academy. She didn't like Scott Robinson and the people he associated with. You could tell that just by the way she looked at him. I don't know if he ever said anything out of the way to her, or if she just sensed he was evil."

Danny shook his head. "Looks like Jacobson's dream of a New Order that would heal the sins of society is falling apart."

"It does that," Margaret replied ruefully.

"If Mr. Robinson was as bad as people claim, I'm surprised he didn't get killed a long time before he did."

Margaret pursed her lips. "I'll bet Clifford gave that a lot of thought over the years."

Danny looked quizzical. "You mean before he actually told my dad to do it?"

She nodded.

"I still can't believe it happened," he said. "Even after Jason said he heard them talking about it."

Margaret nodded understandingly. "It's hard to believe something like that about your own flesh and blood."

"Dad turned into a real monster."

Watching the torment on Danny's young face made Margaret's heart ache for him. Even though he's said he was glad his dad was dead, he still had a lot of underlying feelings to be dealt with. She didn't answer his question. There was no point in adding to his grief.

CHAPTER FIFTY-THREE

The murder of Captain Woolard sparked unbridled controversy over The New Order and the people associated with it. But in spite of the obsessive scrutiny, Clifford Jacobson was relieved that thorn in his side was gone forever. It had been some time since Woolard had proven himself a worthy follower. He had become weak, distracted by his own foolish desires. Now, he was gone and Sybil Kelsey would pay the price.

Jacobson's main concern was finding the source of the fire in the storeroom that had destroyed the evidence he needed to keep the president in line. He shouldn't have insisted that Cal Winslow turn over all those pictures and negatives of the first family. If only he had permitted Winslow to keep the negatives, more pictures could have been made. But the pictures had evaporated in the fire, and so had his leverage. Now, he'd have to devise another way to control Carlson.

———

David Williams escorted Adele and her children to Horace Woolard's funeral. He was surprised by the poor attendance, even though it was cold enough to freeze the antlers off a reindeer. There were more reporters milling around the cemetery than mourners. He recognized a few from the Ledger Star and the Richmond Dispatch, but didn't see any sign of James Kelsey. He supposed James had his hands full, trying to figure out why in the hell his old lady drove Horace out to a secluded cabin in the woods and blew his brains out. It was a puzzler all right, especially considering how intolerable

Sybil found the taking of a life. If James had shot him, it would have made a lot more sense.

———

Sybil sat on the edge of the sterile, single bed. The cotton gown she wore was wrinkled and faded, and her hair, which she'd once spent hours brushing and primping, hung limply around her shoulders. She gazed around, sad and confused, wondering where she was.

A door opened, and a man and woman of average height and appearance, in everyday street clothes, walked in. Sybil's beady eyes shifted fearfully from one of them to the other.

The man smiled broadly. "How are you feeling today, Mrs. Kelsey?"

Sybil didn't respond.

The woman touched her arm. "Dear, did you get any sleep at all last night?"

She didn't answer.

"The woman said, "You didn't eat anything. Aren't you feeling well?"

Still no answer.

The man stepped closer to her and whispered, "Mrs. Kelsey, can you tell us in your own words what happened out there…in the woods?"

Sybil's sunken dark eyes blinked rapidly. "He…he said he'd punish me."

The man and woman exchanged uneasy glances.

"Who told you that?" the woman asked her.

The man hurried from the room and returned moments later with a doctor at his side. "She…she spoke to us," he stammered. "She said someone was going to punish her."

"Probably God," the doctor mumbled wryly.

"The woman spun around and glared angrily at the doctor. "Where's the psychiatrist who's supposed to be assigned to her?"

THE BABY SOLDIERS

"He went to get something to eat," the doctor replied. "I guess it's me or no one."

The man looked concerned. "Maybe we should wait for the other doctor to return," he said timidly.

The woman furrowed her brow. "She may clam up if we wait."

The doctor pushed past her and stood directly in front of the patient.

"All right, Mrs. Kelsey," he said, as though he were bored to distraction. "Tell us just who is going to punish you?"

"God," she replied, shakily.

The doctor threw up his hands and quipped, "See. What did I tell you?"

Then he walked out as quickly as he'd entered.

"What are we going to do now?" the man asked worriedly.

The woman looked glum. "We should have gone to the funeral with the others. We're getting nowhere fast, hanging around this zombie."

Sybil slid off the edge of the bed, her bare feet flat on the tile floor. She padded hypnotically toward the locked window. "God will punish me for killing my baby."

The woman's head spun quickly in Sybil's direction.

"Baby?" she cried. "What baby?"

Sybil smiled faintly. "My baby...and his."

The woman's face colored excitedly. "Whose baby was it, Sybil? Was it your husband's child?"

Sybil's smile remained painted on her lips. "Clifford...Clifford Jacobson. It was his baby."

"Jumpin' Jesus!" the man said. "No one is ever going to believe this."

"When did this happen?" the woman asked her.

"In college. A long time ago."

The man and woman slowly backed out of the room, leaving Sybil to her mental prison.

— 315 —

After David parked Adele's car in the garage, he walked to the kitchen and gave her the keys. "Where are the boys?" he asked.

"They went upstairs to change," she told him. "I think they both put on a very brave front today. I know this has been very hard on them."

David nodded, remembering how he felt when his own father died. He hated the bastard all his life, but when he died, he felt an unexplained loss; a futile wish that things could have worked out differently.

"Can you stay for a while?" she asked. "I need to talk to you."

David knew she was worried about the boys. Hell, he was worried about them, too. It broke his heart to see Jason all banged up because of some lunch room skirmish, or Mark crying, because the kids at school taunted him, calling him a killer's seed. He knew kids didn't dream up those expressions on their own. They probably heard it from their ignorant parents.

Adele walked into the living room and kicked off her shoes. Then she turned to David, and said, "You really don't have to stay, if you have somewhere else you need to be."

David scratched the side of his head. "Adele, you just said you wanted to talk to me. Have you changed your mind?"

She shook her head. "No. I've been doing a lot of thinking about what we discussed before. Nothing has changed, David. I know you told me to take my time before I made a final decision, but I think it would be best for the boys and myself if we moved away from here and all this madness."

He sighed heavily as his shoulders sagged. "The talk will die down, Adele. It might take awhile, but people will soon forget about Horace, and Robinson and Sybil Kelsey. You'll see."

Her eyes appeared as drab as seaweed. "When, David? How many more beatings will Jason have to endure before that happens? And what about Mark? Every time I look at him, he's crying about something. I don't know what else to do," she said, covering her face with her hands.

— 316 —

David put his arms around her, holding her close to him. "I know what you're going through. I love them, too, Adele. I hate to see them hurt as much as you do."

"Then, please don't try to talk me out of this," she sobbed.

"No," he murmured, stroking her hair. "I won't. I just don't want to think about what my life will be like if you and the boys move away."

She stared at him longingly, her green eyes welling with tears. "Come with us, David," she pleaded. "This place has been nothing but grief for you, too. We could make a fresh start somewhere else."

His arms fell away from her. As much as he'd love to do what she asked, he knew he couldn't.

Adele took a deep breath and let it out slowly. "I love you, David," she murmured.

He nodded, wishing there were some way he could reconcile his mind with his heart. "I love you, too," he said. "I just can't leave here, not yet."

She frowned up at him."What do you mean, not yet? What possible reason could you have to stay?"

"Adele, we both know that I won't be free to love you the way you should be loved until I find out why Ann and Ginny were murdered. I have to put that part of my life to rest before I can move on."

She lowered her eyes. "I thought you had decided Horace was responsible for that too."

"I was," he replied. "But after I learned Ginny was pregnant at the time of her death, I had the weirdest feeling that someone else had something to do with it." He exhaled tiredly. "I've been hearing things from the girls who were kidnapped and held at that awful camp that have me running in circles. All I know is, I won't be able to rest until I learn the truth."

Adele took his hand and rubbed it against her cheek. "David, do you honestly think we'll ever be happy?"

"Oh, God, I hope so," he said. "Only a cruel God would keep us apart after everything we've been through."

She snuggled closer, warmed by his embrace. "Will you write to me and let me know what you're doing?" she asked softly

He nodded. "As soon as you let me know where you are."

Adele clung to him, knowing she'd never feel this loved again. When they finally ended their embrace, she said, "I've got a lot of planning to do. Will you help me?"

David nodded grimly and followed her into the kitchen.

Jason ambled into the kitchen, staring at the tile floor. Adele looked up at him concerned. He hadn't said a word since coming home from the funeral.

"Jason, are you hungry?" she asked.

Jason shook his head. Then looked quizzically at David as he penciled notes onto a map. He coughed nervously.

David looked up. "Hi, sport. I'm helping your mom plot her course so she doesn't get you lost."

Jason opened the refrigerator and glanced inside. Then he closed it again. "David, can we…I need to talk to you," he stammered.

David glanced from the puzzled teen to his mother and slowly folded the map.

"I know this has been real tough on you, Jason. You're a lot braver than I'd be if I were in your shoes."

Jason shoved his fists into his pockets, shifting from one foot to the other. "I don't feel very brave," he murmured.

David frowned. "What is it, Jason? If there's anything I can do…"

Jason leaned against the refrigerator door, fidgeting with his fingers. "I don't know where to start. But this is really important… and…and you're the only one I can trust."

David nodded toward the other side of the table. "Do you want to sit down and tell me about it?"

Jason's eyes drifted from David to his mother. "I could tell Danny, but he's not here."

THE BABY SOLDIERS

Adele removed her coffee cup from the table and stood up. "Jason, would you rather I left you two alone?"

"Naw. You don't have to go anywhere," he replied. Dropping into a chair, he lowered his eyes once more. "I don't think you're going to like what I have to say."

Adele gave David a furtive glance. "Maybe I'd better sit down for this, too."

After she was seated, she turned to her son. "Jason, what's this all about?"

He looked sheepishly from her to David. "Remember when I told you about the time, when I followed Dad to Baltimore?"

"Of course, we remember," Adele replied impatiently. "That was a very dangerous thing for you to do."

He sighed helplessly. "Well, that wasn't the only time I followed him."

David shifted to the edge of his seat.

"Good Lord, Jason," Adele cried. "What on earth were you trying to prove? You haven't been driving long enough to roam all over the country!"

He shifted his head from side to side, his sandy curls dangling in his eyes. He'd have to tell them now. There was no other way. "I think I know where they've been keeping the babies," he muttered.

"What!" Adele shrieked.

David reached across the table and touched her arm, trying to calm her. Then he scraped his chair back and stood up. "Jason, are you sure about this?"

Jason fidgeted with a baseball card his brother had left on the table.

"One night, after I came back home, I drove to the place they talked about. I got out and crept up to the building. I was so close. I could hear them crying."

David walked to the other side of the table and put a firm hand on Jason's shoulder. "It's okay, son," he said reassuringly. "Everything is going to be okay."

— 319 —

Jason pushed his hair back as he gazed into his mother's frightened eyes. "I didn't tell you before, because…I knew how afraid you were. You couldn't do anything to help when he…when he was still alive."

Adele closed her eyes tightly. Jason's words pierced her heart. She felt so ashamed. Her children knew she was terrified of their father, so terrified they were afraid to confide in her. Afraid to tell her about the horrible things he had done. She opened her eyes and wiped a tear from her son's pale cheek. "Jason. I'm so sorry. But that's over now. I want you to go ahead and tell David where the children are."

Jason nodded as he rubbed his eyes. "David, do you know where that old prison farm used to be not too far from Emporia?" He opened the map he'd been holding.

David knew exactly where it was. He had transported about a dozen hard-core prisoners there after joining the department.

"Is that where the babies were taken?" he asked, trying to feign a calmness he did not feel.

Jason sniffed as he ran his finger along a blue line drawn on the map. "I saw Dad and some other guy taking babies into the main building one night."

David caught the look of disgust on Adele's face. "How long ago was that?"

Jason shrugged. "Late. Late last summer." He looked at his mother and then shook his head. "You were in the hospital."

David nodded woodenly, seeming to understand why the boy hadn't said anything to her before now. "I can't believe the children have been less than a hundred miles away all this time, and we didn't know."

Adele began to tremble. "David, what are we going to do?"

He folded his arms over his chest and turned to Jason. "We're going to get them the hell out of there. But we're going to need help."

"We'll find Danny," Jason said excitedly. "He'll help us. I know he will."

David nodded. "I know where Danny is. I'll give him a call."

THE BABY SOLDIERS

Adele looked at him puzzled. "Danny's working in Carolina, isn't he?"

David rose to his feet. "Yeah. He and his friends are preparing a safe haven for the missing children. They've been working on it for months." He looked across the table at Jason and winked. "You'd better prepare yourself. You're about to become a hero."

Danny and Amy sat cross-legged on the floor of the hospital's main office sifting through the mound of files which Margaret Hatchey had brought down the previous weekend. When the phone rang, Amy looked at Danny and said, "I think it's your turn."

Danny unfolded his long legs and rose to his feet. While he spoke to the party on the other end of the line, Amy sat querulously, watching his expression change. He grinned from ear to ear and then gave her a thumbs up. Amy had no idea who he was talking to, but she felt certain the news was good.

"That's outstanding," he said. "I'll tell them as soon as I hang up. I'll call you back first thing in the morning and let you know when we'll be there."

Danny hung up and rubbed his hands together.

Amy stood up and walked toward him. "You won the lottery, right?"

He shook his head. "No, it's even better than that."

She narrowed her eyes skeptically.

"That was David Williams on the phone," he said, spontaneously picking her up and spinning her round in circles. "Wait till you hear what's happened."

She laughed. "Danny, if you don't tell me what's going on, right now, I'm going to call Kerry and tell her you've gone mad, so she'd better not come down tomorrow."

Danny burst out laughing and lowered her back to the floor. "Kerry won't be coming anyway. She'll have something a lot more important to do."

— 321 —

"More important?" Amy asked, trying to catch her breath. "What could possibly be more important?"

Danny clucked the roof of his mouth. "Oh, you know," he drawled teasingly. "Important things...such as...bringing her baby home."

At first, it didn't register. Then it dawned on Amy what he said. "Oh God!" she squealed. "They found the babies!"

"Yes," Danny answered enthusiastically. "Jason told David he knew where the babies were."

Amy exhaled heavily, puffing her cheeks. "Now, all we have to do is figure out how we're going to get them away from the animals who took them."

"One step at a time," he said excitedly.

She pulled on her jacket and zipped it up. "You take the top two floors. Find everyone you can and tell them what you've just told me. I'll tell the others."

Amy rushed toward the corridor and looked back over her shoulder. "Danny, find the Trivanes first. Tell them we've got to get ready to roll."

Danny frowned. "Don't you think they should wait here until we come back?"

Amy chuckled. "You can ask them that if you like. But I think I know what their answer will be."

"Amy," he said, as she reached the door.

She turned around.

He looked so earnest as he stood there, staring at her. "Amy, I'm really happy for you. I'm happy for all of you."

The smile she offered froze on her lips. "I've been waiting a long time for this day. I want to see the cold-blooded bastards who stole my baby face to face. You know, Danny, I actually believe I could kill them all. I could blow their brains out without even blinking."

Danny nodded understandingly and headed for the stairs. He was aware his father was partly responsible for Amy's pain. Now, more than ever, he was glad Horace Woolard was dead.

— 322 —

THE BABY SOLDIERS

"David said he'd get in touch with Kerry," Danny told her. "He said he'd pass the information onto Margaret Hatchey, too. Margaret will know what to do once we get there."

Amy raced back toward him and shook his arm. "Come on, Danny. We've got to hurry."

Then she raced from the room and down the hall, her pony-tailed red hair bouncing behind her.

"Amy!"

She spun around exasperated. "Danny, what is it now?"

"I didn't tell David how many of us would be coming."

Amy's laughter echoed through the empty hall. "He'll find out when he sees us."

Danny grinned. "Boy, is he going to be surprised."

———

David Williams parked on the street outside the diner. He could see Kerry talking with someone through the glass window. He had hoped to catch her alone, but he realized how ridiculous that was. The diner was always packed.

He went inside and slipped into a booth that had just been vacated. When Kerry saw him, she picked up a menu and hurried in his direction. "Sergeant Williams," she said, smiling warmly. "We haven't seen much of you around lately."

He smiled contentedly. "Things have been hopping, that's for sure."

Kerry laughed. "Danny said you've been running in circles, trying to keep this city of ours from falling apart."

"I'm running out of glue," he quipped.

"You want a chili dog?" she asked. "The sauce is fresh."

"You mean it hasn't had time to turn into penicillin yet?" He said teasing.

Kerry chuckled. "Well, the last time I checked, it was still red."

"Sounds good. Bring me two."

— 323 —

Kerry disappeared around the counter before he could tell her the real reason he'd come. He could feel the steady beat of drums vibrating from the jukebox on the far end of the diner. For a moment, it sounded like Rock' n Roll. After listening more closely, he realized it wasn't even close. He supposed he was just feeling nostalgic. A group of teens ran past his booth giggling and yelling at one another. When they left, the diner became so quiet he could hear the ice machine churning. He jumped when Kerry reached over his shoulder and deposited a napkin and flatware on the table in front of him. "Your dogs will be ready in a couple minutes," she said.

David looked up, studying her bright face. Kerry was beautiful, he thought. She looked like her mother did when she was young. He pursed his lips, remembering the good times they'd had back then. But that was a lifetime ago.

"Got a minute to sit down and talk?" he asked.

"Sure," she replied, joining him. "The next swarm isn't due to arrive for another twenty minutes."

He toyed with the corners of the paper napkin. "I have some good news for you. I was waiting for things to simmer down in here so I could tell you."

Kerry folded her hands on the edge of the table. "Okay. Let's hear it."

David didn't see any way to work up to the subject. Besides, it would be best just to blurt it out as quickly as possible. "Kerry," he said, inhaling deeply. "The babies have been found."

Kerry shook her head, as though she were attempting to clear a spell of dizziness. "Dear God," she replied. "I can't believe it's actually happened. How? Who found them?"

"Jason Woolard told us just a little while ago."

"Jason?" she cried in disbelief. "How did he find them?"

David shook his head from side to side. "He followed his old man one day. Actually, he's been doing that sort of thing a lot lately. He just didn't bother sharing it with anyone until now."

THE BABY SOLDIERS

She bobbed her head excitedly. "Where are they? When will I get my baby back?"

David raised his hands defensively. "Whoa. Let's start at the beginning."

She nodded excitedly.

"It seems Jason got curious, wondering what his father was doing when he went out at night, so he started following him. The first time he followed him, he found out Woolard was in cahoots with a Reverend Jacobson."

She rubbed a sudden chill from her arms. "Amy told me about him."

"Well anyway," David said. "Jason admitted that wasn't the only time he followed his dad. He saw his dad and some other man carrying babies out to an old prison farm late one night."

Her eyes widened. "I thought they'd torn down those places?"

David grimaced. "Most of them. That was one of Jacobson's promises when he started his rise to power. He promised to have all the hardened criminals in the Tidewater area executed and the rest sent to prisons in other states."

Kerry shrugged. "I guess I was too young to remember when that stuff was going on."

David nodded grimly. "Anyway, Jason said he could hear the babies crying from inside the building. He said he saw some older kids marching out back of the building with rifles on their shoulders. He said they weren't more than nine or ten years old."

Kerry shivered. "Amy heard that the boy babies were being trained to be soldiers."

"Baby soldiers," David mumbled in disbelief.

Kerry grabbed a Kleenex and rubbed her eyes. "I prayed so hard that someday they'd be found. When will we be able to get them and bring them home?"

"Soon," David replied, touching her arm. "Danny and the others are preparing to come back from Morehead City tonight. As soon as everyone arrives, we'll start the wheels turning."

"I want to be there," she said, her voice trailing off.

"I knew you would. I told Danny I'd tell you in person. He said he'd love to see the expression on your face, but he didn't want you to have to wait a minute longer than necessary to hear the good news."

"That sounds like Danny," she replied. "He's a great guy."

Mr. Neely brought the chilidogs to the booth and set them down in front of David. Then he turned to Kerry and said, "I hate to interrupt, seeing you're probably getting arrested and all." He winked at David. "But the rowdies will be here any minute."

Kerry leapt to her feet. "David, can I talk to you later?"

He nodded, "Be at Amy's place around nine o'clock."

She nodded excitedly. "I can't wait until everyone finds out."

David left the remaining chilidog in its Styrofoam container. "I'll take this one with me," he said. "I still have a few more stops to make. Oh, by the way," he said, squeezing out of the booth. "I need Margaret Hatchey's phone number."

Kerry removed a napkin from a dispenser on the counter and scribbled the information on it. She gave it to David. "She may still be in Carolina with the others."

He nodded as he shoved the napkin into his jacket pocket. "I'll see you later."

Tears filled her eyes. "I still can't believe it's really happening."

David watched her walk away, wondering what it must feel like to know that someone you feared you would never see again was alive and so very close. There was a time he thought he'd find Ann and Ginny the same way. Only that day never came. What he'd found instead were decayed remains after five years of empty dreams.

Freezing rain pelted his face the moment he left the diner. David burrowed his head inside the furry collar of his jacket and unlocked the Honda. He sat inside and shivered, waiting for the fan to blow hot air through the tiny vents. Tomorrow, he mused, he wouldn't be as lucky as Amy and Kerry, holding his lost child in his arms. But perhaps tomorrow, he would find the answers to his own questions, and in finding them he would finally find peace.

THE BABY SOLDIERS

James Kelsey hadn't had a moment to himself in days. The telephones never stopped ringing. The irony was that the callers were mostly newspaper reporters, looking for a fresh scoop on his wife, Sybil. He propped his feet on the desk and leaned back in the chair, his fingers laced behind his head. Oh, he could tell them stories all right. He could tell them stories about a woman who hadn't been happy since the day she drew breath. A woman who always talked about the evil in others, but was more filled with hatred than anyone he'd ever known. A vindictive bitch, who was finally reaping what she had sown.

James wondered how she felt confined, alone in that stinking hospital room. It was nothing more than a glorified jail cell. He wondered how she liked wearing baggy cotton shifts with no jewelry. He bet she wasn't bragging about how wonderful Clifford Jacobson was now that he'd proclaimed her as a murderer.

He remembered, even back in college, Jacobson had Sybil wrapped around his little finger. He really had her pegged for a sucker. It embarrassed him the way she chased after Jacobson, even after they were engaged. He was surprised Jacobson hadn't latched onto her himself, considering the stories about her family's supposed wealth. Knowing Jacobson, James figured he probably had her background investigated and discovered the only thing rich about Sybil was her imagination.

When the telephone rang for the umpteenth time, James picked it up, and growled into the receiver. "Hello!"

"Mr. Kelsey?" a demure voice responded.

His eyes widened in recognition. "Kerry, honey, is that you?"

"Mr. Kelsey. I just heard some terrific news. I had to call you. I thought you would want to know."

He sighed heavily. "I could use some good news about now."

— 327 —

A pause followed. "I'm sorry about Mrs. Kelsey. I heard about it on the radio on my way home from work the other day. I can't believe she murdered Captain Woolard."

"Don't get me started," he quipped. "It's a sore subject. Now, tell me your good news."

"Mr. Kelsey, they found the babies," she said.

James rocked back in his swivel chair. "Thank Christ," he murmured softly.

Just when he was beginning to wonder if there was any reason to go on living, Kerry had just given him a perfect one. He had a grandchild. And he was finally going to see him in person. A wide grin spread over his haggard face. "You've just made me the happiest man in the world. I want you to tell me everything."

He clutched the receiver tightly, listening intently to every word she said. His heart hammered loudly. He hadn't been this happy since Robbie was alive.

CHAPTER FIFTY-FOUR

Doctor Kyle Whitley sat near Sybil Kelsey's bed, scribbling information onto a legal pad, in particular her adverse reaction to his questions. Her fingers gripped the edge of the bed, like a hawk clinging to the branch of a Birch tree. Her beady eyes shifted disapprovingly from his semi-bald head to the repulsive orange tie draped over a forest green shirt with gaudy brass buttons.

"How much longer are you planning to keep me here?" she whined, absently picking at the skin on her arms.

He looked up startled. She hadn't uttered a word in days. "I'm afraid you have a long way to go, Sybil. You have so many painful memories buried inside you that need to come to the surface." He smiled reassuringly. "Only then will we be able to help you."

"Help me?" she snorted. "There's nothing wrong with me...nothing some fresh air and a decent meal wouldn't cure."

He grimaced, thinking that if Sybil ever did get well enough to leave the psychiatric ward, her new surroundings would be far worse, and the food deplorable.

"Well," he said, crossing his legs, "Since you're in such a hurry to leave our fine hospitality, I have to ask you some questions."

Her sharp features formed a grotesque mask. "I thought psychiatrists were supposed to listen to people, not ask stupid questions."

He pursed his lips. "We could do it that way, but that technique could take months...maybe years...and you just said you were eager to get out of here."

She sighed heavily. "All right then, ask your damned questions. The faster we can get this over with the better."

He flipped to the next page on his pad and scribbled another note.

"I was hoping you'd tell me about your marriage to James Kelsey, and what led up to it."

Her face shriveled. "That miserable pip-squeak. He never was man enough for me."

Doctor Whitley didn't look up. "Was that because you were in love with another man?"

She inhaled sharply. "Did I say that?"

He placed his pen on the open notebook. "Well, you did insinuate you were in love with another man before your husband came along. Did you tire of him?"

She closed her eyes tightly, causing the lines around them to furrow into deep crevices. "The other man, you mentioned, and I were very much in love. We studied at the University of Richmond together. I loved him even after I married James."

The doctor's gaze remained thoughtful. "I have a note here that says you became pregnant by this other man. What happened to the child, Mrs. Kelsey?"

A pitiful sigh followed. "When I told him I was pregnant, he was mortified. He told me his plans for the future were too important to be compromised by a foolish mistake." She blinked rapidly. "He called our child a foolish mistake? He begged me to transfer to another college immediately, before my condition became obvious." Sybil's laugh sounded more like a bark. "He wasn't going to get rid of me that easily. I wasn't some cheap nobody he could toss aside once he was finished with them. I intended to be a part of his life forever. But he made it quite clear that if I didn't do as he said, we were through."

A long pause followed. "What did you do?"

"I…I had an abortion."

The doctor quickly made another notation. "What did he do when he found out you had aborted his child?"

— 330 —

THE BABY SOLDIERS

She clutched her wrinkled gown. "He threw a fit. What did you expect him to do? Clifford Jacobson despised abortion and anyone who would even consider having one. He still does."

"So," the doctor said cautiously, "he turned against you because you aborted his love child rather than transferring to another university and keeping quiet about it."

Her smile was sinister. "After the abortion, he still wanted me to transfer to another university. But once I explained what would happen to his wonderful career if I let our nasty little secret out... well...you see," she said calculatingly. "There were so many additional expenses."

"So, he eventually forgave you?"

"No," she replied sharply."Not for having the abortion. He never forgave me for that. He told me that God would punish me for that." She lowered her head. "And He has, a hundred times."

"What happened then?" Doctor Whitley asked, studying her intently.

Her back stiffened. "Clifford permitted me to continue working with him on his experiments, but he balked when it came to continuing our personal relationship." Her head swayed from side to side. "He had so many excuses. His work always came first. But I was determined to marry him, so I struck it out, running his errands, begging for money for materials and supplies, and doing everything I could to help the cause."

The doctor looked puzzled. "How does James Kelsey fit into all of this? You did say you married him while you were still at the university?"

She chortled loudly. "James always had the nose of a reporter, even back then. Clifford was afraid James would get wind of his experiments, so he asked me to run interference for him."

"Interference? I don't I follow you. How did that work?"

"Clifford was working on altering defective genes while the fetus was in its early stages, thereby insuring the delivery of a perfectly developed child. Whenever James began sniffing around the lab when

— 331 —

Clifford was doing his experiments, my job was to throw myself at him and draw him away." Her face suddenly pruned. "Like a wanton trollop. Naturally, a man with James's limited sexual experience was overwhelmed by the attention. And Clifford's experiments remained intact."

The doctor looked puzzled. "That explains why you kept Kelsey occupied, but it doesn't explain why you married him?"

She exhaled in exasperation. "One day, while Clifford and I were off gathering research information, James snuck into the lab and found Clifford's notes. He confronted Clifford with them and threatened to have him expelled from the university. Back then, that kind of experimenting was strictly forbidden. Clifford told me I would have to marry James and take him off somewhere, anywhere, so he'd be able to continue his research unhampered."

"So, you married a man you didn't love in order to please a man who didn't love you."

She nodded. "I loved Clifford that much. Yes. I married James. I would have done anything to make Clifford happy."

Anything but leave him alone, the doctor mused.

"I expect he was grateful," Whitley said, enthralled by the story Sybil was telling him. He thought he had heard it all before. But this was even stranger than the other horror stories he'd heard about the infamous preacher over the years.

She folded her hands, rubbing her thumbs together. "When James and I returned from our honeymoon, I continued to work on Clifford's projects, but he became more and more distant. When I asked him why, he told me he didn't want it to look as though he were trying to spoil my marriage." She laughed hysterically once again. "Imagine, spoiling something that should have never happened to begin with."

The doctor scribbled frantically.

"Then I became pregnant with Robbie."

"Robbie? He was Kelsey's child?" the doctor asked, trying to keep the facts straight in his own mind.

THE BABY SOLDIERS

Reluctantly, she nodded. "After that, Clifford began avoiding me completely. The only time he acted human toward me was when he needed financial help, or wanted me to lead a demonstration on his behalf."

"Which you agreed to do without hesitation," he replied amazed.

She nodded. "Yes. I still loved him, in spite of everything."

"So, when he asked you to kill Captain Woolard, you were merely going along with his wishes, the way you had in the past."

"Killing Horace Woolard was no problem," she replied adamantly. "That man was a brute. He treated his family and the men who worked under him worse than garbage."

"If you willingly did everything Clifford Jacobson wanted you to do, why do you suppose he turned you in to the police after you'd murdered Captain Woolard?"

She closed her eyes, shaking her head violently. "That wasn't the reason he turned me in."

He looked up, trying not to appear as confused as he felt. "Why then?" he asked.

"After I killed Horace, I thought he'd be thrilled, that he'd want me again...that things would be the way they used to be between us." She whimpered. "He wanted more alright."

He leaned forward. "What more could he possibly want from you?"

"He wanted me to kill Kerry Trivane and Amy Patterson."

The doctor's face contorted. "Who are they?"

"I don't know Amy Patterson personally, but Kerry Trivane is the slut responsible for my boy being murdered in front of that abortion clinic last year. If he hadn't gone with her that day, he'd be alive today."

Kyle Whitley tapped the pen against his notepad. "But Mrs. Kelsey, you admitted that you had an abortion, too. How could you damn someone else for making the same mistake you had?"

She pressed her index finger against her lips. "No one was supposed to find out about my abortion. It was a secret."

"I see," he said, not seeing at all.

— 333 —

Sybil sat quietly for a moment, running her hands over the edge of the sheet. "I couldn't kill Kerry Trivane. Robbie loved her." She shrugged her narrow shoulders. "He must have had his reasons, although they escaped me." She sighed tiredly. "When I called Clifford back and told him I couldn't go through with it, he threatened to tell James about the abortion I had before we were married. I told him I didn't care. James was too much of a coward to do anything about it anyway."

The doctor noticed her hands trembling. "That must have made the preacher angry," he said. "He was probably afraid he couldn't make you do his bidding any longer."

She nodded fiercely. "He said he couldn't trust me, and that God was going to punish me for my sins."

Doctor Whitley appeared dumbfounded. "Was that when he decided to tell the police what you'd done to Captain Woolard?"

"Yes," she replied weakly. "He told them I was mentally disturbed. It must be true," she said, her rodent eyes shifting from one side of the small room to the other.

"Because here I am, in this pathetic hospital, babbling like a loon."

The doctor rose slowly to his feet. "I can't speak for the police, but I believe you, Mrs. Kelsey. Your story is too incredible to be fabricated."

"Good," she said. "Maybe if you put in a good word for me, I can get out of here and get on with my life."

His warm hazel eyes washed over her face. He bet she'd been a real pistol when she was younger. He had never seen a patient with more misdirected spunk. "Would you like me to call your husband and let him know how you're doing? I can arrange to have him come and visit if you like?"

She stared up at him; her eyes appeared burdened with the pain of a thousand years of injustice. "I don't want James," she replied softly. "I want you to call Clifford. Jacobson and tell him I need him."

THE BABY SOLDIERS

By eight o'clock, all the available parking places near the clubhouse and the swimming pool outside Amy's apartment complex had been filled by friends and converts to the cause. All of them had come to the special meeting to hear about their babies. Amy was pleased to see Rebecca pushing Angie's wheelchair off the elevator, even though she wore a veil over her face. It was one of the few times the two women had ventured out in public, since the fire at the shelter that had left them permanently scarred.

Margaret Hatchey sat in a ladderback chair by the stone fireplace, making a list of things that had to be done prior to the assault on the prison where the babies were being held. Byron had sent her a list of police officers formerly affiliated with Jacobson's organization, and a list of officers who could be trusted. When David Williams arrived, she presented him with both lists, and watched with trepidation as he shook his head.

Danny and Jason Woolard had arrived separately. Amy introduced Jason to the members of the group he didn't know, which included almost everyone. He blushed easily whenever someone shook his hand, or patted him on the back, telling him how grateful they were to him for finding the children. Considering all the flack he'd gotten from Danny and his mother, after they heard he had been following his father, the welcome attention gave him a tremendous rush.

Danny's eyes lit up the moment he saw Kerry. Bernie and Priscilla stood nearby, carefully observing the strangers in the group. Kerry introduced her folks to Rebecca and Angie, and quickly explained what had happened to Angie legs and Rebecca's face.

Kerry smiled when she saw Danny approach."What a great turn out!"

He nodded happily. "I'll say. It looks like everyone made it after all."

David Williams patted Danny on the back. "I think we'd better get everybody seated, so we can discuss our strategy."

Bernie Trivane squeezed Kerry's hand. "Don't worry, honey. Just a couple more days and this will all be over."

— 335 —

Kerry's smile waned as she crossed the long expanse of the club-house. She sat down in one of the folding chairs that Amy had set up for the meeting. In two or three days, she thought dreamily, I'll be holding my baby in my arms. She shivered, thinking that she and Robbie had nearly aborted the child. It seemed so unbelievable now, after all that had happened. Although Robbie had been killed, tonight she felt his presence as strongly as if he were sitting right beside her. "Soon," she whispered. "Soon our baby will be home with me, where he belongs."

Kerry jumped when Danny placed his hand on her shoulder. "Can I see you after the meeting?" he asked. "There's something I..."

She shushed him, when she noticed Amy was trying to start the meeting.

"Will everyone please find a seat," Amy shouted.

After a few moments of shuffling and scraping chairs, the room fell silent.

"I want to thank you all for coming," Amy said. "As you know, the day we've been praying for is finally at hand."

Angie let out a loud whoop. Everyone laughed.

"Day after tomorrow, we will finally get our babies back."

A clamor of applause followed. The noise was deafening. Amy waved her hands to quiet the crowd. "People, please," she cried out. "I don't want to get thrown out of this place. I really like my apartment."

Once the noise subsided, she continued. "Most of you know Sergeant David Williams." She motioned for him to join her. "David has volunteered to have some police officers lead us through the main gates of the prison."

"Way to go, David!" Someone yelled.

David's rugged face flushed as he joined Amy in front of the group. He clutched the papers in his hands. "Hopefully, we'll be able to pull this off without a hitch."

His wandering eyes observed the faces before him, some were familiar, most were strange, but all of them were ready and willing

THE BABY SOLDIERS

to help. "Since talking to Amy earlier, we've been awfully busy trying to pull a plan together."

The excited group applauded his efforts.

"Margaret Hatchey," he said, motioning toward the woman warming herself by the fire, "has given me some invaluable information. A source, which she cannot divulge at this time, was able to provide us with a list of names of the people who were guards at the old prison farm before it closed. We used our own sources to establish that many of the same people are still working there… guarding your babies, no less."

A clamor of protests followed.

"Hear me out," he said, raising his right hand like a traffic cop.

The room quieted instantly.

"As you can well imagine, they don't want any trouble. They don't even want anyone to know what they were doing there. Some of them have families, who have no idea what their jobs entail. And, if they ever found out they were guarding and training young children to become soldiers, they would be ostracized, or worse."

"Worse would be my choice!" Someone yelled.

Someone else shouted, "They're going to pay for this!"

David nodded grimly. "They'll pay all right. Once this is over, the state may have to open all the old prisons again, for their original purpose…housing actual criminals!"

More applause thundered through the room.

"Calm down, everyone," Amy said. "Let David finish."

David nodded his appreciation. "The main thing we have to concentrate on is getting the children out safely. I want everyone to be very careful when we get there. I want you to do exactly as you're told. I don't want anyone going off half-cocked and trying to storm the place on his or her own. We don't want any dead heroes."

"We're with you, David," someone said.

"Good," he replied. "After the children are safe and on their way to the place that's been prepared for them in Carolina, we will go after the leader of this insidious group. The man who systematically

— 337 —

gained the trust of so many unsuspecting people over the years... turning them into virtual sheep. Who among you would be satisfied to put away this sinister shepherd?"

The crowd looked at each other confused. "Who?" They murmured.

His eyes wandered slowly over the attentive group. "The man you want to prosecute is the one who started this crusade of kidnapping women and selling their babies for profit. The man who wanted to be god!"

"Crucify him," Someone cried.

David was about to add something when the doorbell rang. Amy shrugged, then nodded toward Danny. Several of the people in the room gasped, when James Kelsey walked in.

Kerry stood up instantly. "It's all right, everyone," she said. "I invited Mr. Kelsey to come here this evening."

Amy looked irritated. "Kerry, I wish you had discussed it with me first." Then she turned her attention to the rest of the group. "I'm sure that most of you are familiar with Mr. Kelsey. For those of you who aren't, James Kelsey runs the Ledger Star, which hasn't been very favorable to our cause in the past."

Her glare was accusing. "I'm assuming you're here because you've had a change of heart?"

Kelsey's eyes drifted over the wary faces in the room. He was surprised to see so many people he knew, including several members of his own staff. He walked briskly toward Amy and David, feeling a hundred eyes drilling through the back of his head.

He smiled nervously. "Miss Patterson is exactly right," he said timidly. "Until last year, I was totally against your group and everything you stood for." He took a deep breath and then continued. "Now, however, it seems we have more holding us together than tearing us apart. Most of you who fought so hard to keep abortion legal are gathered here to save the very children you planned to abort. A strange twist of fate, wouldn't you say?"

A restless silence followed.

THE BABY SOLDIERS

"If any of you have been keeping up with the news, you are aware that I have taken it upon myself to investigate rumors of subversive activities among certain religious factions in our state and beyond."

"What about that crazy wife of yours?" Someone shouted. "Has she shot anybody else lately?"

James grimaced. Danny gave Jason a sidelong glance, concerned by the reference to their father. Jason shrugged nonchalantly.

James raised his hands, trying to maintain some semblance of order. "I can assure you that killing Captain Woolard was not my wife's idea," he muttered. "She was coerced into doing that by someone more evil and powerful than you could possibly imagine."

"Who?" They chanted. "Who?"

"The same person who convinced Captain Woolard that the principal of Justice Academy had to be eliminated," he answered.

"Scott Robinson?" Someone yelled. "That pervert?"

Angie tightened her fingers around the armrests of her steel chair as she glanced around the room. She wondered how many of the people gathered here had seen the tapes of her and Robinson having sex on top of his office desk. And how many others had experienced the same circumstances. She lowered her head staring at her lifeless legs. She'd never walk again. Her punishment for one brief moment of stupidity would last a lifetime.

Kelsey nodded. "I realize that many of you believe that Robinson got exactly what he deserved."

"You're damned right he did!" someone roared.

"How would you feel if I told you that the same person who ordered Scott Robinson's demise also wanted to kill the girls he had abused, because they were an embarrassment to his organization?"

A frenzy of gasps rippled through the room.

"It's taken a long time to get the proof we needed to bring charges against this freak. But we finally have enough." Kelsey said proudly. "After the children are reunited with their families, my newspaper will tell the story of how this horrible tragedy unfolded. How it was all the result of one man's psychotic dream to become the absolute ruler of a perfect race. Clifford Jacobson."

Margaret Hatchey pressed her back against the chair's hard slats. Her troubled face appeared finally at peace. Her personal dream that one-day Clifford Jacobson would be punished for his crimes would finally come true.

"Mr. Kelsey," someone asked, "are you saying Reverend Jacobson is behind everything that has happened to us?"

"I just knew it," another chimed in. "He was always forcing his demented ideas on everyone."

"I know I still have a long way to go before I earn your respect and confidence," James said, his eyes fixed intently on Kerry. "I think I've come a long way from the narrow-minded slob I was before my son was killed, and his girlfriend kidnapped."

Kerry stood up. "Clifford Jacobson is responsible for that, too," she said.

A tall, slender figure rose in the back of the room. She was unknown to most of the group. Few had made if far enough to meet her in person…at the Nelson Clinic where she worked part-time.

"Jacobson is behind all of it," she said vehemently. "He was responsible for bombing the abortion clinics and everyone inside them. He has killed doctors and nurses and pregnant women by the hundreds. He was responsible for your loved ones being kidnapped and murdered, and humiliated the brave souls who dared to speak out against him." She nodded, acknowledging the newsman. "James Kelsey never stopped tearing away at Jacobson's armor, and it has cost him plenty. I admire him for that."

Kelsey nodded, touched by her comments.

"Jacobson forced your families to abandon their homes and businesses and go into hiding like common criminals." Julie Newman grabbed the back of the chair in front of her, pausing only long enough to catch her breath. "He destroyed my family, too. My brother was a doctor, who volunteered to work at an abortion clinic in his spare time. He felt it was important that those girls receive proper medical attention. He was shot down, murdered by one of Clifford Jacobson's men. "My brother was my hero. He meant more to me than anything in the world."

The room was so quiet, the rumble of the logs in the fireplace sounded like a jet breaking the sound barrier.

"I want to be present when you get your children back," Julie told them. "And I want to be there to see the expression on Jacobson's face when he is found guilty on all charges. God forgive me, but I, too, want my pound of flesh."

David could see he wasn't the only one with tears in his eyes. "Thank you, Julie," he said softly.

Feeling completely drained, Julie sat down. A stranger's hand reached out consolingly and touched her shoulder.

"Julie is an emergency room supervisor at Chesapeake Regional Hospital." David told them. "I first met Julie while investigating Robbie Kelsey's murder. Rebecca and Angie got to know Julie on a more personal level, while they were in the hospital fighting their way back from the fire that destroyed the Haven and killed three of their friends. Julie has no family, now that her brother is gone," David said, fighting back another onslaught of tears."If it's all right with you, we'll adopt her as part of ours."

While everyone rose from their seats and clustered around Julie, David took the opportunity to go to the kitchen and get a drink of water. He was shocked when he found Rebecca sitting at the kitchen table, trembling all over.

"Rebecca?" he asked, hunkering down beside her. "What is it?"

She shook her head. "I'll be all right, David. It's just that when you were talking about Julie and her brother and what happened to me and Angie, I started thinking about the fire at the shelter all over again, and the girls we couldn't save."

He nodded understandingly. "Can I fix you a cup of coffee?" he asked.

She shook her head, forcing herself to her feet. "Amy would have my hide if she walked in here and saw you waiting on me. Taking care of other people is my job."

David slumped into a chair, looking as emotionally drained as Julie had. All the talk about death and Jacobson's involvement made his more certain that ever that the preacher was involved in Ann and Ginny's deaths as well. He had no doubt Horace was involved somehow, but the more he'd heard from the women in the other room, the more convinced he became that Jacobson had orchestrated it. And if his suspicions were correct, he needed to know why?

After the group finished discussing the rescue of the children, they discussed which of them would be responsible for taking the children back to Morehead City and caring for them until their parents could be located. The Trivanes and Margaret Hatchey volunteered to be in charge of the caregivers.

Rebecca's interest was focused on the female babies, the ones who had been sold. After discovering her own child was a girl, Rebecca became more determined than ever to find out who had initiated the illegal adoptions. No one was surprised when she came forward to say the men in charge of selling the babies were a group of lawyers, hand- picked by Clifford Jacobson himself. They were the same lawyers who did all the legal work for The New Order. Rebecca said the lawyers' fates would be far worse than those of the men who guarded the children. Lawyers were accustomed to all the creature comforts money could buy, and their fate would rival the degradation that awaited Clifford Jacobson himself…banished to some stone-cold prison cell, awaiting a prick from the deadly needle.

David returned to the room where Amy and the others were gathered. As other speakers shared their information and their feelings, he glanced over at Danny and Jason, surprised to see they were still there. It was obvious they did not have the same demented genes as their father. Whenever Horace's name was mentioned, neither of the boys displayed any sign of emotion or even recognition. They behaved as though the name meant absolutely nothing to them. David smiled as he thought about how worried Adele had been when Jason told her he was coming here tonight. She didn't want him to be upset by the hateful things that would surely be said about his father. The boys were a lot stronger than she gave them credit for, he thought. He couldn't have been more proud if they had been his own sons.

When the meeting ended, James Kelsey shouldered his way through the crowd until he reached Kerry and her parents. Bernie studied his one-time friend warily. Kerry reached out and took James by the hand. "Thank you for coming, Mr. Kelsey, and thank you for saying the things you did. I know it wasn't easy...after everything that's happened."

James nodded to Bernie and Priscilla, who may well have been Robbie's in-laws had things turned out differently.

"Mr. Kelsey," Kerry said, drawing his attention back to her. "Would you like to come with us when we go to pick up the babies? I...I thought you might like a chance to hold your grandson in your arms."

Her invitation overwhelmed him. His eyes flooded with tears. Bernie put a powerful arm around his shoulder. "What do you say, Grandpa?"

Priscilla stood beside her daughter, smiling proudly.

Everything was going to be all right after all. The child he had blamed for tearing their families apart would be the same child who would bring them together again. James put his trembling arms around Kerry and sighed raggedly. The weight of the world had suddenly lifted from his narrow shoulders. "I can't think of anything in this world that would make me happier."

Danny grinned as he joined the small group outside the apartment clubhouse. "You guys weren't planning to have a party without me, were you?"

"I wouldn't dream of it," Kerry replied, slipping her arm through his."If it wasn't for you, we wouldn't have reason to celebrate."

"That's for sure," Bernie said. "Margaret tells us you've been a regular guardian angel to our little girl for some time now."

— 343 —

Danny blushed. "I didn't do anything. I was just trying to make up for..."

Sensing that Danny was referring to his father's mistakes, James said, "Danny, you can't blame yourself for that. The only wrongs any of us are responsible for are the ones we make on our own."

"Here! Here!" Bernie said.

"May I suggest we get out of here and find some place to eat?" James said, rubbing his stomach. "Suddenly, I feel very hungry."

Danny's eyes glistened, as he replied, "Me, too."

Kerry gave him a playful shove. "Danny, you're always hungry."

The small group walked from the apartment complex arm in arm, their laughter chasing the coldness from the night.

CHAPTER FIFTY-FIVE

Byron Spears emerged from the limousine and straightened his tie. His three-piece blue suit was entirely too dressy for the occasion, but it was the only way he could leave Jacobson's estate without drawing suspicion. Margaret's directions had been precise as usual, although he was sure he was lost after making that last turn onto a winding country road that seemed without end.

The prison farm looked forsaken, so far from the main road. The only thing resembling a traffic signal he'd seen in the past ten miles had been a railroad crossing a few miles back. The warden's quarters, an emergency dispensary, and barns were located on the left side of the road.

The grounds looked much like any other agricultural area. Approximately two hundred head of cattle stood grazing near a stocked fishpond. Beyond the livestock fence were acres of open fields, which produced a fine harvest of corn, peanuts and soybeans in their respective seasons.

Houses in the area were sparse, some were wood framed, others vinyl sided, sitting on wheels. It was the kind of place hard working farmers planted their crops, raised their families and died, leaving their names chiseled on concrete monuments on their own land.

Twenty wide concrete steps climbed up to a set of sturdy oak doors. Byron Spears climbed the steps slowly; beads of perspiration trickled down his face and neck. He wasn't sweating from the heat, but rather from the edgy feeling he always had when entering one of these facilities. It reminded him of a war no one should have fought.

GERRY R. LEWIS

The doors were unlocked, which came as a surprise, and two armed guards were situated directly inside the entrance.

While studying the layout of the grounds and the names of the people he would encounter, he learned that Stanley Keefer, a friend from the old days, would be manning the reception desk this morning. He wished it were a stranger he'd be confronting rather than Stanley. He and Stanley had fought side by side in a hundred wars, and had marched shoulder to shoulder for as many causes. Now, they were on opposite sides of the fence. He was a warrior, experienced enough to know that in a situation like this, anything could happen. But regardless of how things transpired, he hoped that somehow his friendship with Stanley would remain intact. Under the circumstances, that didn't appear likely, but Byron was hopeful none the less.

Stanley Keefer was a tall man, about Bernie Trivane's size, only his bulk had settled in all the wrong places. He was wearing brown slacks and a long-sleeved tan shirt, the mid-section puckering at the buttons. His grin was generous, the way Byron remembered.

"My eyes must be deceiving me," he bellowed, extending a friendly hand. "Byron Hatchey, of all people."

Byron shook his hand. "The name is Spears now. It's been a long time, Stanley. I can't say I expected to see you hanging around one of these places."

"What in the name of all that's holy are you doing out here in the middle of the sticks? I'm surprised Jacobson didn't call and let us know you were coming. We'd have prepared something special for dinner."

Byron rubbed his index finger along the edge of his trim mustache. "Jacobson doesn't know I'm here," he replied. "I'm on urgent business of my own."

The smile faded from Stanley's craggy face. "What kind of business?"

Byron placed his briefcase on top of the desk and opened it to extract a file containing several legal documents. He presented the

— 346 —

THE BABY SOLDIERS

folder to his friend and waited silently while Stanley inspected each page.

Stanley's face wrinkled querulously. "These are from the Attorney General's office?" he said, puzzled. "I don't understand. It says if we do everything we're told, we will receive lighter sentences?" He looked up, his dark eyes intense. "Byron, what the hell is the meaning of this?"

Byron studied Stanley's face. His old friend was far more angry than puzzled. If he wasn't extremely careful, this could go very badly. "It means exactly what it says, Stanley. The state police are on their way now. We're taking the children being held here back where they belong. Anyone attempting to interfere will suffer the consequences."

Stanley slammed the folder down on the desk. Papers scattered everywhere. "Whose bright idea was this?" he asked sharply.

Byron gathered the papers and slipped them back into their folders. "Hard as it may be for you to believe, there's an even more powerful organization out there than Clifford Jacobson's New Order."

Byron felt as though his guts were on fire. He didn't want to argue with Stanley. He'd rather they were in a pub, joking over old times.

Stanley sneered. "There is no such organization. I would have heard."

"I'm sure you haven't heard of this one," Byron replied, remembering Stanley wasn't much of a news hound. "They're freedom fighters, Stan...like we once were."

Stanley's face turned ashen, his breath loud and wheezing. "And just what do these freedom fighters intend to do?"

Byron slid the documents inside the briefcase. "Once the children are freed, they intend to prove Clifford Jacobson is a liar, a fraud, and an evil force beyond measure."

Stanley's eyes narrowed skeptically. Byron could feel the storm brewing behind them. "This is nuts!" he said. "You're one of Jacobson's closest allies? Good lord, Byron, you've been his right arm for years. How could you, of all people, get involved with some ignorant fools who think they can destroy somebody like him?"

— 347 —

Byron turned from his old friend to the window. Outside were a million trees whose branches looked shriveled and dead without their leaves. His eyes took on a hypnotic quality. "There was a time when I believed Clifford Jacobson was the greatest man alive…the same as you and everyone else we knew. He was kind to rich and poor alike. He treated everyone with the utmost respect. He had sound ideas for strengthening the family unit and preserving individual rights. He was going to make our country the strongest and most influential in the world. He had ideas… so many grand ideas."

Stanley sat down hard. The swivel chair cried beneath his weight. "I assume you believe something has happened to change all that?"

Byron loosened his tie, feeling as though he were choking. "Oh, his ideas were fine—as far as it goes. The problem was the man himself changed. He's not the man we all thought he was, or maybe he is the same man, and I wasn't smart enough to see how corrupt he was."

"I don't think he's changed at all," Stanley said haughtily. "He's the same wonderful man he's always been."

Byron studied his old friend's face. He looked like a pouting schoolboy.

"Stanley, do you really believe that?"

"Of course, I believe it!" he snapped. "Look at all the terrific things he's done over the years."

Byron snorted. "You call forcing young girls to have children terrific?"

"It certainly was better than allowing them to murder their children," Stanley retorted.

"What about the innocent people Jacobson murdered?" Byron asked, biting his lip.

"Innocent?" The word sounded like a hiss coming from Stanley's lips. "None of them was innocent. They were out to ruin him and the organization with their selfishness. You know that better than anyone. They sided with the baby killers. And some of them did evil, ugly things."

THE BABY SOLDIERS

"So, you think Jacobson killed those people just to make the world a safer place for the rest of humanity?"

Stanley expanded his wide chest proudly. "We did our share," he boasted. "We brought the children here, and now, we're taking care of them for him."

"Tell me something, Stanley. Why were they brought here?"

"For his important work," Stanley answered belligerently.

"Jacobson's work," Byron said, the putrid taste of bile rising in his throat.

Stanley nodded. "Our leader has great plans for those kids. When we get finished training them, they'll be the best soldiers he could ever hope for."

Byron leaned against the edge of the padded desk, careful not to snag his suit coat on the torn leather. "Any ideas what those long-range goals are?"

Stanley rolled his eyes impatiently. "Byron, are you testing me? Is that what this is all about?"

He turned awkwardly when he heard one of the guards approaching. Byron nodded curtly to the slender man with chiseled features.

The man stopped suddenly, standing at attention as he saluted. "The children are waiting, sir," he said matter-of-factly.

Stanley gawked at the trim guard as though he were insane. "Turner, what are you talking about?"

"The children, Mr. Keefer," the guard replied. "I was instructed to have them packed and ready for pick-up when Mr. Spears arrived."

Stanley stumbled to his feet, and growled, "Who gave you those orders?"

Turner unfolded a green sheet of paper and showed it toward Stanley. "Here it is, sir. It's a transfer order, plain as day."

Stanley glanced from the paper to the sober faced guard at his side.

"Is there a problem?" Turner asked.

"No," Stanley mumbled helplessly. "Carry on."

— 349 —

The guard nodded then spun on his heels, marching down the lengthy hallway.

"I don't like this," Stanley said. "I don't like this one bit. It's deceitful. In fact, it's downright traitorous."

"I'm sorry you feel that way, Stanley. I was hoping that we..."

Stanley shifted to one side. "I can't go against Reverend Jacobson. It wouldn't be right. I made a promise." He snatched a revolver from under the desk, aiming it straight Byron's heart.

Byron, predicting the confrontation, had already drawn his own weapon. He took a deep breath and fired. Stanley's eyes widened in disbelief. He gasped sharply and fell behind the desk.

Byron holstered his weapon and hurried to the other side of the desk. He knelt down beside Stanley, holding his head in his hands. "I'm sorry it had to end this way," he whispered solemnly."There should have been more time for me to explain. Perhaps then, you would have understood why Jacobson has to be stopped." Byron felt like his air had been shut off. "We could have joined forces and fought side by side in this war, too."

Byron felt Stanley's spirit seeping from his body. He clasped the dying man's shoulder tightly and whispered, "Until we meet again, old friend."

Byron stood up trembling; his insides ached with the same loneliness he'd felt the day they told him his sister had disappeared. Then he turned, tucking his briefcase under his arm, and walked down the corridor to meet the others. Two guards fell in beside him. As their footsteps echoed along the tile hallway, Byron lowered his head, hoping they wouldn't see his tears.

The youngest children had been put into playpens in groups of four. The guards and the police officers, who'd accompanied David Williams, wheeled them from the barracks to the main lobby. The children between five and twelve carried their own belongings in burlap sacks, strapped over their shoulders. Most of the children in

THE BABY SOLDIERS

the latter group appeared sullen. This place had been their home, the only home they'd ever known. They muttered among themselves, confused and disgruntled.

Byron Spears and David Williams stood along the wall near the entrance, watching them parade by.

"Do you think we're too late to save them?" David said, just loud enough for Byron to hear.

Byron shook his head sadly. "Only time will tell," he replied. "After everything they've been through, it will probably take a miracle."

David nodded grimly. "Look at their eyes, there's no life in them. And the hypnotic way they march. They're only kids, and they scare the hell out of me. I wonder what kind of plans he had for them?"

Byron couldn't answer. He was so angry he could have spit nails. Couldn't Stanley see what was happening here? Couldn't he see those kids turning into robots, nothing short of killing machines for Jacobson and his New Order? He felt like running back down to the other end of the hall and shaking the death right out of him, so he could stand him on his feet and kill him all over again.

Loud cries of anguish erupted along the corridor behind them, as hordes of volunteers and parents plucked the children from the passing procession. Amy Patterson and Kerry Trivane darted from one playpen to the next, searching for their children. Each child was tagged with a number. Margaret Hatchey stood close-by, holding the record book and explaining how the number system worked.

Kerry looked into one of the playpens and saw a child with the most beautiful, blue eyes staring back at her. He was so big, she thought. He wrapped his perfect little fists around the wooden bars, grunting as he pulled himself to his feet. Number 2682. It was her baby. She squealed happily as she reached for him. Kerry held him close to her breast, tears of happiness spilling from her eyes. "You're safe now, little Robbie," she whispered softly. "Thank God you're alive." Her fingers quivered as she touched his smooth, round face. His corn silk hair wound around her fingertips. He looked just like his dad, she thought. Then she shivered to think that this precious

— 351 —

little child might never have been born at all. There were so many things she wanted to tell him. And she would, someday, when he was old enough to understand. Her baby was over a year old. He'd spent the first year of his life in the care of strangers. His little mouth opened to yawn. Kerry clutched him protectively. She was grateful she'd been given a second chance. From this day forward, she promised to watch over him and protect him from all harm. But more than anything, she would make up for all the times she'd missed holding him and loving him. He was hers, and she would never let him go.

Bernie and Priscilla Trivane wrapped their arms around their daughter and their new grandson. Over the small head bobbing in Kerry's arms, they glanced at each other like guilty conspirators sharing an unbearable secret...regretting the pain their daughter had endured for two years. Pain, they themselves had caused. Their daughter had experienced so much tragedy in seventeen brief years. She'd seen Robbie murdered. And she'd been kidnapped and forced to stay in an awful camp, surrounded by nothing but strangers during the most terrifying time of her life. And worst of all, she had watched helplessly as her baby had been taken from her the moment he was born. Their tremendous guilt weighed heavily on their own consciences. They prayed that Kerry would not hate them for the grief they'd caused, and forbid them from seeing their grandchild. The thought of never seeing Kerry and her baby again would be worse than dying. They tried so desperately not to dwell on the horrible things that had happened, but nothing could stop them from remembering that they alone were responsible for convincing Kerry to have an abortion. Poor Robbie had been in the middle. He'd only conceded because Kerry had given in to them. They could still see Sybil's accusing finger pointing at them, and the way her face contorted when she called them baby killers. And in reality, they were baby killers. They had killed Sybil and James's baby, Robbie, as surely as if they'd pulled the trigger themselves. That startling revelation was something that would haunt them the rest of their lives.

THE BABY SOLDIERS

Kerry hummed softly as she cradled the child in her arms. James Kelsey looked down at him and smiled. "What name have you chosen for him?"

Kerry looked at her son adoringly, and replied, "I've thought of little else since the day he was taken from me. I knew if the good Lord ever let me find him, it would be a sign of a second chance for all of us. I've decided to call him Robbie."

"Robbie," they whispered reverently.

James reached out, touching the baby's hands. Robbie's pink fingers closed around his thumb. "Robbie Kelsey. Well, what do you think about your new name, little fella?" Then he looked at the Trivanes and grinned proudly. "I think he likes it."

Margaret Hatchey walked over to one of the playpens where a small boy lay kicking and screaming, his hands curled into angry fists. She scooped up the unhappy child and carried him toward the noisy reception area. "Amy!' she shouted, holding the child high in the air. "I believe I have something that belongs to you. I'd recognize that set of lungs anywhere."

Amy squeezed between other mothers, grandparents, friends and volunteers until she reached Margaret and the wailing child in her arms. She looked at him and began to laugh as tears rolled down her face. "Oh, Margaret," she said, taking him and holding him close. "He's so big. I know he's mine without even checking the numbers."

Margaret thought her chest would burst from the pride she felt in her heart. She hugged Amy and the toddler. "I never doubted that one day you would find him. You're the most stubborn young woman I've ever known."

Amy looked from the little boy in her arms to the smiling woman she now called friend. "I'll take that as a compliment," she murmured. "But we have Jason to thank for finding the babies. Who knows how long it would have taken if he hadn't been curious enough to follow his father, and then brave enough to come forward."

— 353 —

"That's true," Margaret replied. "As for Byron, Danny and myself, we all knew something, but none of us knew enough. The rare few who were in Jacobson's inner circle, the ones who knew everything, are all dead now."

Amy grimaced. "Everyone but him."

Margaret nodded her head. "You know, the more I thought about the stories my sister used to tell me about him, the more I realized that Clifford Jacobson wanted to become another Adolph Hitler. Clifford had more in common with that maniac than I was willing to admit."

"It'll soon be over," Amy said, kissing her son's chubby face. "Once the world finds out about the appalling things he's done, he'll be through, both him and his precious organization."

Margaret nodded. "We've been looking forward to that day for a long time, haven't we?"

Amy nodded tearfully, holding her child tighter. "Too long."

"Margaret," she said solemnly."I want to thank you for everything. I know you have to be going back to prepare the siege. I just want you to know that..."

Margaret pressed her index finger over Amy's lips. "Don't you dare go getting blubbery on me, young lady. It just wouldn't be you."

Amy burst out laughing. "All right. I promise."

Margaret turned from her new family and walked down the hall, where she finally caught up with her brother. "Byron, I'm so sorry," she said. "Turner told me what happened with Stanley Keefer."

Byron frowned. "You know something, Margaret? Every time you enter a war zone, there's a chance you won't walk away from it. Stanley and I were both trained soldiers, aware that one day our turn would come. I just never thought...I never thought that I would be the one to..."

Margaret felt her chest tighten. She hadn't seen Byron so tormented since Peggy disappeared. She brushed his tears away with her hand. "You and Stanley were friends for a very long time."

THE BABY SOLDIERS

He smiled reflectively. "Yes, we were. Very good friends indeed. I shall carry his memory with me always."

"Where will you go now?" she asked.

"David and I are going to Baltimore as soon as things settle down here. He said he doesn't want Clifford hearing about the raid on his camp second hand. He wants to tell him in person."

James Kelsey heard the last part of their conversation as he joined them. He looked at Byron Spears and grimaced, shaking his hand. It was a lifetime ago, but he remembered seeing Byron and Stanley together on occasion. He'd always envied their friendship. "I wish this could have played out differently," he said. "Stanley was a fine man."

Byron nodded. "One of the best."

"Byron," James said, "would you have time to drop by my office before you go back to Baltimore? I should have the special edition ready by then. I'd appreciate it if you would hand deliver a copy to your boss for me."

Byron chuffed. James Kelsey was as clever at wielding a pen as other men were at wielding swords. "I'll be happy to," he replied, glancing furtively around the room. "Although I'm sure there are at least a hundred people here who would love to have that pleasure themselves."

James nodded grimly. "You can count me among them. I'd love nothing better than seeing the expression on his arrogant face when he finds out he's not god after all. I know there are plenty who will disagree with me, but he's never been much of a man either."

"How much prison time do you think he'll get?" someone asked.

"Considering all the red tape involved between politics, trials and appeals, and how many of his loyal supporters won't believe he's a monster, even though they have proof staring them right in the face." James shrugged. "Who knows."

Byron turned to James. "I'll meet you at your office later. I still have some things I need to take care of."

"That will be fine," James said, reaching for his hand. "The paper will be ready and waiting for you."

— 355 —

Danny Woolard saw Kerry and her folks standing in the parking lot talking to some people he recognized from the group meeting.

"Kerry!" he shouted, hoping she could hear him over the horns bleating from the departing convoy.

She spun around, her face beaming as he ran toward her. By the time he reached her, he was out of breath.

"Kerry," he said, gasping as he looked at the baby in her arms. "Is that him?"

"Yes," she answered proudly. "This is little Robbie." She stared lovingly at her baby and smiled. "Robbie, I'd like you to meet Danny Woolard."

Danny cocked his head to one side. "He's really small, isn't he?"

She laughed. "Actually, I think he's pretty big. Would you like to hold him for a minute?"

"I…I don't know if I can," he stuttered.

"Hold your arms out," she said. "That's the way." Carefully, she lowered her son into them.

Danny held the baby awkwardly. Then he chuckled nervously. "I never held a little baby before."

He looked like he was balancing on a tightrope, while holding a precious Ming vase. His eyes blinked rapidly as he glanced at the Trivanes. He was so terrified he'd drop the baby he didn't dare breathe. "See…see what I got," he stammered.

Bernie turned to Priscilla and roared with laughter. "Do you see the way he's holding that child?"

Priscilla nudged him gently. "It reminds me of the way you held Kerry when we first brought her home from the hospital."

Danny gawked at them in disbelief. "Really?"

"Really," Priscilla replied. "You men all act so tough until it comes to doing something simple, like holding a baby. Then you get all weak-kneed and fall apart."

THE BABY SOLDIERS

Kerry inhaled deeply. "I'll take him back now. I don't want you to have a heart attack or anything."

Danny exhaled heavily, happy to be relieved of his awesome burden. "That felt different."

Bernie slapped Danny on the back. "Not quite the same as holding a sack of potatoes, was it, son?"

Priscilla tugged Bernie's arm. "Bernie, stop teasing that poor boy. He's frightened to death. He looks like he's about to faint."

"Sorry," Bernie muttered. "I guess having a baby around the house is going to be a new experience for all of us."

Danny looked at Kerry and nodded. "Kerry, would it be all right if I stopped by to see you later on this evening?"

She glanced from Danny to her parents. "I...I'm..."

"Sure, you can," Bernie said. "If these two fillies are too worn out to rustle us up anything good for supper, I'll call the Colonel and have him drop by with some chicken and slaw."

"That would be great, sir," Danny said excitedly. "Should I bring anything?"

Kerry grinned impishly, and replied. "Danny, I can think of something for you to bring."

"Anything," he replied anxiously.

"You can swing by Wal-Mart and pick up some disposable diapers."

Danny glanced from one expectant face to another. Then he burst out laughing.

"That will be another first."

CHAPTER FIFTY-SIX

Adele Woolard spent the better part of the day in the closet of the master bedroom, packing Horace's belongings. She looked with grim fascination at all the shirts he'd collected over the years… many of which he'd never worn. Danny was the only one of the boys, who came close enough to fitting into any of Horace's things, but she knew Danny would never wear his father's clothes. Not only were their tastes different, but she seriously doubted Danny would want anything that even remotely reminded him of his father.

She took down the dusty garment bag from the rear of the closet and unzipped it. Her fingers trembled slightly as she touched the shiny lapel on the gray tuxedo and the tiny hole on the lapel, where the boutonniere had been pinned. It was the tuxedo Horace had worn on their wedding day. He was so different back then, she mused. He was gentle and fun. He enjoyed taking long walks along the beach and talking about their future.

"Some future," she mumbled bitterly.

She removed the tuxedo from the bag and folded it into a cardboard box with his shoes and other clothing. After she finished, she would call Goodwill and have them come and pick up his things. If nothing else, perhaps some kids could use his clothes for Halloween costumes. She removed an assortment of slacks in three different sizes. Most of those things should have been discarded years ago, but Horace wasn't the type to part with things, even things he no longer wanted. Whenever she'd suggested cleaning out the closets, he insisted she leave his stuff right where it was. Maybe someday, he'd

THE BABY SOLDIERS

wear those things again. She frowned. Someday was like tomorrow. It never came.

Jason peeked in the closet. "Mom, David's downstairs."

She placed the top on the box and looked at her son. "Honey, will you carry that downstairs for me?"

Jason picked up the box and grunted. "What are you going to do with all this stuff, open a used clothing store?"

"Just doing a little early spring cleaning," she replied.

"Right," he replied sarcastically."Spring cleaning in December."

She followed him down the stairs and found David waiting in the living room. When he saw Jason huffing beneath the weight of the cardboard box, he jumped to his feet. "Can I give you a hand with that?"

"You can open the garage door," Jason said, straining.

David hurried past him and opened the door leading to the garage. Jason dropped the box on the floor beside the others. "Whew!" he muttered. "I hope that's the last one."

Adele chuckled. "Let's just say that's the last heavy one."

Jason wiped his hands down the front of his jeans. "Mom?" he asked thoughtfully. "Would it be all right if I kept Dad's service revolver?"

"I...I suppose so," she stammered. "I didn't think you liked guns?"

"I don't, not really. But when I was a little kid, Dad told me if anything ever happened to him, he wanted me to have it."

She pushed back a wisp of hair from her face. "That's strange. He never mentioned it to me."

Jason chortled. "He probably never thought he was going to die."

"None of us do," she replied absently. She walked back to the living room, and smiled when she saw David standing in front of the bay window. "I wasn't expecting to see you so soon."

Hearing her voice, he spun around. "I just stopped by to tell you how things went at the prison farm today."

Jason's eyes were wide with expectation. "Everything went okay, didn't it?"

— 359 —

David nodded. "It went just fine. You should have been there, Jason. Lots of people wanted to thank you. You're a hero, you know."

Jason blushed as he shifted his feet. "I didn't do anything special."

"I bet you'll change your mind once you read Mr. Kelsey's story in tomorrow's newspaper."

Jason's mouth gaped open. Mr. Kelsey is writing a story about me? Why?"

Adele laughed. "Don't worry, Jason. It'll be something you can tell your grandchildren about someday."

Jason sauntered from the room, groaning, "Grandchildren? Give me a break."

David's eyes drifted slowly from Adele's face to the faded jeans hugging her slender hips. "I missed you today," he said.

"I missed you, too," she replied. "I wish I could have been there to see all those girls reunited with their babies." Then she cast her eyes downward. "But I was afraid if I went it would put a damper on the occasion. When the girls saw me, it would remind them of Horace. They blame him as much as Clifford Jacobson for everything that's happened to them."

David crossed the room and put his arms around her. "That doesn't mean they blame you, too, Adele. You were just as much a victim as they were."

She nodded, rubbing her cheek against his shirt. "No one will ever be a victim of Horace Woolard ever again."

He cupped her chin in his hand, lifting her face to meet his. "Do you still want to move somewhere far away?" he asked.

Adele shook her head slowly. "I was worried about the boys when I told you that. I was afraid they would have a terrible time adjusting...after what happened. But now, I feel that things might work out here after all."

He smiled, relaxed. "I'm glad to hear you say that. There are so many things I want to tell you."

She leaned back, cocking her head to one side. "Such as?"

THE BABY SOLDIERS

"Such as," he said hesitantly. "Things that will have to wait until I get back."

Adele's green eyes narrowed. "Get back? Get back from where?"

"I'm going to Baltimore tonight with Byron Spears. We're planning a little surprise party for Clifford Jacobson."

"David," she said, worriedly. "Promise me you won't do anything foolish."

He chuffed. "As much as I'd love nothing better than beating him so badly his own mother wouldn't recognize him, I promise I'll let the law take care of him."

"The law?" she replied wryly.

"Come on now," he said. "We're not all bad."

She rolled her eyes. "Unfortunately, most of them aren't like you."

His lips brushed her cheek. "That's all going to change real soon."

She nodded smugly. "You know, that's one of the things I like most about you."

"What's that?" he asked.

"Your optimism. You always talk as though everything will work out for the best."

"Adele, if I didn't believe that, there would be no point in going on." He dropped his arms to his sides and turned away. "If only you could have seen those girls today. Kerry Trivane and Amy Patterson in particular." He held his hands out, palms up. "Seeing them holding their children in their arms. It was really something. They never gave up hope they'd find their babies. The relief on their faces was worth a million bucks."

"Children can be a great comfort," she said, then quickly covered her mouth. "Oh, David," she muttered, embarrassed. "I'm so sorry."

He shook his head. "It's all right. What happened to Ginny was one of those instances when my optimism didn't pay off. You know some of those kids we saw today are about the same age Ginny's baby would have been...had she lived."

— 361 —

Adele's eyes narrowed thoughtfully. "David, do you think Ginny could have been murdered on her way to that awful place where the other girls were taken?"

David shook his head. "I don't know. I'm hoping I can get some answers from Jacobson."

"I doubt if he'll tell you the truth, particularly if he was involved. But that still wouldn't explain why Ann was killed, too."

He shrugged. "Maybe Ann and Ginny were going to an abortion clinic...the way Kerry Trivane and Robbie Kelsey were. They shot Robbie because he recognized them. Maybe that's what happened to Ann."

Adele shook her head. "Oh, David, it's all so horrible."

David grimaced. "I always wondered why the kidnappers hadn't killed the girls they kidnapped. Now I know, they were too valuable alive."

"What's going to happen to the children whose parents don't live around here anymore?" she asked.

"They'll be taken to Carolina, to the place Amy and Danny have been working so hard to finish these last few months. Hopefully, it won't be long until their parents are located."

"Ironic, isn't it?" she replied. "Danny helping the same people his father was trying to destroy."

David nodded toward the sofa. "Can we sit down for just a minute?"

She studied his troubled face. "There's something else, isn't there?"

"Some new developments have come up since Horace died," he replied somberly.

"What kind of developments?" she asked, puzzled.

"It has to do with the cabin where Horace was killed."

She nodded grimly. "He bought it so he'd have someplace to go hunting. He took me there once, shortly after we were married. I hated it. All the bugs and snakes. I'd completely forgotten about it until...until he died."

— 362 —

David stretched his arms across the back of the sofa. "After finding Horace's body, the county deputies started nosing around the place." He sighed tiredly, as though he hadn't slept in days. "Adele, they found more bodies."

"Oh God, no!" she cried, horrified. "How long had they been there?"

David stood up slowly and began to pace. "Some of them were so badly decomposed, it was hard to tell." He gazed down at her, and added weakly. "Like Ann and Ginny."

Adele clutched her arms, the color fading from her face. "Now you're more convinced than ever that Horace killed them, or had something to do with them being killed."

"I don't know anything at this point," he answered, his voice drifting. "'Maybe the area was being used as a dumping ground, because it was so remote. Maybe none of the deaths are related at all."

"David," she said, thoughtfully. "The location of Horace's cabin wasn't that far from where the hunters found Ann and Ginny, was it?"

He sat down once again and leaned his head against the back of the sofa. "About one or two miles."

Adele shuddered. "That's too close to be a coincidence."

"Adele, I really have to get going," he said, glancing at his watch. "I still have some things to do before I leave."

Adele walked him to the front door. "How long do you think you'll be gone?"

He stared through the glass panel next to the door. The rain had turned to snow. "Shouldn't take longer than two days." He turned, kissing her gently on the mouth. "I'll call you tomorrow night."

"I'll be right here," she assured him.

"When I get back, maybe we should think about making some plans of our own."

Adele held him so tightly. "Please be careful," she said. "I don't want anything to happen to you."

He kissed her eyelids, her cheeks, her lips. "I'll be careful," he said. "It's been a long time since either of us was happy. I'd like to stick around long enough to see how it feels."

Amy Patterson removed her son from the car seat and carried him up the front walk of the new Haven House. From the outside, it looked like a warm bed and breakfast. The foyer opened into a huge dining area where the mouth-watering aroma of the last meal hung in the air. Off to the left was a brightly painted kitchen with much of the same equipment used in operating a fine restaurant. Several of the women were scurrying around, putting things away after the evening meal. On the far side of the dining area was a long hallway, with individual sleeping quarters on either side.

The moment Rebecca saw Amy, she rushed over to greet her. "Come on everyone! Come see Amy's little Joshua!"

Rebecca took the boy from Amy's arms and held him above her head, so the girls in the kitchen could get a good look at him. "Isn't he beautiful?" she swooned.

Amy touched her arm. "Rebecca, has Margaret called?"

"Not yet," Rebecca replied, making faces at the baby. "I really didn't expect to hear from her until tomorrow."

"I was just hoping," Amy said, removing her gloves.

"I know," Rebecca said, unfastening the baby's hooded coat. "We've all got our fingers crossed that we'll be hearing good news real soon."

"Is Angie here?" Amy asked, glancing toward the kitchen.

Rebecca chuckled. "She's around here someplace. We're going to have to replace the wheels on that chair of hers if she doesn't settle down pretty soon." She laughed. "I can't blame her though. Now that the baby soldier camp has been discovered, she's anxiously waiting for the rest of Jacobson's glass house to come tumbling down."

Amy gritted her teeth. "And it's going to happen a lot sooner than we ever dreamed."

THE BABY SOLDIERS

"When are you leaving for Carolina?" Rebecca asked.

"First thing in the morning…if that's all right with you. I'd like to stay here tonight. I didn't want to spend my first night with Joshua alone in my apartment, and the roads are getting too slippery to drive to Morehead City tonight."

"Sure. We've got plenty of room. Is Kerry going back with you?"

"No. She's going back with her folks. Danny is planning to join them at the house they rented."

Rebecca smiled. "It looks like things are working out just the way you said they would."

Amy shook off her coat. "Yeah. Maybe I should go into business telling fortunes like they do on TV. I'll make so much money with my psychic powers that we'll be able to send all the children to college."

"Hmmm," Rebecca uttered. "Maybe you could spare a few bucks out of your millions to send me to trade school."

"What kind of trade do you have in mind?" Amy asked, shifting her eyebrows up and down like Groucho Marx.

Rebecca rolled her eyes heavenward and sighed. "How about a trade that doesn't involve cooking or cleaning?"

Amy laughed. "What a tragic loss that would be for the rest of us."

"Oh, I was just fantasizing," Rebecca said.

"Tell you what I'll do," Amy said. "Just as soon as all the excitement dies down, we'll transfer you to the bookkeeping department. Then you'll be able to see where all the money goes."

Rebecca kissed Amy's boy and gave him back to his mother. "No thanks. I think I'd rather be a permanent cook and bottle washer."

Amy shrugged as she followed Rebecca into the kitchen. "Well, she said teasingly. "You could always go looking for Mr. Right and get married."

Rebecca gave her a furtive glance. "In case you don't remember, that's how I got in all this trouble to begin with."

— 365 —

CHAPTER FIFTY-SEVEN

Danny Woolard whistled contentedly as he drove along Route 17 on his way to Morehead City. He was beginning to feel more comfortable around Kerry's family all the time. A lot more comfortable than he'd ever hoped. He knew it would be a long time before Kerry would be able to get over everything that had happened to her. But for the first time, he actually felt a glimmer of hope that one day, their friendship could develop into something more serious.

He turned up the volume on the radio and rolled his eyes as he listened to the soothing voice of Johnny Mathis. His mom used to play his records all the time. Danny didn't even know what he looked like. All he remembered was his mother talking about him. Johnny Mathis was one of the few singers whose music the organization hadn't banned from the radio. Danny would have never heard of Elvis Presley, the Temptations, or the Rolling Stones if a friend hadn't squirreled away some CD's his folks were supposed to destroy. Jacobson sure had everyone under his thumb. He'd even banned the daytime soaps women used to watch in the afternoons after finishing their housework. The preacher claimed the soap operas put foolish ideas in their heads...ideas that led to sin.

Danny remembered when his father first joined Jacobson's elite group; the group that was supposed to eliminate the ills of society. He especially remembered the night his father came home from one of those mysterious trips and put his foot through the television set right in the middle of his mother's favorite game show. He was only a kid then, but he'd never forget the fight they had. That was the first time he saw his dad hit her. Witnessing that had killed something inside him. He never felt the same way about his dad after that. Up until that night, Danny idolized his father. He thought his dad was the strongest, bravest man in the whole world. But instead, he learned his father was the kind of man who beat up helpless women, and enjoyed berating everybody else.

Danny slouched down in the driver's seat, thinking about David Williams. David had asked if he'd like to tag along to Baltimore with them. But Danny was afraid the hatred he had for Clifford Jacobson would erupt all over the place if he got within striking distance. He wasn't very good at controlling his temper. In that regard, Danny respected David more than anyone he knew. Even though he knew David was seething inside, he was always in control of his emotions. David would see that Clifford Jacobson got what he deserved...and do it the right way. Danny just prayed the preacher didn't have enough people brain-washed to throw a monkey wrench into the wheels of justice.

When Danny reached Elizabeth City, he put on his turn signal and pulled into Hardees' parking lot. He still had a three-hour drive ahead, and he'd never make it all the way, if he didn't get something to eat.

James Kelsey wasn't in his office when Margaret Hatchey stopped to see him. She placed the sealed envelope on top of his desk, so he wouldn't miss it when he returned. She had a meeting with attorney Judd Donaldson in less than an hour. She took a deep breath and let it out slowly. After telling Donaldson why she wanted to see him, she knew her life would be in great danger. She had hoped Byron would have been able to join her, but it was far more important that he get back to Baltimore as soon as possible. Every hour the preacher remained free gave him that much more time to destroy other lives.

Donaldson's office was on the fifth floor in one of the new high-rise buildings in Norfolk. The reception area offered a spectacular view of Norfolk Harbor, and the impressive yachts that docked there. Margaret figured the yachts probably belonged to lawyers like Donaldson, who paid for them with illegal funds like those obtained from Jacobson's outrageous baby selling scheme.

A neatly dressed woman in her early thirties escorted Margaret into a massive conference room, where she found herself surrounded by floor to ceiling shelves, containing hundreds of leather-bound law books. She sat on the left side of the table near the door in order to make a hasty exit if the need arose. Her dark eyes wandered to the other end of the polished mahogany table, which appeared as long and slick as a bowling alley. The leather chair was so soft and comfy, she felt as though she were sitting on a feather bed. Real leather, she thought, like Clifford Jacobson had in his home. She removed a tissue from her handbag and blew her nose, wondering how many babies you had to sell to own furnishings as fine as these.

Judd Donaldson was dressed in a light gray suit with a silk striped tie and matching handkerchief. He weighed close to three hundred pounds, much too heavy for a man who stood approximately five nine. Margaret's gaze came to rest on his food- stained tie.

The attorney mumbled a curt hello and snorted like a bull as he squeezed into a chair at the head of the table. A wisp of a girl followed him into the room. She wore a basic white blouse and straight black skirt that covered her calves. No eye makeup was visible beneath her horn-rimmed glasses. She carried a legal pad, tucked under her arm. Several pens protruded from the elongated fingers of her right hand. She remained silent as she sat down directly across the table from Margaret Hatchey.

Donaldson glanced at Margaret's non-committal face and then let his eyes settle on his puffy hands.

Margaret had never seen a man wearing so many rings before. His jewelry was even more outlandish than that worn by her former brother-in-law. With his long, grayish hair, Judd Donaldson looked more like an over-the-hill hippy than a prosperous attorney. Even the wiry mustache below his pig-like snout looked phony.

THE BABY SOLDIERS

"Miz Hatchey" he said, his low voice sending chills down her spine. "I believe you've come here to discuss a mutual acquaintance. Is that correct?"

"I told you his name," she replied annoyed. "I don't believe you would have seen me on such short notice if the mutual acquaintance had been someone less important than Clifford Jacobson."

The lawyer attempted to shift in his seat, but his bulk made it impossible. "Mr. Jacobson? Ah, yes. I believe he's a preacher, or something of the sort."

Margaret felt her face flush. "You know damn well who he is!" she replied. Her attention was quickly drawn to a large oil painting, hanging on the wall above the young girl. It looked similar to one she'd seen in an art gallery in Washington DC. "From the furnishings you have in this place, I gather Mr. Jacobson must be a very important man around here."

Donaldson sucked in his breath. "All right, Miz Hatchey. Why don't we stop fencing and get right to the point."

Margaret smiled for the first time since entering the building. "That's precisely why I'm here," she said smugly. "I'd like to discuss your involvement in a crime."

The young woman looked up questioningly.

"Mr. Donaldson knows exactly what I'm talking about," Margaret explained. "I'm talking about a group of young women whose babies were taken away from them after they were born and sold to the highest bidder by your upstanding boss here."

The young woman looked startled. It was obvious she knew nothing about Donaldson's illegal ventures.

Margaret turned to the pasty-faced attorney. "Mr. Donaldson, did you really think that no one would ever find out what you were up to? How many of those babies have you sold for Jacobson and his organization?"

The quivering girl fumbled with her pen, dropping it on the carpet.

"Miss Webber," Donaldson said, distracted. "I don't think you need to record any of this. You may go."

The girl leapt to her feet and scurried from the room, clutching the legal pad tight against her chest.

Pushing himself from his chair, he stood behind it. Then he glared down at Margaret. "That's a mighty strong allegation, Miz Hatchey. I suppose you think you have proof to back up this ridiculous fantasy?"

"No," she answered matter-of-factly."I don't think anything. I do have proof."

His arrogant expression faded. "What kind of proof?"

"I have the names of three sets of adoptive parents, who've admitted coming to you when they wanted to adopt a child. They confessed that you charged them fifty thousand dollars for completing each transaction."

"That's a preposterous lie!" he spat.

She tapped the handbag on her lap. "I have copies of their canceled checks."

He removed a handkerchief from the inside pocket of his jacket and nervously wiped perspiration from his face.

"I also know for a fact that the biological mothers of the children were never paid a dime. Their children were stolen the moment they were born and taken to a secret location until you could arrange to sell them." Margaret's eyes were venomous as she continued to stare at him. "Mr. Donaldson, you are lower than a snake."

He clutched the back of the chair. "And you're insane, Miz Hatchey? I could have you thrown in jail for defamation of character!"

Margaret's laugh was guttural and mocking. "You have no character to malign. Now, why don't you sit back down, and we'll discuss this matter like two civilized adults."

The attorney's face turned from ashen to purple. "Every business transaction that passes through these doors is one hundred percent legal!" he bellowed.

THE BABY SOLDIERS

He dropped into the chair and sighed heavily. "I am a very busy man. Why don't you just tell me what it is you really want?"

"Me?" Margaret replied querulously. "I'd be satisfied to see you and your kind castrated and set on fire."

His face contorted at the thought.

"But then, I'd be no better than you," Margaret added.

His bulbous nose twitched. He rubbed it profusely.

Margaret placed her elbows on the table and steepled her fingers. "I'm aware, of course, you didn't keep all the money you made selling those children."

His mouth gaped open.

"According to the records I observed, you received twenty five percent of the net profits from those sales."

Donaldson struggled to his feet, his fists clenched at his sides. "How could you possibly know that?"

Margaret feigned a yawn to mask her growing fear. "Let's just say I have a friend who made those records available to me. We know everything about your operation, accept the location of the children you sold. So far, we've found about a dozen of them. We want to know the whereabouts of the others. That, Mr. Donaldson, is why I am here."

He studied her for a long time. Then he replied, "And what do I get in return for handing over this so-called information?"

"The information will have to be verified before any deals can be made. After our people are satisfied that you're not holding out on them, we will contact you."

"That's unsatisfactory," he muttered.

She raised a brow. "You don't seem to understand how the game is played. You see, I'm the one holding all the cards."

"You stay right here," he commanded. "I'll see what I can do."

When he brushed her arm on his way out of the room, Margaret shuddered. She could sense his evil presence in the room even after he'd left it. She folded her arms over her chest, trying to calm the rapid beat of her heart. She wondered if he'd return with the information she'd requested, or come back carrying an Uzi. "This could be your last great hurrah for freedom," she muttered wryly.

Moments later, another of Donaldson's assistants, not the frightened Miss Webber, walked into the room and unceremoniously dropped a dozen files on the table in front of Margaret. "Mr. Donaldson instructed me to give these to you," she said. "He said to tell you, he was sorry he wouldn't be able to rejoin you, but he had an urgent matter to take care of."

Margaret rose slowly and gathered the files into her waiting arms."I'm sure he did," she replied demurely.

After hearing about an impending snowstorm, David Williams and Byron Spears agreed to wait until morning to leave for Baltimore. The law enforcement people they needed to see wouldn't be available until then anyway. And Byron knew how treacherous I-95 could be when the roads were icy.

They left David's house at seven o'clock sharp. As Byron's Jeep approached Petersburg, the Interstate traffic became more congested. "We'll be there in a few hours," he told David. "Want to stop and get some coffee?"

David surveyed their surroundings. "Let's wait until we get a little further up the road. If we get off here, it'll probably take another hour to get back on the Interstate."

Byron nodded. "Sounds like you don't want to waste any more time than we already have."

David replied. "You're right about that. I'll feel a lot better when this is over and Jacobson is behind bars where he belongs."

Byron sighed. "Do you really think that's likely to happen?"

David turned to him puzzled. "Don't you?"

Byron shrugged. "Can you imagine Jacobson being tried by a jury of his peers?"

THE BABY SOLDIERS

A car in the outside lane slid on the icy road and headed straight for the Jeep. David grabbed onto the dash while Byron swung the Jeep out of harm's way.

"It is rather scary thinking there might be twelve people out there who are still in awe of Jacobson." David said, not mentioning their close call.

Byron snickered. "If truth be known, there are probably a lot more than that."

David sat back and closed his eyes. "Did anyone ever tell you that you're a real inspiring soul?"

Byron chuckled. "Not lately."

The miles passed in silence.

"That newspaper fellow, James Kelsey, seems to enjoy stirring things up," Byron said reflectively.

"Yeah, James is all right," David muttered.

"Do you know his wife very well?" Byron asked.

"Too well, I'm afraid."

"Do you believe Reverend Jacobson talked her into killing Captain Woolard?"

"You know them both better than I do. You tell me."

Byron chortled. "You'd be surprised how much I don't know. I'm afraid the preacher kept me in the dark about most of his affairs. I lived in the same house with him for years and never saw how badly he was treating my own sister."

"Sister?" David asked, puzzled.

"I didn't mean Margaret. I was talking about my other sister, Peggy. She married Clifford when she was eighteen. Too young to know better."

David pursed his lips. "He probably kept you in the dark because you were an in-law."

"He didn't know," Byron said. "We never told him we were related. He doesn't know Margaret Hatchey is my sister, either."

"I'm impressed," David said. "Someone actually pulled a fast one on the dictator."

— 373 —

"I'm surprised we got away with it as long as we did." Byron replied reflectively.

"You should work for the CIA." David said.

"Who knows, maybe I will." After a short pause, he said, "You know, I always thought Sybil Kelsey would have been great at that sort of thing."

"No way," David said, shocked by the suggestion. "Sybil couldn't keep her mouth shut about anything top secret, or otherwise."

"I didn't see her that way," Byron replied. "To tell you the truth, I was surprised she admitted killing Woolard, even if Clifford forced her to do it."

"Sybil Kelsey was a regular Jacobson groupie," David muttered. "From what James told me, she's been nuts about the preacher for years. They went to college together, you know?"

Byron looked surprised. "I wonder why he didn't marry Sybil instead of Peggy?"

David took a deep breath. "You ever spent much time around Sybil? I mean real quality time?"

Byron thought for a moment."I spoke to her at a few of the organization's meetings, but it was little more than a quick hello how are you, kind of thing."

David nodded grimly. "Well, my friend, if you ever talked to her for any length of time, you'd know why Jacobson would not be interested in a long-term commitment."

"That's interesting," Byron observed. "So why did James marry her?"

David watched a herd of cows grazing on a country slope and wondered how he'd like living in the country. "In the beginning, James thought Sybil had money. She told everyone her family was big in the publishing business. She charmed James right out of his naïve mind."

"And her family?"Byron replied curiously."They weren't wealthy?"

David chuckled. "Sybil's old man was a has-been reporter and a drunk to boot."

THE BABY SOLDIERS

"Sounds like James should have done a little research before he took the plunge."

David grimaced. "When you think about it, it was kind of dumb for a newspaper man."

"You know, David, I think Sybil may have had another reason for killing Captain Woolard."

"Oh? Let's hear it."

Byron lit a cigarette. "I used to see them together in Baltimore, from a distance mind you. But they always looked real cozy with each other."

David's brow furrowed. "Sybil and Horace Woolard? You think they were having an affair?"

Byron shrugged. "Stranger things have happened. Maybe he wanted to call it off and she wasn't ready."

David shook his head. "That's one angle I hadn't considered. So, you think that after they had their little prayer meetings they snuck off to some seedy motel and fornicated?"

Byron sighed tiredly. "You don't believe me, do you?"

David laughed. "No. With a wife as beautiful as Adele at home, why in hell would Horace even consider looking at something like Sybil Kelsey. Christ, I've seen better asses on gorillas.

Byron smiled. "Beauty is in the eye of the beholder, my friend."

"Personally," David muttered. "I'd rather be blind."

The snow on the road was heavier in the mountains. Byron adjusted his speed accordingly.

"Margaret really sounded excited about talking to that lawyer today," David said. "How in the hell did you get a hold of those records?"

"Don't give me credit for that," Byron told him."That was something else I knew absolutely nothing about."

"Then...who..."

"Someone very near and dear to you," Byron replied.

"I can't think of a soul," David said.

"It was the boy."

"Boy?" David said, puzzled. "What boy?"

GERRY R. LEWIS

"The same one who overheard the preacher tell Captain Woolard to take care of Scott Robinson. Margaret said he got into Jacobson's study one day and found the stuff in a locked cabinet behind his desk. He told his brother, Danny, about it."

"Jason!" David exclaimed. "That boy is wiser than his years."

"I hate to say it, but cop is definitely in the boy's blood. He'd make an FBI team look like a group of disheveled boys scouts."

"He could have gotten his skinny little ass killed," David replied.

Byron slowed down for the approaching exit. The green sign on the right advertised five different fast-food restaurants and six filling stations. He turned to David. "You know when Jacobson finds out Jason was the one who broke into his place and stole those records, he's as good as dead."

David frowned. "That's not going to happen."

Byron nodded. "Not if our plans go as smoothly as everything else so far."

CHAPTER FIFTY-EIGHT

The sound of crumbling furniture and broken glass marred the serene ambiance of the hilltop mansion. Files and record books lay scattered about the study. Oil paintings, lay torn and splintered along with the shattered remnants of Tiffany lamps and crystal candle holders.

Red-faced Clifford Jacobson pulled out the last drawer from his desk and watched it bounce off the oak coat rack. The maroon ledger book was nowhere to be found. His shoulders slumped as he stood, snorting like a frustrated bull. He remembered distinctly locking the book away. Those records were off limits to everyone but himself. He stood in front of his desk, jerking his head from side to side, staring at the disheveled mess he'd created. The book had to be here somewhere.

The decline in contributions since Robinson's death had put a substantial dent in the funds needed to run the organization efficiently. If it wasn't for the profits from the baby sales, Clifford Jacobson didn't know how The New Order would survive. Over the past several months, he had taken funds from his personal account and deposited them into the regular business account. He hadn't explained to his followers exactly where the miracle funds had come from, but he had assured them that using his own money was a show of good faith, hoping they would follow suit and do the same. But the results hadn't been as successful as he'd anticipated. His followers were becoming more inquisitive. And he didn't like that one bit. He had to find some way to make them believe in him again.

Jacobson had arranged a meeting with Judd Donaldson to discuss having his share of the profits from the baby market increased. But Donaldson was no fool. He'd want to see proof the preacher needed a larger share. And now, he couldn't find the record book.

The preacher got down on his hands and knees and began rifling through the mound of books and folders, looking for the missing ledger. Beads of perspiration plopped onto the file folders, causing him to wince at the very sight of them. "It has to be here somewhere," he bellowed. "Where the hell are you?"

He looked up startled when he heard the front door open. "Byron?" he called out. "Byron, is that you?"

When he heard the sound of heavy footsteps approaching, he hurried from the study, closing the door behind him. He scowled at the four men in front of him. Byron was standing next to the cop who worked for Woolard at the beach. Sergeant David Williams. The other two were local police officers who had come to his services occasionally, but had never officially joined the congregation.

"Byron," Jacobson said, appraising his unwelcome visitors. "Would you care to explain what these men are doing here?"

Byron took the Virginia newspaper from under his arm and opened it to the front page. His lips tightened as he gave it to the bewildered preacher. "Here," he said. "I believe this pretty much says it all."

Jacobson looked puzzled. Then his gray eyes darted quickly over the headlines.

"James Kelsey again!"

Kidnapped Children Found. Clifford Jacobson and New Order Scam Exposed!

His fists tightened. "What's this about?" he demanded, staring accusingly at Byron.

David Williams looked at the preacher and began to grin. Watching the great Reverend Jacobson squirm was a rare and glorious occasion. He only wished all the people he had hurt over the years could be here to see it, too.

— 378 —

THE BABY SOLDIERS

"Give it up, Jacobson," David said impatiently. "It's over."

Although Jacobson's steely eyes caused most people to tremble, they had no effect whatsoever on the sergeant who stood before him.

"I demand to know where this story came from," he spat.

"Seems your flock isn't quite as gullible as you thought they were," David quipped. "The children you planned to use to further your own ambitions are free now. They've been taken somewhere safe, somewhere you can't use them anymore."

Jacobson's eyes shifted nervously from one of the police officers to the other. "I don't know what you're talking about."

"The facts are right in front of your eyes," David said, nodding toward the quivering newspaper.

"This is nothing but malicious garbage!" Jacobson spat, slinging the paper across the foyer. "That fool Kelsey is responsible for this. It sounds just like him. He'd do anything to discredit me and The New Order." He shook his head. "If it wasn't for what his wife did… Kelsey blames me because his wife is a murderess. Can you imagine, he actually blames me?"

Byron's eyes filled with despair as he approached his fallen leader. "Over the years, I'd heard rumors about pregnant girls who were kidnapped from abortion clinics and imprisoned until their babies were born. Then their infants were taken away from them But I didn't know any more than that." He lowered his eyes. "But I saw the place myself yesterday. I was there with Sergeant Williams and the families of those poor lost children."

Jacobson staggered toward a Victorian chair and sat down heavily. "Byron, I can't believe you'd do this to me," he said hollowly. "After all the things I've done for you over the years. How could you betray me?"

"I don't see things the same way you do," Byron explained. "I haven't for a long time. You're not the man I thought you were."

Deep ridges creased Jacobson's brow as he listened to the shocking words of his trusted servant. He looked at Byron tearfully. "By-

— 379 —

ron, don't you see? I've grown since the organization was formed. I knew what the people needed, and I did my best to fill those needs."

David Williams snorted. "Exactly what do you call filling their needs? Killing them when they didn't agree with your stupid philosophy, the way you killed Robinson and Woolard, and lord knows how many others?"

Jacobson rose to his feet, his arms hung loosely at his sides. "If I wasn't a man of peace, I'd put an end to you and your lies. You are nothing but a mouthy troublemaker like that newspaper idiot, Kelsey. I had nothing to do with what happened to Scott Robinson and Horace Woolard. Why…they were my dearest friends."

"David chortled. "I guess I should be grateful I was never a friend of yours…considering what happens to them."

"This is blasphemy!" Jacobson shouted.

"Not according to Sybil Kelsey," David said. "Sybil said it was your idea to have Horace Woolard killed. She said you promised to give her an important position in The New Order if she killed him."

Jacobson threw his head back and laughed hysterically. "I wouldn't give that woman my used slippers. She's insane! Everyone knows that. Horace brought me hundreds of supporters over the years, why on earth would I want him killed?"

"What about the hundreds of supporters he cost your precious organization when he killed Scott Robinson?" David asked sarcastically.

Jacobson chuffed.

David sat down across from Jacobson and drummed his fingers on the leather armrests. "Captain Woolard's mistake wasn't killing Scott Robinson, was it? You ordered him to do that. His mistake was getting caught."

Jacobson pushed himself out of the chair and lunged at David. The uniformed officers restrained him. "This whole story is preposterous," he said, grunting to free himself. I don't know what you plan to prove, maligning me this way. You're a loser, Williams. You've

THE BABY SOLDIERS

always been a loser. If you were a virtuous man, you wouldn't have raised a little whore!"

David punched Jacobson in the face before anyone could intercept him. Jacobson staggered backward and caught himself on the edge of a wrought iron plant stand. He grabbed his jaw and groaned. "You know what this is going to cost you, don't you?"

David crossed his arms over his chest. "That's nothing compared to the treatment you're going to get when the body builders at the prison get their mitts on you. If it's the last thing I do, I'm going to prove that you were responsible for killing my wife and daughter."

Jacobson took his handkerchief and wiped the blood from his mouth. "Seems as though you're just full of threats you can't prove. Besides," he sneered. "Woolard took care of your wife and your daughter. Seems he wanted some of that precious wife of yours but she fought back. He was so furious when she resisted his advances, he killed her and the girl. Said he didn't need any witnesses."

"He told you that?" David asked frozen.

"Woolard told me everything...eventually."

"You have no proof of me being involved in any wrong-doing."

"My sister has all the proof he needs," Byron said softly.

Jacobson spun around, glaring at Byron. "Your sister?"

A waning grin crept over Byron's face. "I had two of them. You were married to one. As I recall, you told everyone she was crazy, too."

The preacher's mouth gaped open. "That's impossible. You don't have another sister. We checked."

"Not only is it possible," Byron told him. "In fact, you know her quite well. My sister's name is Margaret Hatchey."

Jacobson's eyes fluttered. "Margaret," he replied weakly. "Margaret Hatchey." Suddenly, he looked up. "But Margaret was Peggy's sister...Oh my God!"

"Were you going to say Margaret was one of your most trusted employees?" David taunted.

Jacobson frowned. "Margaret is merely a nursemaid. She knows nothing."

"Margaret has the record book you kept locked in your study," Byron told him.

"How did she get into my study?" he asked, accusingly. "No one can get into my private cabinets, Byron…not even you."

Byron shrugged. "Well, someone did, and that someone turned the book over to Margaret."

"Where is she?" Jacobson asked coolly.

David yawned. "Right about now, she's having a serious chat with your attorney, Judd Donaldson. And knowing Donaldson, I'd say that inflated shark is probably singing like a bird, telling her everything she wants to know about your involvement in selling stolen children."

Jacobson's eyes flickered from David to Byron. The glint of pure hatred turned to panic.

"Okay, fellows," Sergeant Williams said. "Read him his rights and get him the hell out of here."

"One moment," Jacobson said, raising his hands defensively. "Before you do anything rash, grant me a moment to gather a few things from my study to take with me."

Byron looked at David and shrugged.

David thought about it for a moment and nodded. "It's all right, fellas. There's only one way in and one way out. He's not going anywhere."

"Thank you," Jacobson quipped sarcastically.

"You'd better get in there, if you're going,' David snapped. "Make sure you pack your prayer books. You're going to have a lot of time to read them."

The four men stood silently and watched the sullen preacher retreat into his study.

———

Julie Newman sat in a red leather booth close to the buffet counter. She always felt self-conscious when she was the first to arrive at a restaurant. She guessed it was the way people looked at your, pitying you because you were dining alone. She checked her watch. It

THE BABY SOLDIERS

was nearly six o'clock. Kyle was late. He promised he'd meet her at five-thirty. She wondered if he had to go back to the institution to sedate some patient who'd gone berserk. Then she decided there was no point in waiting any longer and grabbed her handbag.

Just as she was about to leave, she looked out the plate glass window and saw his car roll into the parking lot. She sighed relieved.

Kyle hurried inside, breathing heavily. "Julie," he said, breaking into a grin. "I'm sorry I'm late. I had a last-minute emergency."

She nodded. "It goes with the territory."

He slipped into the booth across from her, taking her hand. "Thank you for being so understanding."

She smiled as she studied his face. Kyle Whitley wasn't the most handsome guy she'd ever dated, but he was by far the nicest. His ash blond hair was so thin, she figured he'd be completely bald by the time he was forty. She was an inch taller than him, but that didn't matter. Besides, he had incredible blue eyes, and the other nurses thought he had a terrific sense of humor. In Kyle's profession, a sense of humor was mandatory.

"Have you ordered dinner yet?" he asked, glancing at the menu.

"No," she replied softly. "I was just about to leave and throw a pizza in the microwave when I saw you pull up."

"Ah," he replied. "I guess I should consider myself lucky you weren't thinking of throwing me in the microwave as well."

She laughed. "I told you I wasn't upset. I always thought my job was tough, but I wouldn't trade with you for anything in the world. I'd be too afraid that insanity stuff might rub off on me."

He studied her thoughtfully. "Do you think it's possible my patients could actually drive me nuts?"

"I don't know," she replied. "I've met some psychiatrists who didn't appear to be in any better shape than the people they treated."

"You know what they say," he said, unfolding his napkin.

She looked at him puzzled. "What's that?"

"They say most of us go into the profession, so we can cure ourselves."

"Hmm. I'm going to have to start keeping a closer eye on you."

Kyle laughed easily. "You can watch me all you want. I'd love the attention."

"Speaking of patients," Julie said. "How is Mrs. Kelsey these days?"

A waitress took their order and walked away.

Kyle shook his head sadly. "Not so good, I'm afraid."

Julie nodded. "I can't say I'm surprised. I feel rather sorry for her."

He looked at her in awe. "You do? You feel sorry for Sybil Kelsey? I can't believe it."

Julie frowned. "Clifford Jacobson has had hundreds of people doing his every whim for years. And Sybil Kelsey claims she was in love with him for even longer. She'd be more vulnerable to his demands than all the rest put together."

He nodded thoughtfully. "I suppose you're right."

"I remember seeing her at a pro-life demonstration in front of an abortion clinic one day. She was the most vocal one in the group. Every time she opened her mouth, it was like listening to one of his television sermons. She repeated his speeches word for word." Julie shivered. "I bet she didn't even blink when he asked her to kill Captain Woolard. She would have blown up the entire city if he had asked her."

Kyle picked up his drink and took a sip. "I don't think she'll ever stand trial for murder. She's really out of it. Somehow, she got a hold of this morning's newspaper."

"Oh, Jesus," Julie said. "That story about the missing children and Jacobson's involvement was all over the front page."

Kyle nodded grimly. "She mentioned reading the article her husband wrote. She said Mr. Kelsey blames Jacobson for murdering their son."

Julie sighed heavily. "That was bound to come out eventually. He didn't kill the boy with his own two hands, but he might as well have. I'm sorry Sybil had to see it right now. What rotten timing."

"She went to pieces and shred the newspaper right in front of me."

THE BABY SOLDIERS

Kyle shook his head from side to side. "You know, Julie, I never heard a woman cry like that before. I don't think she really wanted to believe it was true."

"I don't suppose she did," Julie replied. "Finding out the man she loved all these years is responsible for killing her only child. That alone would be enough to drive anyone over the edge." She rubbed her arms thoughtfully. "I wish there was something I could do."

Kyle pursed his lips. "I don't think there's anything any of us can do at this point. Maybe someday she'll come out of it, but only God knows when that will be."

"What about James?" Julie asked. "Does he know about her condition?"

Kyle rubbed his eyes."I called him. He said it was probably for the best. Odd fellow, that one."

Julie forced a smile. "He's been through hell and back, too. I guess he finally got to the point where he can't feel anything...including sympathy."

Kyle chuffed. "And to think, a righteous preacher is responsible for it all."

Julie picked up her fork. "How is your newest patient getting along?"

Kyle's blue eyes widened. "Rebecca? She's a marvel."

Julie's smiled broadened. "That she is. She's the one who should have been a preacher. She's got the right motives."

"I was really worried about her the first time she came to see me. I hate to admit it. I'm glad you warned me in advance about her disfigurement. At least, I didn't gawk at her and make her feel like the freak she claims she is."

Julie cut the tomatoes on her salad into bite-sized pieces. "I'm sure she gets plenty of those looks."

"Rebecca told me someone has offered to pay for her plastic surgery. She said by next year at this time, she'll look like a human being again."

Julie cocked her head to one side. "That's interesting. I wonder who it is?"

"She wouldn't say. But if it's a friend, it must be a damned good one."

Julie stared into space. "There aren't many of those around."

Kyle studied her face. "You're one of those, Julie. You should hear the way Rebecca talks about you."

Julie smiled. "Rebecca likes everyone."

Kyle cleared his throat. "You should hear the way I talk about you…and I don't like everyone."

She laughed. "All right. You made your point."

"Do you have any plans for later this evening?" he asked.

She shook her head. "I can't think of any right now. Why?"

He shrugged. "I was wondering if you might like to go for a walk on the beach? There's something I want to talk to you about."

She looked amused. "You want to walk on the beach? It must be thirty degrees outside."

His sky-blue eyes washed lovingly over her face. "I'll keep you warm. I promise."

She knew he would. He would keep her warm for as long as she wanted. And she knew what he wanted to talk to her about, too. She'd been putting off this conversation for far too long. It was time. She only wished her brother were alive to walk her down the aisle.

CHAPTER FIFTY-NINE

Clifford Jacobson closed the study door, separating himself from the accusing eyes of the men lurking in the hallway. He rubbed his bleary eyes, wondering if he were having a bad dream. Then he gazed numbly at the scattered debris on the floor, while running his shaky fingers through his hair. It wasn't a dream. It was real.

Some rotten thief had broken into his home and stolen the maroon ledger. Now, that he knew where it was, it would be a minor task to learn the identity of the thief.

He'd make Hatchey talk. He knew what her sister's weaknesses were, and had no doubt that beneath her tough exterior, Margaret would be just as easy to break. If she didn't cooperate, she'd end up dead, just like her sister.

He walked slowly to his desk and flipped through what was left of his personal directory until he found Judd Donaldson's phone number. He wondered if Sergeant Williams had lied when he said Margaret had taken the ledger to Donaldson's office to threaten him to spill his guts. He had to know if the devious sergeant had been bluffing to make him confess? Captain Woolard had told him many times that Sergeant Williams was not a man they could trust. Perhaps, just this once, Woolard was right. Jacobson picked up the telephone and punched in the lawyer's office number.

"Donaldson and Associates," a brisk voice replied.

"Nancy, how are you?" Jacobson asked, feigning concern. "May I speak to Judd, please?"

"I'm sorry, Reverend Jacobson. Mr. Donaldson isn't in. He left the office this morning and hasn't returned."

Jacobson spun the wheel on the Rolodex. "Did he happen to mention where he was going?"

"He really didn't say."

The preacher exhaled raggedly. "That's all right, Nancy. I'll try his home."

"He may be packing," she suggested. "He had a meeting this morning with a Margaret Hatchey. After the meeting, I saw him remove his passport from the wall safe."

"Passport?" Jacobson muttered. "He never mentioned he was going anywhere. We were supposed to have a meeting there tomorrow. Is there someone else over there he may have told where he was going?"

"Not that I'm aware of," she replied. "But you know the way things are around here. A major emergency could have come up all of a sudden."

Jacobson frowned. "Major emergency," he echoed hollowly."In the event Judd does check in with you, please have him call me. Oh, never mind," he added quickly. "Just forget I called." Then he hung up.

His eyes darted around the room like a caged animal. There was only one way out. It didn't take a psychic to figure out what his spineless excuse for an attorney was up to. "That no good coward is running off to Switzerland and taking my money with him," he muttered angrily.

Jacobson shuffled to the window and gazed at the grassy hills beyond his estate. Why in the world had he agreed to have iron bars installed on the windows? Yes, of course. Byron convinced him that the bars would guarantee his safety.

"Safety," he mumbled, choking on the word. The devices used to protect his belongings had become a traitor's ploy to trap him. The bars, he mused bitterly, like his trusted servants had been used against him.

THE BABY SOLDIERS

He picked up a small address book from the corner of the desk and placed it in his vest pocket. Everyone important to the future of The New Order was listed in there. Slowly, he canvassed the room. What else should he take? He wouldn't be there long. He wouldn't take any books. He wouldn't have time to read them. He replaced the drawers he'd taken from the desk and tossed as many of the strewn items as he could back inside them. The preacher hated clutter. Besides, he didn't want anyone to know he'd been looking for something badly enough to tear the room completely apart trying to find it. That alone would make him look guilty. He made a mental note to keep his temper in check. He mustn't say anything that would make him appear weak...the way he had a few moments ago with Sergeant Williams.

He shouldn't have said what he'd said about the girl. But he couldn't help himself. The Williams' girl was not pregnant. She'd just been in the wrong place at the wrong time. If Woolard hadn't killed her when he killed her mother, the sergeant may not be as filled with hate as he was.

His cloudy eyes fixed on the revolver on top of the filing cabinet. He walked over and picked it up. Byron had insisted he keep it loaded. An empty gun was no more protection than a small stick. He held the gun to his temple and closed his eyes. It would be so easy to pull the trigger and end his problems for good. Pull the trigger and go away, he thought. He could leave all life's misery and disappointment behind. And those poor wretched souls that he'd tried to save would have to fend for themselves.

"Never!" he said emphatically, dropping the gun back on the cabinet.

My flock would never forgive me for taking the easy way out. He cocked a brow. Besides, wasn't I the one who taught them that taking an innocent life was a sin?

The goal of The New Order had been to strive for absolute perfection among its members. Clifford Jacobson had spent a lifetime polishing the rough stones the Lord had entrusted in his care. But his job was far from done. Even if, by some fluke, he was incarcerated, he would continue to guide them. His followers would continue to nurture and grow even if he had to guide their plight from inside a prison's walls. What a glorious tribute that would be, he thought, saving the least of God's creatures, like Paul did, by walking among them.

A loud tap on the door shook him from his reverie. David Williams opened the study door and peeked inside. "We're ready to go."

Jacobson picked up his bible and held it close to his heart. "I'm ready," he replied, smiling peacefully as he considered his future.

David Williams followed the preacher from the room, puzzled by the eerie smile on his face. He wondered if Jacobson was smiling because he had already figured out his defense strategy. Jacobson was far from illiterate, David mused. If nothing else, he'd probably go for an insanity plea. David nodded to the two officers waiting near the front door and grimaced as they cuffed the preacher and led him out to the patrol car in the driveway. An insanity plea, he thought bemused. The preacher could pull it off easy. Clifford Jacobson was the craziest son-of-a-bitch he'd ever known.

CHAPTER SIXTY

Kerry Trivane carried Robbie up the steps in front of the newspaper office, then took the cramped elevator to the second floor. She wanted to see James Kelsey once again, before heading back to her new home in Morehead City.

James leapt to his feet the moment he saw her. "Kerry," he said surprised. "I wasn't expecting to see you and my grandson again so soon."

She smiled, offering him the small child. "I just came from Amy's apartment. I have all my things packed and waiting in the car. I wanted to stop and see you before we left." She sat down on the arm of a leather chair. "I also wanted to thank you for everything you've done for us."

James blinked back tears. "Is this goodbye? Are you moving away for good?"

She nodded. "We're going back to Morehead City. My folks helped me get my own apartment. It's not very big, but it'll do until I can find something else."

"You...you don't have to do that, you know. You can stay right here. I was thinking of offering you a job here at the newspaper. We could turn one of the storage cubicles into a nursery for little Robbie; that way you wouldn't have to worry about hiring a sitter for him."

Kerry was touched by his thoughtfulness. But at the same time, she knew why he wanted her to stay. He didn't want the only part of Robbie that was still alive to be taken away from him.

"Don't worry, Mr. Kelsey," Kerry assured him. "I plan to come back and visit you often. I want Robbie to know both his grandfathers."

He sighed with relief. "Well, that's something to be thankful for. I sure wouldn't want him to grow up without getting to know who I was."

The tears in his eyes made her heart ache. She shifted uncomfortably, afraid he might break down and cry. She touched his arm. "Robbie will never be farther away than a phone call."

James hugged the baby, kissing his little face. "He looks so much like Robbie did when he was a baby."

Kerry nodded. "I saw the pictures. I think he does, too."

Reluctantly, James gave the child back to her. As he walked them down the hall to the elevator, he said, "I was so excited to see you, I almost forgot to tell you."

Her eyes widened with anticipation. "Tell me what?"

"Sergeant Williams called a little while ago. He managed to get the court to transfer Clifford Jacobson back to Virginia for his trial."

Kerry smiled. "Amy said he could do it. She said the sergeant is what you would call a real mover and shaker."

"And that other friend of yours," he said, rubbing his chin thoughtfully. "Margaret Hatchey is no slouch either."

Kerry looked puzzled. "What do you mean?"

"She went to see Jacobson's attorney about the babies that were sold?"

"I knew she was going. But I hadn't heard how it turned out."

"Well," James shook his head in awe. "After the lawyer high-tailed it out of his office, Margaret called the cops and had them alert the airport authorities. The dumb schmuck showed up about an hour later, carrying copies of the secret records he had given her and about five hundred thousand dollars in cash."

"Thank God!" Kerry said. "Then it's finally over, and all the girls who had their babies sold will be getting them back."

— 392 —

THE BABY SOLDIERS

"It sure looks that way," he said, hugging her warmly. "Off hand, I'd say Clifford Jacobson and his attorney are going to be locked away for a good long time."

Kerry rolled her eyes. "I suppose that means the general population can breathe easy once again."

James smiled ruefully. "Oh, for awhile. Then another nut will climb from under some rock and start the whole sorry business all over again."

The elevator door opened. Kerry climbed aboard and winked at James. "Next time," she said matter-of-factly, "we'll be prepared."

His eyes washed over her and the innocent child in her arms. "I hope so, Kerry. For everybody's sake, I certainly hope so."

Adele Woolard answered the door and smiled with relief when she saw David standing on the porch. He looked tired, and the stubble on his face looked as though he hadn't shaved in a week. She took him by the hand and led him inside. "How did everything go?" she asked.

He nodded as he followed her into the living room. "Pretty much the way we expected. I'm still worried though," he said, falling onto the sofa. "Jacobson is a foxy bastard. It wouldn't surprise me if he didn't have his jury handpicked."

Adele grabbed at the cross on a gold chain around her neck. "You mean there's a possibility he could go free?"

David shrugged. "Who knows? I used to think I had a fairly good grasp on the justice system. The past few months have really opened my eyes."

She squeezed his arm reassuringly. "Well, you'll be retiring soon. Then you won't have to worry about it anymore."

He snickered. "If only that were true. After I retire, I'll probably worry more. So many of the young guys we hire get caught up in easy money scams."

Adele studied his weary face. "You look like you could use a vacation."

GERRY R. LEWIS

He forced a smile. "I've been thinking about that. Maybe we could all go away somewhere for a couple of weeks."

"Where?" she asked excitedly.

"Oh, I don't know…maybe the mountains. I bet the boys would really enjoy going fishing and hiking. Some of those cabins in Tennessee and Kentucky don't even have television sets in them. Just think, we'd be completely free from civilization and all its craziness."

"It sounds wonderful to me," she said. "But I think you'd have a hard time convincing the boys to go anywhere they couldn't watch TV and play video games."

David chuckled. "They'd have so much other stuff to keep them busy, they'd never miss it."

She looked at the pale mark on her finger where her wedding ring had been.

"David, did you find what you were looking for in Baltimore?"

He shook his head. David knew her husband had killed his family, but he'd die in hell before he'd ever tell her.

Suddenly Jason walked into the room and stood in front of his mother and David. His eyes looked glassy, as though he'd been crying. "David," he said, gasping loudly. "There's something I have to tell you."

David leaned forward watching Jason pick at his trembling fingers.

"What is it, son?"

"When…when I followed Dad to Baltimore, I heard him tell…I heard him tell Reverend Jacobson that he…that he…"

Adele stood up, alarmed. "What is it, Jason? Tell us, honey."

Jason shook his head frantically. "Dad told Reverend Jacobson that he killed Mrs. Williams and Ginny."

Adele dropped back onto the sofa as though she'd been struck. "Dear God, no," she muttered.

Jason sniveled. "He said he wanted Mrs. Williams to…you know… and she wouldn't have anything to do with him."

— 394 —

THE BABY SOLDIERS

Adele and David turned to each other, too numbed by what they'd heard to utter a sound.

Jason's shoulders slumped as he continued to cry. "Ginny walked in when he was trying to...and he shot her."

David looked at Jason, tears filling his own eyes.

"Jason, why didn't you tell me sooner?"

Jason wiped his eyes on his shirtsleeve. "Because...because I thought if you knew my dad killed your family, you'd hate us, and you'd never want to see us again."

"Oh, Christ," David muttered, putting his arms around the boy, comforting him. "Everything is going to be all right, Jason. At least, I know what happened now."

Jason sniffed loudly.

David lay his hand on Jason's shoulder "When Ann and Ginny disappeared, I blamed myself. I thought it was my fault. Then after they were found, I didn't know what to think. I suspected Horace had something to do with it. Then I shifted gears and decided that Jacobson had ordered them killed. But I never knew why." His eyes fixed on Jason's. "And you, you poor kid," he said, his voice raspy. "When you learned the truth, you thought I'd hate you if you told me."

Jason nodded.

"It's all over, son," David said softly. "We can't keep living in the past and blaming ourselves for what happened, or what didn't happen. If we do, we'll never be able to see what's ahead for us."

Jason bobbed his head eagerly.

David reached out his other hand to Adele. The three of them stood in a circle, their arms tightly wound around each other. "Jason," David said, "what do you think about all of us going on a little vacation together?"

Jason's eyes widened in disbelief. "Do you really mean it, David?"

David nodded. "I sure do. I thought maybe you and Mark might like to go fishing, someplace far away from here."

"When do we leave?"Jason asked excitedly.

— 395 —

Adele turned from David to her son and smiled. "I think it might be a good idea if we thought about packing first."

"Pack!" Jason said, breaking the circle and running toward the stairs. "Mark, pack your stuff!" he yelled. "David's taking us fishing!"

Adele put her arms around David's neck and kissed him. "Have I told you lately how much I love you?"

He smiled. "I hope you'll remember that once we're out in the wilderness and a wild bear starts chasing us."

Her eyes widened. "David, we won't be running into any wild bears where we're going, will we?"

"Don't worry," he said, holding her close. "Bears are mighty dangerous. But they're nowhere near as dangerous as humans."

THE END

ABOUT THE AUTHOR

Gerry R. Lewis, a native of Pittsburgh, PA, is a seasoned author with a rich background in creative writing, honed at TCC, Virginia Beach and Carteret Tech, Morehead City, NC. Her writing journey has seen her publish numerous articles and short stories in Virginia, North Carolina, True Romance, and True Story Magazine. As a member of The Virginia Writers Club, she contributed to an anthology of short stories and poetry. Gerry's experience extends to journalism, having worked as a reporter in Emporia, VA. Now residing in Franklin, VA, she is diligently crafting her next novel.